BEVERLY CLEARY

First Love

A TREASURY OF THREE FAVORITES

Jean and Johnny

Fifteen

and *The Luckiest Girl*

HARPERCOLLINS*PUBLISHERS*

By the Same Author

JEAN

and

JOHNNY

By BEVERLY CLEARY

Illustrated by
Joe and Beth Krush

Morrow Junior Books   New York

JEAN and JOHNNY

CHAPTER
1

"I HAVE the funniest feeling," remarked Jean Jarrett, who was drying the supper dishes while her older sister Sue washed them. "I keep feeling as if something nice is going to happen."

"That's because this is the first night of Christmas vacation," answered Sue, rinsing a plate under the hot-water faucet and setting it in the dish drainer.

"I suppose so," agreed Jean dreamily, wishing that something nice really would happen. Lately life had lacked interesting ups and downs. Oh, there were little ups like watching Kip Laddish on television, just as there were little downs, too, like the plaid skirt she was wearing. Because she had forgotten to allow extra material for matching the plaid, she discovered, when the pieces of the skirt were sewed together, that the stripes were uneven at every seam. Little ups, little downs—how she wished she could replace them with big ups and downs that would make life exciting.

"What would you like to happen?" asked Sue.

"Oh, I don't know exactly," answered Jean. There was a speck of food on the plate she was wiping. She considered returning the plate to the dishwater for Sue to rewash, thought better of it, and polished off the speck with the dish towel. When it was her turn to wash dishes, she did not like to have dishes returned to her dishwater. "It would be nice to grow a couple more inches, and not have to wear glasses; but at fifteen I don't suppose that will happen. Maybe something like a cable arriving saying that a long-lost uncle has died and left us a fortune."

"That would be nice," agreed Sue. "He could be a terribly romantic figure, a family black sheep we had never even heard of, who had run away at the age of fourteen to Kenya or Bangkok and made his fortune in diamonds or teak or something."

"Or maybe it would be better if he had run away to the South Seas," elaborated Jean. "He could be a pearl king with crews of natives with knives in their teeth diving for oysters."

"Oh, well," said Sue. "How he got the fortune isn't important. What is important is that he died and left it to the Jarretts."

"It wouldn't even have to be a fortune," said Jean. "Just enough so we could have avocado in the salad every single day. And so I could walk into Northgate Apparel Shop just once and buy a plaid skirt with the stripes matched by somebody else."

Sue laughed. "I know what you mean. Money for little extra things. Oh, well," she said, with an airy wave of the dishcloth, "what are the material things in life? We have ingenuity."

Jean giggled. "Especially me. It takes real ingenuity to make such a terrible-looking skirt."

It was Sue who had the ingenuity. Right now she was wearing a skirt she had devised out of twelve red bandana handkerchiefs that she had bought at the dime store. With it she was wearing a white blouse she had made out of a remnant and trimmed with a yard of leftover rickrack. Jean remembered how Sue had schemed, rearranging her pattern several times, to get the blouse out of the short length of material. Even two years ago, when Sue was fifteen, she would have remembered to allow extra material for matching plaid. Sue was that kind of girl: she always knew what she wanted to do and then went about it in the right way.

Both girls were silent, each thinking of nice things they would like to have happen. Sue was right, Jean thought. Money for little extra things was a problem. House payments, life insurance, hospital insurance, money put aside for Sue's freshman year at the University next fall (their father said his girls were going to have a better start in life than he had had), a small check to help their grandmother in the East—all these seemed to consume Mr. Jarrett's pay check almost as soon as he received it. It would help if their father would allow them to earn money baby-sitting someplace besides the two houses next door, but he would not—not since the Friday night some strangers down the street had engaged Sue to stay with their children and had not come home until two-thirty in the morning. Mr. Jarrett, who was a mailman and had to report to the post office at six o'clock in the morning, said he lost too much sleep worrying about Sue in a strange house being responsible for strange children. Kids could get into the darnedest trouble, Mr. Jarrett said. He ought to know. He had seen enough of it in his nineteen years of delivering mail. If his girls were going to baby-sit, they had to do it close to home, where he knew what was going on. Unfortunately for Jean and Sue, their next-door neighbors did not often go out.

Or it would be nice, Jean reflected, if her mother won a really big prize in one of the contests she was always entering—a prize so big she could give up her

Saturday job as a salesclerk in a shop called Fabrics, Etc., which sold remnants and mill ends of dress, drapery, and upholstery material.

"I know what would be nice," said Sue suddenly.

"What?" asked Jean, glancing at the clock. She must not get so carried away in daydreams that she missed Kip Laddish.

"To meet a boy." Sue's voice was wistful. "Not just any boy, but a really nice boy who liked me."

"Yes, that would be nice," agreed Jean seriously, because she understood that this time Sue was not joking. She was a little surprised at her sister's wish, because Sue had never been interested in the boys who seemed to like her. "But what about Cliff?" Jean asked. "He phoned you a couple of times, but you wouldn't go out with him."

Sue made a face. "He always said, 'Guess who this is?' and 'What are you doing next Saturday night?' without telling me what he wanted me to do. Besides, he would have bored me stiff. I am not interested in just any old boy."

"I suppose not." No boy, not even one who could be called any old boy, had ever telephoned Jean.

"Half a minute to seven. Almost time for your program," said Sue. "I'll finish up. We're practically through, anyway."

"Thanks a lot," said Jean gratefully, dropping her

dish towel on the draining board. "I'll finish for you sometime."

At exactly seven o'clock Jean, her chin propped on her fists, was sitting on the hassock in the glow of the Christmas-tree lights in front of the portable television set, the biggest prize her mother had ever won in a contest. This was the moment Jean anticipated every week. And she knew that three doors down the street Elaine Mundy, her best friend, was sitting in front of her television set, too.

The commercial began. A pretty girl faced Jean and, while she smiled radiantly, wiggled her fingers in her soapy hair. The soap, by some magic, rose from her head in a glittering trail of bubbles that turned into a singing, dancing bottle of shampoo. Jean removed her glasses, held them up to the light, and flicked a speck of dust off one lens.

And then Kip Laddish was there in the living room singing straight to Jean. He was *so* good-looking. That checked sport coat, his trade-mark, made him look boyish because it was a bit too large, as if he expected to grow into it. And the way he sang. . . . He looked so serious, almost pleading, and then suddenly he would flash the most wonderful grin, that made Jean feel as if he were sharing a secret with her. It was almost as if he were saying,

I know I don't sing very well, but we don't care, do we?

"Play like you love me . . ." Kip Laddish sang, and Jean sighed. She could hardly wait these next few months until he made his personal appearance in Northgate and she and Elaine went to see him. Without mentioning it to their families, the two girls had made up their minds, as soon as Elaine had spotted his schedule of appearances in a movie magazine, to see Kip Laddish in person and nothing, *nothing* was going to stop them. Elaine was giving Jean a ticket, or rather the promise of a ticket, for Christmas. They had even decided—if they did not lose their courage—to try to get his autograph.

"Play like you love me. . . ." It would be so wonderful if Jean could meet him. Of course that would never happen, but just supposing . . . just supposing she did happen to meet him. Just supposing when he came to Northgate he happened to drive down the street as she was walking along, and somehow he had got lost. Maybe he had stopped for a sandwich or something, and didn't know how to get back on the freeway . . . and there she was, walking along, minding her own business. . . .

The impatient rattle of a newspaper reminded Jean that she was not alone in the room with Kip

Laddish. Her mother and father, as well as Dandy, the dog, were with her. She knew what was coming next.

"What a lot of silly girls see in that half-baked tenor is beyond me," said Mr. Jarrett.

Without taking her eyes from the screen, Jean carefully measured the impatience in his voice. Her trip to Kip Laddish's personal appearance would depend on her father, who, she had an uneasy feeling, might not think highly of such an expedition. "Please, Daddy," she said, knowing that she could not stop what he was going to say. His voice had already registered Impatience, well above Medium but not yet to Explosive. Her father, a kind and gentle man, rarely reached Explosive, but it was wise not to push him too far when he was tired from the rush of Christmas mail.

"He can't even sing," Mr. Jarrett went on. "He probably can't even read music and yet he has the nerve to stand up there in front of a television camera wearing a coat a tinhorn gambler would be ashamed to be seen in."

Jean knew there was some truth in what her father was saying—not about the coat, which was terribly smart although it might look peculiar to someone as old as her father, but about Kip Laddish's singing.

It really was not very good, but that was one of the reasons all the girls liked him so much. It made him seem like a real person, someone a girl might happen to meet someday. A father could not be expected to understand this. "Lots of people like him. His records sell millions of copies," she said defensively, knowing that she risked running her father up from Medium to Explosive. If he reached Explosive, she would have to turn the set off.

Mr. Jarrett snorted an Almost Explosive snort. "If he earns so much money, why doesn't he spend some of it on a haircut?" he asked.

"Oh, Daddy, leave her alone. She'll get over it." Sue had entered the room and now spoke from the wisdom of her seventeen years. "Anyway, I sort of like him myself."

"If the only boy we have to worry about is a boy on a television program, I won't complain," said Mrs. Jarrett. "We can put up with him once in a while if Jean enjoys him."

The rattle of the paper told Jean that her father had resumed his reading and she was free to dream through the rest of the program. Kip Laddish introduced his guest artist, a girl singer in a strapless evening gown. He joked with her a few minutes before she disappeared to permit him to sing another song.

Then the girl appeared in a different dress, a tight dress with the skirt slit up one side, and sang her song. Jean paid little attention to the tune, because she was wondering how the girl managed to sit down in such a skirt. Time out for the tap-dancing bottle of shampoo again. Kip appeared with the girl, who this time was wearing a gown with a halter top and a short, full skirt—how *did* she manage to change in such a short time? Kip put his arm around her while they sang together, and then they twirled around and danced. Kip in his crepe-soled shoes—he always wore crepe-soled shoes—was not a very good dancer either, but he was awkward in such a charming, boyish way. He joined the girl in a few more bars of their song, and then he was alone, singing *Play Like You Love Me* straight to Jean. The bottle of shampoo turned handsprings and the announcer, amused at the antics of the shampoo, urged everyone to buy a bottle and explained that impartial scientific tests had proved conclusively that this shampoo left ninety-seven and one half per cent less dull soap film on the hair than nine other brands on the market. The program was over for another week.

Almost immediately the telephone rang. Jean, certain that it was Elaine who was calling, went into the kitchen to answer.

"Jean? Did you watch?" Elaine sounded as if she were suppressing some strong emotion.

"Yes," answered Jean breathlessly. "Wasn't he *wonderful?*"

"I practically died just watching him," said Elaine and then, speaking pointedly for the benefit of her father, added, "Of course Dad had to rattle his paper and make a lot of rude remarks, but I guess some people just don't appreciate the finer things in life."

Knowing how Mr. Mundy would react to this remark, Jean laughed. "I know," she said sympathetically. "Dad is the same way, but I just rise above it."

"Can you come over for a while?" asked Elaine.

"Sure," answered Jean. "See you in a minute." After Jean had taken her coat from the closet in the room she shared with her sister, she informed her family where she was going and added, "No homework for two weeks!"

"Aren't you going to change your skirt?" Sue, who was so skillful with needle and thread, was disturbed by the unmatched plaid. "The jog in the stripes makes your skirt look as if one half is two inches higher than the other half."

"Oh . . . I guess not," answered Jean. "We are only going to write to our pen pals. Anyway, I have to wear the skirt sometime, and I certainly don't want to wear it to school." She picked up a box of note paper that had been lying on the bookcase and looked inside to make sure she had three envelopes, because she had three letters to write: one to Japan, one to England, and a third, in shaky French, to France. Jean and Elaine always spoke of their pen pals as if the phrase was enclosed in invisible quotation marks. Pen pals were for nine- and ten-year-olds. Their correspondence was on a higher level. By writing to girls in other countries they were improving their languages and promoting better understanding between nations. This, of course, was much more intellectual than just having fun getting mail with foreign stamps.

"Aren't you spending a lot of time at Elaine's?" asked Mrs. Jarrett, looking up from the pad of paper on her knee.

"Not much," said Jean. "I mean, what else is there to do?"

"But you saw her this afternoon after school," said Mrs. Jarrett absently, as she scribbled something on the pad of paper.

"Another contest, Mother?" asked Jean.

"Yes. Why I like Swish detergent in twenty-five words or less," answered Mrs. Jarrett. "Don't you think 'elbow-grease efficiency' would be a good phrase to use? I have heard that winning letters **are** always full of hyphens."

"Sounds good to me," answered Jean, her hand on the knob of the front door.

"Of course I don't like to give the impression that using Swish is work," remarked Mrs. Jarrett critically. "I don't think the judges would like that."

"You could say, 'I like Swish detergent because it makes washday such a whale of a lot of fun,'" suggested Mr. Jarrett from behind his newspaper.

"Oh, I think that is going a little too far," said Mrs. Jarrett seriously.

"Dad is just joking." Jean smiled and opened the door.

"Why not use something that rhymes?" suggested Sue. "Something like, 'I like Swish because when I Swish the clothes I have more time to doze.'"

"You can laugh all you want," said Mrs. Jarrett agreeably, "but just the same, it would help a lot if I could win a new refrigerator. Our old one goes on and off so often I think it must be on its last legs. And don't forget, I won the television set by liking peanut oil in twenty-five words or less."

"Better let Dandy out as long as you are going," Mr. Jarrett told Jean.

Jean snapped her fingers to the beagle, who rose

reluctantly. Dandy, who had half his tail missing, had once belonged to someone on Mr. Jarrett's route. When a car door had been slammed on Dandy's tail and several inches of the tail had to be amputated, the dog could no longer be exhibited at dog shows, and his owners had no further use for him. Mr. Jarrett, who had grown fond of the dog in the course of delivering mail to the owner's house, heard that they wanted to get rid of him and offered to give him a home. When he brought Dandy home, Mrs. Jarrett protested, "But we can't afford to keep a dog." She was still protesting, usually just before payday, but the Jarretts continued to keep and to love Dandy

"Don't stay out late," said Mr. Jarrett.

"I never do stay out late, Dad," answered Jean. Some things were just habits with parents. You would think from the way Mr. Jarrett spoke that his daughters went out with boys.

The day had been smoggy, as December days so often were, but a late afternoon breeze had swept away the ugly haze and left the night clear and sharp. The change in the weather was exhilarating to Jean. As she ran down the sidewalk, the street light behind her making her shadow dance ahead of her, she wished for something more exciting than an evening writing to pen pals.

"Come in," called out Mr. Mundy, when Jean had run up the steps and tapped on the front door.

As Jean stepped out of the cold air into the warm room, fragrant with Christmas greens, vapor formed on her glasses as quickly as if a white curtain had been jerked down before her eyes. She pulled off her glasses and waved them around to let the moisture evaporate.

"Hello there, Half Pint," said Mr. Mundy jovially.

"Mr. Mundy, I'll have you know that I am five feet one and one quarter inches tall," said Jean, who was used to being teased about her size by her best friend's father. "I was measured in gym last week."

"Imagine that," remarked Mr. Mundy. "Pretty soon you'll have to pay full price at the movies."

"Oh, Dad, cut it out," called Elaine from the kitchen. "Jean has paid full admission for years."

"I need Jean's help," said Mrs. Mundy, also from the kitchen. "Come on, Jean."

Cedar boughs were heaped on newspapers on the kitchen floor. On the table lay a stack of Christmas wreaths and a pile of wire coat hangers that had been bent into circles. Mrs. Mundy, a plump, pleasant-looking woman, was wiring greens to the circles while Elaine fastened clusters of gilded eucalyptus buds to the wreaths. Elaine, who took after her father, was tall, thin, slightly round-shouldered, and the kind of girl who could never keep her shirttail tucked in. She said Jean made her feel gawky, all knees and elbows. Jean said Elaine made her feel like someone who should buy her clothes in the children's department. "The long and the short of it," Mr. Mundy often remarked when he saw the girls together, and that was almost every day.

"What would you like me to do?" asked Jean, pleased that they were going to make wreaths instead of writing letters.

"Take the garden clippers and snip off pieces of cedar for me—limber pieces that I can bend around the wire," directed Mrs. Mundy. "When we finish another half dozen I can deliver them to the clubhouse. Our lodge is having a bridge luncheon tomorrow, and I am in charge of the decorations."

"And you know Mom," said Elaine. "Always leaving everything to the last minute."

"Oh, not always," protested Mrs. Mundy, smiling.

The three worked swiftly. Jean enjoyed the fragrance of the cedar. Decorating for a party, even someone else's party, made her feel so festive she was almost sorry to see the last coat hanger camouflaged with green and the last cluster of eucalpytus buds wired into place.

"There," said Mrs. Mundy, with an air of having accomplished something. "Wouldn't you girls like to drive over to the clubhouse with me while I deliver these?"

The girls agreed that a ride across town would be a pleasant change. They put on their coats and carried the wreaths out to the car. Jean found it agreeable to have the illusion of going someplace, of doing something different, even though she was only going along on someone else's errand. Riding in a wreath-filled car on the first night of Christmas vacation seemed a promise of fun and festivity.

"Three and a half months," whispered Elaine, who could be referring to only one thing—Kip Laddish's personal appearance.

"Three and a half months," answered Jean fervently, as she enjoyed the lighted Christmas trees in the windows along the street.

When they reached the clubhouse they saw light streaming from the windows and heard bursts of music as the door opened and closed. "Come on, girls," said Mrs. Mundy briskly. "There's an armload for each of us. We'll just leave them in the kitchen for tonight. I am coming over in the morning with the rest of the committee after the decorations from the dance have been cleared out." The girls, with their loads of wreaths, followed Mrs. Mundy into the building and past the ceiling-high Christmas tree in the lobby into the kitchen, which smelled of stale coffee. They piled their wreaths on the long drainboard beside a row of gallon coffeepots.

"There, that's done," said Mrs. Mundy. "Now I have a few things to attend to in the office. Why don't you girls go in and watch the dance for a few minutes?"

"Yes, let's," said Elaine eagerly, and Jean agreed. It would be fun to see what others were doing for a good time on the first night of Christmas vacation.

The girls slipped through the door into the room where the party was being held. "There are some chairs along the wall," whispered Elaine. "Let's sit there."

The two girls pulled off their coats and sat on the hard folding chairs. "I hope we don't look like wallflowers," murmured Elaine.

"Not in these school clothes. They'll know we aren't part of the crowd," answered Jean. "For us, I guess you could call dancing a spectator sport."

"I see some juniors and seniors from school," observed Elaine, "and a few fellows and girls home from college."

Jean did not answer. She was too absorbed in

the scene before her. It seemed to her an enchant-
ing picture in motion. The room was fragrant with
garlands of Christmas greens, and from the center
of the ceiling hung a revolving ball made of bits
of mirror that cast flakes of light, like confetti, over
the boys in their dark suits and the girls in their
light dresses. Never had Jean seen so many pretty
dresses before—dresses of net and taffeta and lace,
all of them fresh and graceful. And the flowers—
the girls wore flowers on their shoulders or in their
hair or pinned to their sashes. The fragrance of
gardenias mingled with the scent of the greens.

"Some of them are even wearing orchids," whispered Elaine.

"I know." Jean's eyes slid from the flowers to
the shoes—slippers and sandals of silver and gold
and tinted satin. And for every pair of delicate
shoes there was a pair of polished black shoes.

"When I have a formal I want a pair of shoes
dyed to match," whispered Elaine. "You can buy
the shoes at Belmonts' for six ninety-nine, and the
store tints them free."

Jean felt a twinge of annoyance. She wanted to
take in the scene before her without thinking of
the cost of shoes or the problems of matching dye
to swatches of material.

"Kip Laddish has a new record of that piece the

band is playing," said Elaine. "I'm going to buy it when I get my allowance."

The music stopped, and couples drifted to the edge of the room. The flowers, the smiling faces, the dresses dappled by the mirrored light made, it seemed to Jean, one of the loveliest scenes she had ever watched.

And then quite unexpectedly a boy was standing in front of Jean. A tall boy in a dark suit. A boy with a pleasant smile. "May I have this dance?" he asked.

He must be speaking to someone else. Jean felt Elaine nudge her.

"May I have this dance?" he repeated.

"Me?" Jean stared at the boy in disbelief, even though he was standing directly in front of her. A boy—asking Jean Jarrett to step into the scene before her?

"Yes, you," answered the boy, with an engaging smile.

Like a girl walking in her sleep, Jean rose from her chair and stepped forward. The music started. The boy put his arm around her and took her right hand in his left. She laid her left hand on his right shoulder. She was in the boy's arms, a part of the scene she had been watching. She felt as if she had stepped into a dream.

It was then that reality intruded. Jean remembered that she did not know how to dance.

The boy took a step, and Jean stumbled. "I—I'm sorry," she managed to say. "I'm not a very good dancer."

"That's all right," he said cheerfully. "I won't try anything fancy."

But he knows, thought Jean. Two steps, and already he knew she did not know how to dance. Her mind was awhirl. All she could think clearly was, My skirt. My awful homemade skirt with the jogs in the plaid. And she was wearing bobby socks and saddle shoes. Heavy, flat shoes. Sensible shoes that would wear a long time. Her hands grew icy, and her right hand, she now discovered, was sticky from the pitch on the Christmas wreaths. She stumbled. She stumbled again. She wanted to break away from this boy and flee through the crowd, but she did not have the courage. She did not understand how she had managed to get herself into this situation—it had seemed so natural and so wonderful that first moment when she had risen from her chair and stepped toward him—and now . . . this. . . .

The boy simplified his steps until he was walking to music and Jean only had to slide her feet backwards. Then she found she did not know what to do with her face. In her flat shoes she could not see over his shoulder. She was afraid of smearing lipstick on his coat so she thrust her chin upward. She found this awkward and felt that she must be wearing the strained look Dandy wore when he swam and tried to keep his chin out of water. She tried turning her face to the right. Although still not very comfortable, this was better. At least she had a good view of the shirt front of this boy, who-ever he was.

They danced, or rather walked, in silence. Jean wondered desperately how much longer the music would go on. At the same time she was aware that the boy smelled pleasantly of clean wool and soap. Why, I never knew before that a boy could smell good, she thought in surprise. She had not, in fact, thought much about real boys at all. What boy would be interested in a fifteen-year-old girl who could pass for thirteen and who wore glasses, besides? Boys were people who lived in the same neighborhood and went to the same school. Some of them were agreeable to talk to once in a while and some were noisy nuisances. Certainly she had not thought of any of them as dancing partners—that would come in that vague and happy time,

the future. It had been so much easier to dream
about a boy who followed a tap-dancing bottle of
shampoo onto the television screen. With that boy
she would be dancing lightly, gracefully . . . but
with this boy, this real, live boy. . . . Well, it was
all so different from her dreams.

Jean stepped squarely on the boy's toe. "Excuse
me," she managed to say.

"That's all right," he answered.

The music stopped, and Jean felt as if she had
been set free. Then she remembered this was only
a pause, that each dance was divided into three
parts. Feeling that it was only fair to offer the boy
his freedom, she looked up uncertainly at him while
she surreptitiously wiped the palms of her clammy
hands on her skirt.

The boy grinned. "You're catching on," he said.

It was nice of him to say it. Jean did not know
what to answer. She looked down at the floor and
saw that her white saddle shoes were now marked
with black polish. The boy's shoes were streaked
with her white shoe cleaner.

The music began again, the boy put his arm
around Jean, and once more she found herself propelled around the room. She caught a glimpse of
Elaine staring at her and, beside her, Mrs. Mundy

watching with amusement. How ridiculous I must look, thought Jean, seeing herself in relation to the rest of the crowd for the first time, walking around backward in saddle shoes and an old blouse and that skirt—that awful skirt—when all the other girls looked so pretty.

This time the boy stepped on Jean's toe. "I'm sorry," he said pleasantly.

At least he was game. Jean was too miserable to answer.

The music stopped. Two down and one to go, thought Jean, unless she could escape. The thing to do was look this boy, whoever he was, in the eye and excuse herself quickly before the music started again. But when she forced herself to look him in the eye, her resolution wavered. He was so good-looking—tall with dark hair and a jaunty bow tie. Now she knew that she had seen him around school during the past semester. He was a senior, she was sure, but who was he?

"Do you go to Northgate High?" asked the boy.

Jean nodded. He had not remembered seeing her around school—but why should he? And then her courage returned. "Please excuse me," she said swiftly, her cheeks hot. "I really don't know how to dance and I should not have accepted." She turned and as she turned, she thought—she couldn't be sure—that he put out his hand to stop her. She did not wait to find out. She made her way past the other couples, the net and taffeta of the other girls' skirts brushing against her bare legs.

When she reached her chair against the wall, Jean snatched up her coat. "Come on, Elaine," she whispered. "Let's get out of here!"

Elaine followed her into the lobby. "Jean," she said eagerly, "how did you have the *courage?*"

"I don't know," answered Jean weakly. "I just did. Only it wasn't courage exactly. I guess I didn't know any better."

Mrs. Mundy joined the girls beside the Christmas tree. "Jean, you did splendidly," she said warmly.

Jean managed to smile. She knew this was not true, but it was Mrs. Mundy's nature always to look at the cheerful side.

"What was his name?" asked Elaine.

"I don't know," admitted Jean.

"You don't know?" Elaine was disbelieving. "Didn't you ask him?"

"I couldn't," said Jean. "I was too busy thinking about my feet." Those two feet in bobby socks and saddle shoes. "I couldn't talk and think about my feet at the same time. I—I can't even remember what he looked like. Not very clearly anyway, except that he was wearing a bow tie."

"I can," said Elaine. "He was terribly good-looking. He even had curly hair."

"Then why did he want to dance with me?" Jean was genuinely bewildered. Why should a boy want to dance with a strange girl who was not even dressed for the party?

"I don't know," said Elaine. "But he did. That's what counts."

The two girls followed Elaine's mother out to the car. "Jean," whispered Elaine, as they climbed into the back seat, "was it fun, dancing with a good-looking boy?"

"Well . . . no," said Jean honestly. "It was really pretty awful. You know—me in saddle shoes with my hands all clammy and not knowing how to dance."

"I know." There was real regret in Elaine's voice.

Mrs. Mundy pushed the starter button. "Jean, you must be very happy to have had such a nice-looking boy ask you to dance," she remarked.

"Yes," answered Jean, because Mrs. Mundy, a firm believer in positive thinking, would expect an affirmative answer. And yet she really was happy.

That was the funny part of it. She had been miserable, but there was more to her feelings than that. She sensed that Elaine was holding back a flood of questions, because there were some things girls did not like to talk about in front of their mothers.

Jean was glad to have a chance to think about her experience, to try to decide how she really did feel about it. It was surprisingly difficult to remember. She was left with an impression of a boy's pleasant voice, of his dark woolen shoulder and white shirt front, of music and the feel of his toe treading on hers, of other couples moving past and of her own confusion.

All at once it became important that Jean remember everything, every single little detail. She tried to recall what music had been played, but she could not. The only thing she could recall distinctly was the clean wool-and-soap smell of the boy. The rest was just a blur.

It was all so puzzling. Jean had had an embarrassing, uncomfortable experience, and yet it had left her feeling happy. Never before had she felt happy over her own embarrassment. And then she understood. For the first time in her life a boy had singled her out of a crowd. A boy, a real live boy. . . . Why, the future had arrived!

Mrs. Mundy stopped the car in front of the Jarretts' house and, after saying good night, waited until Jean was safely in the house.

The living room was empty. Jean snapped off the light and went to the room she shared with her sister. Sue was sitting in front of the portable sewing machine set up on the table which the girls shared for study and for sewing. On the bed was a row of red and green felt slippers with turned-up toes. On the toe of each was a little bell.

"How perfectly darling!" exclaimed Jean.

"This represents most of my Christmas shopping. I can make them for practically nothing, and they would cost a lot to buy," answered Sue. "I love to make things out of felt. It never has to be hemmed."

Without removing her coat, Jean sat down on the bed and absently picked up a slipper and swung it back and forth to make the bell jingle.

"You look sort of dazed," remarked Sue.

Jean dropped the slipper and looked at her sister. "I guess I am."

"Why?" asked Sue amiably. "Too many Kip Laddish records at Elaine's house?"

"You know, it was the funniest thing," said Jean, "but something nice really did happen."

CHAPTER
2

THE first thing Jean discovered after the dance was that once a boy singles a girl out of a crowd for the first time, her life is never quite the same again. She discovered this when she started to clean her saddle shoes. She shook the bottle of cleaner, poured a little of the fluid onto a cloth, picked up her shoe, and looked thoughtfully at the streaks of black shoe polish on the white leather. Smiling to herself, she put the cap back on the bottle of cleaner and returned the bottle to the closet. There was no hurry about rubbing off the marks the boy's shoes had made on hers. Instead of cleaning her shoes as she always did on Saturday morning, she sat staring dreamily at her smudged toes, while in her mind's eye she saw the boy, whoever he was, in his room just before the dance, giving his shoes a last-minute shine. Perhaps he had been whistling as he bent over and snapped a cloth back and forth across his toes. Then he must have straightened up, put away the polish, slipped into his coat, and paused, still whistling, in front of his mirror to straighten his tie and run a comb through the hair Elaine had said was curly.

Jean enjoyed the scene so much she ran through it once more, this time adding wall-to-wall carpeting to the boy's room and having him tuck a folded handkerchief into his breast pocket. And what about his shoes this morning? Was he polishing off the white marks she had left on the black leather? Maybe that was what he was doing this very minute. It was the beginning of a period of absent-mindedness for Jean.

And then there was the matter of clothes. Jean hung the mismatched plaid skirt in the back of her closet and hoped her mother would not notice that she did not wear it. She longed for a closet full of pretty clothes. Until now she had been satisfied with the dresses her mother made for her or that she made for herself, and with the sweaters that her mother bought at sales. Now Jean looked at fashions in the morning paper and lingered over the advertisements of the Northgate Apparel Shop. She spent a lot of time in the bathroom, where the light was best, looking at the back of her shoulder-length hair in a hand mirror, pulling a comb through her locks, and shaking her head to make her hair swing back and forth like a model in a television commercial for shampoo. Her family often had to pound on the bathroom door and remind her that the bathroom was not hers exclusively.

If the change that five minutes with a boy brought about in Jean was strange, the change that the same five minutes brought about in Elaine was even stranger. While Jean was content to daydream about the real live boy, Elaine prepared to organize. Jean discovered this the Saturday evening after the girls had carried the wreaths into the clubhouse.

Because Mr. Mundy was part owner of a plumbing business and for the sake of his business belonged to a number of clubs and service organizations, the Mundys led an active social life. They often went out on Saturday evening and, rather than leave Elaine at home alone, they usually invited Jean to keep her company. These evenings had fallen into a pattern that both girls enjoyed. Jean arrived late in the afternoon, sometimes with her pajamas and toothbrush, if the Mundys expected to be out late. Mrs. Mundy gave them some

money to buy the ingredients of their own dinner.
The two girls walked to the nearby shopping center to plan their menu and to market, studying
prices and trying to buy as many of their favorite
foods as possible. There were three rules in their
private game: except for seasonings they must not
use anything in the Mundys' cupboards or refrigerator for their meal, they could not add any money
of their own to the sum Mrs. Mundy had given
them, and they must spend every penny of this
sum. To accomplish this required careful figuring
on little slips of paper. On this Saturday they returned to Elaine's house with two pork chops, one
large avocado which was a great bargain because
it was bruised, two artichokes, a papaya which they
selected because neither of them had ever tasted this
fruit, and, to use up the last pennies, three Greek
olives from the delicatessen. The third olive they
would meticulously cut in two.

"You lucky girls!" exclaimed plump Mrs. Mundy,
when she saw the groceries. "The calories you can
consume and not gain an ounce." She tugged at
her skirt as if she felt it might be too tight, kissed
both girls lightly on the cheek, and said, "Have a
good time and don't forget to go to bed. We should
be home by midnight."

"We don't want to see the bedroom light go off

as we drive up the driveway," said Mr. Mundy. "And don't forget to wash the dishes."

"We always wash them, Dad," said Elaine, "unless we burn something and have to soak the pan."

"Jean, do you mind if I tell you something?" Elaine asked, when her parents had left and the girls had set about preparing their meal. She continued, regardless of whether Jean minded or not. "You should wear your bangs shorter."

"My bangs?" repeated Jean, putting her hand to her forehead.

"Yes," said Elaine. "Sometimes you let them get too long and then you go around sort of peering out from under them."

"I do?" Dismayed by this picture of herself, Jean brushed her bangs away from her forehead.

"Yes. You are the gamin type and you should wear them short," said Elaine, unwrapping the pork chops.

Jean laughed, amused at hearing Elaine speak in fashion-magazine language. "I thought a gamin was a ragged little boy."

"You know what I mean," said Elaine impatiently. "Sort of little and . . . well, you know. And another thing—do you have to wear your glasses all the time?"

"I'm pretty nearsighted," said Jean. "Anyway, I

don't mind them too much any more. They have become a part of me."

"But the point is, you could get along without them in the halls at school without actually walking into the wall," Elaine said. "And you want to look your best the next time you see the boy. You're lucky you don't squint, the way some people do when they take off their glasses."

Jean giggled. "Without my glasses I'm not sure I could tell him from the principal."

"Don't be silly. Of course you could." Elaine was very positive. "For one thing the principal is about six inches shorter."

Jean cut the stems from the two artichokes. "Oh, Elaine, what difference does it make? He won't even remember me."

"Of course he will remember you," said Elaine. "He danced with you, didn't he?"

"I wouldn't exactly call it dancing," said Jean, "but he did have a good view of the top of my head. And you know something? I still can't remember what he looked like. I mean—it all happened so fast and I was so surprised I felt confused."

"I remember," said Elaine.

Jean laid down the paring knife and the artichoke she was trimming. "Elaine, what difference does it make? The whole thing was a horrible mistake. He will never look at me again, even if he does remember me—and I almost hope he doesn't. He probably just asked me to dance because he felt sorry for me or something."

"He didn't feel sorry for *me*," Elaine pointed out. "Anyway, I don't think boys ask girls to dance because they feel sorry for them."

Jean was silent. She was turning over in her mind, as she had so many times since the incident, the possible reasons why the perfectly strange boy had asked her to dance. And why he had chosen her instead of Elaine. It might have been better if he had asked Elaine, who at least knew how to dance, because she had joined the junior high school dancing class when she was in the seventh grade. Jean had not been able to, because at the time the Jarretts could not spare the nine dollars that the class cost. But perhaps Elaine was right about the glasses. Maybe she could get along without them between classes. If one boy had noticed her, perhaps another boy might come along. . . .

Elaine gave Jean little time for daydreaming. "Now the first thing you have to do," she said, as she stood with a fork poised over the sizzling pork chops, "is to learn to dance. After dinner we can play some records and I'll show you what I have learned. We can practice all during Christmas vacation. After all, if the boy asked you once, he might ask you again and"—Elaine paused significantly—"he might have a friend."

So that was why Elaine was taking such an interest in Jean's future. Jean carefully slipped the skin from the avocado, leaving the fruit as smooth as green velvet. "I guess it wouldn't hurt to practice," she said. "Not that anything will ever come of it."

And so Jean practiced dancing under Elaine's direction during the rest of Christmas vacation. Step, step, slide, slide, step, step. "This is the basic step," Elaine explained, "but it is more fun with a boy." Step, step, slide, slide, step, step. When Mr. Mundy saw what the girls were doing, he took an interest and insisted on dancing them around the living room a few times. The girls were polite about this, but they did not feel he was much help. His dancing was so old-fashioned.

Jean began to half wish that when school started the boy would recognize her, seek her out, and say something to let her know he had not minded those few minutes spent with her. She wouldn't even expect him to ask her for a date. She would just like to know that a good-looking boy felt friendly toward her and would pay her a little attention beyond saying, "Hi," in the halls. That was the trouble with her and Elaine and a lot of other girls—nobody paid any attention to them. Jean and Elaine had both had a left-out feeling since they had transferred from junior to senior high school. Northgate High School, the only high school in the city, seemed so big, so full of strange faces, that they felt lost in the crowds that swarmed the corridors.

One evening when the practice session ended, Elaine sat down with her long legs over the arm of a chair, helped herself to a handful of peanuts, and began to eat them one at a time. "Wouldn't it be wonderful if we got to be popular?" she asked. "Dates, committees, getting elected to offices, more dates. . . ."

"It's funny," said Jean thoughtfully, "but I don't think I even want to be popular."

"Every girl wants to be popular." Elaine was positive about this.

"I don't." This time Jean was positive too. "I'm too—too quiet. I wouldn't want to call a meeting to order or even read the minutes. And I would be miserable if I had to be a rally girl. Not that there is any danger of that."

"Not me," said Elaine. "I would simply adore

swishing a couple of pompons around in front of the whole student body." She added, with a note of regret, "Except that I am taller than all the yell leaders."

"I would rather be part of the crowd cheering for the team," said Jean, nibbling a peanut.

"And when the school puts on the variety show I would like to be right out in the middle of the stage, with everybody applauding madly," said Elaine, "although I don't know exactly what they would applaud me for. I can't do anything special."

Jean giggled. "You could do that *Captain Jinks of the Horse Marines* tap dance we learned in gym. The one where we had to paw the ground with our feet."

Elaine leaned back against the arm of her chair and laughed. "I want people to applaud, not die laughing," she said. Then she sighed gustily. "I guess I don't have a thing to worry about. Nobody is going to ask me to swish a pompon in front of the rooting section or ask me to dance *Captain Jinks of the Horse Marines* in the variety show."

"I would like to be more . . . a part of things at school. And to have a boy like me," said Jean, reaching for another peanut.

"The trouble with us is that we are the salt-of-the-earth type," said Elaine gloomily. "The type that gets married someday and makes some man a good wife."

Jean laughed at her friend's gloom. "I don't think that is such a terrible fate."

"Well, you know," said Elaine vaguely. "Dishpans, mops. . . ."

"Diapers, budgets," added Jean, thinking that all these things were part of the life she wanted for herself. That was one reason why she was struggling to learn to sew. Still, she understood what Elaine meant. They were girls whom no one would ever expect to dance a ballet, fly an airplane, run for Congress.

"The only thing wrong with us," said Elaine, summing up the situation, "is that we are a couple of late bloomers."

And so, on the day school started after Christmas vacation, Jean, with her bangs cut short and without her glasses, got off the bus with Elaine, walked up the blurry steps, and entered a fuzzy school building.

"Come on, let's go upstairs," whispered Elaine. "If he's a senior, his locker is up there, and if we walk along sort of casually we might see him."

Jean hung back. "Oh, Elaine," she protested,

without much conviction. "If I did see him I think I would *die*."

"No, you wouldn't," said Elaine, taking Jean by the arm. "Come on. We don't have much time."

Jean allowed herself to be led up the steps to the crowded corridor on the second floor. "Now act as if we were really going someplace," directed Elaine, "and pretend you aren't looking for anyone."

Jean laughed nervously. "I don't have to pretend. I can't see very far."

Timidly the two girls patrolled the length of the corridor.

"Come on, let's go back," said Elaine, when they had reached the end. "He must be up here someplace."

Jean knew it was useless to protest in the face of Elaine's determination. And she did not really want to protest, because she wanted to see that boy again. Halfway down the length of the hall, not far from the trophy case, Elaine suddenly clutched her arm. "There he is!" she whispered.

Jean's nearsighted eyes swept the faces around her. "Where?" she asked.

"Pretend you aren't looking," advised Elaine.

"I'm not," said Jean. "I can't."

"Over there against the lockers," whispered Elaine. "In the green plaid shirt."

The plaid shirt emerged from the blur and above it a face, a good-looking face which Jean had seen before and which she now felt too timid to look at for more than an instant. Blushing, she quickly looked away.

Elaine, still clutching Jean's arm, giggled nervously, and the two girls hurried to the stairs, where they ran down the steps to the first floor.

Jean put on her glasses and found it a relief to be once more in a world with clear-cut edges. "Do you think he saw me?" she asked anxiously.

"I don't know. I think so," said Elaine, with her nervous giggle. Then she sighed. "He's *so* good-looking in that plaid shirt."

"I don't care," said Jean. "I'm going to pretend I never saw him before in my life. If he did see me and remember me, he didn't bother to speak. I am just going to forget the whole thing."

Jean did not forget, however, and she found that with careful timing she could make her path cross that of the boy several times a day. Each time she snatched off her glasses just before they met, looked straight ahead, and wished she could control the blush that rushed to her cheeks. She wished . . . she wished a lot of things. She wished that she was the kind of girl people noticed, that she had lots of pretty clothes, that she was three inches taller, two years older, and did not wear glasses.

Elaine did not forget either, and the two girls became tireless collectors of information about the boy. Every afternoon, as they rode home from school on the bus or, if it was not raining, walked so Jean could save her carfare, they compared notes and added to what they had jokingly begun to call his dossier, as if they were characters in a spy movie.

Working together to compile the boy's dossier gave Jean and Elaine the cozy feeling of sharing a delightful secret. Jean had not felt as close as this to Elaine since they were in the fourth grade and had formed the exclusive TEAJ Club. The letters stood for "The Elaine and Jean Club," and it was so exclusive that they were the only members. They had printed the initials on badges, which they had worn to school. They enjoyed the attention the badges had attracted from the rest of the fourth grade, but when the attention diminished because their classmates began to suspect that the club had no other members, the club was abandoned.

Jean filed away in her mind every scrap of information that she and Elaine gathered. She learned that the boy had five different plaid woolen shirts—the kind that had to be dry-cleaned. He usually bought the Dagwood Special instead of the regular cafeteria lunch, except on the days when he went across the street with a crowd of boys and ate a hamburger at the Shack.

Elaine, who was bolder than Jean, usually had more information to add to the dossier. He took chemistry—she had seen him coming out of the lab. His name was Johnny Chessler—he had left his notebook on a table in the library, and she had peeked inside. ("Elaine, what if he had *seen* you?") He knew lots of girls—wouldn't you just know—and he spent a lot of time talking to them in the halls. He lived at 11 Madrone Lane, high enough in the hills so that his house had a view. His telephone number was Toyon 1-4343—she had looked it up in the telephone book. He had a close friend named Homer Darvey, who was much too short for Elaine (wasn't that just her luck?) and was sort of funny-looking, with glasses and crinkly hair, which he wore cut short. She had seen Johnny coming out of a sporting-goods shop with a pair of skis over his shoulder (probably he had rented them for the week end) and he had driven off in a light-blue Chrysler with a white top and license number ENK729. She was sure of the number because she had written it down.

Strangely, once the girls knew Johnny's name, they rarely mentioned it. Johnny was simply "he." This was due partly to caution (they did not want any of the girls at school to know about their interest in Johnny), and partly to their childish pleasure in sharing a secret. Even at home Jean referred to Johnny, when she felt she had to talk about him, as "that boy who danced with me that time."

The girls discovered that by riding the bus to the end of the line and climbing four blocks up the hill, they could walk back past Johnny's house, and this they did. Trying to act as if they were not even looking at the house, they observed it carefully. It was a modern house with a flat roof, and a carport instead of a garage. Because it was built on a steep lot, there was no front lawn but, in its place, a bank covered with low-growing shrubs. Although there was nothing the least bit funny about the house (it was, in fact, a house that both girls admired), Jean and Elaine always burst into a fit of giggles when they were safely past it. One Saturday they even made the walking of Dandy, a most surprised dog, an excuse for going past Johnny's house in hopes of catching a glimpse of Johnny. Jean hoped that if Johnny happened to see them he would realize that Dandy had once been a show dog, even though half his tail was missing now.

And with each shred of information that Jean stored away she found it more and more difficult to forget the boy. Johnny Chessler. Johnny. Jean squeezed her memory hard, and brought back the remembered scent of soap and clean wool and, with it, the memory of his toe treading on hers. It was not what a girl could call a beautiful memory, but it was a memory that Jean clung to. It was the only memory concerning a boy that she had to cling to.

From the school paper the girls learned that Johnny took part in the Saturday-morning broadcast, called "Hi-times," that Northgate High presented over the local radio station. After that Jean, whose share of the Saturday housework was dusting and vacuuming the living room, always turned on the radio and listened, dustcloth in hand, for Johnny's voice. When she heard him speak, introducing a record or interviewing a basketball player, she compared his voice with her memory of the voice which had said, "May I have this dance?" She hung on every word.

Then, early in February, there came a few days of sudden spring weather. The sky was blue, with fluffy white clouds sailing above hills green from winter rains. During lunch period students sunned themselves on the high-school steps or strolled about, enjoying the warmth. It was the kind of day that made a girl wish she could throw away all her winter sweaters and skirts and go out and buy a whole new wardrobe of gay cotton dresses.

Jean, who had eaten her lunch, brought from home, with Elaine, who had bought her lunch, was eager to go outdoors and enjoy the false spring day. The two girls walked aimlessly around the school grounds, enjoying the sunshine and pausing to look at the flowering quince blooming under the windows on the side of the building that got the afternoon sun. The pink blossoms on the bare branches meant that a more lasting spring was not far away. Jean wanted to say to the other trees and shrubs, which were leafless, "Hurry up and bloom!"

It was out at the playing field that the two girls saw Johnny Chessler, with a group of boys who were clowning in the sunshine. They were taking turns seeing how far they could walk on their hands. Confident that Johnny was too busy to notice them, the girls stopped to watch. This time Johnny was wearing his blue plaid shirt, with the sleeves rolled up, and he looked, as always, extremely attractive. Gracefully he bent over, dropped his weight onto his hands, and flipped his feet into the air, spilling change out of his pocket upon the grass. He walked easily ten or twelve feet before he stood up, grinned, and accepted his change from his friend Homer, who had picked it up for him.

The breeze ruffled Jean's bangs. Johnny was *so* attractive. "I wonder how old he is," she remarked wistfully, pushing up the sleeves of her sweater.

"I know how to find out," said Elaine.

"How?" asked Jean.

"Ask him," answered Elaine.

This idea was so farfetched that Jean did not bother to comment.

"And I'm going to," announced Elaine impulsively.

Jean was aghast. "Elaine! You wouldn't!"

"Yes, I would," said Elaine, the light of daring in her eyes.

"Elaine!" protested Jean, seeing that her friend meant what she said. "No!"

Her protest was not heeded. Elaine, her head held high, marched across the playing field and through the crowd of boys, who were now playing leapfrog. Jean watched in fascination and consternation until Elaine approached Johnny. Then, because she could not bear to watch any longer, she turned her back and began to walk toward the main building, hoping that if Johnny glanced in her direction he would not think she and Elaine were together. She wanted no part of this latest inspiration of Elaine's. Sometimes you'd think it was Elaine with whom Johnny had danced.

Jean climbed the steps and entered the building, its nearly empty corridors seeming like dark tunnels after the bright spring sunlight. She walked to her locker and had just finished twirling the combination on the lock when she heard Elaine's hurried footsteps.

"Jean!" gasped Elaine, her face crimson from hurrying and from excitement. "I did it!" She leaned back against the row of lockers and clasped her notebook to her chest. "Just wait till I tell you!"

"Elaine, you didn't tell him I wanted to know, did you?" demanded Jean.

"Oh, no. Nothing like that," said Elaine, taking a big breath. Apparently she had a lot to tell. Either that, or she was enjoying making a big anecdote out of a small experience. "Well, I walked across the playing field and through this bunch of boys clowning around, and I walked up to him—he was standing by the backstop—and I stood right in front of him. He was talking to some fellows and he didn't notice me. Well, there I was, and I had to do something with all the other fellows looking at me, so I reached out and poked his arm with my finger as if I was ringing a doorbell or something—his sleeve was rolled up and his arm was brown and sort of hairy, *you* know—and all the fellows stopped talking and looked at me. Honestly, I just about *died!* But there I was, and I had to do something, didn't I?"

"You said that before," Jean reminded her.

"And so I just came right out with it. 'How old are you?' I asked. And wait till I tell you what he said!"

Jean waited.

"He grinned sort of a lazy grin and said—these were his exact words—'I'm seventeen, but tell *her* I'm nineteen.' And I said, 'Thank you,' and got away as fast as I could." Elaine, her story at an end, was out of breath.

"Oh—" was all that Jean could say. What did Johnny mean? That he had missed none of it—the strolls through the upstairs hall to catch a glimpse of him, the giggling, whispered conferences when they had seen him? Probably he had seen Elaine write down his license number and thought that Jean had asked her to spy on him. "Oh, Elaine," said Jean miserably. "Why did you have to go and do it? He probably thought I asked you to."

"But don't you see?" said Elaine. "He has noticed you!"

"I guess he couldn't help it, the way we watched him and giggled as if we had never seen a boy before," said Jean, in a flat voice. "Well, now we know we aren't invisible. We must have thought we were. Let's just forget the whole thing." It wasn't as though she had ever really known Johnny, or anything like that. To him, she was just a girl he had danced with once (but why? *why?*) and now he must think she was a very silly person. And he would be right. She *was* silly.

"I don't see why you feel that way," said Elaine. "I thought you would be pleased that he had noticed you. I would be."

"I am never going to look at him again," resolved Jean. "Well, my next class is in the annex. I guess I might as well go out before the halls are mobbed."

"If that's the way you feel," said Elaine humbly, "I am terribly sorry. I just thought. . . ."

Jean walked toward the bright square of light made by the open door at the end of the corridor. Students were beginning to straggle in from outdoors. Automatically Jean nodded and spoke to acquaintances, but her mouth and eyes refused to smile. How could she ever have behaved as she had? Why, everyone in school must know she had a crush on Johnny! And everyone must know how hopeless it was, because Johnny was a senior, attractive and popular in his collection of expensive woolen shirts. And who was she? Just a fifteen-year-old girl, small for her age, and noticed by practically no one at all.

As Jean walked through the doorway and emerged from the dark hall into the sunlight, she almost had to close her eyes because of the sudden brightness. At the foot of the steps, as she was turning toward the annex, she bumped into a boy. "Excuse me," she said, and stepped to the right. Unfortunately, the boy stepped to his left at the same moment. Then they both stepped to Jean's left and Jean was suddenly aware that she was facing a blue plaid shirt. This boy was Johnny.

"Say, what is this, a minuet?" asked Johnny, and then smiled when he recognized Jean. It was a genuine smile, warm and friendly. "Oh—hi," he said. "How's the cute girl?"

"Hi," answered Jean, and fled toward her classroom in the annex. She wondered where she had found the breath to speak that one syllable, because now she could scarcely breathe. Johnny had smiled and had actually spoken to her! He had called her a cute girl. Maybe Elaine was right after all. Maybe she ought to be pleased that Johnny had noticed her.

As she slipped into her seat, Jean's emotions were in a snarl. Johnny had remembered her, or anyway noticed her at school, and now he had smiled and spoken and called her a cute girl. Nobody had ever called her a cute girl before. Cute? What did it really mean? It was a word she had often used carelessly, like all the other girls, but she had never thought of it as a boy's word. Kittens were cute. Puppies were cute. Hats were cute.

Jean slid out of her seat and walked to the dictionary on the stand by the blackboard. She turned toward the end of the C's and ran her finger down the columns until she came to the word *cute*. She studied the definition intently: "cute (kūt), adj., cuter, cutest. 1. *U.S. Colloq.* Pleasingly pretty or dainty." Pleasingly pretty or dainty. Then the word really was a compliment!

Jean, who had been called Midge or Half Pint so often that she had come to think of herself as insignificant, now felt herself blossoming. A boy had called her a cute girl, which meant pleasingly pretty or dainty, *and she had been wearing her glasses.* She began to feel that she really was pleasingly pretty or dainty—in the United States in a colloquial or conversational sense, of course.

Suddenly Jean laughed out loud. Colloquially in the United States was the very best way for a girl who lived in California to be pleasingly pretty or dainty.

"The dictionary is funny?" remarked the boy in the nearest seat.

"My favorite joke book." Jean smiled blithely.

"Dames," muttered the boy, and although he tapped his forehead he returned Jean's smile.

Jean felt as if the boy were noticing her for the first time. Prettily and daintily she slid into her seat.

CHAPTER
3

AFTER the near collision on the steps, Johnny began to speak to Jean whenever he saw her at school. Every word he spoke increased her happiness— someone was noticing her at last. "Hi. How's the cute girl?" he would drawl, while she colored in the light of his smile. Sometimes he would say simply, "Hello, Jean." This made her even happier, because the words told her that Johnny had taken the trouble to learn her name. She imagined him stopping someone in the hall and asking, "Say, who is that girl over there? The cute one."

One cloudy afternoon late in February, Jean, quite by accident, made an important discovery. The last class of her day was Clothing I. Her project for this class was a dress with set-in sleeves, a problem that had given her considerable trouble. No matter how many times she basted those sleeves into the armholes, they persisted in puckering at the shoulders. That afternoon Jean had grimly ripped out her basting threads twice, and by pinning the sleeves every quarter of an inch (so that was the secret!), she finally had them basted smoothly into place.

Jean took her work to Mrs. Rankin, the sewing teacher, to have it approved, but she was put off while her teacher interrupted the class to make an announcement. The Costume Club, whose adviser was Mrs. Rankin, needed members, and anyone who studied Clothing was eligible. Jean, who always thought of clubs as activities for other people but not for herself, paid little attention to this announcement. Sue was taking extra courses in typing and shorthand and did not have time for clubs, and so Jean, used to following in her sister's footsteps, had not thought about joining any clubs either. By waiting with her sewing in hand until Mrs. Rankin was through speaking, Jean finally had her work approved, but by that time the class was nearly over and all the sewing machines were occupied.

Jean made up her mind that she was not going to leave until she had those sleeves stitched into her dress. She was tired of sleeves, she was tired of the dress, and she wanted the whole project out of the way. She whiled away the time tidying her sewing box. This had been an exasperating afternoon.

"Are you going to join the Costume Club?" whispered Mitsuko Yamoto, who sat across the table from Jean.

"No, I don't think so," said Jean, without thinking at all.

"I am," said Mitsuko. "Everybody says it is lots of fun to be behind the scenes at the senior play and the variety show and things. The school rents most of the costumes and all the club has to do is press them, fit them, and see that the right people get into them."

"Come on, Jean, why don't you join?" asked another girl who shared the table.

Someone vacated a sewing machine—fortunately one of the good ones—and Jean, intent on her sleeves, hurried to get it before someone else did and did not bother to answer the girl's question. She stitched slowly and carefully. While she stitched in the right sleeve, the bell rang, but she went on working. She was about to stitch the left sleeve when Elaine came into the sewing room.

"Oh, there you are," said Elaine. "I've been looking all over for you. Aren't you going home?"

"Not until I finish this sleeve," answered Jean. "I

have had to rip it out so many times I don't dare try to hurry with it."

"I guess I'll run along," said Elaine. "Mother wanted me to come straight home today so we could do some shopping."

Jean successfully stitched the sleeve, put away her sewing things, gathered up her books, and hurried out of the room, very nearly bumping into Johnny and his friend Homer Darvey, who were walking down the hall. "Oh—hello," she said, startled at seeing Johnny.

"Hi," answered Johnny, with a grin.

"Hi," echoed Homer.

Because the two boys were obviously leaving the building by the same door she always used, Jean found herself walking with them. In a panic she tried to think of something to say.

"Do you take sewing?" Johnny asked.

"Yes," answered Jean, longing for witty words to spring to her lips.

"I didn't think girls knew how to sew any more," remarked Johnny.

"Oh, yes," answered Jean. "Practically everybody sews. Girls, I mean." It was silly to feel so confused, just because she was walking down the hall with a boy—two boys—but Jean could not help it.

"I was just telling Homer about my trip to the mountains last week end," remarked Johnny, as they left the building and walked down the steps.

"Do you ski?" asked Jean, knowing very well that he did.

"Every chance I get," answered Johnny. "I drove up early Saturday morning with some fellows. One of them has a cabin."

"Then you must have run into that storm I read about in the papers," said Jean, pleased that she could add to the conversation.

"I'll say we did," said Johnny. "It looked pretty threatening when we got there—the wind was blowing and the clouds were getting lower all the time—so we decided to get in some skiing before we took time to unload our food or our sleeping bags. Well, I was up on the mountain when the storm broke. The wind must have been blowing sixty miles an hour when I came down that mountain, and the snow was so thick it seemed to be coming from all directions at once. I didn't know whether I was going to make it back to the cabin without hitting a tree or a boulder, or not. And I wasn't sure where the other fellows were."

"Weren't you scared?" asked Jean.

"Some, but I knew that if I kept going downhill

I would come to the cabin," said Johnny, his gestures suggesting skiing.

Jean could see him, slim and handsome in his ski clothes, skiing through the blizzard. "What happened? Did you make it all right?"

"It took some doing, but I finally got down that mountain," said Johnny. "I could hardly see the cabin. Well, the way the snow was drifting I thought we might get snowed in before the week end was over. Then I remembered the sleeping bags and all the food in the car, and I thought I better get it unloaded before the car got buried. So I left my skis on the porch and sort of felt my way over to the car. I had just opened the door to take out a box of groceries from the floor of the back seat, when I happened to look up and there was the biggest bear I have ever seen. He was so close I could have shaken hands with him."

"Johnny!" exclaimed Jean. "What did you do?"

"I can tell you I didn't waste any time getting into that car and slamming the door," Johnny went on. "Well, that bear went prowling around the car—I guess he must have smelled the bacon. Bears like bacon, you know. Well, there I was shut in the car with the bear snuffling around. Sometimes the car would shake and I knew he was trying to break in.

I was really caught in a trap. I couldn't chase the bear away, and I didn't dare get out." Johnny paused dramatically.

Jean waited in suspense for Johnny to go on with the story. He smiled down at his eager audience, enjoying the suspense he had created.

Then Homer spoke. "Except that bears hibernate in the winter," he said seriously.

Jean and Johnny stared at Homer and then shouted with laughter. His statement of fact was such an anticlimax.

"Homer, I have never had the rug pulled out from under me quite so fast," said Johnny, slapping Homer on the back. "Oh, well. It was a good story while it lasted."

Earnest, earth-bound Homer, with no imagination at all, thought Jean. How like him to spoil a good story. "But maybe this bear had insomnia," suggested Jean. "Maybe he couldn't sleep, so he got up to fix himself a snack."

"Thanks, Jean. You're my pal," said Johnny, smiling down at her as they stood on the sidewalk. "Well, so long."

"So long," said Homer.

"Good-by," said Jean, and stood a moment watching Johnny as he walked toward the parking lot with Homer. Johnny was everything she had hoped he would be—interesting, full of fun, the kind of boy who would make up for a girl's shyness. Jean chose to walk home along a street lined with cherry trees flowering like pink clouds in the sharp breeze. That was one of the nice things about Northgate. In the flat part of town the streets were lined with different kinds of flowering trees. Jean could walk to school on a plum street and walk home on a cherry street. Jean reached out and caught a pink petal as it drifted to the ground. Johnny had walked down the hall with her!

After that Jean took to lingering in the sewing room after school, so that she could leave at the time Johnny might be coming down the hall. At first Jean made up excuses for not being able to leave when Elaine came for her, but finally, when she saw that Elaine's feelings were hurt she whispered, so none of the other girls would hear, "Look, Elaine, if I leave just a little later, sometimes I run into Johnny and he walks down the hall with me."

"So that's it! I was afraid maybe you were mad at me about something." Comprehension sparkled on Elaine's face. "Don't worry about me. I'll keep out of your way." Naturally in a situation like this a boy took precedence over a girl. "Good luck and happy hunting!"

"I'm not using a bow and arrow." Jean could not

help laughing at Elaine's expression. "I knew you would understand," she said seriously, thinking that one of the reasons she valued Elaine's friendship was Elaine's cheerful acceptance of whatever she wanted to do.

Once Jean found Johnny and Homer waiting for her outside the classroom door. Actually *waiting* for her! This, Jean felt, was significant, and after that if she did not see the two boys, she waited for them to come. When Jean could find no reason for lingering any longer by the door of the sewing room, when she had reread half a dozen times the schedule of classes posted outside the door, when she had started to leave and stopped, pretending to go through her notebook looking for something she might have forgotten, she walked home alone—and missed the companionship of Elaine.

"Hasn't Johnny come yet?" one of the girls in the sewing class asked Jean one afternoon.

"Johnny?" Jean pretended surprise. "Oh, I wasn't waiting for Johnny."

Once Homer appeared alone. Jean could not avoid walking out of the building with him. "Where's Johnny?" she asked.

"Trying out for the variety show," answered Homer.

Jean remembered hearing the announcement of the tryouts in the morning bulletins for the past week. The show was to be built around the theme "Through the Years," and any student or group of students who had an act could try out. Jean, who had no desire for the spotlight, had passed over the announcement without giving it any thought. Now her thoughts fell quickly into logical sequence: Johnny, variety show, costumes, Costume Club, the club's new member as of the first thing tomorrow morning—Jean Jarrett! It was the most natural thing in the world.

"What kind of an act is he trying out with?" Jean asked.

"It isn't an act exactly," explained Homer. "They need someone to be the narrator. You know, sort of hold the acts together, and he is trying out for that part."

What sort of costume would a narrator wear? A circus ringmaster's costume? A different costume for each act? Top hat, white tie, and tails? How handsome Johnny would look in evening clothes! "Don't you want to be in the show?" Jean asked, because she felt she had to make conversation with Homer as they left the building. Boys like Homer never took part in variety shows.

"I'm already in it," said Homer. "I play a violin in the orchestra."

"That's nice," said Jean vaguely, as they reached the foot of the steps. "Well—good-by." She did hope Johnny would wear evening clothes.

The next day Jean found Johnny and Homer waiting by the sewing-room door. Johnny told her that he had been chosen to narrate the variety show and she told him that she had been sure he would get the part and that since she was a member of the Costume Club, she would be seeing him at rehears-

als. Everything, she felt, was working out very nicely indeed.

Then there was one dreadful day when Jean, who had waited too long by the sewing-room door, was about to give up and leave when she saw Johnny and Homer coming toward her with another girl, a girl named Peggy Jo. Johnny, who was smiling at Peggy Jo, was engrossed in telling her something that required broad gestures.

Jean felt a pang of pure despair. She now had a rival for her brief walk with Johnny, and that rival was Peggy Jo, who was tall, quiet, and beautiful, but a girl who wore her beauty carelessly as if it were of no interest to her. Her long fair hair was twisted into an untidy knot at the nape of her neck. She was wearing a baggy brown skirt and a tan suède jacket that needed cleaning. She looked, Jean thought, like a girl who would not bother to wash her face before going to bed. But for all her carelessness there was something about Peggy Jo that made people aware of her. What that something was Jean did not know, but she did know that she herself lacked this quality. That made it even harder to see Johnny walking with Peggy Jo.

Jean was about to slip back into the sewing room, to allow Johnny to pass without seeing her, when Johnny looked directly at her. Jean was embarrassed to have him see her waiting for him when he was with another girl. She hesitated, not knowing how to handle the situation, and while she hesitated Johnny winked at her. He looked straight into her eyes and winked. And suddenly everything was all right again. That wink told her that Peggy Jo did not really matter, that he liked Jean, and that he could not really help it, because Peggy Jo came along and walked down the hall with him.

Jean smiled at Johnny and walked out of the

building alone. She wondered where Elaine was, and thought how much fun she and Elaine used to have talking over the events of their day as they walked home from school. It almost seemed as if she and Elaine were growing apart lately. Elaine seemed so busy—she had even managed to get a part in the variety show. A group of girls from her gym class planned to perform an Indian hoop dance and had asked Elaine to join them. It was scarcely a part to bring an applauding student body to its feet, but Elaine, a long-legged and enthusiastic Indian, was ostentatiously busy with rehearsals. Jean hoped that as a new member of the Costume Club she would not only see more of Johnny but also of Elaine.

Then one Friday when Johnny and Homer had walked out of the building with Jean, Johnny turned to her and instead of saying good-by, said, "Are you doing anything tomorrow night?"

"Why . . . no," admitted Jean.

"I thought I might drop around awhile if you are going to be home," said Johnny.

"I—I would love to have you," answered Jean, frantically trying to think what she could do with her family when a boy came to call. "I mean—I really would."

"I'll see you around eight," said Johnny.

"That will be nice," answered Jean, expecting him to ask where she lived.

Johnny grinned. "So long," he said. "I'll see you tomorrow night." Apparently he already knew where she lived.

"So long," said Homer.

Jean wasted a second's thought, as she did almost every day, in wondering what Johnny saw in an unimaginative boy like Homer. Then, elated, she hurried straight to Elaine's house. "Guess what!" she burst out, when Elaine met her at the door.

"You have a date with Johnny!" guessed Elaine.

It was blissful to be able to answer yes.

"Come in and tell me everything. Absolutely everything!" said Elaine.

"There isn't an awful lot to tell," admitted Jean and told Elaine what little there was to tell.

"Golly. He really asked you for a date. Now maybe there is hope for me." Elaine did not try to conceal her admiration. "I was going to ask you over for supper tomorrow night, but now that you are busy, I think I'll ask Maxine instead."

When Jean reached her own small house, she had no recollection of having walked there. She had been thinking about the house and how tiny it was and how awkward it would be trying to entertain Johnny, with the whole family sitting in the living room. She walked into the bedroom, where Sue was sitting at their table studying several leaflets advertising dress patterns, the sort of leaflets given away at pattern counters in department stores.

Jean could not wait to break the news. "Sue, guess what. Johnny Chessler is coming over to see me tomorrow night!"

"Johnny *Chessler?*" exclaimed Sue.

"Yes." Jean could not help feeling indignant at the way Sue spoke. "Is there anything wrong with that?"

"No. No, of course not," Sue said slowly. "Was *he* the boy who danced with you that time?"

"Yes." Jean's feelings were still slightly ruffled.

"Oh. I knew you were interested in the boy who danced with you and I knew you talked to Johnny once in a while, but. . . . Well, it just never occurred to me that they were the same boy," Sue explained. "Johnny is in my English class and . . . I just never thought about you and Johnny together, is all."

Jean looked speculatively at her sister. Sue was such a quiet girl, it was not often easy to tell what she was thinking. Could it be, Jean wondered, that

Sue liked Johnny herself? Poor Sue, it wasn't going to be easy to have her younger sister dating first, especially since Sue had already said she wanted to meet a nice boy. Well, that was life.

Sue studied a page of dresses designed in Paris. "I can't picture anyone I know wearing these," she remarked and then said, as if it had been Jean's date with Johnny that she had been thinking about all the time, "What are you going to do with him when he gets here?"

"I don't know exactly," Jean confessed. Then she lowered her voice and asked, "What am I going to do about Mother and Dad? There's no place for them to go." Tactfully she refrained from saying, "And you, too."

"Don't worry about me," said Sue, as if she had heard the unspoken words. "I can sew or study in our room. But I don't know about Dad. . . ."

Once more Jean went over the house in her mind. A living room not much larger than a nine by twelve rug, a dining room that was practically part of the living room, two bedrooms, one bathroom, a kitchen that was just a kitchen and not a family room like those pictures in house and garden magazines, a breakfast nook that showed how old the house was, because houses were not built with breakfast nooks any more. That was all. It would help if the breakfast nook was a breakfast room, but it was not. It was so awfully . . . nooky.

"Dad may be a problem," agreed Jean, wishing that a rumpus room or a family room or any kind of extra space would suddenly attach itself to the house.

"Maybe we could move the television set into the breakfast nook and pretend we wanted to see something during supper," suggested Sue. "If we didn't move it back, Dad might just happen to sit there and watch it."

"That won't work," said Jean, pleased that Sue was entering into her plans in spite of any feelings she might have about the date. "You know Dad won't allow television during meals."

"I guess you're right," said Sue. "But don't worry. We'll think of something."

"We'll have to," said Jean, "but I don't know what. I can't expect Mother and Daddy to go to bed at eight o'clock, just because Johnny is coming over to see me."

Sue pushed aside the fashion leaflets and smiled at her sister. "We'll manage Dad somehow," she said. "He may be strict in some ways, but underneath it all he is just an old softy."

"But you never can tell what he is going to be strict about," Jean reminded her sister. "Look how he feels about baby-sitting."

Jean waited until suppertime to break the news to her mother and father. When everyone had been served she said as matter-of-factly as she could manage, "A boy named Johnny Chessler is coming over to see me tomorrow night."

"Why, how nice, dear," said Mrs. Jarrett. "Chessler? I don't recall hearing the name. What is he like?"

"Well. . . ." Jean hesitated, wondering how to describe a boy like Johnny to her mother and father. She did not know how to explain that Johnny was handsome and charming and all the things a girl would like a boy to be. "He—he is nice-looking, with curly hair, and he wears the most beautiful woolen shirts, the kind that have to be dry-cleaned, and he is—oh, I don't know. . . ."

"You are telling us what he looks like," said Mr. Jarrett, "but what I want to know is, is he good enough for my daughter."

"Oh, Daddy," said Jean with a nervous laugh. Her father was teasing, she knew, but she understood him well enough to know that beneath his banter was a serious note.

"And what *I* want to know," said Sue, "is how she is going to entertain a boy. We can't all sit around the living room and stare at him."

Jean mentally thanked her sister for bringing up this touchy problem.

"No young whippersnapper is going to drive me out of my house," said Mr. Jarrett.

The sisters exchanged a glance that said they understood their father was not entirely joking. "Now, Dad," said Sue, "don't start playing the heavy father."

"We'll manage somehow," said Mrs. Jarrett reassuringly. "Of course the girls will be entertaining boys and we will have to figure out a way for them to do it."

"I'll stay in my room and study," volunteered Sue. "I have to do it sometime this week end and it might as well be then. That will remove me from the scene."

"Your father and I will want to meet him," said Mrs. Jarrett.

"Of course," agreed Jean. "He would think it was peculiar if I didn't have any family around at all."

Mrs. Jarrett sighed. "I do wish we could buy a larger house. Or at least build onto this one. Perhaps I should enter that contest I saw announced the other day."

"What is the prize this time?" asked Mr. Jarrett. "Not a live kangaroo like you thought you might win for naming that airline."

"I thought it was rather ridiculous at the time," said Mrs. Jarrett. "The winner receives his weight in gold. Or rather the equivalent in money for writing the last line of a limerick about a new kind of home permanent."

Mrs. Jarrett's family shouted with laughter. "You don't have to enter a contest," said Mr. Jarrett. "You are worth your weight in gold already."

"Have some more potatoes, Mother," urged Jean. "Just in case you win."

"Every little ounce would help," said Sue. "How about some more dressing on your coleslaw?"

"Just don't forget—I won the television set," Mrs. Jarrett reminded her family.

"But nobody has said what I am going to do with Johnny," Jean said, bringing the conversation back to the original problem.

"Just who is the fellow, anyway?" asked Mr. Jarrett.

"A boy at school." Jean resigned herself to answering questions of this sort from her father.

"If he wants to call on Jean, I am sure he is a very nice boy," said Mrs. Jarrett soothingly.

"Do you know him?" Mr. Jarrett asked Sue.

"Yes," answered Sue. "He's in my English class."

This seemed to mollify Mr. Jarrett. At least he did not ask further questions about Johnny.

"But *nobody* has said what I am going to do with him." Jean cast an anxious glance at Sue, who could be counted on to understand and help out.

"We could all have a lively game of old maid or lotto," said Mr. Jarrett.

"Daddy!" Jean could not help sounding stricken. What a dreadful idea, suggesting that Johnny play old maid or lotto with her family. He would never want to come again.

Mr. Jarrett patted Jean's hand. "Don't worry, daughter. I was only joking. Of course you may entertain your young man." It sounded so quaint and old-fashioned, his saying "your young man."

"The breakfast nook," said Mrs. Jarrett as Jean and Sue rose to clear the table. "It is the only place for us. We'll move the television set in here before Johnny comes and after we meet him, we can come back here, and your father can watch his television programs while I work on a contest."

Jean and Sue exchanged a smile in the kitchen. "Whew!" mouthed Jean silently.

"What are we having for dessert, Mother?" asked Sue.

"Vanilla pudding," answered Mrs. Jarrett. "There

is a jar of strawberry preserves open. You might put a dab on top of each serving to give it a little color."

"Let's call it blancmange," suggested Sue. "It sounds so much more glamorous. When I used to read in *Little Women* about the March girls' taking blancmange to Laurie when he was sick, I thought it must be a great delicacy."

"Why, so did I!" exclaimed Jean. "I felt terribly disillusioned to find out it was plain old vanilla cornstarch pudding."

"I suppose this boy is going to eat us out of house and home," commented Mr. Jarrett, as the family began to eat the vanilla pudding, or blancmange.

"That is just in the funny papers. At least I think it is," said Jean, "but I suppose I should give him something to eat. I hadn't thought of that."

Jean thought it over. She had a vague notion that when a boy came to see a girl, the girl usually took him into the kitchen to raid the refrigerator. The Jarrett refrigerator, unfortunately, did not merit raiding. Vanilla pudding and cold meat loaf were hardly the sort of things a girl could offer a boy. And the milk. . . . It was stored in half-gallon cartons which Mrs. Jarrett bought at the market, because she saved two and a half cents a quart, just as she bought butter in one-pound pieces because it cost five cents less than a pound of butter divided into quarters. Jean did wish they could have milk delivered in bottles from a dairy. It seemed to her that quartered butter and milk in bottles always looked so elegant in a refrigerator.

"I think you should fix something ahead of time," said Sue, who also must have been taking mental inventory of the Jarrett refrigerator. "Something you can whisk onto the table. That is what I would do if he were coming to see me."

"What table?" asked Jean. "Mother and Dad will be in the breakfast nook. Eating with a boy in the dining room is too formal."

"Serve it from a tray on the coffee table," said Sue.

"I think that is a very practical suggestion. Now don't worry, Jean. I am sure it will all work out." Mrs. Jarrett patted her daughter's hand.

Jean looked around the table at her mother, smiling at her so reassuringly, at her ruddy-complexioned father, who was so tenderhearted underneath his sternness, at Sue, who had helped her, even though it must hurt to have her younger sister have the first date. Jean was completely happy. She not only had a date with Johnny, she also had the most wonderful, understanding family in the whole world.

CHAPTER

4

Mrs. Jarrett, in galoshes and her wet-weather coat, stood by the drainboard enjoying a last-minute sip of coffee before she left for her day of selling yardage at Fabrics, Etc. "It is such miserable weather I doubt if we will be very busy today," she remarked, "even though we are having a good sale of seersucker mill ends. There are some very good buys—pieces that would make up into sturdy pajamas for children."

Sue, who was stacking the breakfast dishes, looked out the kitchen window into the gray morning. "Poor Daddy, delivering mail in this awful weather."

" 'Neither snow, nor rain, nor heat—' " began Jean, as she carried her plate from the breakfast nook into the kitchen.

" '—Nor gloom of night stays these couriers from

94

the swift completion of their appointed rounds,'"
finished Sue and her mother in unison. Mrs. Jarrett
plucked a couple of dead blossoms from the brightly
blooming African violet on the window sill.

"I'll have a pot of hot coffee waiting for him when
he gets home this afternoon," volunteered Jean.

"That's my good girl." Mrs. Jarrett smiled at her
youngest daughter. "Have you thought what you
are going to serve in the way of refreshments this
evening?"

Jean was happy to have the conversation turned
to the evening that lay before her. "I had thought
of that dessert made of chocolate cookies with
whipped cream between, because it is supposed to
stand awhile before it is served, and I could make it
after lunch," she said, as Sue began to wash the
breakfast dishes. "Or is that too expensive?"

"I think we can manage." Mrs. Jarrett opened a
cupboard, took down a canister and pulled out some
of the housekeeping money, which she handed to
Jean. "This should be enough. You might even buy
a small jar of maraschino cherries, too."

"Thank you, Mother," said Jean. "I'll make enough
so we can have some for supper, too." It did not
seem right to use so much of the housekeeping
money for herself and Johnny.

"And, Jean," Mrs. Jarrett continued, "be sure to plan some way to entertain him. You might get that old Chinese checker set out of the garage and set it up on the coffee table."

"Oh, Mother," protested Jean. "Nobody plays Chinese checkers any more. That went out with bustles."

"Not quite," said Mrs. Jarrett. "Johnny doesn't have to play if he doesn't want to, but it might make things easier if you had something on hand in case you need it." Mrs. Jarrett set her empty coffee cup on the drainboard for Sue to wash. "I hope Johnny has a good time this evening. I am so glad boys are beginning to come to the house."

Jean felt that her mother's use of the plural was a little optimistic.

"What are you going to do today, Sue?" asked Mrs. Jarrett.

"Straighten our room and then go downtown to the main library to gather material for my term paper," answered Sue. " 'Should Capital Punishment be Abolished?' "

"I didn't know high-school students were still abolishing capital punishment," remarked Mrs. Jarrett, as she opened the back door. "Well, good-by, girls. I'll try to catch the five thirty-three bus so we can have an early supper."

"Good-by, Mother," answered Jean. "I hope you sell lots of remnants."

Jean set to work cleaning the living room and dining room, and soon discovered it was much more fun to clean house for a boy than for her family. She forgot about the weather and set about trying to make the living room attractive. She ran the vacuum cleaner and used an attachment to remove Dandy's hair from the chair he slept in when no one was looking. At ten o'clock she turned on the radio to hear the Hi-times broadcast and sat, toying with the vacuum-cleaner attachment, lulled into a daydream by the smooth flow of Johnny's voice. It was too bad the program wasted time playing records—she would much rather listen to a full fifteen minutes of Johnny.

The day grew so dark that Jean had to turn on the light to dust when Hi-times was over. She had not realized the shabbiness of the furniture until now, when she tried to see her house through Johnny's eyes. She turned the cushions of the couch to find the least worn sides. She scrubbed the soiled spot on the back of her father's favorite chair with ammonia and water and then shoved the chair over a thin spot in the carpet. Her father should not object just this once, since he was going to spend most of the evening in the breakfast nook anyway. She dusted with unusual thoroughness, remembering to wipe off the window sills and the rungs of the dining-room chairs. Dustcloth in hand, she paused to look critically around the room. It was comfortable, even if it was shabby, but it needed something to brighten it, something to divert the eye—Johnny's eye—from the walls in need of a fresh coat of paint. She wished she could think of a way to hide the crack in the plaster over the door into the hall.

Jean went to the bathroom at the rear of the house and looked out into the yard in hope of seeing a few flowers that she could cut. The day was even more forbidding than she had realized. The small lawn was sodden, and the few geraniums along the fence were beaten down as if they would never have the courage to rise again. Juncos had stripped the berries from the cotoneaster in the corner of the yard, so there was no hope of creating an interesting arrangement from a few of its branches. Then Jean remembered her mother's African violet on the kitchen window sill. Its fuzzy green leaves and purple blossoms would make a spot of life and color.

Jean carried the African violet into the living room, where she tried it in front of the mirror over the mantelpiece, on the coffee table, on a lamp table, and finally back on the mantelpiece, where it stayed because, reflected in the mirror, it was almost as good as having two plants.

"Oh, Johnny, oh, Johnny, dum de de dum," Jean hummed, as she turned the plant so the most blossoms would show. Probably her mother was right about the Chinese checker set, even though Johnny might think it terribly old-fashioned of them to keep the game around. If she found conversation difficult—not that she would with a boy like Johnny, but *if* she did—she could casually make the first move, smile at Johnny, and say, "Your turn. Isn't it a quaint old game. My father simply adores it and insists we keep a set in the living room all the time." Or something like that. The more Jean thought about it, the more certain she became that this was exactly what she would have to do, except that she would have to omit the line about her father's adoring Chinese checkers. Conversation with her whole family within earshot might be difficult. She would like to spend the evening talking to Johnny, getting to know him better. She particularly wanted to find out why he had asked her to dance that evening in December, but this sort of conversation would be impossible, unless her father happened to watch a good noisy western on television and they could talk under cover of gunfire from the breakfast nook.

Jean shoved Dandy, who appeared restless, out the back door into the storm and let him in again a few minutes later. Then as she dragged the dusty checker box out of a pile of cartons in the garage, she found another worry nagging at her. Because her father had to get up at five o'clock in the morning on work days in order to eat breakfast and be at the post office by six, he was inclined to yawn, sometimes rather noisily, by nine-thirty in the evening. Wouldn't it be dreadful if he started yawning from the breakfast nook while she and Johnny were talking? She was positive that Johnny's father, whom she pictured as a tweedy commuter with a brief case, never yawned.

When Sue had not come back from the library by lunch time, Jean prepared herself a peanut-butter sandwich, poured herself a glass of milk from a carton, and ate her chilly lunch standing beside the floor furnace with her skirt ballooned out by the hot air.

After lunch she put on her sneakers and raincoat to go to the market to buy the chocolate cookies, whipping cream, and maraschino cherries. The rain slanted against the street in sheets and she had to leap the gutters, which boiled with muddy water rushing down from the hills. She thought sympathetically of her father, his mail pouch protected by the cape on his black raincoat, who had been walking in this weather all morning. For herself she did not care. She felt exhilarated by the bad weather and even found a childish pleasure in getting her sneakers wet. What difference did it make? By evening it would all be over and when Johnny arrived the stars would be out and sparkling through the atmosphere that was now being so thoroughly washed. It almost seemed as if the whole world was being washed clean for Johnny. In the market she smiled radiantly, for no reason at all, at the boy who packed her groceries in a bag, and was surprised when he smiled back. Smiling at a boy was not so difficult after all.

Jean enjoyed puttering around the kitchen preparing dessert for Johnny. She stacked the cookies carefully with layers of whipped cream between, frosted them with graceful swirls of more whipped cream, and topped each small tower with a red cherry. She made five servings, three for her mother and father and Sue to eat for supper, and two for herself and Johnny later in the evening. She would be too excited to eat dessert with her family anyway.

When the kitchen clock told her it was almost time for her father to come home, Jean got out the percolator, measured coffee and water into it, and set it over one of the burners on the gas stove. While she waited for the coffee to perk, she leaned on the window sill of the breakfast nook and scanned the sky for even one light spot in the dark clouds. It was a soggy, soggy day and for the first time Jean began to wonder if it really would clear up before eight o'clock. The coffee began a few tentative eruptions into the glass percolator knob before it settled into a rapid perk. Come on, weather, thought Jean intently. Clear up, clear up, clear up for Johnny.

The kitchen was filled with the fragrance of hot coffee, and Jean, who timed coffee by her sense of smell rather than by the clock, turned down the heat under the percolator. Her father should be home by now. Clear up, clear up for Johnny, she went on thinking. Through the window she saw Sue, her umbrella held low against the wind, hurrying up the driveway, and hastened to open the back door for her.

"M-m-m, hot coffee!" exclaimed Sue, handing her wet umbrella to Jean, who thrust it into the sink to drip. "I'm starved. I skipped lunch, because everything cost so much downtown. Where's Daddy?"

"He hasn't come home yet," answered Jean, thinking that the cold air had made Sue's face glow until she was actually pretty. "How would you like me to make you a delicious peanut-butter sandwich, specialty of the house?"

"Would you?" asked Sue gratefully, as she glanced at the kitchen clock. "He shouldn't be this late even if the weather is awful."

"At least all the dogs that don't like mailmen will be inside on a day like this," observed Jean, spreading peanut butter with a lavish hand. "Want some coffee with your sandwich?"

"Love it." Sue removed her wet coat and hung it on a corner of the kitchen door so it would dry over the linoleum. Then she clasped both hands around the hot cup Jean handed her. "This feels good. My hands are practically numb, they are so cold."

"Get the information for your paper?" Jean cut the sandwich diagonally and laid it on a plate.

"Enough to make a good start, even though the book I need most is out," answered Sue, carrying the sandwich and coffee into the breakfast nook. "And, Jean, you will never guess who I ran into in the reference room!"

"The reference librarian?" guessed Jean, joining her sister at the breakfast table with a cup of milk flavored with coffee.

"Silly," said Sue. "No. Kenneth Cory. I hadn't

seen him for ages. Not since he moved out of the neighborhood."

"You mean Old Repulsive?" The words escaped Jean's lips almost involuntarily. The expression that crossed Sue's face made her instantly regret that she had recalled the nickname the neighborhood children, with the cruelty natural to childhood, had once given this boy.

"Yes, Old Repulsive. Only he isn't any more," said Sue. "I almost didn't know him at first. You know how he used to have buck teeth with bands on them? Well, his teeth are straight now. And his skin isn't all blotchy the way it was when he was in high school, either. And he wears a crew cut, so his hair doesn't stick out like porcupine quills the way it used to."

"Where does he live now?" asked Jean, more from politeness than from interest.

"His family moved up into the hills," answered Sue. "He's going to the University now. He's going to be an entomologist."

"Is that the study of bugs or words?" asked Jean. "I never can remember."

"Insects," answered Sue.

This confirmed Jean's feelings about Old Repulsive. He was exactly the kind of boy she would expect to study insects.

"He talked to me quite a while," said Sue, and added almost shyly, "I think he likes me."

"Do you want him to?" Jean hid her dismay upon realizing that her sister was so eager to have a boy like her that she would snatch at this one.

"Yes," said Sue thoughtfully, "I do."

"I hope he does like you." Jean kept the stiffness she felt out of her voice. How fortunate she was to have a good-looking boy like Johnny like her. There was something pathetic about Sue's eagerness to make Kenneth sound attractive, as if perhaps she wanted to catch up with her younger sister.

The girls heard a car turn into the driveway. Jean, glad to have the disturbing conversation about Old Repulsive interrupted, got up to set the coffeepot back on the burner to reheat.

"What happened to you?" both girls asked their father, as soon as he opened the back door.

Mr. Jarrett removed the black raincoat and handed it to Sue, who carried it into the bathroom to drip into the tub. "It was that little lady near the end of my route," he said, stooping to pull off his rubbers and to pat Dandy, who had come running, his half a tail wagging, at the sound of his voice.

"The one with the son in New York who never writes?" Jean took a cup and saucer out of the cupboard.

"Yes," answered Mr. Jarrett. "She came out on the porch in this rain to ask if I was positive I didn't have a letter from New York for her. She was so sure she would get one today. She said she had a hunch."

"She says that every day," said Sue, coming out of the bathroom.

"I know." There was regret in Mr. Jarrett's voice, and his daughters knew he would have liked to bring the lady a letter from her son every day. "She was so disappointed that when I got back to the post office I looked around and sure enough, there was a letter for her from New York. Airmail. I got to thinking about this poor woman living all alone and spending the whole week end wishing she had that letter. So when I left the office I drove out to her house and gave it to her. I wish you could have seen her face when she saw that return address."

Jean and Sue smiled affectionately at their father. "We might have known," said Sue. "Last week it was the lady who was watching for the colored slides of her trip to Europe, because she was having company that evening and wanted to show them."

"And the week before it was the girl watching for the letter from the sailor in Okinawa," added Jean, pouring a steaming cup of coffee for her father.

"It was a small thing to do, and it made her happy.

I only wish it had been a thicker letter." Mr. Jarrett accepted the coffee with a grateful smile for Jean. "Are you ready for that young man of yours?"

"Yes," answered Jean. "Now if the weather will just clear up before tonight."

But by the time Mrs. Jarrett came home from work it was obvious that the storm would not only continue but would probably grow worse. Squalls of wind dashed rain against the living-room and dining-room windows. Rain gurgled out of the gutters on the roof, and drops fell down the chimney and plopped into the cold ashes in the fireplace. The branches of the trees that lined the street bowed and lashed and tossed.

"I hope the roof doesn't leak." Mrs. Jarrett sounded worried. Their roof, as they all knew, was old, and although Mr. Jarrett had patched it last summer, it needed reshingling.

Jean began to be uneasy. Perhaps Johnny would not be able to come after all. She listened for cars on the street, and it seemed a very long time before one passed. A branch torn from a tree blew against the house. At the back of her mind was the worry that she was not attractive enough or interesting enough for a boy to come through a storm to see. Don't be silly, she told herself sternly. "Neither rain, nor snow, nor heat, nor gloom of night. . . ." Now she was being even sillier. Johnny was not a mail-man.

Jean tried to shut out the fear that the telephone might ring and it would be Johnny breaking the date. She wondered if Elaine and Maxine had had fun marketing for their supper and how many Greek olives they had had money for when everything else had been purchased. She wondered if Elaine missed her and if Maxine liked avocados as much as she did.

When supper was over and the dishes washed, Jean took one last reassuring peek into the refrig-erator at the two desserts she had saved for herself and Johnny. So far he had not telephoned to break the date, so maybe everything was going to be all right after all. She went to her room to change her dress.

Sue was already sitting at the table with a pile of books and notes in front of her. "Term paper," she said.

"May I extend my sympathy?" asked Jean, who admired her sister for starting her term paper in the middle of the semester. She changed into her best blouse and a bright cotton skirt. She brushed her hair and carefully arranged her bangs. The rain was still beating against the windows. "Isn't this a terrible night?" she said, wanting and yet not wanting to discuss with Sue the possibility that Johnny might be kept home by the weather.

"Mm-hm," murmured Sue, her head bent over her notebook. A blast of wind seemed to shake the house.

Jean tiptoed out of the room. In the living room she found her father kneeling on the hearth, starting a fire in the fireplace.

"I thought this might be a good time to get rid of some of the cartons and a couple of orange crates that were cluttering up the garage," Mr. Jarrett said. "They won't last long, but I thought a little fire might brighten things up."

"Good idea, Daddy." Jean could not help being touched. This was her father's way of showing that he, too, was pleased that a boy was coming to see one of his daughters. The papers and cartons caught fire, making the room seem more pleasant and the storm less threatening. While Mr. Jarrett broke up the orange crates, Jean sat down on a chair near the front door, got up, and moved to the couch. She did not want Johnny to look through the glass door and see her sitting there as if she couldn't wait to open the door. She looked around the room at the fire, the African violet blooming cheerily on the mantel, the

Chinese checker set waiting on the coffee table, and was satisfied. Their house might be small, but it was homelike—tonight one could even call it cozy—and no one would notice the crack in the plaster or the worn places in the carpet. Her father, who was outdoors so much, was better-looking than most men his age and no one would ever guess, looking at her mother, that she had stood on her feet all day selling remnants.

At a quarter to eight Jean walked across the room and straightened a book, just to get a glimpse of herself in the mirror over the mantel. Johnny was right. She was a cute girl. Eight o'clock came. Jean grew tense. Eight-fifteen. Above the sound of the wind and the rain and the gurgling gutters Jean heard a car approach, and pass on down the street. Had Johnny forgotten? Of course not. It was needless to worry when he was only fifteen minutes late. "This is the worst storm we have had this year," Jean observed, laying the ground for excuses in case Johnny really did not come.

Eight-thirty. Jean's mouth was dry and her hands were cold. She longed to say brightly, as if it did not matter, Well, it looks as if Johnny isn't coming. She could not. Not yet. Give him another five minutes. Or ten.

Raindrops hissed into the fire. "Didn't you say this fellow was coming at eight?" asked Mr. Jarrett.

"Yes," said Jean miserably, knowing that her father did not really mean to be tactless. "At least I think that was what he said. I might have misunderstood." The pieces of orange crate burned through, broke apart, fell into coals. When ten more drops hissed into the fire Johnny would come. No, better make it twenty. One . . . two . . .

Mrs. Jarrett looked up from the pad of paper on her knee. "Do you think it would sound all right to say a cold cream leaves your face with a gossamer glow?" she asked.

"Yes, Mother." Jean was not thinking about her mother's question. Johnny had not asked for her address. Perhaps he was in a telephone booth someplace, calling all the Jarretts in the book. How many Jarretts were there, she wondered, and did she dare go look? Her mother's words finally penetrated. "I mean, no," she amended hastily. "Gossamer doesn't glow. At least I don't think it does. I think it would be all right to say gossamer soft but I don't think you can say gossamer glow."

"I guess you are right," said Mrs. Jarrett. "But I do think alliterative phrases stand a better chance of winning." Then, as if the subject had been on her mind all the time, she said, "Don't worry, dear. In a storm like this Johnny could easily be delayed. Perhaps his car won't start."

"Maybe," was all Jean was able to say. Any excuse was better than none. The three sat in silence, listening to the wind and the rain, the sound of burning wood crumbling into coals. Every time Jean heard tires on the street her heart felt like something trying to beat its way out of a cage.

By ten minutes to nine the fire was reduced to hot ashes. That fire had been her father's contribution to her evening, Jean thought sadly. Whatever would she say when Elaine telephoned in the morning? And Elaine would telephone. The very first thing. Jean pictured herself answering the telephone, chattering brightly. Elaine, it was all the most *ghastly* mistake. Ghastly in a *hilarious* sort of way, if you know what I mean. There we sat by those dying embers, listening for a car to stop, and all the time I had the wrong day. Except that she did not have the wrong day and even if she did, she would not talk to Elaine that way. That was the way Elaine talked when she was trying to turn an incident into an event.

Mr. Jarrett yawned.

"I—I guess he isn't coming." With tremendous effort Jean contrived a wry half-smile. "Maybe he was just—joking or something." Maybe that was it. Why should a boy who wore shirts that had to be dry-cleaned want to come to see a girl like her?

Mr. Jarrett was busy poking the dead fire. Mrs. Jarrett bit her lip and looked at Jean, her eyes dark with sympathy—sympathy that Jean appreciated and at the same time resented. Part of her wanted to bury her face in her mother's lap the way she had when she was a little girl, and another part of her wanted to hold her head high and say proudly, I'm fifteen—I can manage my own affairs.

The telephone rang. None of the Jarretts seemed able to move. It rang a second time and a third.

"Answer it, dear," said Mrs. Jarrett, on the fourth ring.

Numbly Jean walked into the kitchen and picked up the receiver.

"Hello, Jean?" It was Johnny all right.

"Oh, hi, Johnny," Jean said in a strangled voice.

"Look, Jean. I'm sure sorry, but I am not going to be able to make it tonight after all." Johnny sounded genuinely contrite.

"That's all right, Johnny." It wasn't all right, but what could a girl say?

"No, it isn't all right," insisted Johnny. "I feel ter-

rible about it. Some people from out of town arrived and Dad says I have to stick around. You know how it is. Old family friends and all."

"Sure, Johnny." Jean felt somewhat better. Johnny really did sound sorry, and anybody's family could have out-of-town friends arrive. Even on a night like this. Of course they could.

"I'll make it up to you sometime," said Johnny, almost tenderly. "Honest."

"Oh, that's all right," said Jean, beginning to feel that it was all right.

Johnny lowered his voice, as if he did not want anyone to overhear what he was saying. "Jean? Did I ever tell you what a cute little nose you have?"

Jean smiled into the telephone in spite of herself. "No, I don't think so." Unconsciously she lowered her voice too, and enjoyed a delightful sense of conspiracy.

"Remind me on Monday and I'll tell you," said Johnny softly.

Jean laughed. "I'll do that." At least she would get to see him day after tomorrow.

"Look, Jean," said Johnny, his voice still low, "I've got to go now. I'm sure sorry and I'll see you Monday."

"See you Monday," agreed Jean. "And I'm sorry you couldn't make it."

Reluctantly Jean went into the living room to repeat Johnny's conversation, omitting the part about her cute little nose, to her mother and father.

"What a shame," said Mrs. Jarrett mildly.

"It seems to me he could have phoned a little sooner," said Mr. Jarrett.

Jean had tried to ignore this thought.

"We don't know," said Mrs. Jarrett. "Perhaps he couldn't."

"It seems to me if a boy really liked a girl—" began Mr. Jarrett.

"Now, Jim," interrupted Mrs. Jarrett.

"It's all right, Daddy," said Jean earnestly. "Really it is. He said he would make it up to me and he would see me Monday. And he sounded truly sorry."

Mr. Jarrett, who still did not look convinced, changed his manner abruptly. "I'll bet I can still beat my daughter at Chinese checkers," he said jovially.

"No, thank you, Daddy. Not tonight. I—I don't feel like playing." Jean could not play checkers with her father, not after she had planned to play with Johnny. Poor Daddy, his attempt to make her feel better was so sweet and so clumsy, but she did wish he would not try to be understanding. She didn't *need* to feel better, because everything was perfectly all right. There was no reason to make an issue out of Johnny's not being able to come. It wasn't as though he hadn't wanted to come.

Jean stood uncertainly in the doorway, not knowing how to use the remnant of the evening. While she stood there listening to the storm she discovered that she was tired, very tired. "I guess I might as well go to bed," she said.

"Good night, dear," said Mrs. Jarrett gently.

Now Jean had to face Sue, who looked up from her books when Jean opened the door of their room. "Too bad, Jean," said Sue quietly.

"Oh, it's perfectly all right," said Jean, trying to sound vivacious in spite of her weariness. What was wrong with her family that they could not see there was nothing to be sorry about? Why did they have to go around being so sympathetic? They were treating her as if she were an invalid or something. The way they were behaving, they would probably start tiptoeing and speaking in hushed voices—and bringing her dishes of blancmange.

Well, they could just stop being so understanding, Jean thought crossly as she turned back her bedspread. Lots of girls would be glad to have Johnny look forward to seeing them on Monday. To have Johnny make a date was something, even if he did have to break it. Jean walked over to the mirror and studied her nose. Johnny was right. It was a cute little nose. She wondered why she had never thought so before. And her family could just stop being so horribly understanding.

CHAPTER
5

ALTHOUGH Jean had made up her mind that this was
one Monday when she would not wait for Johnny
after school, not for more than two seconds, anyway,
she was overjoyed to find that Johnny was as good as
his word. He arrived at the door of the sewing room
almost as soon as the bell had rung, and after looking
inside this feminine precinct, he actually entered,
causing all the girls who were putting away their
sewing boxes or finishing seams on the sewing machines to look up. Boys did not often venture into
the clothing class.

Jean was so flustered she dropped her thimble.
This would show her horribly sympathetic family,
when she happened to mention it at the dinner
table! "This afternoon when Johnny came into the
sewing room to find me," she would begin.

"He's *darling*," whispered Mitsuko, as Jean bent to pick up the thimble. "You're lucky."

Undisturbed by the stir he was creating, Johnny made his way to Jean's table, where she was stuffing her tape measure and spools of thread into her sewing box with trembling hands.

"Hi," said Johnny, looking down at Jean.

"Hi," answered Jean, coloring because she felt as conspicuous as if she were on a stage. She stowed

her sewing box in her drawer and shoved the drawer
shut.

"I always wondered what went on in here," remarked Johnny.

"And now you know," said Jean lightly, and
smiled up at him.

Johnny put his hand on her elbow (actually put
his hand on her elbow!) and walked with her out of
the sewing room while the other girls watched. "Did

I ever tell you you have a cute little nose?" Johnny asked softly.

"I believe you may have mentioned it at some time or another." Jean felt that her conversation was improving rapidly. Dear, charming Johnny. However, she was puzzled by an uneasy feeling that she had lost or forgotten something. For a moment she could not think what it was and then it came to her. She had not forgotten anything at all. Homer was missing. "Where's your friend?" she asked.

"He got lost," said Johnny briefly.

Jean did not pursue the subject, because she was not really interested in what had happened to Homer. She was so happy to have Johnny all to herself for a change and she was more interested in her nose than in Homer. Johnny not only walked out of the building with her but accompanied her to the bus stop, waited in the crowd for her bus to arrive, and then waved to her after she had climbed on the bus and paid her fare. Just wait until she told her sympathetic family! As Johnny said, when he waited for the bus with me. . . .

Except for Thursday, when Johnny and several other boys made the tape recording of the Hi-times program to be broadcast Saturday morning, Johnny met Jean and accompanied her to the bus stop every day that week. He was always interesting to talk to. He told Jean more about his experiences skiing and about the time he became entangled in seaweed while skin diving off Point Lobos.

On Friday Jean waited expectantly for Johnny to say something about a date, but he did not. She realized there was no reason why she should not invite him to come to her house Saturday evening. Probably that was what she should do, since he might still be embarrassed because he had been forced to break the date with her. "Johnny," she began as the bus pulled up to the curb, but she was caught in the crowd that surged toward the door of the bus.

"Were you going to say something?" Johnny called.

"No," Jean called back, over her shoulder. "I mean—good-by." A girl could not very well yell an invitation to a boy from the steps of a bus. Disheartened, Jean paid her fare and was lucky enough to get a seat. Three other students not so fortunate promptly piled their books on her lap, and from beneath the books Jean reflected on her disappointment. She also reflected ruefully that she had spent more money on carfare that week than she had intended to, but when a boy walked her to her bus stop and waited for the bus with her, she could not very well tell him that she walked home whenever she could, to save carfare.

When Jean reached her house and was changing from her school clothes, she looked gloomily at her books on the study table and wondered if she could be noble and get her homework out of the way now, or leave it until Sunday evening. This was a question she considered every Friday after school. Sue, who was always prompt and efficient, would do most of hers today, she knew, but she was not Sue. She liked to postpone her homework as long as possible, in spite of all the sensible arguments for doing it promptly.

While Jean was debating with herself (go on, get it out of the way so you can forget it; no, I don't feel like doing it now, because I would rather think about Johnny), Sue came home from school and walked into the bedroom with a large brown-paper bundle which she dropped on her bed.

"What's that?" asked Jean, pulling up the zipper on her skirt. She would have preferred a button and buttonhole on the waistband instead of hooks and eyes, but she had not come to buttonholes yet in her clothing class.

"The Jarrett sisters seek their fortunes! We don't need any long-lost uncle." Sue seemed unusually gay as she pulled the string off the bundle and laid back the paper, revealing a quantity of fabric in two colors, red and turquoise-blue.

Jean leaned over and fingered the material, which she found to be a heavy rayon crepe, scarcely appropriate for dresses and certainly not suitable for drapes or bedspreads. "What in the world are you going to do with all that material in those colors?" asked Jean. "There must be enough to slip-cover an elephant."

"That material," said Sue, "represents our fortunes." She sat down on the bed and held a length of red material against her cheek, as if she enjoyed the feel of it. "We are going to make stoles for the *a cappella* choir to wear over their dark-blue robes."

"Us?" said Jean. "But we aren't in the choir."

"We don't have to be." Sue went on to explain. "You see, the choir needs new stoles, and anybody in Advanced Clothing who wants to can make them. Not many of the girls in the class were interested, but I thought it would be a wonderful chance to earn some money—they will pay us a dollar and a quarter apiece—and so I brought home a pile of the material and a pattern. They aren't hard to make. They are red, with a turquoise edging two inches wide on the inside edge. The hardest part will be getting the edging straight, but I know you can do it if you baste."

"Why, Sue, that's almost too good to be true!" Jean rapidly calculated that four stoles equaled five dollars. "How many do they need?"

"Over a hundred. Tall, medium, and short," answered Sue. "My teacher said when I finished this material I can take home some more."

"And Daddy can't possibly object," Jean pointed out. "Come on, what are we waiting for? Let's go to work!"

Her homework held at bay for a while and her disappointment over Johnny temporarily out of her mind, Jean enjoyed spreading the bright material on the table, pinning on the brown wrapping-paper pattern, and cutting with long slashes of the scissors. She picked up an unsewn stole and buried her nose in it. "Mmm," she breathed. "I just love the smell of new material."

"So do I," said Sue from the closet, where she was getting out the portable sewing machine. "I wish someone would bottle it for perfume, so I could dab it behind my ears."

Jean pinned the shoulder seams of a stole. "What would you name the perfume?" she mused. "Silken Scent?"

"No, I don't think so," said Sue, as if the matter was of great importance. "I think I would name it after a fabric. Crepe de Chine would make a good name. Or Peau de Soie."

Jean giggled. "We sound like Mother working on a contest."

Sue lifted the sewing machine from its case and set it on the table. "Who knows? Maybe Mother will run across a perfume-naming contest and we can offer her our prize-winning suggestions. She has thought up names for almost everything else. Why not perfume?"

The evening passed quickly for both girls, and by bedtime Jean had the satisfaction of having earned three dollars and seventy-five cents with her two hands. Sue, who was not afraid to make the old sewing machine roar down the length of a seam, had completed four stoles and cut out two more.

On Saturday morning, after they had finished their household chores, Jean and Sue continued sewing on the stoles. They cut, pinned, basted, and stitched until their room was a tangle of color.

"Do you think we could say the money we earn is stolen money?" asked Sue.

"That is practically the worst pun I have ever heard," said Jean, and laughed. Four stoles equaled five dollars or a new slip, a pretty blouse, material for a cotton dress. Eight stoles equaled a ten-dollar bill, something Jean almost never had in her possession. There were so many things a girl could do with ten dollars. With luck, and a sale, she could buy a ready-made cotton dress, a dress that was not cut out by a pattern that had to be altered for a girl who was shorter than average. Jean was rapt in the limitless possibilities of a ten-dollar bill, when the doorbell rang. "I'll get it," she said, because Sue was using the sewing machine.

When Jean opened the front door she found Johnny standing on the porch. "Why, Johnny!" She could not keep her surprise from showing.

Johnny grinned engagingly. "I was just cruising around and I wondered if you would like to go down to the drive-in for a Coke."

"Now?" Jean still could not quite believe that Johnny was really standing on her doorstep.

"Sure," said Johnny. "Why not?"

"Why not?" agreed Jean, delighted. "Just a minute. I'll get my sweater." She was quite sure her father would not object to her going to the drive-in in the daytime.

In the bedroom, Jean whispered, "It's Johnny! He wants me to go to the drive-in for a Coke!" Oh, the joy of saying Johnny wanted her to do something!

"At quarter of ten in the morning?" Sue did not sound entirely approving.

"Sure. Why not?" Jean snatched her sweater and jerked a comb through her bangs.

"Have fun," said Sue.

"I shall," answered Jean, almost defiantly. It was too bad there were not two Johnnies, one for each of them, but that was the way things were. They couldn't all be lucky.

Jean and Johnny walked down the steps to the Volkswagen in the driveway. "I've always wanted to ride in one of these little cars," Jean told Johnny, as he held the door open for her.

"This is Mom's car," he said. "She keeps it for a pet." Johnny folded his long legs into the small car and backed it down the driveway. "It doesn't really have a motor. It's powered by a gnome turning an egg beater. It's much cheaper than gas."

"And here I thought that noise coming from the back of the car instead of the front was the engine," said Jean, "and all the time it was an egg beater. What do you feed the gnome? A saucer of milk, or is that just for brownies?"

"This gnome likes Cokes and French fries," answered Johnny.

Jean basked in being alone with Johnny, but when he drove into the parking area of the drive-in and brought the car to a halt between two white lines, Jean felt as if she had run out of conversation. Too shy to look at Johnny, she read the signs posted on the front of the drive-in. "Jumboburgers—¼ lb. beef on bun 37¢." "French fries 14¢." "Porkchopettes 79¢."

"Two Cokes," Johnny yelled out the window, to the carhop who was approaching. She smiled, nodded, and turned back. Johnny glanced at his watch. "We're just in time," he remarked, and turned on the radio.

"Time for what?" asked Jean.

"Hi-times," he said. "Don't you listen?"

"Every Saturday," answered Jean, embarrassed that the actual presence of Johnny had made her forget the program.

The theme song and then Johnny's voice came out of the loud-speaker. "Good morning. This is Johnny Chessler, your Hi-times announcer broadcasting by tape-recording from the control room of Northgate High School." Johnny listened intently.

Jean listened too, relieved of the burden of conversation. Now she had a chance to think about what she wanted to say to Johnny when the program ended. She wanted to talk to him, to find out more about him, and most of all, to learn the answer to the question that had fascinated her since December. Why had he asked her to dance with him? This was her opportunity if she could only manipulate the conversation. It was too bad she couldn't have a script writer, like the Hi-times program.

When the carhop set the tray on the car door beside Johnny, Jean accepted a Coke from Johnny and silently sipped it through the straw. There really was no reason why she couldn't come right out and ask Johnny about that evening at the clubhouse.

"Now that the cast of the variety show has been chosen and rehearsals will start next week," said Johnny's voice, "committees have been appointed to start the ball rolling on another event on the social calendar of Northgate High School—the Girls' Association Dance, which will be held on the eleventh of April, in the gymnasium. Hawaiian Holiday is the theme, and this time the girls invite the boys. Smile for the ladies, boys, and maybe you will be lucky enough to get an invitation." Johnny listened to every word.

And probably half the girls in school will ask Johnny to go to that dance, thought Jean unhappily. There was no use even thinking about it herself—

she knew she would never have the courage. She stirred the ice in her Coke with her straw and told herself, I'll just say casually, Johnny, do you remember that night at the clubhouse when you asked me to dance? And he will say, Yes, Jean, what about it? And I'll say, How did you happen to ask me to dance when I was so obviously not a part of the crowd? Or maybe she shouldn't ask. Maybe it would be better not to recall the episode at all.

Jean sipped her Coke slowly, trying to make it last, while she listened to Johnny's voice on the radio and stole glances at Johnny himself, absorbed in his own words. He had such a regular profile and was so attractive with his curls tumbling over his forehead that way. And it was pleasant to hear Johnny's voice coming out of the loud-speaker instead of Johnny, because she was spared the anxiety of conversation, of wondering if she had said the right thing, of weighing the meaning of Johnny's words. Yes, this was a pleasant moment, sitting in a car in the drive-in sipping a Coke as if she came to this popular spot every day. She could not help marveling that the words she was hearing had been spoken by Johnny on Thursday, recorded on tape, preserved for two days, and were now being played from a radio station. Gradually she, too, became en-

grossed in the sound of Johnny's voice. As the words flowed by, Jean ceased to listen to their meaning and listened only to the stream of pleasant sound. Then his voice stopped to allow the playing of a record.

"Oh, Johnny!" exclaimed Jean, turning toward him. "You sound marvelous!"

"You really think so?" Obviously Johnny was pleased by her admiration.

"Oh, yes," said Jean. "With your voice you should be an announcer or an actor."

"I do the best I can with the scripts the literary club writes." Johnny frowned slightly. "The trouble is, they don't realize some of the problems of radio broadcasting, so I've got to learn to be more careful with my enunciation in phrases like 'Girls' Association.' Those *s's* made too much of a hissing sound," he said critically.

"Nobody would ever notice," said Jean.

The record ended. Johnny interviewed the drama coach, who said he thought this variety show was going to be one of the best Northgate High had ever staged. When the program was over, Johnny turned to Jean. "Like it?" he asked.

"Oh, yes," said Jean. "You were every bit as good as a professional announcer and better than lots of them."

Johnny grinned. "Did I ever tell you you are cute?"

Johnny's voice issuing from Johnny's mouth was much more satisfactory after all, even though Jean did not know how to answer. If she said yes it would sound as if she treasured his casual remarks—which she did, but was not going to let him know it. And if she said no, it would sound as if she was seeking compliments—which she longed to do. Instead of answering, she looked down at her Coke and smiled.

"Did you know you have dimples when you smile like that?" asked Johnny.

"Have I?" Jean decided this was a good moment to risk asking the question. "Is that why you asked me to dance that night at the Christmas party?"

Johnny laughed. "Partly, I guess. You looked so cute and eager, sitting there watching."

Jean stored this away to mull over at her leisure. "I thought I looked terrible in my saddle shoes and that awful plaid skirt," she said, laughing lightly. "I had been helping with some decorations for a party the next day, so I wasn't dressed up." She handed Johnny her empty Coke glass to set on the tray. Johnny did not need to know that it was Elaine's mother's party and not her own.

Johnny looked searchingly at Jean as if he were memorizing her features. Jean was both flattered and flustered. "I know I must have been terrible to dance with." She forced a gay laugh. "But I have improved a lot since then. I have had some practice." It certainly would not hurt to let him know that she had learned to dance since that night. Never mind how she had learned. A girl did not have to tell a boy everything.

The carhop removed the tray from the car door, depriving them of the right to occupy one of the drive-in's parking spaces, even though the lot was almost empty at that hour in the morning. When Johnny started the car and headed toward her house, Jean was disappointed, because she had hoped they might drive around for a while. She considered saying it was such a beautiful spring day that it must be possible to see for miles from the hills, but rejected the remark as being too obvious. When Johnny let her out of the car and walked her to the front door, she asked, "Won't you come in?"

"No, thanks. Not this time," he said, smiling down at her. "I have to be getting home. Mom needs the car."

This time! That meant there would be a next time. "Well—thanks for the Coke." Jean was reluctant to let Johnny go. "And it was fun listening to the program."

Johnny smiled at Jean as if he were amused in an

affectionate sort of way. "See you around," he said, and was gone.

Jean closed the door and watched from the window while Johnny backed down the driveway. She had had a date with Johnny! And she had found out what she wanted to know. It was true that she was a little disappointed that he had brought her home so soon and had not asked her for another date, but. . . . Oh, well, there was always next week. Humming *Play Like You Love Me,* she walked into the bedroom.

"Back so soon?" asked Sue, as she silenced the roar of the sewing machine.

"Johnny had to take the car back. His mother needed it," Jean explained, as she dropped her sweater on the foot of the bed.

"Oh." The sewing machine began to race down the length of a seam again.

Jean stood in front of the mirror that hung over the chest of drawers she shared with Sue, and looked thoughtfully at herself. She looked down, smiled demurely the way she had smiled for Johnny in the car, and tried to peek out from beneath her lashes to see how she had looked to Johnny.

"What are you looking like that for?" asked Sue curiously.

Jean had not noticed that the sewing machine had stopped once more. "Was I looking any special way?" she asked innocently, as she turned from the mirror. It was unfortunate that a girl could not have one shred of privacy in her own home. She sat down, picked up a stole, started to baste, discovered she was basting a long facing to a short stole, and put her work down again. She felt too restless to settle down to sewing.

"There," said Sue, folding a finished stole and glancing at the clock on the table between the two beds. "I think I'll stop for now. I have to go downtown."

"What for?" asked Jean, knowing Sue did not spend carfare unnecessarily.

"I need some more material from the main library for my term paper," explained Sue. "I just received a reserve card saying the book I tried to get last week is in now."

When Jean had the house to herself she felt an unaccustomed freedom. She seized an armful of red and turquoise material and threw it into the air just for the joy of watching it fall in a brilliant heap upon her bed. Johnny, Johnny, Johnny, she thought. She brushed and combed her hair as meticulously as if she expected Johnny to ring the doorbell at any moment. She wandered into the kitchen and opened the refrigerator, to see what she could find for her lunch. It was early for lunch, but she could not think of anything else to do. She stared dreamily at the covered dishes of leftovers, the cartons of milk, a tomato-juice can half full of bacon fat, and wished they all would turn into avocados, artichokes, and delicious little tea-party sandwiches. They did not, so she poured herself a glass of milk and made a peanut-butter sandwich. She was scarcely aware of what she was eating.

When Jean finished her lunch she could not think of anything she wanted to do. She reread the head-lines of the morning paper, but wars and labor un-ions and bills before Congress were too remote from her springtime mood. She turned on the television set and got an exercise program that happened to be on. "Come on, girls, let's get up off those chairs and firm our thighs," directed a muscular young man. "Right hand on hip, swing your left leg out to the side. One, two. One, two. That's right. One, two. One, two." Jean halfheartedly slimmed her thighs for a few measures of organ music before she turned the set off again.

Feeling that Sue was lucky to have an excuse for going downtown to the library, Jean was seized by a desire to leave the house, to be out in the sunshine. Maybe she didn't have any reason to go to the library downtown, but she could walk to the branch library to do some reference work for her history class. Jean picked up her notebook and, followed by Dandy, left the house, but even as she tried the door to make sure it was locked she knew that she would not do any work when she reached the library. The walk was pleasant, however, for her thoughts were filled with Johnny.

At the library Jean did pause beside the encyclopedias long enough to think how much she did not want to open one of those heavy volumes today. She wandered into the periodical section and thumbed through the fashion magazines. How wonderful it must be to be as tall as a fashion model and to wear, even for a little while, such lovely clothes: evening gowns, slim suits, hats like flower gardens. None of these was meant for her, but in the back of one of the magazines, in a section called "Important Clothes for Little Money," Jean found a photograph of a saucy-looking model wearing a dress she longed to own. The full skirt was gathered onto a simple waist that had a little round collar and buttons down the front. The fabric was pink, printed with clover blossoms in a deeper shade, and there must have been five yards in the skirt alone. The price was forty-nine dollars and ninety-five cents. And they call that little money, thought Jean. To her, forty-nine dollars and ninety-five cents seemed like a fortune. It was—let's see—forty *a cappella* choir stoles.

Then, because Jean did not really want to be in the library at all, she returned the magazine to the rack and, mentally wearing the clover dress, she started homeward, followed by Dandy, who had napped on the library steps. What she really wanted more than anything was to talk to Johnny again, and as she walked, her imaginary skirt silken against her legs, she looked up at the trees, which had shed their blossoms and were now putting forth sweet green foliage and thought, Why not? She would have the house to herself. All she had to do was make up an excuse to telephone him. Why shouldn't she hear his voice once? Maybe if she talked to him, he would ask to come over. It took Jean only a moment to hit upon an excuse for telephoning Johnny. She would hear his voice in person, over the telephone, and on the radio—all in one day! She lived in a wonderful age indeed.

As soon as Jean unlocked the front door, she dropped her notebook on a table and went straight to the telephone. She did not need to look up Johnny's telephone number. She knew it as well as she knew the license number of his father's car. With a trembly finger she dialed Toyon 1-4343 and waited, with her heart thumping, for Johnny to answer.

After the second ring a woman's voice said, "Hello?"

Jean had been so preoccupied with Johnny that she was unprepared for this woman's voice.

"Hello?" the woman repeated impatiently. In the background Jean heard Johnny call, "Hey, Mom!"

Silently Jean replaced the receiver. She could not bring herself to ask for Johnny. Then, annoyed with herself, she sat biting at her thumb and wondering why she had been so foolish. There was no reason why she should not ask to speak to Johnny. No reason at all. Now that she knew he was home she would try again after a decent interval—say about five minutes—and if his mother answered a second time, she would calmly ask if she might speak to Johnny.

In exactly five minutes or three hundred seconds by the clock, Jean dialed again. In Johnny's house the telephone rang and rang and rang again. Jean tried to picture how it looked, in the kitchen or on a table in the hall, calling angrily for someone to come and lift the receiver. Or perhaps in a such a large house there were two telephones, both of them demanding to be answered. Five rings. Six rings. The receiver was lifted! Jean thought her heart would stop.

"Hello?" It was the woman's impatient voice again.

"May I please speak to Johnny?" asked Jean.

"Just a moment." Mrs. Chessler, if that was who she was, spoke crisply.

"Hello?" Johnny's voice at last.

"Oh—hello, Johnny. This is Jean." Somehow Jean got the words out, even though she did not seem to have the breath with which to speak them.

"Oh, hi, Jean." Johnny sounded casual, friendly, and not at all surprised to hear her voice.

"Johnny, I was wondering—" began Jean. "I was wondering—if I left my sweater in your car. I mean—I thought I took it with me and now I can't find it anyplace. I've looked everywhere, and well, it just occurred to me I might have put it over the back of the seat and it could have fallen back onto the floor."

"Hold on a minute, Jean," said Johnny, "and I'll go out to the garage and have a look."

"All right, Johnny," Jean waited, feeling the beat

of her own heart. Had there been a note, a grace note, of amusement in Johnny's voice?

"Hello, Jean." Johnny was on the line again. "Sorry. It isn't there, and Mom says she didn't see it when she took the car out a little while ago."

"Oh, dear," said Jean. "I wonder what I could have done with it. I've looked everywhere."

"I'm afraid I can't help you," answered Johnny.

Was that impatience in his voice, too? Jean could hear the sound of a faucet running and the rattle of pans, telling her that Johnny's telephone was in the kitchen. Jean waited a moment for Johnny to say something—any little remark that could prolong the conversation—but she heard only the rush of water.

"Well, thanks a lot, Johnny," Jean was forced to say when the silence had stretched to an awkward length. "Sorry I had to bother you."

"That's all right, Jean," said Johnny.

"Good-by, Johnny."

"Good-by."

As Jean sat for a moment with her hand on the telephone she clung to that last word, letting it ring through her mind so she could examine every inflection, every nuance, in those two syllables. Impatience was there, she was quite certain, but naturally a boy would not want to have a long conversation with a girl when his mother was in the same room. Although Jean tried to persuade herself that this was true, she knew with a terrible certainty that she had made a mistake. She had not fooled Johnny one bit and, what was worse, she had not been able to keep wistfulness out of her voice. Johnny sounded perfectly friendly, and she could have lost her sweater, couldn't she? Yes, but she had not. In her heart Jean knew that Johnny had seen through her maneuver.

That was that. With a sigh of regret Jean decided that she might as well spend the rest of the afternoon sewing on *a cappella* choir stoles. Next time—if there was a next time—she would know better. She left the telephone and went to the bedroom, where she was startled to see Sue lying on her bed, with her head propped up on her hand, reading a book. "Oh—hello, Sue," she said, realizing that Sue must have overheard her telephone call. "I didn't know you were home."

"I ran into Ken Cory at the library and he gave me a ride home," said Sue. She looked levelly at Jean and said, "Your sweater is lying on your bed."

"Why, so it is!" Jean tried to cover up her feelings by picking up the stole she had been basting together. "I could have sworn I had lost it."

Sue sat up and closed her book. "Jean," she said. "Please don't."

Jean moistened her finger tip and tied a knot in her thread. "Please don't what?" she asked, although she knew very well what Sue was talking about.

"Please don't chase Johnny." There was real concern in Sue's voice.

That concern put Jean on the defensive. "I'm not chasing him," she said, and her voice was cool.

"Oh, Jean!" exclaimed Sue. "Who do you think you are fooling, phoning a boy on such a made-up excuse?"

Jean flung the stole on her bed. "Is there anything so terrible about phoning a boy?" she demanded. "Is there?"

"No, there isn't anything so terrible about it," said Sue, "but I don't think it was the thing to do when you didn't really have a reason to phone him."

"*You* don't think it was the thing to do! Just because you are two years older you think you know everything." Jean did not like the sound of her own voice. She did not want to quarrel with Sue, especially when Sue was right; but that, for some obscure reason, was exactly why she was quarreling. "And what about you? You probably went to the library

this morning hoping to meet that awful Kenneth Cory."

Sue lowered her eyes an instant, just long enough to tell Jean her guess was right. "Hoping to meet a boy and telephoning him are not the same," said Sue. "And anyway, Ken had spent the whole morning in the library, hoping I might come in again. He said so. And he isn't awful. He's a whole lot nicer than that Johnny Chessler."

"He isn't either," protested Jean. "Johnny is the nicest boy I know."

"Did he make a date with you?" asked Sue.

"Well, no, not this time," admitted Jean.

"Ken is coming over this evening to take me to the movies," said Sue quietly, "and what is more, I expect he will really get here."

Jean had no answer for this. Both girls sewed in silence in the small bedroom, which seemed stifled by their hot words. Their house was not large enough to hold a quarrel.

Jean mulled the argument over in her mind. It seemed as if suddenly everything she did or said

was wrong. First she had made the mistake of telephoning Johnny, and now she was calling the boy
her sister liked awful. She felt mixed-up and miserable, and she did not know what to do about it.
Couldn't Sue see what a desirable boy Johnny was
and how much all the girls admired him?

"Sue," ventured Jean at last, "don't you like
Johnny at all?"

"Jean, can't you see?" Sue sounded almost sad.
"Johnny just isn't good enough for you."

"Why, how can you say that?" demanded Jean.
"Practically every girl in school likes Johnny. I'm the
one that isn't good enough."

"Jean, don't think that way about yourself,"
begged Sue. "You are much too nice to be satisfied
with . . . crumbs from a boy like Johnny. I don't
know how to say it exactly, but Johnny—oh, I don't
know. Maybe we better just forget it." She looked
miserable too, as she bent over a stole.

"Johnny what?" persisted Jean.

"Well, for example," said Sue. "One day in
English he told Miss Pritchard that he didn't see
any reason for wasting his time on trivial assignments."

"Maybe Miss Pritchard's assignments are trivial,"
said Jean. "Maybe he was right."

"He doesn't get A's. Anyway, it wasn't just that," said Sue unhappily. She put down her sewing and looked pleadingly at Jean. "Don't you see—he doesn't really like you."

"He does like me," said Jean stiffly. Or he had liked her before she had made the mistake of telephoning him. "I know he does."

"How do you know?" asked Sue.

"He—he expects to see me after school every day," said Jean.

"You mean you hang around the halls hoping he will come by," said Sue. "Naturally he is flattered. What boy wouldn't be?"

"He always says, 'Hi, how's the cute girl?' And—"

Sue interrupted. "He says that to all the girls. He even says it to me."

It immediately became urgent for Jean to prove that Johnny really did like her. "And he said that night at the clubhouse dance, when Elaine and I were sitting there, that he asked me to dance because I looked so cute and eager."

"In other words you looked as if you were asking, 'How much is that doggie in the window?'" said Sue. "And Johnny gave the little girl a break."

This stung Jean. "Well, I don't care. He does like me. I know he does. And I am going to ask him to go to the Girls' Association Dance with me. So there!" Instantly Jean regretted her last two words. It was such a childish phrase, one that she and Sue had often used in disagreements when they were little girls. On second thought Jean regretted the whole rash statement.

Sue jerked at a basting thread. "Go ahead and ask him," she said, "but he won't go with you."

"Yes, he will." Jean sounded much more positive than she felt.

Sue unreeled an arm's length of thread from a spool. "If you really want to take him to the dance," she said slowly, "I hope he goes with you. Maybe I am wrong, but I don't think so. And I don't like quarreling."

"Neither do I." Jean went to the sewing machine to stitch a stole. It would be difficult to talk while the sewing machine was running, and right now she did not feel like talking. She slipped one end of the stole under the foot of the machine, dropped the foot, and began to stitch. While the machine hummed she found that in her thoughts she was still arguing with Sue. She explained to Sue that Johnny really did like her. It wasn't easy to put into words, but she could tell in little ways—the way he looked at her, the way he always, or almost always, left the building by the door nearest the sewing room. And he didn't have to do that, did he? There were at least six exits from the building, weren't there? So you see. The advantage of an imaginary conversation was that the person argued with did not have the opportunity to advance any unwelcome points to support his side of the debate. Jean could always win an imaginary debate.

When Jean finished stitching her seam she glanced at her sister, who was basting another turquoise edging to a stole. Sue was frowning slightly, as if her thoughts were on something more serious than basting together two pieces of rayon crepe. I'll bet she is going right on with the argument too, thought Jean wryly.

The girls sewed silently, and while they sewed Jean thought, Johnny, Johnny, please go to the dance with me, even if I was foolish enough to phone you on a flimsy fibbing excuse. He had to accept. He could not turn her down, not after this conversation with Sue.

But first Jean, who was no longer sure Johnny liked her, had to find the courage to ask him.

CHAPTER
6

JEAN spent an uncomfortable week end. Her argument with Sue hung in the air like a threatening cloud on a bright day, spoiling their pleasure in working together on the choir stoles. After supper Jean continued to sew alone, but sharing a room with Sue forced her to watch Sue's blithe preparations for her first date. She could not understand Sue's attitude, which was serene as well as happy. Sue knew exactly what she wanted to wear, and she had no trouble getting her lipstick on. One would think she went out with a boy every night of the week. When Jean could not bear to watch Sue another moment, she gathered up her basting thread and material and took them into the living room. Sue would probably be glad to have the bedroom to herself, and Jean could duck out of sight before

Ken came. She did not know why, but she did not want to meet her sister's friend.

Jean was so gnawed by the fear that Johnny might be angry with her for telephoning him, and so worried that she might not have the courage to ask him to go to the dance with her and that he might refuse her if she did ask him, that she lost track of time and was surprised when the doorbell rang.

"Answer it, somebody," Sue called.

Because Kenneth could see her through the glass door, there was nothing for Jean to do but put down her sewing and open the door for him.

"Why, hello, Jean!" Kenneth's voice was deeper than she had remembered.

"Won't you come in?" asked Jean. "Sue will be ready in a minute."

"I haven't seen you since you were a little girl," remarked Kenneth, as he stepped into the living room. "You've grown so much that I am not sure I would have known you if I'd seen you on the street."

Kenneth could not have said anything that would have pleased Jean more. While he spoke to Mrs. Jarrett and shook hands with Mr. Jarrett, Jean folded her sewing and at the same time appraised this boy her sister liked. Sue was right. He wasn't awful at all. The ugly duckling had turned into . . . not exactly a swan, but a young man with poise. He seemed grown-up, compared to the boys at school, and although he was not handsome, or even particularly good-looking—there were still some scars on his face from the skin trouble he had had when he was younger—his face was agreeable because it was so. . . . What *was* the word? Kind, perhaps. Or gentle. But strong, too. He was genuinely glad to see all of Sue's family, and when Sue entered the room and he helped her on with her coat, Jean thought he acted as if her sister was someone precious to him. And Sue . . . the way she glowed when she looked at Kenneth. . . .

As soon as Sue and Kenneth had gone, Jean did the only thing a girl could possibly do when her sister had a date, and she was left at home worrying for fear the boy she liked was angry with her. She went into the bedroom, muffled her face in her pillow, and had a good cry. Then she dried her eyes and sewed furiously on *a cappella* choir stoles the rest of the evening.

The first thing Monday morning, Jean managed to just happen to meet Johnny in the hall. "Why, *hello*, Johnny," she said, registering great surprise.

"How's the cute girl?" asked Johnny, with his lazy grin.

Did he really say this to all the girls? "I'm fine except—"

"Except what?" asked Johnny.

"Johnny—you aren't mad at me or anything, are you?" Jean began bravely, determined to get at least one of her worries out of the way this morning.

"Mad at you?" Johnny leaned against a locker and looked down at Jean. "What for?"

"For—telephoning you about my sweater." Jean carefully examined the corner of her notebook, which was beginning to fray. "I mean—I thought I had lost it and I thought it would be all right to phone you. I—I just hoped I didn't make you mad or anything."

"Why should I be mad?" Johnny sounded amused. "What was wrong with that?"

"Nothing, I guess, only I thought you sounded sort of—oh, I don't know. Funny." Jean realized she was saying too much. She could have been mistaken about the tone of his voice over the telephone. Maybe he had not been impatient after all. It would be a graver mistake to accuse him now.

"Funny little girl." Johnny sounded almost affectionate.

"I just didn't want you to be mad or anything. I mean—" Oh, *shut up*, Jean told herself. She should stop trying to say what she meant. Babbling on like this was only making things worse. She smiled up at Johnny. "It was nothing, really. I guess I was just imagining things. Well, I have to hurry or I'll be late for English." So *that* was all right, she thought, and found her heart was not as light as she had hoped it would be. She would consider the significance of the phrase "funny little girl" later, when she had time. Now her next problem was to find courage to ask Johnny to go to the dance.

Before Jean found that courage she was swept into the activities of the Costume Club. She attended rehearsals of the variety show and watched acts being pruned and altered to fit the theme "Through the Years." Indians war-whooped, cowboys gathered around a wastebasket to sing campfire songs, colonial ladies and gentlemen in modern school clothes danced the minuet. The Dance Club, whose members had studied modern and ballet dancing, had trouble deciding what they should do; they felt that anyone could do a square dance, and their talent should be used for something more unusual. They argued with one another and with Mr. Kohler, the director, until a member of the stage crew, a muscular type who could not see why a bunch of girls had to make such a fuss about a dance, said in obvious disgust, "Aw, go haunt a house."

The girls decided that haunting a house was exactly what they would do. The art department could design a set that suggested a crumbling Victorian mansion and a few moss-hung trees, and they would compose a bat dance. Still better, at the first of the act, the lights would be bright and some of the girls in Victorian dresses would perform a dance that suggested a game of croquet. Then they would dance off, the lighting would gradually grow dim and eerie (some blue spotlights should do it), and the bats would flit out of the wings to haunt the house.

Because Jean was new to the club and had no particular duties at first, she sat in one of the front rows of the auditorium near the orchestra pit, where, to her amusement, Homer was engrossed in a book, oblivious to the rehearsal when not actually playing his violin. The members of the cast began to ask her to hold their valuables while they rehearsed their act and Jean found herself guarding a lapful of wallets and purses. No sooner had the minuet group finished and collected its belongings from her lap, than the Charleston dancers dumped their valuables upon her. Jean did not mind. It was such fun to be participating, even in this small way, that she wondered why she had not thought of joining a club before. She now felt as if she were a part of the school, and not just a girl who attended classes.

And through it all, Johnny, the narrator's script in his hand, was present. "Testing. One, two, three. Testing." He spoke frequently into the microphone, and his voice filled the auditorium.

Elaine, too, was part of the crowd. Unfortunately, Mr. Kohler decided that a boys' war dance would make a more effective opening for the show and assigned the girls who had planned to do the hoop dance the part of Indian maidens who stood on papier-mâché rocks and watched the dance. After rehearsing her motionless part, Elaine walked down off the stage and dropped into the seat beside Jean. "How!" she said, raising her arm in an Indian salute.

"How!" answered Jean.

"I'm frustrated by my role," Elaine said, in a world-weary voice. "There is no scope for my talents just standing there like Minnehaha or somebody, on that lover's leap by the shores of the shining big sea water or whatever it is supposed to be."

"Too bad. All you have to do is look at boys," said Jean wickedly. "And aren't you thinking of Old Nokomis?"

"The boys are a consolation," agreed Elaine, "but

the trouble is, they don't look at me. And speaking of boys, have you asked him yet?" Elaine had heard about Jean's dilemma on the way to school.

Jean looked at Johnny, standing in front of the curtain with his script in hand. He looked so attractive and so important that she wondered how a mere wallet holder would ever find the courage to offer him an invitation. "No," she admitted.

"Don't put it off too long," cautioned Elaine. "You don't want some other girl to grab him. Well, I've got to run. Mom is expecting me."

A fat and battered wallet slid from Jean's lap and disappeared under the seat ahead of her. She piled the rest of the purses and wallets on the seat that Elaine had vacated and got down on her hands and knees to pick up the wallet, which was so stuffed with bits of paper, small change, a comb, and a lipstick that its snap had popped open. As Jean picked up the wallet and started to close it, she could not help noticing a plastic-protected snapshot inside. Still kneeling on the floor, she paused, unable to stop herself, to look at the picture, which was dog-eared beneath the plastic, as if it had been held in a girl's hand many times. It was a snapshot of a boy sitting on some wide steps—the steps of a school, perhaps. His shirt was unbuttoned at the throat and he was leaning forward, his hands clasped between his knees as if he happened to be sitting there in the sun when someone came along and snapped his picture. Someone he liked must have been holding the camera, because he was smiling.

Ashamed of herself for looking into someone else's wallet, Jean snapped it shut, returned to her seat, and gathered up the property she was guarding. She continued to watch the rehearsal, but her thoughts persisted in returning to that snapshot somewhere in the heap on her lap. It seemed to her that knowing a boy well enough to carry his picture in her wallet must be one of the happiest experiences a girl could have.

On the stage Johnny read from his script. "And now time dances on! Allemand right and dos-a-dos—" There was a suggestion of a square-dance caller's singsong in his voice. On the next-to-the-last word Homer closed his book and picked up his violin. On the last word he began to play *Turkey in the Straw*, with the other violinists. The curtain parted on the square dancers.

Johnny Chessler, thought Jean, I elect you the Boy Whose Snapshot I Would Most Like to Carry in My Wallet.

As the show took shape Jean had more to do. No

longer a mere holder of wallets, she helped take inventory of the costumes in the storeroom behind the auditorium, to see what the school had on hand that could be used for the show. When the Costume Club decided it could make the costumes for the Indian maidens, she stayed after school to stitch the brown outing-flannel dresses and to snip the lower edges into fringe. She also helped make up the list of costumes to be rented, including a suit of evening clothes for the narrator. She could hardly wait for the dress rehearsal.

The day the costume rental company's truck backed up to the side door of the auditorium was an exciting one. As the workmen carried racks of costumes into the building, the room backstage became crowded with crinolines, pantalets, Indian headdresses, bat wings, white wigs, parasols, several horse costumes, and parts and pieces of costumes that Jean did not recognize. There was one costume she looked for and did not find—the costume for Johnny. "Where are the evening clothes for the narrator?" she asked Mitsuko, as the two girls were pressing ruffles on some Gay Nineties dresses at the ironing boards in the sewing room. "It was on the list, and I didn't find it anyplace."

"Mr. Kohler crossed it off," answered Mitsuko.

"He decided Johnny didn't need to appear. That would save the rental of one costume, and it would be more effective if the audience just heard his voice. The disembodied voice of time marching on, I guess."

That was a disappointment, but one which Jean did not have time to dwell on. Because she was not a particularly skillful seamstress capable of fitting coats and bodices, Jean was assigned the job of handing out costumes to members of the cast. This was a task which Jean enjoyed. She stood behind the Dutch door, and as members of the cast requested their costumes, she located on the racks whatever it was they were to wear. Touching the various fabrics was a pleasure, and it was interesting to see how inexpensive materials had been used to achieve the greatest effect. Jean had handed out a Civil War uniform (Confederate—tall) across the Dutch door, when Johnny looked in to see what was going on. Maybe this was her moment to ask him.

Peggy Jo appeared behind him, and Johnny stepped aside. "Blue dress with hoop skirt," said Peggy Jo.

"Blue dress with hoop skirt coming up," answered Jean, glad of the opportunity to disappear behind a rack of costumes to try to calm herself. She had to ask him, and he had to say yes. Now—as soon as Peggy Jo leaves. Johnny, will you go to the Girls' Association Dance with me? She had the words lined up on the tip of her tongue, ready to be spoken.

While Jean slipped the blue dress from its hanger, a chorus of war whoops came from the Dutch door. Well, thought Jean, that takes care of that. A girl could not ask a boy to go to a dance with her when a bunch of Indians were whooping over his shoulder. When Jean carried Peggy Jo's costume to the Dutch door, Johnny was gone. Feeling let down, Jean set about gathering up an armload of war bonnets. Surely the next time she saw him. . . .

Elaine, who was wearing her outing-flannel dress and had a turkey feather stuck in a band around her head, elbowed her way through the group of Indians, clasped her hands, and sang, " 'For I'll be calling you—oo—oo—oo.' "

Jean wished Elaine was not so anxious to call attention to herself. The boys would only laugh at her.

"Let's scalp her," suggested one of the Indians.

"There isn't time," said Jean, smiling at the Indians as she shoved their costumes across the Dutch door. Smiling at boys, now that she was taking part in a school activity, was getting easier every day. "Go try on your costumes."

Elaine lingered by the door while half a dozen girls who were to be bats came to collect their chartreuse leotards and black wings.

Jean consulted a list. "Your fingernails haven't come yet," she told the bats, "but the rest of your costumes are ready to try on."

"What fingernails?" asked the bats.

"The bats all wear glittery fingernails eight inches long," answered Jean.

The bats were entranced with the thought of eight-inch fingernails.

"Did you ask him?" whispered Elaine as soon as the bats had trooped off to the dressing room.

Jean pretended to find something wrong with a beard that one of the boys was to wear in the Rip Van Winkle skit. She was beginning to be annoyed by Elaine's intense interest. She was so—so pushy where boys were concerned. You would almost think she was the one who was going to ask Johnny.

"Well, did you?" insisted Elaine. "I saw you talking to him."

"No, Elaine," said Jean. "I haven't."

Elaine must have sensed the change in Jean's feeling toward her, because she sounded crestfallen when she spoke. "Oh. I just wondered, is all."

"There were so many people around." Jean did not want to hurt Elaine's feelings. "Don't you think

the bats will look spooky with their long fingernails?
I think the haunted-house number will be one of
the best in the show."

"Yes," said Elaine, whose feelings had been hurt.
"Yes, I guess it will."

Gradually the show took shape. Scenery was
painted, the orchestra rehearsed, lines memorized,
dances perfected, songs sung. After Jean checked
out the costumes for fitting, she checked them in
again. While various parts of the show rehearsed in
the gymnasium or the band room or wherever they
could find space to work in, Jean assisted with several of the simpler alterations. She basted up the
hems of some dresses worn by square dancers and
sewed an artificial rose on the hip of a dress from
the 1920's, to be worn in the Charleston number.

And then came the afternoon of dress rehearsal,
the day that Jean would surely ask Johnny to go to
the dance. She had to ask him. She was tired of waiting for exactly the right moment, weary of carrying
the question on the tip of her tongue. The worst he
could do was to say no, and if that was the way it
was to be, she wanted to find out now. She did not
want this awful suspense to spoil her fun the night
of the actual performance.

The minute school was out, Jean rushed to the
costume room to start handing out the costumes.

This time, because the cast was going to run through the entire show, from beginning to end, it was important that everyone be dressed on time. Out in the auditorium the orchestra was tuning up. Backstage there was the sound of hammering and the shout of "Heads!" that always preceded the lowering of a piece of scenery. Johnny, may I take you to the Girls' Association Dance? Once more Jean lined up the words on her tongue as she handed costumes across the Dutch door. Johnny, will you go to the Girls' Association Dance with me? Outside in the auditorium Mr. Kohler shouted, "Will the singers *please* stand under the *microphones?*"

Mrs. Rankin, adviser of the Costume Club, pushed open the lower half of the Dutch door and entered the room. "All right, girls, let's try to issue the costumes a little faster," she said briskly. "We can't waste time this afternoon. Jean, I'm putting you in charge of the bats' fingernails. Take this box to the dressing room and give each bat ten fingernails, and after rehearsal see that you collect ten fingernails from each girl."

"Yes, Mrs. Rankin." Jean certainly wouldn't have a chance to see Johnny in the girls' dressing room. That question on the tip of her tongue seemed to grow heavier by the minute.

On her way to the dressing room she caught a glimpse of Johnny, surrounded by a group of admiring girls. Jean's acrobatic heart managed to leap because she was looking at Johnny and at the same time to sink because there were so many girls with him. This was not the moment. Scurrying down the hall with her box of fingernails, she found consolation in the thought that there was safety in numbers. All those girls couldn't be asking Johnny to go to the dance. Not at the same time.

The dressing room was a whirl of activity. Girls in their slips waited for members of the club to help them with their hoop skirts. Indian maidens ran around in their bare feet. Girls in the long-waisted, short-skirted dresses of the 1920's, knees close together, stood in front of the mirrors, kicked up their heels in the steps of the Charleston, and collapsed on the benches in fits of giggles. The bats, all twenty of them, were wearing their chartreuse leotards with black bands crisscrossed from waist to shoulder, and helping one another fasten on their black wings.

"Anyone ready for fingernails?" asked Jean, opening her box.

"Oh, look!" cried the bats, as they clustered around Jean.

Jean began to hand out the sparkle-encrusted

plastic fingernails to the bats, who slipped them over their finger tips and held out their hands for admiration. "Aren't we glamorous?" they crowed, twinkling their finger tips for everyone to see. Girls in less exotic costumes crowded around to admire.

"You look positively Fu Manchu," said Elaine.

"Lo, the poor Indian in her brown-flannel nightgown," answered a bat, as she flitted over to the mirror to admire herself.

Mrs. Rankin bustled into the dressing room with an armload of white wigs. "All right, minuet girls.

Here are your wigs. We have to return them in good condition, so it is not necessary to let the entire student body try them on. We are not going to take time for full make-up today. Three of each group report to the make-up room, so we can get the effect. Jean, if all the bats have their fingernails, see if you can't help some of the other girls."

Jean, who had hoped to escape from the dressing room to someplace backstage where she might see Johnny, looked around for someone to help.

"I need help, Mrs. Rankin," said Peggy Jo. "The hem is coming out of my skirt and I am afraid I will trip on it."

"There is your chance, Jean," directed Mrs. Rankin. "Are all the jitterbug girls wearing saddle shoes and white socks? We don't want any ballerina slippers in this number."

With needle and thread Jean went to the assistance of Peggy Jo, who had accidentally caught her foot in the hem of her sweeping skirt of the 1860's. Outside in the auditorium Mr. Kohler called out, "Don't forget we are timing this show!" Jean knelt and quickly basted up the hem of Peggy Jo's blue brocaded gown. When she stood up she paused to admire the tall girl in the dress with the drop shoulders. "You look lovely," Jean said truthfully.

Even with her blond hair skinned back in an untidy
knot, Peggy Jo was beautiful.

"Thank you," said Peggy Jo, her eyes on the
mirror.

Jean studied her a moment. "Maybe I shouldn't
suggest it," she said shyly, "but I think your hair
would look awfully pretty with that dress if you
wore it down instead of pinned up."

"Oh, yes, Peggy Jo," said Mitsuko enthusiastically,
as she tied a sash for one of the square dancers.
"Please take down your hair."

"All right." Peggy Jo quickly pulled the pins out
of the knot, so that her fair straight hair tumbled
over her shoulders.

"Look!" cried a Charleston girl. "Peggy Jo has
taken her hair down."

"Isn't it beautiful?" asked Jean admiringly.

"But I can't wear it this way," protested Peggy Jo,
studying herself in the mirror.

"Give me your comb," said Jean. "Maybe I can
fix it."

Peggy Jo dug her comb out of her purse and
handed it to Jean.

"I think she should wear it hanging straight down
her back," said one of the girls.

"With a flower over one ear," added another.

Jean combed back the hair so that it hung straight and heavy. It must be wonderful to have such beautiful hair, so thick and soft to touch.

Mitsuko produced a pink camellia, which she said she had snitched from a bush outside the auditorium (the gardener shouldn't mind this once, because it was for art, wasn't it?) and helped Jean secure it behind Peggy Jo's ear with bobby pins.

"Perfect!" exclaimed the girls, and Jean agreed.

Peggy Jo smiled at herself in the mirror and said nothing.

"Everyone out front," cried Mrs. Rankin. "Now as soon as your number is over, come backstage, change your clothes, turn in your costumes, and *quietly* return to the auditorium by the side door. Minuet girls, be careful of those wigs. Bats, don't tear your wings, and be sure you turn in your finger-nails to Jean Jarrett after your act. We don't want any nine-fingered bats during tomorrow night's performance. Now hurry along."

The cast and the members of the Costume Club crowded out of the dressing room, through the backstage area, and down the steps at the front of the stage. Jean saw Johnny standing by a micro-phone in the wings.

"Hey!" exclaimed Johnny, when he saw the bats. "You can haunt my house any time."

"Hi, Johnny," said Peggy Jo.

Johnny whistled.

"All that and a Chevrolet, too," remarked a stage-hand.

Jean, carried along by the crowd, felt a twinge of some uncomfortable emotion. It wasn't envy and it wasn't jealousy. It was more a feeling of dissatisfaction with herself, a foolish feeling because she neither expected nor wanted to be the kind of girl boys whistled at. And she was bothered by something else. Maybe some people did make fun of feminine intuition, but Jean knew—as certainly as she was wearing white saddle shoes—from the way Peggy Jo looked at Johnny, that Peggy Jo liked Johnny and liked him a lot. And I helped make her even more beautiful than she usually is, thought Jean.

"Hi, Jean," Johnny called, as she descended the steps into the auditorium.

Jean smiled radiantly. "Guess what I am," she called gaily. "Vice-president in charge of bats' fingernails!" It was good to know she was not completely overshadowed by Peggy Jo.

"Hi, Jean."

Jean looked around and located Homer, his violin resting on his knee, sitting in the orchestra pit.

"Oh—hi, Homer," she answered, thinking that he

must have just had his crinkly hair cut. Or perhaps *mowed* was a better word.

"House lights!" bellowed Mr. Kohler. The auditorium grew dim. The orchestra played a medley of music used in the show, and then the voice of the invisible Johnny filled the auditorium.

> "Welcome one and all!
> Come with us year by year
> From then to now, from there to here,
> In song and dance and skit.
> We hope our show will make a hit."

Jean's admiration was wholehearted. Johnny was every bit as good as any announcer she had heard on radio or television. The curtains parted on the Indian scene, and after noticing with amusement Elaine standing on an artificial rock in her brown outing-flannel Indian dress, Jean drifted off in a daydream in which Johnny was saying, and she was replying, Why, yes, Jean, I'd like to go to the Girls' Association Dance with you and don't worry about transportation. I can get the car. Oh, Johnny, that will be wonderful! That's all right, Jean. I am looking forward to going to the dance with you.

If only it would happen that way.

It seemed to Jean that the show had scarcely begun when the bats were leaping and twirling eerily through the moss-hung trees. She pulled herself out of her daydream long enough to admire the effectiveness of the glittering fingernails, which were her responsibility. And then it was time to slip through the side door and around to the dressing room.

The bats, breathless from dancing, came crowding into the dressing room and flung themselves down on the benches. "How did we look from out front?" someone asked Jean.

"Eerie. Just the way you should look," answered Jean, holding out her box. "Fingernails, please."

"I think we should wear black leotards," said another girl. "Whoever heard of a chartreuse bat?"

"Maybe you are right," agreed another girl. "Don't you think so, Jean?"

"What?" asked Jean, who had been thinking about Johnny.

"Don't you think black leotards would look better?" repeated the girl.

Jean was flattered to have her opinion asked. "No," she said, after considering the matter. "All-black costumes in the dim light would not be nearly as effective. Fingernails, please."

"I guess you are right," mused the bat.

Plainly the bats were in no hurry to part with their fingernails. "Fingernails, *please*," said Jean.

"Can't we wear them awhile?" pleaded a bat, twinkling her fingers. "I have always wanted to have really long fingernails, but my mother won't let me. She's so mid-Victorian about things like that."

"No," said Jean, feeling desperation growing within her.

Girls from other acts were coming in to change their costumes, and the dressing room was once more a scene of confusion. Each girl wanted to discuss her part with anyone who would listen. Jean looked into her box. She had collected fingernails from not more than half a dozen bats.

Jean made a decision. If she was ever going to ask Johnny to go to that dance, she had to do it now. That very minute. She set her box on a bench, stepped up on the bench, clapped her hands, and as the voices subsided and she had attention for an instant, she announced resolutely, "All bats will deposit their fingernails in this box at once. Mrs. Rankin's orders."

I am not acting like me at all, Jean marveled, as she hopped off the bench and pushed her way out of the dressing room. That was the thing to do, she de-

cided—go right on not acting like herself. Be somebody else for a change. She ran down the hall and
up the steps to the area backstage. She heard the
cowboys singing and caught a glimpse of their campfire, red electric bulbs under crumpled paper this
time, instead of a wastebasket, and saw their horses
standing in the background. A ripple of laughter
went through the audience as the horses stepped
out of the shadows and began to dance. But Johnny
—where was Johnny?

"Only members of the stage crew are supposed
to be backstage," someone reminded Jean.

Jean paid no attention. She had to find Johnny.
Now. She tripped over a prop and as she bent to rub
her leg, she saw Johnny leaning against the wall in
the wings toward the front of the stage, waiting for
his cue. While she made her way around the artificial rocks that had been removed from the stage
after the Indian number, the cowboys and horses
finished their act and after the curtain had been
drawn, trooped into the wings.

Jean got around the last rock, stood in front of
Johnny, looked him straight in the eye, and in her
determination spoke almost belligerently. "Johnny,
will you go to the Girls' Association Dance with
me?" This was not the way she had meant to sound

at all, but at least her tongue was free of the weight of those words she had carried about with her all through rehearsals.

"Narrator!" bellowed Mr. Kohler, from the rear of the auditorium. "We are wasting time! Where is our narrator?"

Johnny grinned at Jean and tweaked a lock of her hair before he answered, "Sure, Jean. I'll go with you." Then he turned on the microphone and filled the auditorium with his voice.

Jean stood where she was, stunned and elated by her good fortune. Johnny had accepted! He really had. Johnny Chessler was going to the dance with Jean Jarrett. *Johnny Chessler.* She could hardly wait to tell the news to Sue.

Then, because Jean was conscientious, she turned and climbed around the rocks once more and ran on light feet back to the dressing room to count the bats' fingernails.

CHAPTER

7

THE days following the variety show were happy ones for Jean. Sue, who had said with good grace, "All right, I'm wrong," when she heard that Johnny had accepted Jean's invitation, had another date with Kenneth Cory and had decided that she could, if she really put her mind to it, slip-cover her father's chair, which was really terribly shabby. Jean, thinking how the house would look when Johnny came to see her, said that Sue was absolutely right: that chair was a disgrace. Mrs. Jarrett suggested that it might be easier to upholster than to slip-cover, because the old cover could be used for a pattern. Sue agreed, and after Mrs. Jarrett had found a good buy at Fabrics, Etc., the two girls and their mother fell to work on the chair. Mr. Jarrett muttered good-naturedly that a man couldn't even call his favorite chair his own when he lived in a houseful of women, but as long as he wouldn't have any place to sit for a few days he had better do something about the cracks in the plaster over the door into the hall, and while he was at it he might as well give the living room and dining room a coat of paint.

Because Jean actually had a date with Johnny now, she felt free to join him and his friends during lunch hour. Johnny continued to meet her outside the sewing room after school and to walk out of the building with her. That week Jean felt she had only one problem, but that problem, unfortunately, was serious. She had no transportation for the dance.

It was not until Thursday evening that Jean found courage to broach the subject to her father. She did not often find her father alone, but this evening Sue, who had done her homework after school, was in the bedroom stitching on the new upholstery. Mrs. Jarrett was in the breakfast nook going through the advertisements in the evening paper and making a list of bargains to be the basis of her weekly shopping list. Mr. Jarrett was in the living room painting the walls with a roller. It seemed like a perfect opportunity.

"By the way, Daddy," began Jean, perching on the arm of a chair covered with an old sheet. "Maybe you have heard me mention it already, but

Johnny is going to the Girls' Association Dance with me. . . and I wondered if you would mind driving us in the car."

Mr. Jarrett dipped the roller into a tray of paint and rolled it back and forth. "Jean," he said, keeping his voice low, "I want to have a little talk with you."

"Yes, Daddy," answered Jean in a whisper, as her hopes wilted. Her parents so rarely found it necessary to have little talks with their daughters that her father's words sounded ominous. Without transportation she could hardly take Johnny to the dance.

"Jean, I don't want you running after this fellow, Johnny," said Mr. Jarrett, running the roller over the wall above the mantel.

"Daddy, the girls are *supposed* to ask the boys to go to this dance." Jean glanced apprehensively at her father, who was too busy watching his work to look at her. Didn't he understand these things? "The boys can't ask the girls this time."

"I haven't noticed Johnny taking you any place," said Mr. Jarrett.

"I see him every day after school," said Jean, "and he came over one Saturday and took me out for a Coke. I told you about that. And last Friday was the variety show, so he couldn't make a date that night. And it wasn't his fault he couldn't come over that time he was supposed to. His father. . . ." Jean's arguments diminished into silence. Nervously she twisted her fingers.

"Would you rather have braised short ribs or shoulder lamb chops?" Mrs. Jarrett asked from the breakfast nook. "They are both on special this week end."

When neither Jean nor her father answered, Sue called from the bedroom, "Let's have shoulder lamb chops. Braised short ribs are just stew meat with bones. And don't forget to put soap powder on the list. We are just about out."

"Anything else you can think of?" asked Mrs. Jarrett.

"Isn't some market having a special on asparagus?" asked Sue.

"I'll see," replied Mrs. Jarrett. "Asparagus would taste good for a change."

Shoulder lamb chops and soap powder, at what was practically the most important moment in her whole life! Jean searched her father's face for some sign that he might give her an affirmative answer to her question. It would be so much easier if they lived in a house big enough for two conversations at the same time. . . .

"I'm not going to have my girls running after

boys," said Mr. Jarrett. "Let the boys run after you."

Jean stifled an impatient sigh and forgot to whisper. "Daddy, I'm *not*. Just tell me, will you drive us to the dance?"

"How late does this dance last?" asked Jean's father.

And now they had to go into that. "Midnight," answered Jean.

"Midnight!" It was easy to see that Mr. Jarrett did not approve.

"Daddy, it is Saturday night," pleaded Jean. "It isn't as though it was a school night or you had to go to work the next morning."

"It seems to me that midnight is pretty late for a fifteen-year-old girl to be out," said Mr. Jarrett.

"Not on Saturday." Jean did not want to argue with her father but she could not avoid it. She wanted a promise of transportation, not a discussion of proper hours for fifteen-year-olds. Surely this was not one of those times when her father would be unusually strict, the way he was about baby-sitting.

"Oh, come on, Daddy," Sue called from the bedroom. "Say you'll drive them. It's just this once."

Honestly, the walls in the house were practically tissue paper. Nevertheless, Jean hoped that Sue's word would help.

Mrs. Jarrett came into the living room with her

grocery list in her hand. "I'll chauffeur them," she said. "I don't mind."

"Would you, Mother?" asked Jean eagerly, appreciating the offer all the more because Saturday was Mrs. Jarrett's most tiring day at Fabrics, Etc.

"I'll be glad to," said Mrs. Jarrett. "I'm anxious to know what kind of boy Johnny is."

If that wasn't just like a mother, thought Jean. Oh, well, never mind. That was the way mothers were, and there wasn't much a girl could do about it. She finally had a promise of transportation, and that was the important thing.

Mr. Jarrett wiped a speck of paint off the bricks on the front of the fireplace. "All right, but she has to be home by midnight. I know it will mean leaving the dance early, but midnight is plenty late enough for a girl her age." He still did not look as though he approved.

There are times when it is best for a girl to give in gracefully, and this was one of them. "All right, Daddy," agreed Jean. She had a date, she had transportation. Let the problem of leaving early take care of itself when the time came. "I'll be Cinderella, but I won't leave my slipper behind, because we can't afford to scatter shoes around."

Jean felt so lighthearted that she skipped down

the street like a little girl on her way to Elaine's house, where she was going to study and keep Elaine company, because the Mundys were going out for the evening. After Jean told Elaine her good news, the girls settled down with their books at the kitchen table.

It was not long before Elaine looked up from her Spanish book. "What a silly sentence. 'Mary is carrying her cat in a basket.' Any cat I know would jump out before she had gone two feet. It isn't a basket with a lid, either, because there is a picture. By the way—have you forgotten about Saturday afternoon?" she asked.

Saturday afternoon? "What about Saturday afternoon?" asked Jean, unable to recall what it was she was supposed to remember.

"Kip Laddish's personal appearance," said Elaine.

"Oh—Elaine." Jean was genuinely contrite. "I completely forgot. I am terribly sorry." It seemed to her that Kip Laddish had gone out of her life a long, long time ago. It had been weeks since she had even remembered to watch his program.

Elaine looked speculatively at her friend. "Tell me something," she said slowly. "You don't really want to go, do you?"

Jean hesitated. She and Elaine knew one another

too well not to be honest, but at the same time, she did not want to hurt Elaine's feelings. Her hesitation was answer enough.

Elaine's usual exuberance faded. "You don't want to go. I can tell."

"Elaine . . ." Jean began, and found she did not know what to say. Going to the personal appearance of a singer who made popular records now seemed like such a childish thing to do that she felt ashamed that she had ever wanted to go in the first place. Why, they had even planned to try to get his autograph—it embarrassed her to even think of that now. However, she did not want to disappoint Elaine, who had given her on Christmas morning an envelope containing a hand-printed certificate saying that Elaine Mundy promised to give Jean Jarrett one (1) paid admission to the personal appearance of Kip Laddish.

"I know how it is." Elaine smiled ruefully. "Things are different when you have a real boy to think about. Not that Kip is unreal, exactly, but for us he might as well be somebody we imagined."

"I'll go with you, Elaine," said Jean. "I just forgot, is all."

Elaine shook her head. "It wouldn't be the same now that you have Johnny."

Jean could not deny the truth of this. And she was glad she no longer wanted to stand in line with a lot of giggling girls to see a singer who needed a haircut. It seemed a silly waste of time and money. Why, I have gone through a stage, thought Jean triumphantly. I must be growing up.

Elaine, who was never disheartened long, seemed to perk up. "Now the trouble is, I owe you a Christmas present."

"Oh, Elaine," Jean laughed. "That's all right. It's enough that you wanted to take me."

"No," said Elaine seriously. "I'll think of something to take the place of a ticket for the personal appearance."

"Don't worry about it," said Jean and then, because she wanted to change the subject, asked, "Have you heard from any pen pals lately?"

"A letter from the English girl, Cynthia," replied Elaine. "She wants to know if we have many skyscrapers in Northgate."

Jean giggled. "I wonder if the Pacific Insurance Building counts."

"Or there is the Medical-Dental building," said Elaine. "That is five stories high, but I don't think either one of them exactly scrapes the sky. Cynthia also wants me to describe an American drugstore.

She has heard they sell everything and she wants to know if they really do."

"You could tell her that the Low Cost sells Easter bunnies, garden hose, and split-leaf philodendron. That ought to answer her question," said Jean, thinking that she had been too busy sewing on stoles and dreaming about Johnny to write letters. "I haven't heard from any of my pen pals lately."

"I wonder if they have Easter bunnies in England," remarked Elaine. "Cynthia also sent a snapshot of herself. She was standing in what looked like a park, holding her hand out to a deer."

Snapshot—Johnny, ran Jean's thoughts, because any subject could remind her of Johnny. Johnny, the Boy Whose Snapshot I Would Most Like to Carry in My Wallet.

"I guess I should send her a snapshot of me, but I don't have any recent ones," said Elaine, "except that one Dad took of me when I was wearing my shorts at the mountains last summer and I look like Ichabod Crane or something. Oh, well. Don't forget we are supposed to be studying."

Jean bent her head over her book, but an idea was stirring in the back of her mind.

"Ah, this is better," remarked Elaine, and began to translate, " 'Here comes John's dog. The cat jumps out of the basket. Run, run, cat.' I knew that cat wouldn't stay in a basket."

"Elaine, if we had a camera I could take your picture," suggested Jean. The idea was taking definite shape. "Cynthia might like a picture of you taken at school." The idea was now ready to hatch. "Lots of people take cameras to school in this good weather, and I could take your picture during lunch hour when everybody is outside milling around. And then—maybe we could sort of casually snap Johnny's picture. I mean—if you wouldn't mind. I would love to have his snapshot and I would pay for the film developing out of my stole money."

"And then you could carry his picture in your wallet." Elaine took it from there. "And leave your wallet open accidentally on purpose so everybody could see that you are carrying Johnny's picture in it!"

"Well, not exactly," said Jean. "Everybody knows that I don't really know Johnny that well. But I would like to have his picture to keep in my corner of the mirror." For some inexplicable reason Jean felt that owning a snapshot of Johnny would help her to feel more sure of him.

"You don't have to pay for anything. The picture will be my **Christ**mas present to you," said Elaine enthusiastically. "I'll take Dad's good camera, if he will let me, and we'll take a good picture."

Since the girls were supposed to be studying, the implications of this remark did not strike Jean until the next morning, when she stopped for Elaine on the way to school. Elaine came to the door with a camera in a brown case slung over one shoulder. Over the other shoulder she carried a tripod. "I have the light meter in my pocket," she said.

"Oh, Elaine, not the tripod," protested Jean. "Nobody takes a tripod to school."

"We want to take a good picture," Elaine pointed out. "This is your Christmas present."

That was the trouble with Elaine. Her co-operation was too wholehearted. "But I don't want Johnny to think we planned to take his picture," Jean explained. "It wouldn't look casual if we have to set up a tripod and everything. I would rather snap his picture quickly when he wasn't even looking."

"Well—all right." Regretfully Elaine left the tripod behind. "He usually hangs around that urn by the front steps after he eats his lunch. Maybe we could catch him then."

Jean agreed that this would be a good time to take Johnny's picture. "Maybe it would be better if you took the picture," she suggested as they started toward school. "Then he could think—if he noticed you, that is—that you were just taking a picture of a bunch of kids on the steps of the school. You know. Like those snapshots they publish in the back of the yearbook."

"That's a good idea," agreed Elaine. "That way maybe you could be in the picture too. You could walk over and ask him something, and I could creep up and snap the picture without his knowing it."

"I think that might work." A snapshot of herself and Johnny, to be able to see the two of them in black and white—this would be even better than having one of Johnny alone. And maybe if—no, not if, *when*—she got to know Johnny better she could tell him about the snapshot. And maybe he would remark, Say, I'd like to have a copy to carry in my wallet. And she would say, I'll have a copy made for you, Johnny. And he would say eagerly, Would you? I'd sure like to have a picture of us together.

At noon Jean and Elaine hurried through their lunch, which to Jean was tasteless. Her thoughts were not on food that day. Then they went to the "Girls," where they combed their hair and carefully refreshed their lipstick. "Let's hurry and take your picture before Johnny and his gang get there," said Jean anxiously. "Do I look all right?"

"You look fine," answered Elaine. "Now remember, just be casual when you walk over to Johnny. Don't jitter or he will suspect something is up."

But when Jean and Elaine reached the front steps of Northgate High, they found that Johnny and some of his friends were already there. "Hi, Johnny," said Jean, and whispered to Elaine, "I'll go ahead and take your picture first, the way we planned."

Elaine removed the camera from its case and handed it to Jean. "You look in here and press here," she instructed Jean before she leaned against the geranium-filled urn at one side of the steps and smiled fixedly into the camera.

"Smile at the birdie," Johnny called across the steps. Knowing that Johnny was watching made Jean's hands tremble as she peered into the finder.

"Come closer," said Elaine. "For outdoor close-ups you are supposed to be five feet away from your subject."

Still looking into the finder, Jean moved closer and tripped on the steps.

"Hey, look out!" cautioned Elaine. "That's Dad's good camera."

"Sorry." Jean was ashamed that Johnny had seen her being so clumsy. She managed to center Elaine in the jiggling finder and to snap the picture.

"I just know I had my eyes closed." Elaine's voice was a shade too loud, as if she was eager to call attention to herself.

"I'll take another," offered Jean, hoping that Johnny would lose interest and turn his attention elsewhere.

"Maybe you better," agreed Elaine. This time she sat on the steps, crossed her ankles, and gazed off into the distance.

Some of the boys with Johnny whistled. "A regular pin-up girl," one of them said, and the others laughed.

Still self-conscious because Johnny was watching, Jean once more centered her friend in the finder that refused to stand still, and pressed the button. "That should be a good one," she said, not because she thought it could be a clear picture when her hands had been trembling, but because she wanted to say something that would make her appear at ease in Johnny's eyes.

"The light meter," said Elaine as she took the camera from Jean. "We forgot to use the light meter."

"Does it really matter?" asked Jean, not anxious to take Elaine's picture a third time.

"I don't know," admitted Elaine, "but Dad always uses it." Then she said under her breath, "Go over near Johnny and act nonchalant."

"Elaine, I *can't*," whispered Jean, losing her courage. "He will guess what we are up to."

"No, he won't. I'll do it so he will never guess. Now go on." After this assurance Elaine said, in a clear, firm voice, "Well, I guess I'll take some snapshots around school. If they are any good maybe the yearbook can use them."

Jean did not move.

"Go *on*," whispered Elaine.

Reluctantly Jean started toward Johnny. In a way, it must be nice to be like Elaine, who was never bashful, instead of always feeling too shy to do the things she wanted to do. "Hello, Johnny," said Jean. "I just wanted to tell you it is all right about transportation for the dance. Mother said she would drive us."

"That's good." Johnny grinned down at Jean.

"I just thought I would tell you," said Jean. She enjoyed standing beside Johnny—after all, she did have a date with him. Out of the corner of her eye she could see Elaine focusing the camera. Jean, who could not think of a thing to say to Johnny, felt her smile grow strained. She glimpsed Elaine holding up the light meter. Hurry, Elaine, Jean thought desperately. Never mind the light meter. Just take the picture any old way.

"Hey, Elaine!" It was Homer who called out from beside a pillar at the top of the steps. "You girls forgot to wind the film."

Elaine groaned and the crowd laughed. Wouldn't you know, thought Jean.

It seemed to Jean that the crowd grew every minute. And Johnny would probably guess that the reason she had forgotten to turn the film was that she was flustered because he was watching. At the same time the thought flashed through her mind that Homer must have been standing there taking in the whole performance.

Elaine wound the film and looked into the finder once more.

Jean, suffering because this snapshot had taken too long and attracted too much attention, found herself, like an animal caught in the glare of headlights, unable to move. Snap it, Elaine, she thought. Snap it and get it over with before Johnny guesses what we are doing.

"Elaine, you will have better light if you move out of that shadow," Homer called from the top of the steps.

Homer, you keep out of this, Jean thought fiercely,

as Elaine did as she was told. At least, Johnny seemed unconcerned about it all. It was just possible that he still thought Elaine was taking a picture of the front of the school. Still facing Johnny, Jean turned her eyes toward Elaine to see what was keeping her from taking the picture this time.

At that moment Elaine pressed the button. Jean quickly looked up to see if Johnny had noticed, and found that Johnny was smiling directly into the lens of the camera. He had not only noticed, he had posed. Jean's feelings were in a state of confusion. The snapshot should be a good one—of Johnny, at least—if Elaine had the right distance and had made the right adjustments, but Johnny must have guessed what they were doing. She wondered what he thought.

"This time I'll remember to turn the film," Elaine remarked to the crowd, but by this time only Jean was interested.

"Let's go around to the playing field," suggested Johnny, to the group around him. "Some of the track team is practicing."

"Good idea," agreed someone, and the group started to move from the steps.

Does Johnny mean me, too, Jean wondered.

"Coming, Jean?" asked Johnny, as the others started to go around the building

"Yes," answered Jean happily. She glanced back at Elaine, whose eyes were saying so plainly, Include me. Please include me.

Johnny put his hand casually on Jean's shoulder, but Jean's instant pleasure was spoiled by the longing look on Elaine's face. Poor Elaine, standing there with the camera in her hands and one side of her hem sagging. It should have been so easy to say, You come, too, Elaine, but somehow Jean could not make the words come out. She felt too insecure with Johnny and his friends to include Elaine. As she walked along with Johnny she tried to catch Elaine's eye, to receive a glance that would show that Elaine understood her feelings.

But Elaine was busy fitting the camera into its case, the camera that now held the precious impression of Jean and Johnny on its film. It hurt Jean to watch her and she felt ashamed of her own behavior. Elaine looked so forlorn with her hem sagging. Somehow, Jean would have felt better if Elaine's hem had been straight.

CHAPTER
8

WITH twenty dollars in *a cappella* choir-stole money saved, Jean decided to splurge. Why not? Her first school dance was an important event, a milestone in her life and she wanted to look her best for Johnny. She wanted to read in his face the thought that he had never seen her look so nice before. This time there would be no pattern spread out on the study table, no careful planning to get a dress out of half a yard less material than the pattern called for, no struggles to sew in a zipper. This time Jean would take her twenty dollars, go into a shop, and buy a dress ready-made so that she could be sure ahead of time how she was going to look. It was going to be blissfully luxurious to go forth with money in her pocket, money that was going to buy not only a new dress, but a new adventure as well.

However, Jean was uncertain of her own taste in clothes, timid about going into a dress shop alone. She needed someone to go with her, but who? Elaine? She would like to do something to make up to Elaine for the way she had treated her, but Elaine was the kind of girl who shopped with great enthusiasm and somehow bought all the wrong things. Not that this bothered Elaine, who thought nothing of wearing a plaid coat over a print dress. Her mother? No. Her mother was inclined to be a little old-fashioned in her choice of clothes. Sue? Sue, who had had more experience in sewing, had a good eye for smart lines and becoming colors, but Jean was not sure that she would want to go on this shopping trip, because she was not sure how Sue felt about Johnny. It was always so hard to tell what Sue was thinking. She had managed a graceful show of pleasure when Johnny had accepted Jean's invitation, and she had made no further references to the quarrel about whether he would or would not. Probably her thoughts were so full of Kenneth that she no longer bothered even to think about Johnny.

"Sue?" asked Jean from her end of the study table.

"Hmm?" replied Sue from the other end of the table.

"I want to take my stole money and buy a dress

to wear to the dance. A dress-shop dress," said Jean. "Would you come with me?"

"I'd love to," answered Sue, looking up from her books. "Try on lots of dresses, and we will make an afternoon of it. I adore looking at pretty clothes, and it will be lots more fun with money to spend."

Jean knew what Sue meant. Both girls had often visited shops to get ideas for their own sewing, but without money to spend they had always felt like intruders. They had entered hoping the clerks would all be so busy that they could look at the dresses on the racks without assistance. If a clerk did insist on helping, they managed to invent a reason for leaving. And one of the nicest parts of this shopping expedition would be the companionship of a sister who understood.

Saturday turned out to be an exhilarating day, warm and bright, with an occasional breeze to remind Jean that this was still spring, that summer had not come. A beautiful day, and twenty dollars that she had earned all by herself! Anything could happen. Jean felt like skipping all the way to the bus stop.

When the girls got off the bus, they wandered along the main street, pausing in front of windows, uncertain which store to try first. In some shops the windows were full of house dresses, in others the clothing was too old for a fifteen-year-old girl. "Let's try Northgate Apparel," said Sue impulsively.

"Isn't that pretty expensive?" Jean was doubtful. These days twenty dollars, a lot of money to her, did not seem like much to other people. She knew that from looking at the fashions in *Vogue*.

"Lots of good shops carry inexpensive dresses," said Sue. "Anyway, I have always wanted to go in there, so why not?"

"All right," agreed Jean, who wanted to squeeze every bit of adventure out of her two ten-dollar bills. "What are we waiting for?"

Together the girls pushed open the heavy glass door of Northgate Apparel and stepped onto the thick carpet. The shop was cool and filled with soft music that seemed to come from nowhere. They breathed the dry fragrance of new clothes.

"Remember," whispered Sue. "Try on lots of dresses."

"I feel like an impostor," Jean whispered back.

There were few customers in the shop. Several saleswomen, in smart beige or gray dresses with touches of white at the neck, were sitting on chairs at one side of the shop. One of them rose and approached the girls. "Good afternoon," she said. "May I help you?"

"Well. . . ." Jean licked her lips. Her resolution

to try on lots of dresses wavered. This place was much too elegant for her pocketbook. "Yes . . . I am looking for a—a dress." When the clerk looked as if she did not quite understand, Jean added hastily, "I don't mean a school dress or anything like that." She did not want this woman to think she would come to a shop like Northgate Apparel for a school dress.

"An afternoon dress, perhaps?" queried the clerk.

"Yes, only I'm not going to wear it in the afternoon," said Jean, uncomfortably conscious that her saddle shoes were scuffed under their layer of fresh white cleaner. She wanted an afternoon dress to wear in the evening—that sounded ridiculous, but she could hardly say she wanted an evening dress. That did not sound right, either.

"A dress to wear to a dance," said Sue, taking over. "A school dance."

"I understand," said the clerk. "If you will be seated, I will show you some of the things we have that might be suitable. What size do you wear?"

Jean was not prepared for this question. "Well . . . I take a size twelve pattern, but patterns don't run the same as dresses. And I always have to shorten the patterns," answered Jean, and wished she had not. The clerk did not need to know she was not used to shopping for dresses.

"I think perhaps a nine." The woman looked appraisingly at Jean. "Or even a seven."

When the clerk disappeared, the girls sat down on two gray chairs separated by a table that held copies of *Vogue* and *Harper's Bazaar*. "I hope she does understand," whispered Jean. "Everything looks so expensive." She took comfort in the thought of her slip, a new one that she had been saving since last Christmas for some special occasion.

The saleswoman appeared with several dresses over her arm, one of which she hung on a stand in front of the girls. It was blue linen with embroidered white flowers scattered across the waist. Jean managed to catch a glimpse of the price tag dangling from the sleeve. The dress cost thirty-nine dollars and ninety-five cents. Jean and Sue exchanged a glance that said, Oh, dear, this won't do at all.

"No, I don't think so," said Jean.

The clerk hung a pale yellow dress in front of it. The dangling tag read twenty-nine dollars and ninety-five cents.

"Well . . . no," said Jean, feeling more and more uncomfortable.

Sue was braver. "Don't you have anything for less?" she asked.

"How much did you have in mind?" asked the clerk kindly.

Jean decided she might as well be honest. If the shop did not have anything she could afford, they could leave, couldn't they? It wasn't as though she had no money at all. "I have twenty dollars," she said. Twenty dollars seemed much smaller than it had before they had entered the shop. "I don't suppose you have anything for that."

"Oh, yes. We have lots of dresses at that price. It is the small size that is the problem. Not many people are lucky enough to have a trim little figure like yours." She smiled reassuringly at Jean. "I'll see what I can find."

Jean relaxed. This woman, she felt, really did understand. And it was pleasant to know that she had a trim little figure. She would remember this the next time someone called her Half Pint. A girl wearing a smock appeared and silently removed the dresses the clerk had hung on the stand. "Those dresses are awfully plain to cost so much," whispered Jean.

"Plain things always cost more," Sue whispered back.

The clerk returned with a pink dress, hung it on the rack, looked at Jean, and then critically at the dress. "No," she said definitely. "It won't do at all. Pastels are wrong for you."

Jean, who had thought the dress pretty, looked at the clerk in surprise.

"With your coloring you need unusual colors, odd colors that most people can't wear," said the clerk firmly.

"I do?" Jean had always liked pink and blue. She remembered the dress printed with pink clover that she had admired in a magazine in the library. Was that wrong for her?

The clerk disappeared once more.

"She's right. You aren't the pretty type," said Sue, and then added hastily, as if she feared she might hurt her sister's feelings, "I mean you are not the— the fluffy type."

Jean sighed. "I know what you mean."

The clerk appeared with another batch of dresses over her arm. "I found these in our patio shop," she said, and hung a dress of an unusual shade of green, almost an olive green, on the stand. Jean could see that it was a smart dress, but somehow it was not what she had pictured for herself. "Well . . ." she said doubtfully. "I sort of had a gathered skirt in mind."

"No, not for you," said the clerk definitely. "Little girls are so often overwhelmed by too much skirt." She hung on the stand a pale beige dress of polished cotton with a twisted sash of brown and apricot.

Jean knew that this was her dress. It was not at all the sort of dress she had planned to buy, but she knew at once that it was right for her. "Oh, yes," she said happily. "That is—if it doesn't cost too much."

"It is only seventeen ninety-five," said the clerk, "and it just came in today. We think it has a lot of style for the price."

The girls followed the clerk to the fitting room. "It has to fit," Jean whispered to her sister. When the clerk had left them alone, Jean slipped out of her dress and slid the new dress on over her best slip. When Sue pulled up the zipper for her, Jean faced three views of herself in the mirror. Even though the skirt was too long and her scuffed shoes looked even more shabby, she was completely satisfied with what she saw. "I love it," she said ecstatically, and twirled around for the joy of watching three reflections of the dress in motion. "It is so simple and—"

"Becoming," finished Sue.

"Of course it is too long." Jean knew this was not a real obstacle.

"We can shorten it ourselves," said Sue. "Alterations are terribly expensive."

Jean ran her hands over the polished cotton. "I suppose . . ." she hesitated, not wanting to say the words, but feeling that she should. "I suppose we could make it for a lot less." They could, but it would not be the same.

"We could," agreed Sue, "except I don't think we could find a pattern like it. Or any material exactly that color."

Jean smiled gratefully at her sister because she had answered this argument for not buying the dress.

The clerk swept aside the curtain of the fitting room. "Why don't you come out and look at yourself in the big mirror in the daylight?"

Jean's resolution to try on lots of dresses was completely forgotten. She knew she was going to buy this dress, but she could not resist walking out of the fitting room in it. She was even more delighted with the dress in the daylight. In front of the big mirror Johnny's words, "How's the cute girl?" ran through her thoughts. Now she wondered why she had been surprised to hear him speak the words. She was attractive. She did not need Johnny to tell her. In the reflection she noticed another clerk and a customer glance at her and then pause to look more closely. They, too, recognized that the dress was becoming, that she was an attractive girl.

Jean could find no reason for prolonging this satisfying moment. "I'll take the dress," she said, smiling radiantly at the clerk.

"You have made a wise choice." The clerk returned Jean's smile. "A flared skirt is right for you. You would be lost in a lot of gathers."

I'll remember that, thought Jean gratefully, and I'll remember what she said about color, too.

"And if you don't mind my making a suggestion," continued the clerk, "some linen pumps tinted to match the brown in the sash would set the dress off."

Pumps with heels to make her look taller! If only Jean had enough money.

"I'll lend you the money," said Sue, reading her sister's thoughts.

"Would you?" Jean was touched by her sister's generosity. Since it was settled that she was taking Johnny to the dance, Sue wanted her to look her best and to have a good time.

"I hope you have a wonderful evening," said the clerk, when Jean had taken off the dress and paid for it. "I know there won't be a sweeter-looking girl at the dance."

"Thank you," said Jean, flushing with pleasure as she accepted the box containing the dress that she had earned with her own hands.

The girls left the shop and walked down the street

to Belmonts', the shoe store that advertised free tinting of shoes. They chose a pair of linen pumps that made Jean, who had never worn high heels before, feel as if she were going to pitch forward on her face. When the salesman assured her that the shoes fit correctly, she opened the box from the dress shop and carefully matched the sash to the right shade of brown on the salesman's color card. The shoes would be ready for her to pick up two days later.

"That will give me time to practice walking in heels," Jean told Sue, as they left the shoe store. Then she gave a sigh of pure happiness. A date with Johnny, a pretty new dress, and high heels—all at the same time. And most wonderful of all, now she really believed that she was attractive. The world was brighter, her footsteps lighter. It had been such a happy afternoon that she was reluctant to let it end. "Sue, let's splurge some more," she said impulsively. "I'll treat you to a Coke at Snow's—if you will lend me twenty cents."

Sue laughed. "And recklessly spend two whole dimes?"

"Just fling them to the winds," answered Jean. She and her sister rarely spent money on Cokes. Money, they had learned, could quickly be dribbled away on little things that had no real value.

Having made up their minds, Jean and Sue walked
into Snow's, an establishment that was part candy
store and part soda fountain. "Mmm. Smell the
chocolate," remarked Jean, as she chose a small
booth. When the waitress, who wore a starched
bow on top of her head, handed her a menu, she
read it, because it made such delicious reading, even
though she knew she had only a dime to spend. She
felt luxurious just reading the prices.

When the waitress had taken Jean's and Sue's orders, two women sat down in a booth that was separated from the girls' by a shoulder-high partition.
While the pair settled themselves, Jean noticed that
they were both well dressed and had smart haircuts.
The face of one of the women was unnaturally
pink, as if she might have spent part of the afternoon
under a hair dryer. She wore a neckpiece made of the
skins of several small animals biting one another's
tails, which she pushed back as if she did not enjoy
the feel of the fur against her flushed skin. The other
woman wore an expensively simple black dress, a
choker of pearls, and a flowery hat.

The waitress set two Cokes on small plates covered with paper doilies and placed two paper-covered straws in front of Jean and Sue. The girls
smiled at one another across the table. A dress in an

elegant box on the seat beside Jean, Cokes served on paper doilies—so much luxury for one afternoon!

"The *calories*," murmured Fur Neckpiece across the partition, as she studied the menu.

Once more Jean and Sue exchanged glances, this time of amusement. Jean felt a little smug, because she did not have to worry about calories. She had a trim little figure. The clerk said so. Slowly she pulled the wrapper from the straw. The cute girl with the trim little figure was enjoying herself, and she wanted to make the Coke last as long as she could.

"Oh, well, I feel reckless," said Flowery Hat. "I'm going to have a hot fudge sundae and let the calories fall where they may."

"On me they always fall in the wrong place," answered Fur Neckpiece, "but I think I'll have one too, and just feel guilty while I eat it."

Jean felt sorry for the two women, who could afford hot fudge sundaes but could not wholeheartedly enjoy them. Poor things. It must be dreadful to be middle-aged, able to afford those nice fattening sweets, and have to worry about calories. How much nicer to be fifteen and have a trim little figure!

"Tell me," said Flowery Hat, "how is that handsome son of yours?"

Fur Neckpiece laughed lightly. "He's still the same old charmer."

"Madly pursued by all the girls?" asked Flowery Hat.

"Oh, my, yes," answered Fur Neckpiece, in mock weariness. "And by one girl in particular. Poor little thing."

"Doesn't he like her?" Flowery Hat asked.

Fur Neckpiece poured hot fudge from a pitcher over her ice cream. "I suppose he is flattered. After all, what boy wouldn't be? It is really too funny for

words. She has a friend, and the two of them walk past our house, although I am sure they live nowhere near—probably they hope to run into him—and they giggle."

Jean let her straw stand in her Coke. She knew with a terrible certainty who the girl was they were talking about. Jean Jarrett was being gossiped about over two hot fudge sundaes. If only Sue were not there to listen, too.

"And she invents excuses to telephone," Fur Neckpiece continued. "When I was a girl I wouldn't have dreamed of telephoning a boy. I didn't have to. They telephoned me."

"What is the girl like?" asked Flowery Hat.

"Oh, just a girl—no one you would ever notice," answered Fur Neckpiece.

Jean had no appetite for her Coke. This could not be Johnny's mother, because things like this did not happen, but who else could she be? Everything she said fitted like—like that shoe everybody said you should wear if it fits. This shoe was custom-made.

"She even asked him to go to a school dance," Fur Piece went on.

Jean lifted her eyes to Sue, who was looking at the doily under her Coke while she sipped through her straw. Sue's face was grave.

"Of course the dance is girl's choice, but she asked him so far ahead he had to say yes." Fur Piece poured more hot fudge over her ice cream and scraped out the pitcher with her spoon.

"I think your new dress is terribly becoming," said Sue, in a clear voice, because she did not want to give the two women the impression that she and Jean were eavesdropping.

"Yes, isn't it?" Jean managed to say, and missed part of the conversation in the next booth. Once more Jean looked at Sue, whose face was filled with concern. If Sue is going to start being sympathetic, I can't bear it, Jean thought. I simply can't bear it.

"He's really a very good-natured boy," the mother of the charmer was saying. "But he was hoping another girl would ask him. Of course, there wasn't much he could do, when this girl asked him so far in advance."

Was two weeks too far ahead? Surely not, but Jean was not certain, because she had never asked a boy to go to a dance before. Jean longed to look more closely at the boy's mother, but she did not dare turn her head. And then the wild thought crossed her mind that perhaps the woman had recognized her as the girl who walked past Johnny's house and giggled. Perhaps she was saying all this for her particular benefit.

Jean longed to say to Sue, Come on, let's leave, but her tongue felt too stiff to speak, her feet too heavy to walk. When she picked up her Coke, her hands shook so that the ice rattled in the glass, and she had to set it down again. And there was Sue, beginning to look sympathetic. Jean longed to melt and disappear with her ice. Her world had been reduced to ravelings.

"Poor Roger," remarked Flowery Hat. "He will always be pursued by girls."

Roger. The boy they were talking about was not

named Johnny! His name was Roger. Jean's relief was so enormous it left her feeling weak. Those two women were not talking about her at all. They were talking about some other girl. Some other girl entirely. Jean lifted her Coke with hands that still trembled, and took a small sip through her straw. She looked across the table at Sue and saw relief written on her face, too. Jean managed a feeble smile.

"Yes, I suppose girls always will chase him," agreed Fur Piece.

There was no reason why Jean should continue to listen to this conversation, but she was so fascinated she could not help herself.

"It seems to me that Roger is old enough to take care of himself," said Flowery Hat and added, with amusement in her voice, "Are you sure you aren't afraid he likes her?"

"Oh, really!" Fur Piece was impatient.

This exchange boosted Jean's spirits enough to allow her to look at Sue, who had finished her Coke, with an expressionless face that showed she was concealing what she felt. "Shall we go?" asked Jean.

The girls left the booth and paid their check at the cash register by the candy counter. The gaiety and anticipation that Jean had felt when she entered

Snow's was gone, and the fragrance of chocolate now seemed too warm and too sweet. She felt the incident looming between herself and Sue.

"Talk about ups and downs," said Jean, as they walked toward the bus stop. "I have really had it today." When Sue was silent, she burst out, "Why don't you say it? It might as well have been me they were talking about."

"But it wasn't you." Sue's voice was gentle.

"I know." But as they boarded the bus a voice within Jean repeated, It might as well have been you. There was little comfort in knowing she was not the only girl who had chased a boy.

Jean found a seat, clasped her arms around her dress box, and rested her chin on it. She wondered if Johnny really wanted to go to the dance with her after all. What had he said? "Sure, Jean, I'll go with you." As if he was bestowing a favor upon her. And perhaps he was. He knew lots of girls, and she didn't know many boys. It just happened that Johnny was the first boy who had ever paid any attention to her.

And as Jean looked back over the past weeks she realized that the attention Johnny had paid her had not been worth the uneasy vigils in the halls at school, or the ordeal of asking him to go to the dance. Why, trying to find the right moment to ask him to go to the dance had actually spoiled some of her fun in her small part in the variety show. No, Johnny's condescending, "Sure, Jean, I'll go with you," was not worth the strain between herself and Sue, Elaine's hurt feelings, her father's concern.

"Jean, don't feel that way," begged Sue, when they got off the bus. "You are lucky, you know."

"I am?" said Jean. "I thought you didn't like Johnny."

"I don't much," admitted Sue.

"Then why do you say I'm lucky?" asked Jean.

Sue smiled. "When I was fifteen I liked a boy. It seems funny now. He was a tackle on the football team—all chest and not many brains—the kind who stood on the front steps at school and bragged. I thought he was wonderful and cut out his picture every time it was in the paper and tagged him around all semester. He knew I liked him, but nothing ever happened. So you see, you are luckier than I was."

"Why, Sue!" Jean had never suspected her sister of this sort of behavior.

"You were in junior high then," said Sue. "I finally caught on that I really was pretty miserable and that at least half the boys at school didn't even seem to be interested in girls. There didn't seem to be anything anyone could do about it, and I decided next time I would wait for a boy to come along who liked me. Everybody meets somebody sometime, even if it doesn't happen when you are a sophomore. And then one day Kenneth waited for me in the library and everything turned out the way I had dreamed it would. But just the same it would have been nice to have had one date with that tackle."

Jean laughed. "I used to see those clippings from the sport section. I thought it was school spirit, and it really was love."

"Crush is a better word," said Sue. "Or maybe it was rocks in my head or a bee in my bonnet. Anyway, it wasn't love."

As the girls entered their house, Jean thought Sue sounded as if she was sure now that she knew what love was. Jean went into the bedroom and was distracted from her thoughts by the sight of a flat box wrapped in Christmas paper and tied with a red ribbon, lying on her bed. That box, so inappropriate to a warm spring day, saddened Jean. It told her that no matter how she had treated Elaine, Elaine's heart was big enough to want her to have the snapshot of Johnny.

Jean dropped her dress box on the bed, sat down,

and read the card on Elaine's package. "Merry
Christmas to Jean from Elaine." That was all. No
joking remark, no funny note. Carefully Jean untied
the ribbon and rolled it up to save for a small package next Christmas. The candy-cane paper, she decided, was not large enough to save, so she tore it
off the box. Inside, as she had expected, lay a snapshot on a cushion of crumpled tissue paper. Jean
picked it up and studied it. Johnny did look so natural and so handsome as he smiled into the camera.
Johnny . . . he was so attractive . . . if *only*. . . .
Jean broke off that train of thought to study herself
in the snapshot. She looked strained as she faced
Johnny and at the same time tried to look at the
camera—strained and unhappy, and that was how
she had felt, too. And that was how she must have
appeared to Elaine and Homer and all of Johnny's
friends on the steps of the school that day.

"What's that?" asked Sue curiously, as she entered
the bedroom.

"Just a joke," answered Jean, rising from the bed
and dropping the snapshot into her top drawer.
"Just a silly joke." Jean knew then that she no longer
wanted to take Johnny to the dance.

CHAPTER
9

JEAN, who had found it difficult to invite a boy to go to a dance, found the problem of uninviting him even more difficult. She turned the matter over in her mind all through supper. She was only vaguely conscious of what her father was saying.

"There is this new family on my route," Mr. Jarrett was saying, "with a little boy—he must be about four years old—and this morning he stopped me and said, 'Mr. Mailman, have you seen my dog? He didn't come home last night.' "

Jean was thinking she could hardly go up to Johnny in the hall and say, Excuse me, Johnny, but I don't want to go to the dance with you. A girl couldn't come right out and say a thing like that. She should have an excuse like—like breaking a leg, or being called out of town, or catching the measles.

"And when I reached the bottom of the hill near

the end of my route," Mr. Jarrett went on, "another little fellow ran out to meet me. He said, 'Mr. Mailman, see my dog.' He was leading the first little boy's dog by a piece of clothesline tied to its collar."

"What did you do?" asked Sue.

"I had a little talk with the boy's mother. She said she would take the dog back to the first boy in her car, but since her own boy was so happy about the dog, she would get him another."

"A dog that likes mailmen, of course," said Mrs. Jarrett.

Jean smiled absently, more because she was aware her father had finished an anecdote than because she had really listened.

"What's on your mind, Jean?" asked Mr. Jarrett.

"Is something on my mind?" Jean asked, embarrassed that her father had noticed her lack of interest.

"Something is bothering you," answered her father.

Maybe this was one of the times a family could help. "Well . . . I have decided I don't want to take Johnny to the dance after all," said Jean reluctantly, "and I don't know what to do about it."

"But why, dear?" asked Mrs. Jarrett.

"I just don't, is all," answered Jean, searching for

an answer to give her mother. "I don't think it would be any fun."

"Of course it would," said Mrs. Jarrett. "Jean, you have to get over being so shy sometime. Sue is having such a good time with Kenneth. I think you should have some fun too."

"Mother, it isn't because I am shy," insisted Jean. "I—I just don't want to go is all. Anyway, it is different with Ken and Sue."

"But, dear, you have asked him and he has accepted," said Mrs. Jarrett. "You can't break a date just because you have changed your mind. How would you feel if a boy treated you that way?"

"He did, sort of," said Jean. "That night he was supposed to come over."

"You don't really know the circumstances of that evening," Mrs. Jarrett pointed out. "There is no reason to believe he wasn't telling the truth."

"I suppose not," said Jean hopelessly. A girl could not tell her mother that she had chased a boy, and that she was hurt by his condescending acceptance of her invitation. Funny little girl. Sure, I'll go with you. How could she explain that?

"You wear your pretty dress and your new shoes and take him to the dance and have a good time," said Mrs. Jarrett.

"Your mother is right—not that I ever thought much of this fellow Johnny," said Jean's father. "But it wouldn't be right to break the date. Take him this time and let that be the end of it. You don't have to go out with him again."

Reluctantly Jean admitted that her mother and father were probably right. Later, in the kitchen, when she and Sue were washing and wiping the supper dishes, Jean whispered, "I couldn't tell them Johnny probably wouldn't even care."

"It will be all right," answered Sue reassuringly. "Four hours isn't forever, and after that you can drop him. Anyway, those women weren't talking about you."

"They might as well have been," said Jean unhappily, as she polished a glass. "You know that."

"You take things too hard," said Sue. "Maybe it wasn't that way at all. You heard only the woman's version of the story."

"Maybe." When you were fifteen, it seemed difficult to take things any other way.

When the dishes were dried and put away, Jean picked up a letter she had received from her Japanese pen pal that afternoon, and walked over to the Mundys' house to try to make amends for the way she had treated Elaine. "Hi, Elaine," she said, when her friend opened the door. "I thought I would run over and thank you for the Christmas present. You certainly got the pictures developed in a hurry. Wasn't it simply awful of me?"

"Come on in." Elaine seemed glad to see Jean. "It was good of Johnny, though."

Jean saw that Elaine was alone. "Elaine—I'm terribly sorry about the way I treated you the day we took the snapshots. I should have asked you to go around to the playing field too."

"Oh, that's all right," said Elaine. Apologies were as embarrassing to receive as to give.

"Besides," said Jean quickly, to bring an end to the awkward moment, "I brought over a letter I received this afternoon from my Japanese pen pal. I thought you might like to read it. She wants to know if Northgate is near Hollywood. I guess she doesn't realize how big California is."

Elaine took the letter and began to read. "Well, what do you know!" She laughed and looked up from the letter. "She says she is 'particularly interesting in knowing how coeds make date with boys.' Only she spells it *d-e-t-e*. What are you going to tell her?"

The humorous side of this question had not struck Jean until this moment. "You know, that might be a little difficult to explain," she said, and began to laugh.

Elaine giggled. "You can never explain it in one letter. You will have to write an encyclopedia."

Laughing with Elaine helped to erase Jean's worries. "It would take a whole volume to tell how I made a date with Johnny. And now that I have bought a new dress (at Northgate Apparel, too, by the way) and some pumps with heels, I have changed my mind about wanting to take him."

"You're crazy," said Elaine flatly. "Absolutely mad." Then she added, in a voice that expressed her eagerness for information, "What made you change your mind?"

"I just did," answered Jean vaguely. "I got to thinking that Johnny didn't really care whether he went with me or not."

"But that is not the point," protested Elaine. "The point is that even if you know he doesn't really want to go with you, or even if you don't want to go with him, you should go so that you will be seen. Lots of girls would like to go with Johnny, and everybody knows it. And if you are seen at a school dance with him, everybody will think you rate. And maybe somebody else will ask you the next time."

Perhaps Elaine was right. A girl never would have

any fun if she did not make the most of whatever opportunities came her way. But Johnny as an opportunity had not really come Jean's way. She had run after him. Jean wished she were not so uncertain about everything.

"Besides, you have a new dress," Elaine pointed out practically. "And a pair of pumps with heels."

"Yes, there is the dress," agreed Jean. Her lovely plain dress with the shoes tinted to match the sash. Where would she ever wear them if she did not wear them to the dance?

"I think you are lucky," said Elaine. "I don't have anyone to ask at all. Oh, sure, I know some boys, but if I asked one of them to go to a dance with me he would probably run away screaming."

"Oh, Elaine, don't be silly," said Jean.

"Maybe not screaming exactly," admitted Elaine, "but he would probably be thinking like mad to make up an excuse. I couldn't stand to see him suffer."

"Oh, Elaine," protested Jean, not wanting her friend, who had so many good qualities, to have such a low estimate of herself.

"It's true. I don't know a single boy who would like to go to a dance with me." Whenever Elaine was gloomy she was thoroughly gloomy. "Oh, well, you know me. I always like to see the young people have a good time." Elaine attempted to be jaunty about the whole thing. "You go to the dance and tell me about it."

Laughing at Elaine raised Jean's spirits sufficiently to enable her to decide, I will go. She would go and wear her dress and have what fun she could and after that she would never go out of her way for Johnny again.

"Anyway, things will be better next semester," said Elaine, "because I have decided to learn to play the flute."

"The flute!" Jean could not help laughing. Elaine did have some of the wildest ideas. "How will that help?"

"If I can play the flute I can play in the band," said Elaine. "And the band is full of boys--a lot of them tall. And the band has a lot of fun. It even gets to go on trips sometimes. Maybe none of the boys will notice me, but at least I'll belong to something and be doing something and not just wandering around like a lost soul dreaming about a television singer. Besides, a flute is easy to carry."

"You know, Elaine," said Jean, "I think you have something there. I haven't felt so left-out since I joined the Costume Club."

Elaine whistled *Yankee Doodle* into an imaginary

flute. "Weren't we silly back in the days when we used to dream about Kip Laddish?" she asked, and both girls found this remark extremely funny.

On Monday, after school, Jean, who found that her change in attitude toward Johnny gave her a feeling of independence toward him, did not linger in her clothing classroom in the hope of meeting him on her way out of the building. She managed not to see him at all that day. On Tuesday afternoon he was waiting for her when she came out.

"Oh—hi," said Jean, with more calm than she had ever felt before in speaking to Johnny.

"Hi, there," Johnny answered, looking down at her with a disarming smile. "I've missed you."

"Have you?" answered Jean with composure, while she thought, Have you really, Johnny, or are you just saying it? This new detachment toward Johnny gave her ego a tremendous boost. Who was Johnny Chessler anyway? Just a boy.

"Say . . . Jean," Johnny hesitated, and then, leaning lazily against a locker, smiled down at her. "I know you aren't going to believe what I am going to say."

Jean returned his smile. "Probably not," she said lightly. Even though her feelings toward him had changed, she still found him attractive.

"My grandmother is pretty sick," said Johnny,

"and I am not going to be able to go to the dance Saturday night. Dad says it wouldn't be right for me to go when she is so sick, and all."

Jean felt her face turn scarlet. Why, *why* hadn't she broken the date first? Now no one would ever believe she had wanted to break it, even if she told anyone, which, of course, now she could never do. His grandmother! Jean was suddenly more angry than hurt, not because he was breaking the date, but because he was offering such a flimsy excuse.

"Anyone with your imagination should be able to think up a better excuse," she told him.

"See?" said Johnny. "You don't believe me, do you?"

"No, Johnny," said Jean levelly. "I don't believe you, but it is all right. You don't have to go to the dance with me."

Surprise flickered across Johnny's face. He had expected Jean to show disappointment, to protest, perhaps to plead. That glimpse of surprise helped to support Jean's pride. "And now I am going to tell you something *you* won't believe," she said, pleased with her unexpected poise. "I have been wanting to break the date with you." She noted more than a flicker of surprise on Johnny's face.

Johnny smiled his lazy smile. "How come?" he

asked. "How come you have changed your mind?"

Jean looked Johnny straight in the eye. "Because I have thought it over and decided I don't want to go with you, because you don't really want to go with me."

"You have more spunk than I thought you had." Johnny grinned, and ran the tip of his finger down Jean's nose. "And you know something?" he drawled. "You're cute when you're mad."

Oh! "I'm glad you think so," answered Jean and, turning, walked away from Johnny with her head held high. Let him laugh if he wanted to. Johnny, she was sure, would not believe her, because it would be difficult for Johnny to believe any girl did not like him. Nevertheless, she felt better for speaking the words.

Jean hurried down the hall to Elaine's locker.

"Why—hello." Elaine sounded surprised. "I thought you would be waiting for Johnny."

"I'm through waiting for Johnny," answered Jean.

"You didn't break the date after all?" asked Elaine, as she snapped shut the padlock of her locker.

"No, I didn't break it," said Jean. "Johnny did."

Elaine turned to face Jean. "Oh, Jean! How awful."

"It isn't awful at all," said Jean calmly. "You know

I didn't want to go with him. And now I don't have to."

"But to have *him* break it—" Elaine was so outraged she did not finish the sentence. "I mean, a girl has her pride. He can't treat you that way." Elaine scowled, and said urgently, "Jean, you've got to go to that dance. You've *got* to go and wear your dress, just to show Johnny! It is bound to get back to him that you went to the dance after all."

Jean doubted this, but she felt herself infected by the intensity of Elaine's feelings. "But who could I ask?"

"There must be somebody," said Elaine. "*Think.* Think hard."

"I'm thinking," said Jean, "but it doesn't help." There was that boy in her English class who had been friendly, but he had already been asked, she knew. And a boy in math—no, she didn't know him well enough and besides, she thought he was already going steady. And of course there were no boys at all in Clothing or in the Costume Club.

"What about one of the Indians from the variety show?" suggested Elaine.

"No," said Jean. "There was such a bunch of them that I don't remember any one especially."

"Homer!" said Elaine triumphantly.

"Homer?" echoed Jean.

"He's a boy and he knows you," said Elaine.

"Yes, but—Homer. I never thought of him as a boy to dance with," protested Jean.

"You can start," Elaine informed her.

So Jean leaned back against a locker, her books clutched in her arms, and thought about Homer as a boy to take to a dance. It was not easy, because she had always thought of him as a boy who tagged around after Johnny. Or used to. Now that she thought about it, she had not seen them together lately.

"He's not really homely, or anything like that," Elaine pointed out. "And he shouldn't mind your glasses, because he wears glasses himself. And he has nice manners. He isn't anybody you would be ashamed to be seen with."

"N-no," said Jean. He was not anyone she was especially eager to be seen with, either. Still, there was nothing actually wrong with him now that she took the trouble to think about him. Perhaps the only thing wrong with Homer was that he was so easy not to think about. Like me, thought Jean. I am awfully easy for boys not to think about.

"Remember your dress and your high heels," said Elaine, as if she were dangling bait in front of Jean.

Jean was tempted. "What if he has a date?"

"He won't have," said Elaine confidently. "Go on, Jean. Ask him for—for the sake of womanhood. You don't want to be downtrodden by someone like Johnny, do you?"

Jean could not help laughing. "Oh, Elaine, the way you put things! All right. I'll ask him for the sake of womanhood. The worst he can do is turn me down."

"Good!" Elaine was jubilant. "You'd better ask him right away."

"Before I lose my courage?" asked Jean.

"Partly," admitted Elaine, "and because you can't wait until the day of the dance to ask him. It wouldn't look right."

"Elaine, I can't telephone him." Jean did not think she could ever bring herself to telephone a boy again.

"Ask him the first thing in the morning and *don't change your mind.*"

"I won't" Jean sounded less certain than her promise. Together the girls walked down the hall. Jean found it pleasant to be walking the familiar route with Elaine once more, instead of lingering outside her clothing classroom, hoping that Johnny's whim might bring him toward her. She had never found any real pleasure in those uncertain moments, and now she wondered why she had waited at all. She felt as if she had suddenly been set free. As they passed the foot of the central stairs, both girls saw Homer descending from the library, a book in his hand.

"Here's your chance," whispered Elaine, and disappeared.

Here goes, thought Jean, glad that she would not have time to change her mind. "Hi, Homer," she said, when he had reached the bottom of the stairs.

"Hello, Jean," Homer answered. He hesitated and then started to walk down the hall.

"Homer—could I talk to you a minute?" Jean asked nervously.

"Why sure, Jean." Homer turned back.

"Homer—" Jean had to force herself to utter the words. "Homer, would you go to the Girls' Association Dance with me?" The invitation was offered, and now the worst that could happen was his refusal. She could take it bravely if she had to.

"Why—" Homer's face turned crimson.

Just the way mine does sometimes, thought Jean.

Homer's face relaxed into a smile. "Why—sure, Jean," he answered, looking flustered. "Gosh, that would be *swell!*"

"Swell," said Jean, weak with relief.

"I mean—that would really be *swell*," said Homer.

He honestly means it, thought Jean. How different was his reaction from Johnny's . . . and how pleasant it was to watch. Jean and Homer looked at one another and this time Jean really observed him. He is a nice boy, she thought, and he has long eyelashes behind his glasses. She felt ashamed that she had not taken the trouble to look at him before.

"Golly, I never expected a girl to ask *me* to go to a dance," Homer blurted out.

Jean was touched by Homer's humility. Then she remembered Johnny, and wondered if Homer knew she had asked him first. If he did not already know, he was sure to hear it. Jean did not want this boy's feelings to be hurt. She bit her lip for a moment while she decided that the best thing to do was to tell him herself. Right now.

"Uh . . . Homer," she began. "I guess maybe I had better confess. I asked Johnny first and then he—he broke the date."

If Homer was disappointed, he concealed his feelings from Jean. "That's O.K.," he said awkwardly. "I guess there are some fellows who just naturally get asked first."

"I don't suppose anybody will believe me, but I

was sorry I had asked him and I really wanted to break the date myself," Jean explained. "I mean, I am not heartbroken or anything like that because he broke the date." Naturally a boy would not enjoy going to a dance with a girl whose heart was breaking over another boy.

"That Johnny!" was all Homer said.

"My mother will drive us," said Jean. "I'm not old enough to get a license."

"That's all right. She doesn't need to go to that trouble," said Homer. "I can get our car."

"Could you really?" asked Jean. It would be lots more fun to go in the boy's car.

"Sure," said Homer. "I'll be glad to."

Jean did not know what to do with the conversation next. Homer had accepted and he would supply the transportation. There seemed nothing more to discuss.

"I'm sure glad you asked me," said Homer, "even if I wasn't first."

The wonderful part was, he meant it.

"Well, I have to go now," said Jean. "I'll probably see you before Friday."

"Sure," said Homer. "I'll see you around school."

As they parted Jean turned to watch this boy walk down the hall. There was no mistaking it. His walk was jauntier than she had ever seen it before. Elaine was by her side, seeming to appear from nowhere.

"What did you do?" asked Jean. "Disappear in a puff of smoke?"

"I went into the nearest room. I thought it was the right moment for me to tactfully disappear," Elaine explained. "Did he say yes?"

"That's right." Jean looked thoughtfully at Homer, who was going out the door at the end of the hall.

"Hooray!" exclaimed Elaine. "That will show old Johnny."

Jean wondered. Probably Johnny would not even know, because the activities of the Jeans and Homers were scarcely news around Northgate High. And if he did find out, she doubted very much that he would care.

"Tell me about it." Elaine was always impatient for details. "He didn't just say yes and walk off. What happened?"

"You know something, Elaine?" said Jean wonderingly. "He *wants* to go to the dance with me. He really does."

"And now you can wear the dress!" Elaine sighed happily. "And the heels."

"Yes, I can wear my dress," said Jean dreamily. Maybe Homer wasn't a boy she would have chosen to take to the dance if she had had the whole school to choose from, but he was a boy who really wanted to go with her. He was actually enthusiastic and wasn't afraid to show it. Jean smiled to herself. Maybe Homer wasn't the handsomest boy in school or the most popular. She didn't care. He was a nice boy and he was eager, really eager to go to the dance with her. And that, Jean discovered, made up for a lot of things.

CHAPTER
10

JEAN practiced wearing her brown linen pumps. She walked across the carpet, she walked on the bare floor. She danced forward, she danced backward, she whirled in circles, and all the while the phrase, "She walks in beauty," whispered through her thoughts.

Mr. Jarrett rubbed the soles of Jean's new shoes with sandpaper and, feeling more secure, she wore the shoes every possible moment until it was time to dress for the dance. Without her saddle shoes she felt light enough to float. It was a joy to slip into the new dress, now shortened to a becoming length, and have Sue pull up the long zipper for her. Carefully she knotted the brown-and-apricot sash.

"Your turn for the mirror," said Sue, who had had first turn at the bathroom and who had now finished dressing. She and Kenneth were going to drive across the bay to see some old movies that were part of a series called "The Development of the Motion Picture as an Art," which was being shown at a museum. "You look darling and I hope you have a wonderful time with Homer."

Jean smiled into the mirror at her sister, who seemed to shine with happiness tonight. "Thank you. And I don't have to hope you will have a good time. I know you will." She combed her bangs into place before she asked, "You really like Kenneth, don't you?"

"Mm-hm," answered Sue. "He's—he's just wonderful, that's all."

"I'm glad," said Jean sincerely and wistfully. It would be so nice if she could feel that Homer was wonderful too.

The doorbell rang. "He's here!" Sue snatched her coat from the closet, and was gone.

Jean enjoyed having the bedroom to herself. She fluffed the ends of her hair and admired her dress all over again. Johnny and the clerk in Northgate Apparel were right. She was attractive. It was funny, too, because she had the same brown hair and the same too short nose that she had always had, and yet now she was different. She felt attractive. Maybe wearing glasses and being too short did not matter as much as she had believed. I am attractive, she told herself. I believe it now. But in the back of Jean's mind lurked an unhappy thought. If she was attractive, why didn't Johnny want to go to the dance with her?

"Jean, why don't you come out and let us see how you look?" Mrs. Jarrett called from the living room.

Feeling suddenly shy in front of her mother and father, Jean made her entrance.

Mr. Jarrett whistled.

"You look lovely, dear," said Mrs. Jarrett. "That dress is most becoming."

"Thank you," said Jean. It was comforting to know her family was proud of her.

"And I can tell you one thing," said Mr. Jarrett. "That fellow Johnny is going to be sorry he changed his mind."

"No danger," said Jean. "He won't be there."

"Not that I ever thought he amounted to a hill of beans," said Mr. Jarrett, as he reached into his pocket and pulled out his wallet. He took out two one-dollar bills and handed them to Jean. "Since this is a girls' affair, you had better take this along. A boy gets pretty hungry dancing."

"Thank you, Daddy." It was thoughtful of her father to do this and just before payday, too. Jean took the money into the bedroom and slipped it into the pocket of her coat—really her mother's coat, borrowed for the occasion. Maybe Homer would like to go to the drive-in after the dance, because that was where everybody went.

The doorbell rang for the second time that evening. Where had the moments flown? Jean had not had time to start being nervous about Homer's arrival, and here he was already. She snatched up the coat which she dropped on a chair in the living room, and hurried to open the door. "Hello, Homer," she said. "Won't you come in and meet my mother and father?"

Jean, who had rehearsed this introduction in her mind for several days, managed it smoothly. Reading approval on the faces of her parents, she tried to view Homer through their eyes and saw a serious-looking boy in a white shirt and gray flannel suit, with his hair mowed short. Because he was wearing a necktie he looked more grown-up than he looked at school, and he was quite at ease with her parents, which surprised Jean. Somehow, she had expected him to blush and stammer.

"Shall we go, Jean?" Homer asked, as he picked up her coat.

"Have a good time, children," said Mrs. Jarrett,

as Homer put his hand on the doorknob. Jean, who was often annoyed with her mother for what she considered the careless use of the word *children*, did not mind this time. It was a loving word, the way her mother spoke it, and Jean felt that now her mother was extending her warm feelings to include this boy who was happy to go to the dance with her daughter.

"Take good care of my daughter," said Mr. Jarrett.

"Oh, Dad," laughed Jean, embarrassed by her father's remark.

"I will, sir," said Homer seriously.

Jean experienced a pleasant feeling of being cherished. After she had walked successfully down the steps in her high heels, and she and Homer were seated in the car, he handed her a clear plastic florist's box that protected one perfect white camellia. "I know this isn't a formal dance or anything like that," he said bashfully, "but I—uh—thought you might like a flower anyway."

"Why, Homer—" A boy had given her a flower! "Homer, it's lovely!" Jean would never have guessed that Homer was the kind of boy who would give a girl a flower.

"Do you really like it?" asked Homer, as he

started the car. "I wasn't sure whether it was the thing to do or not."

"I love it," said Jean. This waxy camellia was more than a perfect blossom to Jean. It was thoughtfulness boxed in plastic, and after Johnny, Jean found a boy's thoughtfulness a lovely thing to hold in her two hands. She held the gift carefully all the way to the gymnasium, where she left the box (which of course she wanted to keep forever) in the car. After she had checked her coat she pinned the camellia to her dress with the stem up, took it off, and repinned it with the stem down.

When Jean joined Homer at the edge of the dance floor and handed him her coat check, she was suddenly frightened. "Homer, maybe I should tell you," she said hesitantly, listening to the beat of the orchestra. "I'm not a very good dancer."

"Neither am I," Homer confessed cheerfully. "Not this kind of dancing. I'm pretty good at folk dancing."

Nevertheless, Jean felt her palms grow cold as Homer dropped her coat check into his pocket. Her mouth felt as dry as Kleenex and she made an excuse to step over to the drinking fountain. The water seemed the most delicious she had ever tasted. She longed to postpone the moment when she had to step onto the dance floor, but they had come to dance, and dance they must. Fortunately there were not many couples on the floor yet, so there would not be many people to bump into. And Jean had the satisfaction of knowing that she was becomingly dressed. That helped a lot.

Homer put his arm around Jean, took her hand, and together they moved onto the floor. Almost immediately Jean stumbled. "Excuse me," they both said at the same time, and laughed nervously.

They started to dance again. Homer stepped squarely on the toe of Jean's new pumps.

"Excuse me," repeated Homer, "but you are always supposed to start with your right foot. I start with my left."

"Oh, excuse me," apologized Jean, recalling that Elaine had told her this. They began actually to move along with the other couples. Homer's hand, Jean discovered, was as cold as hers, and she took comfort in knowing that a boy could be nervous too. They stumbled once more, and both said, "Excuse me."

"Look," said Homer. "Let's lay a few ground rules. No more apologies. We'll just do the best we can."

Jean felt a wild desire to giggle, but when they

had circled the gymnasium floor once, she had a real sense of achievement. We made it, she thought triumphantly. When the music stopped she surreptitiously rubbed her cold, moist hand on her skirt. Homer, she noticed, rubbed his hand on his coat.

"Look," said Homer once more. "Maybe I shouldn't say it, but couldn't you sort of relax? I am supposed to do the leading, you know."

"I'll try," said Jean contritely. Dancing with a boy was a lot different from dancing with Elaine. When the music began once more, Jean tried to be limp.

"That's better," said Homer.

Jean was encouraged, but gradually as she danced she felt herself stiffen. Relax, she told herself sternly and managed to be less tense. Homer's dancing, she soon discovered, was as regular as the beat of a metronome. When she could be sure he would not try any unexpected steps, she felt encouraged and even glanced at him. Why, he shaves, she thought. How silly of her! Of course he shaved. He was a senior and must be seventeen. She somehow had never thought of him as old enough to have a beard. Should they, she began to wonder, be carrying on a conversation?

"I thought there would be a larger crowd," she said experimentally, not at all sure she could dance and talk at the same time.

"It will get larger later," explained Homer. "It is the herd instinct in reverse. Half the crowd is afraid to come before nine for fear they might be the first ones here."

Jean wondered how Homer knew this. Around and around the floor they circled. Jean's feet, unaccustomed to high heels, began to hurt. She thought perhaps she should have bought a larger pair of shoes and caught herself leaning heavily on Homer's shoulder to relieve the pressure on her toes. Quickly she straightened. Her poor, poor toes.

When the music stopped, Jean slipped off one shoe and wiggled her toes. *Ahh*. Bliss. Pure bliss. Now for the first time Jean was able to look around her. She noticed on the bleachers a number of pairs of girls' shoes, and when she looked at the girls on the dance floor, she discovered many had been dancing in their stocking feet.

"That crunching sound you have been hearing," remarked Homer, "is the sound of toes being stepped on."

Jean could not help admiring the girls who were such good dancers they could risk their toes. When the music started, Jean managed to shove her foot into her shoe, which was a size too small. Around and around they danced, repeating the same steps over and over. Jean began to feel that she was getting to know Homer's gray flannel shoulder very well. Around and around. There was no hope of a change of scenery, because no one traded dances as Jean had expected. Around and around. Either Jean's feet were growing or her shoes were shrinking. The whole situation suddenly struck Jean as being hilariously funny and she wanted to laugh. Politeness, however, prevented her from showing how she felt. School dances weren't supposed to be funny. Naturally she could not let Homer know that she thought it was ridiculous to dance around and around with one gray flannel shoulder. She began to wonder how many laps around the gymnasium made a mile.

Suddenly Jean stiffened and was aware that Homer had not only noticed her quick intake of breath but was staring in the same direction, toward the checkroom door, where Johnny was standing with Peggy Jo. Johnny was looking intently at Peggy Jo, who was almost as tall as he was. She said something, and they both laughed. Then Johnny put his arm around Peggy Jo and they began to dance, easily and gracefully.

The pleasure was completely drained from Jean's

evening, which had begun to seem like a private joke that she had been enjoying in spite of her toes. All that was gone, now that she knew Johnny thought so little of her that he would break a date to go with another girl. Did he think she was such a—a mouse that she could not ask another boy? Or didn't he care? And what was she supposed to do now? She could not face Johnny. That she knew.

"Did you think he wouldn't come?" asked Homer mildly.

"I guess so," admitted Jean, stumbling on Homer's foot. Don't let Johnny see me, she thought fervently. Just don't let him see me. She danced with her eyes on Homer's shoulder, hoping that if she could avoid seeing Johnny, that somehow he would not see her. Each step was more painful than the one before, and when the music stopped, Jean stood on her right foot and wiggled the toes of her left foot while she stared wretchedly at the basketball foul-line painted on the floor.

"You don't want to see Johnny, do you?" asked Homer bluntly.

Jean stood on her left foot and wiggled the toes of her right foot. "No," she confessed shamefacedly.

"Why?" asked Homer. "He should be embarrassed. Not you."

Why? How could a girl explain to a boy that it was humiliating not to be wanted, and even more humiliating that a boy did not care about her feelings. And yet she knew Homer was right. "I just feel funny about it, is all," Jean said lamely. Thoughtful Homer, who had been kind enough to bring her a flower—Jean had to think of him, too. She could not spoil his evening, when he had been so glad to come with her.

Jean smiled shakily, and the music started once more. When Jean caught a glimpse of Johnny on the other side of the gymnasium, she found herself smothering a ridiculous feeling of wistfulness. It would be so wonderful to be dancing with a tall, good-looking boy like Johnny, a boy whose dancing was graceful and not like the beat of a metronome. If only Johnny had been some other kind of boy. . . .

The music stopped and inevitably, when Homer dropped Jean's hand, she found herself facing Johnny. She could not miss the surprise, followed by embarrassment, that crossed Johnny's handsome face. So he hadn't thought she had enough spirit to ask another boy to go to the dance. Well, she would show him! "Hello, Johnny," she said coolly. "Hello, Peggy Jo."

"Why—hello, Jean," answered Johnny. There

was an awkard pause. Peggy Jo smiled, apparently unaware of the situation.

"Hi, Johnny," said Homer.

Jean felt a little wicked. "Isn't it miraculous the things they do with wonder drugs these days?" she asked, looking directly at Johnny.

"Wonder drugs?" Johnny did not know what she was talking about.

"Yes. Your grandmother—I am so glad she is feeling better," said Jean with a smile.

"Uh—yes," said Johnny, and Jean was happy to see that he was embarrassed.

"Jean, would you like some punch?" asked Homer.

"Yes, thank you," answered Jean. The uncomfortable moment was over. She had been able to face Johnny after all. Her relief was followed by an unexpected feeling of gaiety, as she accompanied Homer to the little grass shack made out of crepe paper, and accepted a paper cup of pineapple punch from Homer. It was so cold and refreshing that for an instant Jean wished she could pour it over her toes.

"What was that about wonder drugs?" Homer asked.

"Oh, that—" Jean laughed. "Johnny used a sick grandmother as an excuse for breaking his date with me, and I couldn't resist reminding him of it."

When Homer threw back his head and laughed, Jean laughed with him. Over his shoulder Jean caught a glimpse of Johnny looking toward them, as if he was surprised to see them enjoying themselves. What did Johnny expect me to do, Jean thought in annoyance. Sob my little heart out? She smiled warmly at Homer.

Homer drained his cup of punch before he spoke. "Jean, let's face it. We aren't having a good time."

"Why, Homer—" In her consternation, Jean did not know what to say. She felt as if she had failed, because everyone who came to a dance was supposed to have a good time. That was what dances were for. "Homer, I am terribly sorry."

"What are you sorry about?" Homer asked. "There's nothing so terrible about that, is there? Maybe we just aren't the kind of people who have a good time at a dance. I think it is pretty stupid

myself, the way a lot of people come and don't dance
at all, or don't trade dances. I belong to a folk-dance
group that is lots more fun than this, because everybody mixes."

Jean found that in her heart she agreed with
Homer, but what could they do if they left the dance
now? It was only nine-thirty. Nobody went home
at nine-thirty. It even seemed too early to suggest
going to the the drive-in.

"Look, Jean," said Homer eagerly. "Would you
like to see my pigeons?"

"Your pigeons?" repeated Jean. What on earth
was Homer talking about now?

"Yes. My homing pigeons. I have six in a cote in
the back yard at home," Homer explained.

"I didn't know you kept pigeons." Jean was stall-
ing for time to think. She wanted to leave the dance,
but she wondered what her mother and father would
say about her going to a boy's house. She had no
idea, the problem was so unexpected.

"It would be all right for you to come," said
Homer. "Mom and Dad are home. They have some
friends there."

This settled the problem in Jean's mind. "I would
love to see your pigeons, Homer," she said.

"Swell," said Homer. "Let's get your coat."

As they left the checkroom, Johnny and Peggy Jo danced by. Johnny grinned lazily at Jean over Peggy Jo's shoulder, and winked. Oh, stop it, Johnny, thought Jean, and repinned her camellia to her coat, stem up this time.

When they climbed into the car, Jean realized that she did not even know where Homer lived. How heavenly it was to be able to take off both her shoes! They drove through the business district and took a road that wound uphill, twisting and turning until at last Homer drove up a steep driveway. Jean had to shove to get her shoes back on again. As they got out of the car Jean paused to look at the lights of the city below and of the cities in the distance strung together by necklaces of lights on the bridges across the bay. Jean breathed deeply. It was good to be out of the gymnasium, which always smelled faintly of sneakers and sweeping compound, and into the night air, so much cooler up here in the hills and scented with eucalyptus.

"Come on in and meet Mom and Dad while I get the flashlight," said Homer, leading Jean toward the front door.

"Well, you are home early," remarked Mr. Darvey, when Homer had taken Jean into the living room and introduced her to his parents and their guests.

"I wanted to show Jean my pigeons," said Homer. He seemed at ease in a roomful of adults—much more at ease than he ever appeared at school.

"But the dance can't be over this early." Mrs. Darvey was concerned over her son's early return. "What happened?"

"Jean and I decided we would rather look at pigeons," said Homer easily. "Come on, Jean." He led her into the kitchen, where he found a flashlight in a drawer. They went out the back door and walked across a lighted patio.

Jean had an impression of blooming rhododendrons and azaleas and, beneath the flowering shrubs, masses of blue and yellow violas. "What a lovely garden," remarked Jean, as she followed Homer along a path that led into the dark.

"Mom's a spring-garden fiend," said Homer, lighting the way for Jean. "Nothing much blooms the rest of the year, but it is sure beautiful now. Mom says the seasons are so indefinite in California that she tries to make up for it with a good rousing springtime."

Under a cluster of eucalyptus trees they came to the pigeon cote, a neat structure stained gray to match the house. Homer opened the door and flashed the light inside. Six sleeping pigeons stirred

on their perches, blinked, and flapped their wings.
Homer reached inside and brought out one pigeon.
"This is Papa Pigeon," he said. "Would you like to
hold him?"

Jean took the uneasy pigeon in her arms and
gently stroked the iridescent feathers.

"Papa Pigeon is the father of those two," said
Homer, pointing. "And that one is Mama Pigeon."
He lifted out another bird. "This one we call Ugh.
He was the first squab I raised, and when he hatched
he was the weirdest thing I had ever seen. He had
a great big beak, all out of proportion to his skinny
little body, and his skin was covered with yellow
hair. But he grew fast and is a beauty now."

"And do they really come home?" asked Jean.

"Always," said Homer. "We have a lot of fun on
Sundays when we go for a drive. We take them along
and release them in the country, and no matter which
way we take them, they always circle around for
a while and then head for home in the right direction."

One by one Homer removed the pigeons for Jean
to stroke. She had not realized how soft and smooth
feathers were. "Just like satin," she murmured, running her hand down a glossy back. "Smoother than
satin." The pigeon flapped its wings and for a

moment Jean was afraid it might slip out of her fingers. Homer took it from her and returned it to the perch. "And did you build the pigeon cote?" she asked.

"Last summer," answered Homer. "I drew up the plans and Dad helped me build it." He closed and fastened the door of the cote and led the way back toward the house.

Jean put her hand in her pocket and felt the money her father had given her to treat Homer. "Homer," she said hesitantly, "would you like to go to the drive-in? I mean, I made the date and I—I would like to treat you."

"Let's not go to that crummy place," said Homer. "Come on in the house and I'll make you a milk shake."

"All right." At first Jean was a little hurt by Homer's rejection of her invitation, but the more she thought about it, the more she began to feel that Homer was right about the drive-in. She began to feel a kind of admiration for this boy who would come right out and say he did not like the most popular meeting place of high-school students, and who saw nothing wrong with leaving a dance he did not enjoy. Jean had always felt critical of herself because she was not like everyone else at school.

In the kitchen Homer took Jean's coat after she had unpinned her camellia. "What kind of milk shake would you like?" he asked.

"I like any kind," answered Jean, as she pinned the camellia, stem down, to her dress. She would not like to say she liked chocolate milk shakes if the Darveys did not have any chocolate syrup.

While Homer was opening the refrigerator, Jean looked around at the kitchen, which was larger than the Jarretts'. Instead of curtains, the windows had shades, made of pink-and-white striped ticking. I must tell Mother, thought Jean. Shades like that, instead of curtains, were attractive and would save a lot of ironing, too. Her mother could watch for a remnant of pink-and-white ticking . . . or yellow-and-white might look prettier in their kitchen. . . .

Homer removed a carton of ice cream and a box of strawberries from the refrigerator. "We have bananas, too," he said, "and there is a dish of pineapple in here if you like pineapple milk shakes."

"They all sound good," said Jean.

"I'll tell you what I'll do," said Homer. "I'll use all three." He spooned ice cream into an electric blender and added a banana, a few strawberries, and a slice of pineapple. He flipped the switch, let the blender whir a moment, and poured two milk

shakes into two tall glasses. "We even have straws,"
he said, opening a cupboard.

"Paper-covered straws!" exclaimed Jean.

"That's right," said Homer. "All the comforts of a
soda fountain." He sat down at the table across from
Jean, and together they peeled the paper from their
straws and began to sip their milk shakes.

"Mmm. Good." said Jean. "Banana-strawberry-
pineapple milk shakes are my very favorite from
now on." It was fun to be sitting in a kitchen that
looked like a magazine illustration, drinking a milk
shake that a boy had made. "You are right about
the drive-in," she said. "It is a crummy place. I
just never thought of it that way, because . . . well,
everybody goes there. I guess I thought liking the
drive-in was compulsory."

"You sure look nice in that dress," said Homer.

"Why—thank you, Homer." Jean had not expected
him to be the kind of boy who would notice a girl's
dress.

"I like it because it is sort of streamlined," said
Homer seriously. "It isn't a lot of material cluttered
up with stuff."

Even though Jean laughed at Homer's masculine
description of her dress, she found it pleasant to
have a boy appreciate her appearance.

"The color is nice too," said Homer. "Plain and not a lot of swirls and swooshes and little pink rosebuds, like most girls wear."

Jean smiled at him over her milk shake. "I am sure my sewing teacher would like to hear you describe girls' dresses."

"Maybe I don't know the right words, but I know what I like." Homer grinned at Jean and smoothed out the paper wrapper of one of the straws, which he handed to Jean. "Here is a souvenir for you."

"Thank you," she said gravely. There was something she very much wanted to ask Homer. She thought it over a moment and decided there was no reason why she shouldn't ask. "Homer, tell me something. You and Johnny used to be friends. What happened?"

"Sure we were friends." There was some bitterness in Homer's voice. "My dad lets me take the car and Johnny's dad won't. Oh, sure, I know I used to think he was great and tagged around after him and all. He was popular and I guess I thought some of it would rub off on me."

"But he took me out in his car once," said Jean.

"Just once, and I'll bet it was in the daytime," said Homer. "His mother lets him take her car when his dad isn't home. He had his license taken away because a cop picked him up for doing ninety on the freeway."

"Johnny drove ninety miles an hour on the freeway!" Jean was shocked.

"And then Johnny got sore at me that night he asked to come over to see you. He wanted me to go along and I wouldn't. I figured he asked you for a date, and you wouldn't want me coming along, too."

"That stormy night," reminisced Jean. "I remember it rained all day."

"And he said he didn't want to walk to your house in the rain," Homer went on, "and I said that was his problem. Johnny got sore, and after that he didn't bother about me." Homer grinned across the table at Jean. "I'll bet he was sopping when he got there."

Jean bit her lip and looked into her empty glass. "He didn't get there, Homer," she said quietly, hurt because Johnny had not been willing to go through rain and gloom of night to see her. She could not help thinking of her father, who delivered mail in all kinds of weather and even gave extra service to the people on his route without complaining.

"I'm sorry, Jean," said Homer. "I didn't know. Like I said, after that Johnny was sore at me and I didn't think so much of him, either. And I got to thinking about a lot of things. Things like what was so wonderful about a fellow like Johnny and what was so wonderful about being popular. There are lots more interesting things to do besides hanging around a drive-in or cruising around town in a car."

"Homer, does Peggy Jo have her own car?" Jean asked suddenly. "It seems to me I heard someone say something about it during the rehearsal of the variety show."

"Yes, she does," answered Homer. "A hard top."

"Oh." That explained a lot to Jean. Johnny did not want to bother going to a dance with a girl whose mother had to drive them. Now that she knew the real reason he had broken the date, the unhappy question lurking in the back of her mind was banished.

"What are we talking about Johnny for?" Homer demanded. "Johnny is Johnny's greatest admirer."

Why, that is true, thought Jean. Johnny liked Johnny, and the reason he had liked her was that she had been a good audience. An audience was important to Johnny, she realized, now that she looked back on the last few months, and she had certainly hung on every word he spoke. "Yes, let's not talk about Johnny." Jean unwound the wrapper of the straw from her finger. "Maybe I should be starting home. Dad said I had to be in by midnight." Since she and Homer had left the dance, time had gone surprisingly fast. Jean had heard the Darveys' guests leave some time ago.

"Sure, Jean," said Homer with a grin. "I promised your father I would take good care of you."

In the living room, while Homer got her coat, Jean said good night to Mr. and Mrs. Darvey.

"Good night, Jean," said Mrs. Darvey. "I am so glad Homer brought you home. I hope you will come again."

"Thank you." Jean smiled shyly at this woman who liked a good rousing springtime. She could tell that Homer's mother and father liked her. Awkwardly she unfastened the camellia from her dress and pinned it to her coat.

When Homer turned the car into the Jarretts' driveway, he turned off the motor and switched off the lights. Jean waited for him to get out of the car, but when he did not, they sat in silence. Jean began to feel uncomfortable. Her mother and father and the people next door must have heard them drive in and might be thinking that Jean, on her first date, was parked in the driveway with a boy.

"The people next door just had their house painted," said Jean to break the silence, even though she knew Homer would not be interested.

Homer did not answer.

"I mean—you can still smell the paint," said Jean, because a girl had to say something at a time like this. "I thought you might have noticed it."

Homer laid his arm across the back of the seat and turned to Jean. "Jean," he said earnestly, "would you consider kissing me?"

"*Kissing* you!" The words were startled out of Jean. What a funny idea—kissing Homer. Jean's impulse was to jump out of the car and run up the steps into the house.

"Yes," said Homer seriously. "I wondered if you would be interested."

Interested! Homer made kissing sound as impersonal as—as discussing a current event. Jean could not imagine kissing Homer. And if she did, with both of them wearing glasses there would be an unromantic clash of spectacle frames. Or did couples who both wore glasses say, Excuse me while I remove my glasses? And if they did, *then* what did they do? Hold them? Or pull out their cases, fold their glasses, and put them away, saying, Now I am ready to be kissed. Had Homer thought of this, she wondered. The way he was behaving, they would probably have an impersonal discussion of the problem. Jean, he would say, since you have agreed to kiss me, perhaps we should remove our glasses. Yes, Homer, she would answer, that is an excellent suggestion. *Oh.* What was she thinking of anyway? She wasn't going to kiss Homer.

"Well?" said Homer. "You haven't answered."

"Why I. . . . " Jean did not know what to say. She did not want to hurt his feelings, because she liked him. And anyway, she had probably already hurt his feelings by sounding horrified when he mentioned kissing. She had not meant to sound that way, but in her surprise she could not help it. "I mean. . . . Well, no thank you. What I mean is, this is just our first date and everything—" Jean stopped. Would he think she expected him to ask her for a second date? Or would he—this was worse —think she was leading him on? What was a girl supposed to do at a moment like this? She wished she knew.

"I didn't think you would," said Homer seriously, "but I didn't think it would hurt to ask."

"No, I guess it doesn't hurt to ask," said Jean, so relieved to get through this awkward moment that she felt for the second time that evening a wild desire to giggle. Elaine would die laughing. Except that this time she was not going to tell Elaine, because even though she thought the situation was funny, there was something so likable about Homer that she would not want anyone to make fun of him. Not ever.

A square of light from a bedroom window fell on the driveway, telling Jean that her father must have turned on the bedroom light to look at the time. The car clock said ten minutes to midnight.

"Homer, I think I had better go in," said Jean.

Homer got out of the car, went around, and opened the door for her. This time Jean could not bear to shove her feet into her pumps. She picked up her shoes and her florist's box and stepped out of the car in her stocking feet. They walked up the steps and when Jean had unlatched the door she stood with one hand on the knob. Her parents, she was sure, would hear the click of the lock and know that she was about to come in. "Thank you for going to the dance with me," she said, feeling that this was proper, because she had extended the invitation. With etiquette out of the way, she laughed and said, "I know the dance was pretty awful, but I really did have a good time at your house. I loved seeing your pigeons and the milk shake was fun, too."

"I'm sure glad you asked me," answered Homer. Then he hesitated. "Jean—would you like to go out again sometime? With me, I mean?"

"Yes, Homer, I would," answered Jean.

"Swell." Homer sounded both pleased and relieved. "Maybe next Saturday afternoon we could take the pigeons out over the hills and release them."

"I would love to. And I—I hope your feelings aren't hurt, or anything, because I didn't—" ventured Jean, and stopped.

"That's all right." Homer understood what she was talking about. "Good night, Jean."

"Good night, Homer. And thank you again for the flower." Jean stepped into the living room, closed the door, started to turn off the light, remembered that Sue probably had not come in, and walked in her stocking feet to the kitchen, where she removed the bruised camellia from her coat and laid it next to a carton of eggs in the refrigerator. Then she tiptoed into the bedroom, sat down on the bed, and began to rub one aching foot.

So that was the way it was, Jean thought. A girl went out with a boy she did not much care about, and her evening did not turn out at all the way she had imagined. In many ways it was disappointing, even painful, and yet when it was over, it was all right. She liked the boy and he liked her. And she would be happy to go out with him again, even though no date with him would ever be the kind of date a girl dreamed about. Homer would always do and say unexpected, disconcerting things, but that was the kind of boy he was. And a girl would not have to analyze every remark, every quirk of his eyebrow, when she went out with a boy like Homer. She would not have to wonder if he liked her just a shade less than he had the day before if he happened to say, Hi, instead of Hi, Jean.

Jean was still sitting on the bed tenderly massaging her foot when she heard a car stop in front of the house, and in a few minutes the front door opened and Sue tiptoed down the hall.

"Hello," whispered Jean.

"Hi," answered Sue, silently closing the door. "Did you have fun?"

"Yes and no," answered Jean. "Mostly yes. Did you?"

"Oh, yes," sighed Sue, and dropped down on her own bed. "I had a wonderful time. Just wonderful. We saw *The Great Train Robbery* and some old Chaplin comedies."

Jean thought she had never seen her sister look so pretty, and she knew that prettiness was not caused by old movies. Jean rose from the bed and walked gingerly to the closet. She wished she were floating on a cloud like Sue—then her feet might not hurt so much. She removed her coat and as she did so, she put her hand in her pocket and took out the paper covering from the straw. She hung her coat in the closet, but instead of throwing the straw covering into the wastebasket, she smoothed it out and read the words printed on it. *Sani-straw. Pat. U.S. Off.*

"You know something?" said Sue dreamily.

"What?" asked Jean, absently winding the flattened paper tube around her finger.

"Ken kissed me good night," whispered Sue.

Jean looked curiously at her sister, radiant because Ken had kissed her. It must be a lovely feeling. "I guess Ken changed a lot as he grew up," she reflected.

"Mm-hm." Sue slipped off her coat and kicked off her shoes. "A whole lot. He makes the boys at school seem childish."

"Sue, how did you feel that day you ran into Ken at the library?" Jean asked.

"Oh, I don't know. Surprised that he had changed so much, and not sure what to say to him." Sue pulled her dress off over her head.

"You didn't feel all full of pinwheels at the sight of him?" persisted Jean.

"Pinwheels and Fourth of July sparklers? Of

course not, silly. I just thought he had turned out to be an awfully nice boy," said Sue.

"Do you think you would have liked him as much if you had gone out with him two years ago?" There was so much Jean wanted to know.

"You are certainly full of questions tonight," answered Sue. "No, I don't think I would have liked him very much two years ago. He wouldn't have grown up enough. And now if you want first turn at the bathroom you had better stop playing with that piece of paper, and get started."

"You go first," said Jean, still toying with the wrapper from the straw. Maybe that was what a lot of girls should do—all they could do, really—wait for the boys to grow up. And in the meantime there were other things to do . . . the things she and Elaine had always enjoyed doing together . . . and now there was Homer and his flock of pigeons.

Jean decided she really would keep the straw wrapper for a souvenir. She opened her top drawer and took out a Japanese lacquered box, which held the odds and ends she did not quite know what to do with, but still did not want to throw away: her junior-high school graduation diploma, a paper napkin from a birthday party, a ball-point pen that

needed a refill. As she removed the box from the
drawer, her eye fell on the snapshot of Johnny
which she had thrown into the drawer and half forgotten about. Now she picked it up and studied it
critically. How charming he looked smiling into the
camera, and how miserable she looked facing Johnny
and trying to peek at the camera at the same time!
All that was behind her now. The real Johnny would
always do what Johnny wanted and never mind how
other people felt. The Johnny she had admired was
no more real than Kip Laddish on the television
screen.

Jean started to tear the snapshot in two, hesitated,
and looked at it a second time. Johnny, the boy she
neither liked nor admired, and yet . . . she would
never forget Johnny. It was Johnny who had noticed
her, singled her out of the crowd, had made her feel
that she was attractive. In a way, it was Johnny who
had made her aware of herself. She could not forget
that. If only Johnny had been a different kind of
boy. . . .

Jean picked up a pair of manicure scissors from
the dresser and carefully snipped off her half of the
snapshot and dropped it into the wastebasket. She
lifted the lid of the lacquered box and dropped into
it the wrapper of the straw. Her glance lingered on

Johnny's half of the snapshot, which she laid on top of the wrapper. Silently she closed the box and shut it in her drawer. Good-by, Johnny, she thought. I am not sorry I knew you. Maybe she should be sorry, but she wasn't. In her heart she knew she would remember Johnny. Always.

FIFTEEN

BEVERLY CLEARY

FIFTEEN

Illustrated by
JOE *and* **BETH KRUSH**

MORROW JUNIOR BOOKS
New York

Library of Congress Catalog Card Number: 56-7509

34   35   36   37   38   39   40   41

CHAPTER

1

TODAY I'm going to meet a boy, Jane Purdy told herself, as she walked up Blossom Street toward her baby-sitting job. *Today I'm going to meet a boy.* If she thought it often enough as if she really believed it, maybe she actually would meet a boy even though she was headed for Sandra Norton's house and the worst baby-sitting job in Woodmont.

If I don't step on any cracks in the sidewalk all the way there, Jane thought, I'll be sure to meet a boy. But avoiding cracks was silly, of course, and the sort of thing she had done when she was in the third grade. She was being just as silly as some of the other fifteen-year-old girls she knew, who counted red convertibles and believed they would go steady with the first boy they saw after the hundredth red convertible. Counting convertibles

and not stepping on cracks were no way to meet a
boy.

Maybe, when she finished her job with Sandra,
she could walk down to Nibley's Confectionery
and Soda Fountain and sit at the counter and order
a chocolate coke float; and if she sipped it very,
very slowly a new boy might happen to come in and
sit down beside her. He would be at least sixteen—
old enough to have a driver's license—and he would
have crinkles around his eyes that showed he had
a sense of humor and he would be tall, the kind of
boy all the other girls would like to date. Their
eyes would meet in the mirror behind the milk-shake
machines, and he would smile and she would smile
back and he would turn to her and look down
(*down*—that was important) and grin and say . . .

"Hello there!" A girl's voice interrupted Jane's
daydream, and she looked up to see Marcy Stokes
waving at her from a green convertible driven by
Greg Donahoe, president of the junior class of
Woodmont High School.

"Hi, Marcy," Jane called back. People who said,
"Hello there," to her always made her feel so unimportant.

Greg waved, and as the couple drove on down
the hill Marcy brushed a lock of hair out of her

eyes and smiled back at Jane with the kind of smile a girl riding in a convertible with a popular boy on a summer day gives a girl who is walking alone. And that smile made Jane feel that everything about herself was all wrong. Her yellow cotton dress was too—well, too little-girlish with its round collar and full skirt. Her skin wasn't tan enough and even if it were, she didn't have a white piqué dress to show it off. And her curly brown hair, which had seemed pretty enough in the mirror at home, now seemed childish compared to Marcy's sleek blond hair, bleached to golden streaks by the sun.

The trouble with me, Jane thought, as the hill grew steeper, is that I am not the cashmere-sweater type like Marcy. Marcy wore her cashmere sweaters as if they were of no importance at all. Jane had one cashmere sweater, which she took off the minute she got home from school. Marcy had many dates with the most popular boys in school and spent a lot of time with the crowd at Nibley's. Jane had an occasional date with an old family friend named George, who was an inch shorter than she was and carried his money in a change purse instead of loose in his pocket and took her straight home from the movies. Marcy had her name mentioned in the gossip column of the *Woodmontonian* nearly every week. Jane had her name in the school paper when she served on the clean-up committee after the freshman tea. Marcy belonged. Jane did not.

And if I were in Marcy's place right now, Jane thought wistfully, I wouldn't even know what to say. I would probably just sit there beside Greg with my hands all clammy, because I would be so nervous and excited.

Jane reached the end of Blossom Street and paused to catch her breath before starting to climb the winding road to Sandra's house. She looked back through the locust trees at the roof of her own comfortable old house in the center of Woodmont. In recent years this pleasant village had begun to grow in two directions. Toward the bay, on the treeless side of town, there was now a real-estate development called Bayaire Estates—block after block of small houses, all variations of one ranch-style plan, which Jane thought of as the no-down-payment-to-veterans neighborhood, because of the advertisements on billboards along the highway. On the other side of the Purdys' part of town, where Woodmont rose sharply into tree-covered hills, there were also many new houses, referred to in advertisements as "California modern,

architect-designed, planned for outdoor living."
These houses were being built into the hillside
among the gracious old redwood homes, now called
"charming rustics."

It was toward one of these new houses in the
hills that Jane now walked so reluctantly. Sandra
Norton and her parents had lived in Woodmont
only a few months, having recently returned to
this country after two years in France, where Mr.
Norton had been the American representative of
an airline. Already Sandra was notorious among
Woodmont baby sitters. The last time Jane sat with
the eight-year-old girl, Sandra had grabbed a Flit
gun full of fly spray and aimed it at a new chair
upholstered in pale fabric. Before Jane wrested the
Flit gun from Sandra she was drenched in fly spray.
Afterwards she had laughed about the incident
and turned it into a funny paragraph for a baby-
sitting (baby-running was really a better word)
article she had written for Manuscript, the Woodmont High literary club. Nevertheless, it was not
an experience she would care to repeat.

When Jane reached the Norton house, which
was set on a flat area bulldozed out of the side
of the hill, she found Sandra, dressed in a cow-girl
costume, in the front yard bending over a bed of

snapdragons. Her blond hair, with its uncared-for permanent wave, hung like raveled rope on either side of her thin little face.

Jane walked across the tender new lawn. "Hello, Sandra," she said cheerfully. "What are you doing?"

"Catching flies and shutting them up inside snap-dragons," replied Sandra, without looking at Jane. An angry buzzing came from the blossoms in front of her.

Jane noticed Sandra's mother looking impatiently through the picture window so she hurried to the front door, which Mrs. Norton opened at once. She was wearing a silk suit the color of sand and a tiny pink hat smothered in flowers and misted with veiling. Jane felt young and dowdy beside her.

"Hello there, Jane," said Mrs. Norton breathlessly. "I was so afraid I couldn't get anyone to look after Sandra, and I didn't want to miss the hospital guild's tea and fashion show. See that Sandra takes a nap. She went to the city with us last night and she's a little bit tired today."

"Yes, Mrs. Norton," answered Jane. That made two people in a row who had said, "Hello there."

Mrs. Norton swept past Jane, leaving a cloud of expensive scent (probably Chanel Number Five, Jane decided, since Sandra's mother had been living

in France), and then she paused. "Oh, yes—and
don't let Cuthbert out of the house. We just had
him bathed at the veterinarian's and I don't want
him rolling in the dirt. It takes weeks to get an
appointment to have a dog washed. It's worse than
trying to get an appointment at the hairdresser's."
Her high heels clicked down the brick walk. "Good-
by, chick," she called to Sandra.

"I want you to stay home." Sandra stared unhappily at her mother.

"I'll be back before you know it," Mrs. Norton
said with artificial gaiety, and hopped into her car.

Jane was alone with Sandra. She walked across
the grass to join the child, who was still occupied
with the buzzing snapdragons. "Come on, Sandra,"
she said. "I'll help you let the flies out of the flowers
before we go into the house for your nap."

Sandra, who was holding a fly by the wings,
pinched open the mouth of a blossom and popped
the fly inside. "My mother said I didn't have to
take a nap," she told Jane.

Now what do I do, Jane wondered. That was the
trouble with baby-sitting. Mothers always told sitters what to do with their children, but they rarely
told them how to do it. Perhaps if she did not
mention the nap she could entice Sandra into the

house and read to her until she fell asleep. "If you were a fly, would you like to be shut up in a snapdragon?" Jane asked, to change the subject.

"No. That's why I'm doing it," said Sandra. "My mother said Julie was going to sit with me."

"Julie couldn't come, because she had to sit with Jackie," Jane explained. Julie was her best friend. The two girls often handed over baby-sitting jobs to each other. The only reason Jane was sitting with Sandra today was that she and Julie felt that some day they might be broke enough to really need to sit with Sandra and so in the meantime it would be a good idea to keep Mrs. Norton's business.

"I'd rather have Julie than you," said Sandra flatly.

Maybe she would, thought Jane. Julie was such a comfortable, cheerful person that all the children liked her. But this was not getting Sandra into the house and persuading her to go to sleep. And if she could not do that, Jane knew that she was in for a long and difficult afternoon. "I know what," she said brightly, as if she had just had an idea.

Sandra looked at her suspiciously. She was, Jane knew, a child who had had many baby sitters and was undoubtedly onto all the tricks of getting her to mind.

"Let's go in the house and see what Cuthbert is doing." Jane held out her hand to Sandra. Into the house—that was the first step toward a nap.

"He's asleep under the coffee table," said Sandra. "That's all he ever does. He's a dumb dog. I'd rather have a horse." Sandra stared at Jane as if she were taking her measure to see just how far she could go with this sitter.

Why is it, Jane wondered, that substitute teachers and baby sitters are so often targets for children?

"O.K., let's go in the house," agreed Sandra suddenly.

Jane could not help wondering uneasily what the glint in Sandra's eye meant. She hoped she could figure out a way to get Sandra to sleep quickly, because there were so many things indoors that she could get into mischief with—knicknacks that could be broken, lamps to be knocked over, lipstick for marking wallpaper. After the experience with the Flit gun Jane knew she could not trust Sandra for one instant.

Jane glanced around the Nortons' living room, so different from her own home, where everything was comfortably worn. "A house is meant to be lived in," her mother often said. Here everything looked brand-new, as if the furniture had been delivered only the day before. The wooden pieces were square and simple and, except for a few cushions in brilliant colors, everything in the room was carefully neutral. Over the fireplace hung a painting made up of drips and dribbles, splotches and splashes, in the same colors as the cushions. The room looked, Jane decided, interior-decorated. Not even the layer of dust or the heap of magazines and newspapers on the coffee table or the overflowing ash trays made the room seem as if a family really lived here. And isn't it funny, Jane thought; if I were blindfolded and set down in the house of any one of my baby-sitting customers I could tell where I was by the odor of the house. The Nortons' house smelled of fresh plaster and wallpaper and stale cigarette smoke.

Cuthbert was, as Sandra had predicted, asleep under the coffee table. Now the fat pug dog rose and shook himself, scattering his hair over the carpet. He was an ugly little animal with a black face on a tan body, popeyes, and a nose so upturned that it was difficult for him to breathe. Panting asthmatically, he ran toward Jane, his kinky tail wagging, his bulging eyes beseeching her for attention. She knelt and patted his head. Cuthbert was overcome with emotion; his breathing rasped louder, and he ran back and forth under the edge of the coffee table to scratch his back. Then he collapsed on the rug and panted.

Sandra opened the front door. "I'm going to let Cuthbert out," she cried. "Here, Cuthbert!"

"Oh, no, Sandra," protested Jane. "Your mother said not to. He's just been washed."

But Cuthbert was not going to miss this rare opportunity for freedom. As fast as his short little legs would carry him, he scrambled out the front door and down the steps.

"Oh, Sandra," said Jane reproachfully, and ran after the dog, who had scurried down the brick walk and across the lawn.

"Go on, Cuthbert!" shrieked Sandra, jumping up and down in the doorway. Cuthbert scuttled under a bush.

Don't roll in the dirt, Jane pleaded silently. Please don't roll in the dirt when you've just been washed. She got down on her hands and knees and crawled under the bush toward the dog, who puffed and wheezed as he watched her with his bulging eyes.

"Don't let her get you, Cuthbert," screamed Sandra.

A branch caught in Jane's hair and while she worked to disentangle it, Cuthbert stopped wheez-

ing and began to bark. A car horn tooted on the road.

Oh! thought Jane, as she looked toward the curb. Oh, no! Greg and Marcy, headed up the hill in the green convertible, were looking at her and laughing.

"Hi," Jane called, trying to sound gay.

"Why don't you bark back at him?" Marcy asked, and Greg laughed and drove on.

Jane felt her face grow hot with embarrassment. Greg's laugh she did not mind, because it was a friendly laugh; but she did not like to be laughed at by a girl riding in a convertible. She wished she had come back with an answer, something like, "I

only bark in English and this dog has been living in France." Jane sighed. That was the trouble with her. She always thought of the right answer too late, or if she did think of it at the right time she was too shy to say it.

Jane dived farther under the bush and caught Cuthbert by one foreleg. He yapped hoarsely and hysterically while she dragged him out and picked him up. He wheezed and snuffled as he tried to wriggle out of her grasp, but she held him tight. Then his chunky little body relaxed and he struggled to get enough air through his turned-up nose. Poor thing, thought Jane; I believe he's relieved to be

caught. He wouldn't know what to do with his freedom if he had it.

She hurried up the brick walk with the fat little
dog in her arms. And this was the day I was sure I
would meet a boy, she thought. And now look at
me—all rumpled, with leaves in my hair and grass
stains on my skirt. Jane noticed apprehensively that
Sandra was no longer in the doorway. Certainly the
child would not be sleepy after the excitement of
making her sitter chase Cuthbert. But she found
Sandra sitting quietly in a chair looking at a copy of
Vogue. Jane carefully shut the door and shoved
Cuthbert under the coffee table.

"Hello," said Sandra, as if she were surprised to
see Jane so soon. Cuthbert began to snore.

"Hello." Jane eyed her charge. Sandra's thin little face did look tired—so tired that Jane felt sorry
for her. Since she was willing to sit quietly looking
at *Vogue,* perhaps she was one step closer to a nap.
"Why don't we go to your room?" Jane suggested
gently. "I'll read to you."

When Sandra ignored her and went on reading
Vogue, Jane sat down. To have Sandra fall asleep
over *Vogue* was too much to hope for, she knew,
but she did not know what to do next. Sandra put
her feet on the coffee table.

"Oh, Sandra, I wouldn't put my feet on the table if I were you," said Jane.

Sandra stared at her over the top of the magazine. "Say table in French," she demanded.

"*La table*," answered Jane, giving the article as well as the noun, as she had been taught to do in her one year of high-school French. Well, she thought hopefully, maybe we can work out a nice quiet game with French. I'll say something in French and then Sandra can say something in French. Maybe that will amuse her.

"Say chair," ordered Sandra.

"*La chaise*," answered Jane promptly. Those A's she had earned in two semesters of French were going to come in handy after all.

"Window," Sandra said.

"*La fenêtre*." That was easy. Practically the first word Jane had learned in French.

"Curtains," demanded Sandra.

Jane paused. Curtains? Oh, yes. "*Les rideaux*."

Sandra looked impressed and Jane relaxed. This could go on for a long time, and as long as Sandra asked the French for ordinary objects in the living room she was confident that she could answer.

"Dog." Cuthbert's snoring called Sandra's attention to the dog.

"*Le chien.*"

"Book."

"*Le livre.*"

Sandra put down *Vogue* and began to wander around the room looking for new objects to name. "Desk," she said.

Jane started to say *le pupitre* but remembered that was the word for a pupil's desk. "*Le bureau,*" she answered, pleased with herself for remembering the difference. However, she had begun to notice that the room was full of objects that her French vocabulary was not equal to. "Now you tell me the word for rug," she suggested, because she herself did not know the word and did not want to risk revealing her ignorance to Sandra.

"*Le tapis,*" answered Sandra promptly and in an accent more authentic than Jane's.

"*C'est bien!*" cried Jane, feeling that she sounded like her own French teacher, even though she had no idea whether Sandra was right or not.

"You speak French sort of funny," observed Sandra critically, as her eyes darted around the room looking for a difficult object to name. Her eye fell on a heavy crystal ash tray on the desk. "Ash tray," she said.

Ash tray? Tray of the ashes? It was not the sort

of phrase one learned in first-year French. Jane gave
up. "I'm sorry, Sandra. I don't know how to say ash
tray in French."

Sandra picked up the overflowing crystal tray.
"Say it, or I'll dump it on the rug!"

Jane began to feel uneasy. Maybe she could make
up something, some syllables that sounded foreign.
No, Sandra would know the difference. "I'm sorry,
Sandra," she said. "I just don't know it. Put down
the ash tray and let's try something else."

Sandra looked defiantly at Jane. Slowly she tipped
the ash tray so that ashes and lipstick-stained cigarette butts cascaded onto the beige carpet.

"Sandra!" cried Jane.

Sandra set the ash tray back on the desk and
snatched a bottle of ink out of a drawer. "Say bottle of blue ink," she ordered, as she loosened the
top of the bottle. "Say it or I'll dump it on the rug!"

That's one I know, Jane told herself, but the words
would not come to her lips. She could read *Permanent Blue Black* on the label of the ink bottle.
She looked in despair at the ashes and cigarette
butts on the pale carpet—wall-to-wall carpet, yards
and yards of it. The permanent blue-black ink would
fall in a permanent blue-black puddle and seep
slowly . . . If she made a grab for Sandra and tried

to get the bottle away from her, the ink was sure to spill in the scuffle.

"Say it!" Sandra sounded ominous.

"Uh . . . *le* . . . *la*," was all that Jane could utter. Oh, why couldn't she think! Bottle? Bottle? What *was* the word for bottle? "Wait a minute," she pleaded desperately. "It's on the tip of my tongue." It was, but she could not find it. And Sandra, she knew from her experience with the fly spray, was ruthless.

"You don't know it." There was triumph in Sandra's voice. "I know something you don't know! I know something you don't know!"

Jane was desperate. She could not think and she was afraid to move. Those yards and yards of beige carpet . . . It would be ruined and she would be responsible. Yards and yards of carpet covered with permanent blue-black stains . . .

At that moment Jane heard the back door open. "Good afternoon, Mrs. Norton," a boy's cheerful voice called. Cuthbert scrambled out from under the coffee table and ran yapping joyfully into the kitchen.

Startled that someone should burst into the house without knocking, Jane still was unable to move. She could only think, The ink, Sandra, the ink. Don't

spill the ink. *Please* don't spill the permanent blue-black ink.

There was the sound of the refrigerator door opening and closing and a voice saying, "Hi there, Cuthbert. How's the fellow?"

Jane knew she should investigate, but she could not leave Sandra with the ink bottle in her hands. "Who is it?" she called out in a weak voice.

"The Doggie Diner," the strange voice answered, and a boy appeared in the dining-room doorway. "Oh, excuse me. I thought you were Mrs. Norton," he said.

If only this intrusion would distract Sandra from the ink! "The Doggie Diner?" Jane echoed, and then felt stupid for doing so. She knew that the Doggie Diner was a small business that delivered horse meat to the owners of dogs in Woodmont and nearby towns. It was just that she was so startled to have a boy appear from nowhere. And, now that she took her eyes away from the ink bottle long enough to look at him, a very nice strange boy.

"I brought Cuthbert's meat. Mrs. Norton likes me to walk in and put it in the refrigerator for her," he explained, looking questioningly at Jane.

"Oh. I'm—I'm sitting with Sandra." Jane felt that the way he looked at her required an answer.

"Yes, and she can't say bottle of blue ink in French, so I'm going to dump this on the rug," said Sandra.

"Oh, Sandra," pleaded Jane wearily, "please put the ink down."

Sandra tipped the bottle at a dangerous angle. Now that she had an audience she was going to make the most of her scene. "Say it," she ordered. "Say it right now."

"*Utpay atthay ownday!*" commanded the strange boy in a sharp voice.

Sandra turned from Jane to stare at him. "What did you say?" she wanted to know.

Utpay atthay ownday? Utpay—of course! Suddenly Jane laughed. The boy was saying, "Put that down," in pig Latin and he had succeeded in diverting Sandra. "*Esyay, Andrasay, utpay atthay ownday,*" she said, and smiled gratefully at him over Sandra's head.

Sandra turned to Jane. "What are you saying? I can't understand you." She looked close to tears.

"I was telling you to put the ink down," answered Jane.

Sandra was intrigued by this language she could not understand. "Say some more. You've got to say some more."

"You didn't put the ink down," Jane pointed out, and looked at the strange boy again.

"Yes, put it down," he said, and Jane felt a ripple of pleasure that this boy was standing by her when she needed him. Reluctantly Sandra walked over to the desk and set the ink down. Jane and the strange boy exchanged looks—relief and gratitude on her part, amusement on his.

"Well, so long," said the boy, and disappeared from the dining-room doorway.

I mustn't let him get away like this, thought Jane, and ran to the kitchen just as he was going out the back door. "Thanks a lot," she called out to him. "I don't know what I would have done if you hadn't come along."

"That's O.K.," he said. "I've got a kid sister and I know how it is." And with that he was gone.

Jane looked out the kitchen window in time to see him jump into a red truck with *Doggie Diner—Fresh U. S. Government-inspected Horse Meat Delivered Weekly* painted on its side. And in a moment the truck was disappearing around a bend in the road.

Well, thought Jane. Well! I did meet a boy today! A new boy who is old enough to have a driver's license!

"Say some more," demanded Sandra, bringing Jane's thoughts back into the kitchen.

"Come to your room and I'll say some more." Jane spoke gently, but she had made up her mind to be firm with Sandra from now on. She had the upper hand and she was going to hang onto it as long as she could. "Come along."

Somewhat reluctantly, Sandra followed Jane to her room and sat down on the bed, which was covered by a spread woven with a design of cattle brands. The influence of the interior decorator had not reached Sandra's room. Her walls were hung with pictures of blue rabbits and pink kittens that would glow in the dark, and beside her bed was a child-sized papier-mâché figure of Bugs Bunny with a real radio set in the middle of its stomach. "Say some more," pleaded Sandra.

"*Imetay orfay ouryay apnay.*" Jane took advantage of Sandra's interest to kneel and remove the child's shoes.

"What did you say?" Sandra asked.

"I said it's time for your nap."

Sandra scowled and looked as if she were about to say it was not time for her nap. Instead she said, "Is it a foreign language?"

Jane smiled. "Not exactly. It's more like a secret language."

"A secret language?" Sandra asked eagerly. "Do you really know how to talk a secret language?"

"Yes," replied Jane, thinking how tired Sandra looked. She unfolded the blanket at the foot of the bed. "Lie down and let me cover you up and I'll say some more things in the secret language."

Wearily, Sandra flopped back with her head on the pillow. "Say my name," she requested, as Jane pulled the blanket over her.

"*Andrasay Ortonay,*" Jane told her.

"That's pretty," was Sandra's comment. "Say your name."

"*Anejay Urdypay.*" Was Sandra really beginning to look drowsy? Jane watched the little girl's eyelids begin to droop. "*Ogay otay eepslay,*" she said softly.

Sandra's eyes closed and then opened again as she struggled against sleep.

"Sandra," whispered Jane, "what is the name of the boy who brought Cuthbert's meat?"

"I don't know," said Sandra drowsily, and closed her eyes.

Jane sat watching her for a moment. Poor kid, she wasn't really a monster. She was just a tired little girl who had lived in too many places and had too many strange baby sitters. Jane tucked the blanket over Sandra's arms. Well, she thought, I'm certainly bright. She had wanted to meet a new boy and when she finally did meet one she didn't even find out his name. All she knew about him was that he delivered horse meat and had a younger sister.

Jane sat staring at the Bugs Bunny with the radio in its stomach, but she did not really see it. Instead, she saw the boy standing in the doorway grinning at her. And when I did meet him, her thoughts ran on, I was rumpled and covered with dirt and grass stains and worried about the Nortons' rug. That was no way to make an impression on a boy. Then she smiled to herself. If any of the boys she already knew delivered horse meat for the Doggie Diner, she would think it was a big joke. Maybe it was funny, but somehow she did not feel like laughing at this boy's job.

Why, I know lots of things about him, Jane thought suddenly. The boy was at least sixteen, because he had a driver's license. He had a nice smile and merry eyes—greenish-gray eyes. He had brown hair with a dip in it. He was not really tall, but he was tall enough so a medium-sized girl could wear heels and not feel she had to scrooch down when she walked beside him. He was outdoors a lot, because he was so tanned, and he must be new in Woodmont, because she had never seen him before. He looked like a nice boy, full of fun and—best of all—when he saw she was having trouble with Sandra, he understood. One might say they spoke the same language!

But what good does it do me, Jane thought sadly. This was the kind of luck she always had. The boy was sixteen, and nice and understanding, but she didn't even know his name or where he went to school or what town he lived in. But there must be some way she could find out. She didn't know how, but there must be a way. And she was going to find out.

Jane glanced once more at Sandra to make sure she was sleeping soundly. Then she tiptoed out of the bedroom to clean up the ashes Sandra had dumped on the carpet and to let the flies out of the snapdragons.

CHAPTER

2

"Pop, have you ever thought about getting a dog?" Jane asked that evening, after baby-sitting with Sandra and meeting so briefly the boy who delivered horse meat for the Doggie Diner.

"Can't say that I have," answered Mr. Purdy from behind the evening paper. From time to time he stroked Sir Puss, the large tabby cat that was stretched out on his lap. Meticulously Sir Puss licked a paw and scrubbed it behind his ear. When Jane spoke he paused to stare at her disapprovingly for a long moment before he resumed his routine of licking and scrubbing.

That cat acts as if he understood what I said and knew what I was planning, Jane thought. "Well, don't you think it would be a good idea to have a dog?" she asked.

"What for?" Mr. Purdy asked.

"For a watchdog," Jane suggested.

"In Woodmont?" Mr. Purdy lowered the paper and looked at his daughter through a cloud of pipe smoke. "Nobody even bothers to lock doors in Woodmont. I don't know what we would want a watchdog for." He raised the paper again as if that ended the discussion.

"Dogs are nice pets," Jane persisted. "Lots of people keep dogs just because they like them."

"We have a nice pet." Mr. Purdy dropped one half the paper to pet Sir Puss, who rested his chin on his master's knee and closed his eyes with a look of self-satisfaction on his tiger face.

"But dogs are different," said Jane. "They are loyal and faithful and—"

"Yes, I know," Mr. Purdy interrupted. "I've read about what noble animals dogs are too. Man's best friend and all that. They rouse sleeping people in burning buildings. They drag little children out of fish ponds. They also dig up gardens. I have enough trouble with the neighbors' dogs running through the begonias and burying bones in the chrysanthemum bed without spending perfectly good money on a four-legged force of destruction of our own."

"We can get a dog free at the pound," Jane ar-

gued. "We wouldn't have to spend money on a
fancy dog with a pedigree and everything. We could
just drive over to the pound and pick out a nice
plain dog that needs a good home." As far as Jane
was concerned, the only qualification a Purdy dog
needed was a good appetite.

Mr. Purdy rubbed his cat under the chin. "Now
take Sir Puss, here," he said. "There's a pet for you.
The handsomest cat and the best gopher hunter in
Woodmont. And he wouldn't stand for a dog. He
would run a dog off the place."

"Some cats get along with dogs," Jane pointed out.

"Not Sir Puss," said Mr. Purdy. "He's too old and
set in his ways."

"And I don't like to think what life would be like
if I had to let a dog in and out, in and out, all day,
too. Sir Puss keeps me busy enough opening doors,"
said Jane's mother. "Jane, why this sudden interest
in a dog? You've never mentioned one before."

"Oh, I don't know," answered Jane vaguely. "I
just thought a dog might be nice to have around."
Well, that took care of that. Neither her father nor
her mother would consent to a dog, so there was no
chance of the Purdys' having horse meat delivered
by the Doggie Diner. And no chance of her getting
to know the strange boy that way. She would have

to think of some other way. And she must think of it soon. If he had recently moved to Woodmont and would be entering Woodmont High in September, it would be a good idea to get to know him before school started and all the girls saw how attractive he was. Half a dozen girls had probably seen him already and were wondering how they could meet him—girls who were smooth like Marcy. Or maybe they had met him already. And how could a girl meet a boy who delivered food for dogs if her father wouldn't keep a dog?

Sir Puss yawned and stretched luxuriously on Mr. Purdy's lap. It seemed to Jane that she had never seen a cat look so self-satisfied. She had loved him since he was a kitten and she was only four years old; she and Sir Puss had grown up together, but at the moment she felt a twinge of annoyance at him for spoiling her plan. As she sat watching the cat settle himself for a nap, she turned her problem over in her mind. The delivery of horse meat had seemed like such a good answer until the cat spoiled it.

Jane watched Sir Puss twitch one ear in his sleep, and suddenly the sight of the well-fed cat gave her an inspiration. "Say, Pop," she said, trying not to sound too eager, "I saw an ad in the paper that said the Doggie Diner delivered horse meat for pets.

Wouldn't it be easier to have horse meat delivered
for Sir Puss than to get lamb liver from the market?
The delivery boy could walk right in and leave it in
the refrigerator."

"Goodness, Jane," exclaimed Mrs. Purdy. "I
wouldn't want to keep horse meat in the refrigerator
with our food."

"And Sir Puss likes liver," Mr. Purdy added. "He
wouldn't eat horse meat."

"His food is no trouble. I always buy his liver
when I get our meat." Mrs. Purdy looked curiously
at her daughter. "You've never taken an interest in
the cat's diet before. What's come over you tonight?"

Another good idea that would not work. "Oh,
nothing. I just saw this ad and got to thinking," said
Jane, realizing that she had better be careful what
she said, or her mother would start asking a lot of
tiresome questions like who was the boy's family and
what did his father do and a lot of things she couldn't
answer until she got to know him. If only she knew
the boy's name she could look him up in the telephone book and just happen to walk by his house,
and he might just happen to be outside washing the
car or mowing the lawn or something. She would
glance at him with a faintly puzzled expression as
if she had seen him someplace but couldn't quite

remember where. And he would look up from whatever he was doing and say, "Why, hello. Aren't you the girl who was baby-sitting at the Nortons'?" And she would say . . . But she did not know his name and even if she did, he was probably so new in town that his family would not be listed in the telephone directory yet. Or he might not even live in Woodmont. He might live in some other town and when school started he would be part of the school-bus crowd.

Or she could find out where the Doggie Diner was located and just happen to walk past about the time he might be through work. Jane considered this idea and discarded it as being too obvious. A business that cut up horse meat would not be in a part of town where she could go for a walk without having people wonder what she was doing there.

Or she could happen to walk by the Nortons' house about three o'clock on Friday afternoon when he might be delivering Cuthbert's food again. Jane thought this over and decided the plan had both advantages and disadvantages. She could easily go for a walk in the Nortons' neighborhood without looking out of place. However, the truck probably would not arrive at exactly three o'clock and she could not very well walk up and down in front of

the Nortons' as if she were picketing their house.
The neighbors would begin to wonder what she was
doing. Nevertheless, a leisurely stroll up their street
next Friday afternoon could do no harm. He might
happen to drive by and see her and think, Why,
there's that girl I spoke to at the Nortons'. He would
stop the truck and say, "Hi there. Going to Sandra's
house? If you are I'll give you a lift." And she would
say . . .

And then Jane had an even better idea. If she were
baby-sitting with Sandra she would be sure to see
him. She turned this over in her mind. Could she
stand another afternoon of Sandra—another afternoon of trying to maneuver her into doing what she
was supposed to do when Sandra was so clever at
outwitting sitters? To see that boy again, yes. It
would not be easy but she could do it. The boy
would arrive with Cuthbert's food and say, "Hi! I
didn't expect to see you here again," and of course
he would look as if he were glad she was there again.
And she would laugh and say . . .

Jane realized there was another reason for wanting to sit with Sandra Friday afternoons—she might
keep some other baby sitter from meeting the boy.

"Well, I guess I'll phone Julie," Jane remarked
casually.

"Don't talk all night," said Mr. Purdy.

Jane kicked off her loafers and dialed Julie's number. "Hi, it's me," she said, when Julie answered. Jane could picture her friend at the other end of the line with her loafers kicked off, too, and her freckled face smiling expectantly. "Look, Julie, if Mrs. Norton wants somebody to sit with Sandra again next Friday, I've got dibs."

"Jane!" shrieked Julie into the telephone. "Have you lost your mind?"

"I don't think so," answered Jane. "Not yet, anyway."

"What happened?" Julie asked. "Has Sandra reformed or something?"

"Lots of things happened." Jane pulled her knees up under her chin and prepared to make certain no one else would sit with Sandra. "She shut up a lot of flies in snapdragons and let Cuthbert out when he had just been washed and she dumped an ash tray on the carpet and she threatened to pour ink all over the living-room floor and—"

"That's enough," cried Julie. "You can have her any time Mrs. Norton wants a sitter, but I still think you're crazy. Or did Mrs. Norton pay double or something?"

"No, she paid the usual," answered Jane. "And for once she had the right change."

There was a moment of silence at Julie's end of the line. "Then there must be a boy in it someplace," announced Julie. "There can't be any other reason."

"At Sandra's? How could there be?" Jane made her voice sound innocent.

"There must be," insisted Julie. "There can't be any other reason why, of your own free will, you would offer to sit with Sandra."

"Have you ever seen a boy there?" asked Jane.

"Jane!" Mr. Purdy's voice was warning her that she had talked long enough.

That was the trouble with this house. A girl couldn't even carry on a telephone conversation with any privacy. "Well, I have to say good-by now," Jane said hastily. "Pop is beginning to bellow."

"Yes, I know how it is." Julie's voice was sympathetic. Then she added insistently, "It must be a boy, but if he's worth an afternoon of Sandra I wish you luck."

"I'll call you tomorrow. 'By." Jane was glad to hang up. She was willing to share her secret with her best friend, but she did not want to discuss the new boy in front of her mother and father, who would be sure to ask a lot of questions about him that she could not answer. And, on second thought, she did not really want to discuss him with Julie. Not yet. Not until she had a date with him. Jane sat staring at the telephone, deep in her thoughts of the strange boy, until she heard her mother speak to her father.

"I'm so glad Jane is interested in baby-sitting." Mrs. Purdy spoke softly, apparently unaware that her daughter was listening.

If Mom only knew, thought Jane, with a twinge of guilt.

"So many girls her age are boy-crazy," Mrs. Purdy continued. "Like Marcy Stokes. I don't know what has come over that girl in the past year. She used to be such a good student and now all she thinks about is boys and clothes."

Well, I know what has come over Marcy, Jane thought. She no longer wears bands on her teeth and she has a figure and a definite personality. She's tall and slim, casual and just a touch bored, with sun-streaked hair and exactly the right clothes. The kind of girl all the boys go for. The cashmere-sweater type. But this, Jane knew, was something she could never explain to her mother, who would say, "But Jane, you have a cashmere sweater."

Mrs. Purdy went on in a voice so low that Jane had to strain to catch her words. "I'm glad our daughter is a sweet, sensible girl."

Mom, how could you, thought Jane. Sweet and *sensible*—how perfectly awful. Nobody wanted to be sweet and sensible, at least not a girl in high school. Jane hoped her mother would not spread it around Woodmont that she thought her daughter was sweet and sensible.

The telephone at Jane's elbow rang so unexpectedly that she jumped before she was able to pick up the receiver. "Hello," she said almost absent-mindedly, because her thoughts had drifted back to the strange boy who had smiled at her across the Nortons' kitchen.

"Uh . . . is this Jane Purdy?" asked a voice—a boy's voice.

An electric feeling flashed through Jane clear to her finger tips. The boy! It was *his* voice! She was sitting there thinking and wishing, and suddenly there he was, on the other end of the line. *He* was calling *her!* Jane swallowed. (Careful, Jane, don't be too eager.) "Yes, it is." Somehow she managed to keep her voice calm. To think that she and this boy she wanted so much to know were connected with each other by telephone wires strung on poles along the streets and over the trees of Woodmont! It was a miracle, a real miracle.

"Well, uh . . . I don't know whether you remember me or not, but I delivered some horse meat to the Nortons' when you were sitting with Sandra. My name is Stan Crandall."

Stan Crandall. *Stan Crandall!* "Yes?" Ah, good girl, Jane. Calm, polite, just the faintest touch of surprise in her voice. "Yes, I remember."

"I called Mrs. Norton and asked her for the name of her sitter," the boy explained.

Oh. Oh, dear. Hang onto yourself, Jane. Maybe his mother is looking for a sitter for his little sister. And what if his mother is looking for a sitter? I'd get to see him, wouldn't I?

"I know this is probably sort of sudden." The boy hesitated. "But I was wondering if you would care to go to the movies with me tomorrow night."

He didn't want a sitter. He wanted her! Jane's thoughts spun. She had better ask her mother. No, that would lead to a lot of tiresome arguments about just who was this Stan Crandall. She couldn't keep him dangling on the telephone while she tried to explain to her mother and father. Besides, she was practically sixteen, wasn't she? She couldn't be tied to her mother's apron strings forever, could she? She had a right to accept a date with a perfectly nice boy, didn't she?

"I would love to go," said Jane.

"Swell." There was relief in the boy's—in Stan's—voice. He had been afraid she might turn him down! "Would seven o'clock be all right?" he asked.

"Seven would be fine," answered Jane.

"Swell," he repeated. "I'll see you then."

"All right," agreed Jane, and hesitated. She felt she should say something more, but she could not think what. There did not seem to be anything more to add to the conversation. "Good-by," she said. "Thank you for calling."

"Good-by," he said, "and thanks a lot."

Once more Jane sat staring at the telephone. This time she was filled with a confidence that was new to her. Stan Crandall. Stanley Crandall. He liked her! He had seen her once, and even though she had been rumpled and grass-stained and having a terrible time with Sandra, he liked her well enough to go to the trouble of finding out her name and calling to ask her to go to the movies. Jane smiled at the telephone and gave a sigh of pure happiness. *Stan Crandall!*

"Jane, what were you saying about seven o'clock?" Mrs. Purdy called from the living room.

Jane stopped smiling. Here it comes, she thought. She might as well get it over. Her mother and father would *have* to let her go. They had to. She couldn't bear it if they wouldn't. Jane walked into the living room determined to be firm with her mother and father and said, as calmly as she could, "I'm going to the movies tomorrow night at seven o'clock."

"With some of the girls?" asked Mrs. Purdy.

"No. I'm going with a boy named Stanley Crandall." Jane tried unsuccessfully to keep a note of defiance out of her voice.

Mr. Purdy put down the seed catalogue he was studying. "And who is Stanley Crandall?" he demanded.

"Yes, Jane," said Mrs. Purdy. "Just who is this Stanley Crandall?"

Oh, Mom, do you have to refer to him as "this Stanley Crandall"? Jane thought. It sounded so awful, as if she had picked him up on a street corner someplace. "He's a perfectly nice boy," she said.

"Where did you meet him?" inquired Mrs. Purdy.

"At the Nortons'," replied Jane.

"Is he a friend of theirs?" persisted Mrs. Purdy.

"Not exactly. At least I don't think so."

"Then how did you happen to meet him at the Nortons'?"

Oh, Mom, do you have to act like the FBI, or something, just because I'm going to the movies tomorrow night with a perfectly nice boy, Jane thought. "He came in a delivery truck," she said.

"From Jake's Market?"

Jane stared at the corner of the living-room ceiling. "No. Not from Jake's Market," she said patiently.

"Jane Purdy!" said Mrs. Purdy sharply. "Will you please get that look of exaggerated patience off your face? Your father and I are not morons. We only want to know for your own good who this boy is."

Her own good. Everything around here was always for her own good. Well, they would have to know the truth some time. "He was delivering horse meat for the dog from the Doggie Diner."

Mr. Purdy gave a snort of laughter. "Aha! Horse meat!" he exclaimed. "The plot thickens!"

Jane tried to wither her father with a glance but succeeded only in giving him a look of despair. How could he be so callous when she was in the middle of a crisis?

"Really, Jane," said Mrs. Purdy weakly. "Horse meat!"

"And what's the matter with horse meat?" cried Jane. "Delivering horse meat is a perfectly honest way for a boy to earn some money. It's no worse than baby-sitting. You always said honest labor was nothing to be ashamed of." Jane stared defiantly at her mother and father. "You just don't want me to have any fun!" Jane knew when she said this that it was not true. Her mother and father were both anxious for her to have a good time, but somehow this was the sort of thing she had found herself saying to them lately. She was sorry, but honestly, the way a girl's mother and father could take a beautiful feeling of happiness and practically trample it in the dust!

"We're not forbidding the banns just because the boy delivers horse meat," said Mr. Purdy mildly, as he lit his pipe and flicked out the match.

"Oh, Pop," said Jane impatiently. "I don't want to marry him. I merely want to go to the movies with him."

"Horse meat!" Mrs. Purdy began to laugh. "He delivers horse meat!"

Jane turned on her mother and said almost tearfully, "It's U. S. government-inspected horse meat!"

"I'm sorry, Jane." Mrs. Purdy managed to stop laughing. "There is no reason for you to get so worked up. It isn't the quality of the horse meat that we are questioning. We only want to know something about the boy. Surely that's not too much to ask."

"Well, he's new in Woodmont," said Jane, somewhat mollified, although still ruffled because her mother had laughed at a perfectly honest way for a boy to earn some money. "And he's an awfully nice boy."

"But Jane, how do you know he's a nice boy?" Mrs. Purdy asked. "You never saw him before. You don't know his family or anything about him except that he delivers horse meat. That isn't much of a recommendation."

How could she explain to her mother that because a boy had a dip in his hair and a friendly grin and wore a clean white T shirt she knew he was a nice boy? "He just is," was all Jane could say miserably. "I can tell. And anyway, I'm going out with him, not his family."

Mrs. Purdy did not look convinced, so Jane went on. "He's not the type to ride around in a hot rod and throw beer cans out along the highway. Mom, I *know* he's a nice boy. He looks clean and intelligent and—well, *nice*. And he looks like he's fun to be with, too. Not like the boys I've known all my life. Not like George, who just thinks about his old rock collection and chemistry experiments."

"Now, Jane," said Mrs. Purdy, "don't underestimate George. He's a nice boy with real interests.

He may not seem very exciting to you now, but he's the kind of boy with a purpose, the kind of boy who will be a doctor or a scientist when he grows up."

"But Mom, I don't want to go out with a boy I have known practically since I was in my play pen, and I don't care what George is like when he grows up. I want to go to the movies on Saturday night with a boy who is fun *now*."

"Why, Jane," Mrs. Purdy protested. "You've always had a good time at the little dancing parties you have gone to."

"Little dancing parties! Mom, those are for children."

"And you have gone to the movies and school affairs with George," Mrs. Purdy pointed out. "I thought you liked him."

"I do like George," Jane insisted. "I just don't like to go out with him. He's too short and that lock of hair always sticks up. At the spring dance at school all he talked about was his rock collection, and he's a horrible dancer. He sort of lopes around and I had to scrooch down so I wouldn't tower over him. And his mother and father came to pick us up, because he isn't old enough to have a driver's license and they came early because they wanted to *watch* the dance, and it was just too embarrassing, and then when they were leaving the gym his mother said to his father in a loud voice, 'Wasn't it a lovely party for the children?' Everybody looked at George and me and I felt about six years old and it was simply ghastly. *That's* why I don't like to go out with George."

"Oh," said Mr. Purdy. "I see."

Jane looked quickly at her father to see if he was laughing at her, but his expression was serious.

"I suppose it was a little awkward," said Mrs. Purdy, "but just the same, I don't want you running around with a boy we know nothing about."

"But I'm not going to run around with him. I'm going to walk five blocks in a straight line with him to the movies. That isn't running around."

Then Jane's father spoke up. "I think that by now Jane is old enough to recognize a nice boy when she sees one. And as she has pointed out, they are only going to the movies."

Jane looked gratefully at her father. Good for Pop! He understood.

"But she's had so little experience," protested Mrs. Purdy.

Experience! How was a girl going to get any experience when her mother was so old-fashioned she didn't even want her daughter to go to the movies with a boy unless she personally knew his whole family tree for a couple of generations?

"Does this boy have a car?" Mrs. Purdy asked.

"I don't know," answered Jane truthfully, fervently hoping that he did own a car or at least have the use of one.

"It's all right if you walk to the movies," said Mrs. Purdy, "but I don't want you riding around in a car with some strange boy."

"Yes, Mom." The battle was won, although somehow Jane had known from the beginning that she would win. She was actually going to the movies with Stan, the new boy, the boy with the friendly smile and the dip in his hair. In less than twenty-four hours she would be with him. The problem of the car she would meet when she came to it. If Stan did arrive in a car, she could easily suggest that since it was a nice evening (and it would be a nice evening, it had to be), they could walk to the movies. The theater was only five blocks from her house. And in the meantime her mother and father would see for themselves what a nice boy he was and maybe the next time . . .

There has to be a next time, thought Jane, as she curled up in a chair with a book in her hand.

I couldn't bear it if there isn't another date. And another and another. She saw herself chattering with a cluster of girls in front of the lockers at Woodmont High. "Stan and I had the most wonderful time . . ." "Last night Stan and I . . ." "And Stan said to me . . ." "Oh, yes, Stan gave me this . . ." (Gave her what? An identification bracelet? His class ring?) "Stan dropped over last night and we . . ." "I thought I'd die laughing when Stan . . ."

"Jane, hadn't you better think about going to bed?" Mrs. Purdy asked.

Her mother's voice scarcely touched Jane's thoughts. Still standing by the lockers at Woodmont High, Jane answered, "I guess so," and walked dreamily toward the bathroom to start putting her hair up in pin curls. "Stan and I always . . ." "Stan and I . . ."

CHAPTER

3

IT WAS not until the next morning that Jane began to have qualms about her date with Stan Crandall. First of all, she decided that her hair simply would not do, so she washed it and put it up in pin curls, each one clamped with two bobby pins.

"Why, Jane, I thought you washed your hair day before yesterday," remarked Mrs. Purdy.

"Did I? I don't remember," fibbed Jane, staring critically at herself in the mirror. Carefully she plucked six hairs out of her left eyebrow and five out of her right.

Then she opened her closet and studied her wardrobe to see what she owned that would be suitable to wear to walk five blocks to Woodmont's only movie and perhaps to Nibley's afterwards. One by one she examined her dresses. Her best navy-blue silk printed with white daisies was too dressy. Her gray suit—well, no. That was more for wearing to the city. Her pale-blue princess dress—certainly not. Not that old thing. Her yellow cotton—no. Stan had already seen it. Besides, the round collar looked so babyish. Her dirndl and peasant blouse wouldn't do either. Once more she went over her wardrobe. She did not have a thing that was exactly right to wear on her first date with Stan Crandall. Not one single thing—and neither did she have enough money from baby-sitting to buy a new dress.

Jane decided to approach her mother. "Mom, if I give you the six dollars and a half baby-sitting money that I have, could I charge a dress and pay you the rest later?" she asked.

"Why, Jane, you have a closet full of clothes. More than lots of girls in Woodmont."

This was the sort of thing Jane might have expected from her mother. "Well, may I, Mom? I haven't a thing to wear tonight."

"I don't think so, dear." Mrs. Purdy was pleasant but definite. "There are lots of girls who would be glad to have your pretty clothes. Besides, you are only going to walk five blocks to the neighborhood movie."

That was Mom, always dragging "lots of girls"

into arguments. And you'd think she could understand how important those five blocks were. "But, Mom—"

"Jane," sighed Mrs. Purdy, "I don't know what's come over you. It wasn't so long ago that I had a terrible time getting you out of play clothes and sneakers."

And now that I want to dress up, you won't let me charge anything, thought Jane, and it was her turn to sigh. Sometimes she, too, wondered what had come over her.

Jane spent half an hour pressing her blue princess dress and suffering qualms about herself. What would she say to Stan? She could ask him how long he had lived in Woodmont and where he had lived before. That would take up part of the time, but what could she talk about after that? The Teen Corner in the newspaper advised girls to ask questions about boys' interests, but she couldn't come right out and say, "What are you interested in?" If she said, "Are you interested in sports?" he might turn out to be a Rugby fan or excited about something else she knew nothing about. Maybe she had better start reading the sport sections after this. And if he did take her to Nibley's, would she know how to act? Going there in the eve-

ning with a boy was not the same as dropping in with Julie after school.

Cleaning her white Capezio slippers and painting her nails with Rosy Rapture polish took a good part of the afternoon. It was not until nearly three o'clock, as she wafted her damp finger tips back and forth to dry them, that Jane began to have qualms about Stan. What if he came in a T shirt and jeans? Or one of those gaudy sport shirts with the tail hanging out? A plain sport shirt with the tail tucked in would be all right for a movie date in Woodmont, but not a T shirt or a figured sport shirt. But he won't, he can't, she thought. He was not that kind of boy. And all at once she was no longer sure what kind of boy Stan was. Maybe he was the kind who would drive up and toot and expect her to come running out—as if her mother would let her. Or maybe he would chew gum and snap it and guffaw at the love scenes in the movie. Maybe he wouldn't know how to talk to her mother and father, or maybe he would walk on the inside of the sidewalk and let her walk beside the curb. Maybe he would turn out to be like George and buy ice-cream cones to eat on the way home and lick his cone the way George did. Maybe he even had a rock collection like George and, like George, a scientific mind. Maybe she would have to listen to him tell about finding an unusual piece of contorted gneiss in the Sierras. George never picked up rocks that were just pretty. He always found specimens that he called by the exact scientific name.

Then Jane looked around the Purdy living room and wondered if she should try to get her mother to call in an interior decorator, now that she was going to have dates. She decided against it. The rug was worn by the door and one chair was pretty shabby where Sir Puss insisted on sharpening his claws on it, but the room was pleasant and comfortable.

Just before dinner Jane took the bobby pins out of her hair, because her father did not allow her to come to the table with her hair in pin curls. He said it spoiled his appetite to realize he had a pinhead for a daughter. It was not until she was seated at the table that Jane began to have qualms about her parents. Between bites of salad she considered them with a feeling of great detachment, as if she were seeing them for the first time. On the whole, she found them presentable, but she did wish her mother would put on some stockings and wear a dress instead of that striped cotton skirt and red blouse. It was so undignified for a mother who was practically forty and very old-fashioned to go around with bare legs, even if they were tanned, and to wear such gay clothes. Stan might think she didn't know how to dress. And her father—if only he wouldn't try to be funny when Stan arrived! His jokes were all right for the family, but he should realize that he had been out of college sixteen years and was too old to go around trying to be funny in front of company. Stan's father probably didn't make jokes all the time and Stan might think it was undignified. Jane barely touched the casserole dish, even though it was her favorite—the one her mother called "It Smells to Heaven." There were onions in it and Jane did not want to breathe onions on Stan at the movie.

After dinner Jane decided the blue dress would not do at all. It was terrible, and how could she ever have thought she could wear it? She hastily pressed a pink blouse to wear with her suit. As soon as she had it pressed she realized it was all wrong and of course she would have to wear the blue dress. Hurriedly she locked herself in the bathroom, where she took a shower and washed her face carefully with a deep pore cleanser. She examined her face critically in the mirror and plucked one more hair out of her right eyebrow.

"Jane, you aren't the only member of the family who uses the bathroom," Mrs. Purdy reminded her through the bathroom door.

"O.K., Mom." Jane scurried into her room. She slid the blue dress over her head and slipped into her clean white shoes. It took four attempts to get a straight part in her hair. Then, with a lipstick brush which she kept hidden from her mother, who was inclined to be old-fashioned about make-up, Jane outlined her lips with Rosy Rapture, which all the girls were wearing this summer. She filled in the outline, studied the effect in the mirror, and then blotted off some of the color so she could get out of the house without her mother's saying, "Really, Jane, I do wish you wouldn't wear so much lipstick." A light dusting of powder on her nose came next. Finally she studied herself carefully and snipped off two wisps of hair with her manicure scissors. Then she was ready.

At five minutes to seven Jane walked into the living room and looked around with a critical eye. She was pleased to see a bowl of fresh begonias, vivid as flames, on the coffee table. Thank goodness her mother had changed to a dark linen dress and had put on stockings, and her father, who was wearing a plain tan sport shirt, had put on his horn-rimmed glasses to read the evening paper. He looked almost dignified. Even Sir Puss was stretched out on the rug, languidly patting at his rubber mouse with one paw and behaving properly for a cat. Now if they would all stay that way and not move until Stan came, everything would be all right.

"Well, how about it, Jane?" her father asked jovially. "Do we pass inspection?"

"Pop, just this once, please don't try to be funny," implored Jane as she sat carefully on the edge of a chair so she would not wrinkle her dress. Her mouth was dry and her hands felt cold. Her thoughts were anxious. In five more minutes . . . he did say tonight, didn't he . . . tonight and not next Saturday? In three more minutes . . . Please, Stan, don't be late! And please, please be as nice as I think you are.

At exactly seven o'clock Jane heard someone coming up the front steps. She had not heard a car stop in front of the house, so that was one problem she would not have to meet this evening.

"Hist!" said Mr. Purdy in a stage whisper from behind his paper. "I hear footsteps approaching."

"Pop!" begged Jane, starting from her chair even though she had anticipated the sound of the doorbell. Sir Puss jumped up and glared, annoyed at this disturbance of his peace.

Jane opened the door. "Hello, Stan," she murmured, suddenly feeling shy. "Won't you come in?"

"Hello, Jane." Stan stepped into the living room. He was even more attractive than Jane remembered. His greenish eyes and the dip in his hair were the same, but he was wearing gray flannel slacks, a white sport shirt, and a green sweater—not cashmere, but a good-looking wool. His manner no longer seemed easy and casual as it had yesterday

when he delivered the horse meat. Now he appeared serious, even a little nervous, as if he, too, were not quite sure how this date might turn out. He was a boy any girl would be proud to introduce to her parents.

"Uh . . . Mother, may I present Stan Crandall?" said Jane carefully.

"Hello, Stan," said Mrs. Purdy warmly, and Jane was proud of her.

"How do you do, Mrs. Purdy?" Stan answered.

The anxiety that had tormented Jane all afternoon now began to fade. "And Father, this is Stan Crandall."

Mr. Purdy rose from his chair and extended his hand. Stan stepped forward to shake hands and, as Jane watched helplessly, seeing what was about to happen, he trod squarely on Sir Puss's rubber mouse. The mouse gave out a piercing squeak. Stan jumped and turned red to the tips of his ears.

"Oh!" gasped Jane, embarrassed and ashamed that she had not foreseen this. That cat!

Gamely Stan grasped Mr. Purdy's hand and said, as if nothing had happened, "I'm pleased to meet you, sir."

"Won't you sit down?" invited Mr. Purdy. Stan glanced uncertainly at Jane and remained standing.

In her relief that introductions were over, Jane leaned against the end of the sofa. So far so good, in spite of the rubber mouse. Now what happens, she wondered. Should they talk awhile, or should she suggest that they leave, or should she wait for him to suggest it?

Mr. Purdy sat down again, but Stan remained standing. "That's a handsome cat you have," he remarked.

Sir Puss stared balefully at the visitor, then sat down, hoisted his hind leg, and began deliberately to wash.

Inwardly Jane squirmed with embarrassment. Leave it to Sir Puss! You'd think he was the most important member of the family, the way he acted. Why, oh, why did he have to choose this particular moment, when everyone was looking at him, to wash his bottom? And be so industrious about it. Why couldn't he wash his face prettily? And why did Stan have to stand there so awkwardly? Why didn't he sit down?

"Yes, he's a mighty fine cat," agreed Mr. Purdy. "And he's a good hunter. Keeps the garden free of gophers."

Jane shifted her weight from one foot to the other and wished her father would not get started

on Sir Puss. If only Stan would sit down instead
of standing there looking so ill at ease. Jane wished
desperately she could push him into a chair. He
should know better than to stand there when her
father had asked him to sit down. Then she caught
her mother's eye. Mrs. Purdy frowned ever so
slightly and looked meaningfully at the place beside her on the sofa. Jane understood the message
and, crimson with embarrassment, hastily sat down.
Of course she should have realized that a boy with
such nice manners as Stan's would not be seated
while she was standing. How could she ever have
done such an awkward thing? Now Stan would
think she didn't know any better. In spite of her
humiliation, Jane was tremendously relieved when
at last Stan sat down.

"Yes, he's a great cat," Mr. Purdy went on, as if
a crisis had not taken place before his eyes. "He
always wants to be praised when he catches a
gopher. If he can find an open window he will
jump into the house with the gopher in his mouth.
He weighs fourteen pounds and he lands with a
thud that wakes up everyone in the house. You
might say—"

Pop, implored Jane silently, not that joke. Please,
not that old joke. It was all right for the family,

but maybe Stan hadn't read the poem about the fog coming on little cat feet. He might not get the point.

"You might say," Mr. Purdy went on, "that what we need around here is a cat that comes on little fog feet."

Stan laughed—a natural boyish laugh. In spite of her annoyance with her father, Jane smiled. So Stan had also read the poem in his English I class. That was good to know. It gave them something in common. Now if she could just get her father to stop talking about Sir Puss and keep him from getting started on his begonias, maybe they could go on to the movies. But now that Stan was finally seated, how on earth was she going to get him up again? If she stood up he would probably get to his feet too, but that did not seem the way to do it. Sitting down and standing up had always been such a simple process until now. Suddenly life seemed unbearably complicated.

Not knowing what else to do, Jane smiled timidly across the room at Stan, who seemed to understand. "Perhaps we should go," he said, "if we want to catch the beginning of the movie."

"Yes, I think we should," agreed Jane. She rose from the sofa, an act that brought Stan to his feet. She went to the hall closet and pulled her short white coat from a hanger. Another uncomfortable moment came when Stan took the coat from her to help her into it, and her arm missed the left sleeve twice before she groped her way into it. She was sure Stan would think she was not used to having a boy help her on with her coat. And how right he would be!

"Mrs. Purdy, is it all right if I have Jane home by ten-thirty?" Stan asked.

Jane could tell her mother was pleased to have Stan ask this question. She herself would have preferred Stan to think she was old enough to come in whenever she wanted to, but on the other hand, if she wanted more dates with him, it was a good idea to please her parents. And it was pleasant to feel protected as long as it was Stan, and not her parents, who was doing the protecting.

"Yes, I think ten-thirty is late enough for her to be out," said Mrs. Purdy. She smiled encouragingly at Stan, while Jane did some rapid mental arithmetic. About two and a half hours for a single feature, cartoon, and newsreel, fifty-five minutes at Nibley's, and five minutes to walk home.

"I'll have her back by then," Stan promised.

"Have a good time, kids," said Mr. Purdy.

Kids! Pop *would* have to call them kids. Oh, well,

thought Jane, what difference did it make? She was starting out on a date with Stan, and he was every bit as nice as she had thought he would be.

"I hope you don't mind walking," said Stan, when they were outside. "Dad won't let me have the car very often."

"It's a lovely evening to walk," answered Jane. So his father did let him have the car sometimes! "Have you lived in Woodmont long?"

"A little over a month," said Stan. "We lived in the city, but my folks decided to move over here to get out of the fog. Dad commutes to the city now."

"We have fog here too," said Jane, to keep the conversation going. She noticed that Stan walked on the outside of the sidewalk.

"Yes, but not like the fog in the city. It really dripped, out where we lived."

Jane wanted to find out as much as she could about Stan in the five blocks to the movie. "Where do you live in Woodmont?" she asked.

"On Poppy Lane," he said. "It's sure nice over there. We have an acacia tree in the front yard and a big fig tree in back."

Poppy Lane. About a mile from the Purdys'; on the other side of the shopping district, but in the same kind of neighborhood. If the Crandalls had a fig tree in the back yard, their house must be fairly old, like the Purdys', and that meant they were neither very rich nor very poor. Just average. Jane smiled to herself. Things were working out better than she had dared hope.

By the time they reached the Woodmont Theater, Jane had learned that Stan, besides his younger sister, had one who was two years older than he was and that he would enter his junior year at Woodmont High in September. In the meantime, he had this job working for the Doggie Diner, because his cousin owned the business and because he liked dogs and planned to be a veterinarian when he finished college. He does have a purpose, Jane told herself triumphantly. Conversation was not so difficult, after all, and the five blocks were much too short. Stan was soon pushing his money through the hole in the glass window of the Woodmont Theater ticket booth.

Afterwards Jane realized she had been too busy turning over in her mind all she had learned about Stan to remember much about the movie they saw together. It began with a schoolmarm getting out of a stagecoach while a lone horseman rode into town, and it ended with a kiss against a technicolor sky, and in between there was a fight in a saloon, shooting on the street, the sound of horses' hoofs in the night, and something about a mortgage. What Jane did remember clearly were the admiring glances of several Woodmont High girls who had seen them take seats just before the lights were lowered, and Stan's shoulder above hers, and the way their elbows kept bumping accidentally until she folded her hands in her lap. She did not want Stan to think she was the kind of girl who expected to have her hand held just because she was sitting in the dark with a boy.

After the movie Stan said, "How about stopping at Nibley's? We still have time."

"O.K.," agreed Jane happily, and the two walked half a block down the street to Nibley's Confectionery and Soda Fountain. Once inside, Jane could not decide whether it would be better to sit in a booth in the back, where she would be sure to have Stan all to herself, or whether it would be better to sit toward the front, where she could show him off to the rest of the crowd. She nodded and spoke to a boy who had been in her history class, a girl from her gym class, and two more from her registration room, and hoped she was behaving as casually as if she were used to walking into Nibley's with a good-looking boy. The girls spoke to Jane, but they looked at Stan. Jane noticed wistfulness, envy, or just curiosity on their faces—depending, Jane decided, on whether they were with other girls, boys they didn't like much, or dates they really liked. It was, Jane felt, a very satisfactory experience.

Jane was surprised that Stan, who had lived in Woodmont only a month, knew so many people and could call them by name. They couldn't *all* have dogs that ate Doggie Diner horse meat. Stan guided her into the only unoccupied booth, which was toward the front. Jane looked around her at the signs painted on the mirror behind the milkshake machines and remembered that only yesterday she had imagined herself sitting at the counter catching the eye of some strange boy in that mirror. Now she felt sorry for the girls who were sitting together at the counter sipping cokes and watching the door to see who would come in next. The jukebox began to play *Love Me on Monday*, and Jane watched its colors turn and shift and thought how much they looked like the fruits that boiled in the kettle when her mother made jam. The slow, rolling-boil stage, the cookbooks called it. Jane brushed this irrelevant thought out of her mind.

She was wasting precious time that she could spend talking to Stan.

"What would you like?" Stan asked, as Mr. Nibley himself appeared to take their order.

"Well, hello there, Janey," said Mr. Nibley jovially. "Aren't you out pretty late?"

Jane smiled weakly. Oh, Mr. Nibley, she thought desperately, *don't*. Don't let Stan know I don't come in here with boys after the movies all the time. That was the trouble with a town like Woodmont. Everyone in the older part knew everything about everyone else. Mr. Nibley had known her since she had to be lifted onto a stool and he had to lean over to hand her an ice-cream cone. He probably thought she was about eleven years old now.

As Stan asked for a chocolate shake, Jane found she was too excited to eat. "A dish of vanilla ice cream," she said at last. Tonight a chocolate coke float seemed too childish to order.

"Why, Janey, what's the matter?" asked Mr. Nibley. "Don't you like chocolate coke floats any more?"

"I don't feel like one tonight," Jane said aloud. In her thoughts she was saying, Mr. Nibley, did you *have* to go and tell Stan what I usually order? And please go away. I want to talk to him.

"Say, Janey, I just happened to think," Mr. Nibley said. "Do you happen to know what kind of fertilizer your father is using on his begonias this year? I don't seem to get the same results he does."

Fertilizer for begonias! "No, I don't, Mr. Nibley. I never noticed," answered Jane. Go away, Mr. Nibley, she thought. *Go away.*

But when Mr. Nibley did leave, Jane found she did not know what to say. Talking to Stan when she faced him in the light was much more difficult than talking while walking beside him in the dusk. She smiled across at Stan, who smiled back at her. Jane glanced down at the initials scratched in the paint on the table and raised her eyes again. How smooth and tan, almost golden, his skin looked. It was funny she had not noticed before that his eyelashes were thick and the crest of the dip in his hair was faded to a light brown. And on his right wrist—a strong-looking wrist—was a silver identification bracelet. Maybe some day . . .

"You were having quite a time with Sandra when I first saw you," Stan remarked.

Jane laughed. "Perfectly awful. You saved my life. I don't know what I would have done if she had really dumped that ink all over the carpet."

This was better. Feeling more at ease, Jane told Stan about her experience with Sandra and the fly spray.

Stan was amused. "Mrs. Norton has just as much trouble with Sandra herself," he said. "Do you baby-sit often?"

"Once or twice a week," Jane explained. "My friend Julie and I have built up a sort of business." She did not mind telling this to Stan, because he had a part-time job himself. There were some boys at Woodmont High who would look down on a girl who baby-sat regularly.

Mr. Nibley set the vanilla ice cream down in front of Jane and, by not looking up, she managed to avoid conversation with him. She took a small bite of ice cream and looked across at Stan, who was peeling the wrapper off a pair of straws. He looked like a boy who was enjoying his date.

"Well, if it isn't Stan Crandall!" cried a girl's voice, and Jane, looking up, saw Marcy Stokes and Greg.

Wouldn't you know it, thought Jane. Marcy *would* have to come along now, when everything was going so smoothly. And at the same time her mind recorded the fact that Marcy already knew Stan. Leave it to Marcy.

"Oh, hello there, Jane," exclaimed Marcy, with

a note of surprise in her voice that made Jane feel as if she were the last person in the world Marcy expected to see at Nibley's with a boy.

"Hi, Jane," said Greg. "Mind if we join you? There aren't any empty booths."

"Sure. Come on," said Stan, sliding over in the booth. "Jane and I will be leaving before long anyway."

Marcy slipped into the booth beside Jane, and Jane felt that everything about herself was all wrong. Marcy's simple black cotton dress and the white cashmere sweater tossed over her shoulders made Jane, in her pastel dress and white coat, feel prim and all bundled up.

"Just coffee, Mr. Nibley," said Marcy. This made Jane, who was nibbling at her vanilla ice cream, feel like a small girl who was being given a treat. She did not drink coffee. To her it was a bitter beverage that grownups—no, that wasn't the word—that older people drank.

Marcy flung back her sun-bleached hair with an impatient gesture and smiled lazily at Stan, as if Jane and Greg were not there. "We sure had fun at the beach that day, didn't we, Stan?" she asked.

"We sure did," agreed Stan.

What beach? What day? Jane wondered miserably if Marcy's just-between-us-two smile meant that she had already had a date with Stan.

"Except we ran out of sandwiches," was Greg's comment. "Next time you women had better remember you're packing a lunch for men, not boys."

"Such as?" drawled Marcy.

So Greg had been there too, and at least one other girl. Jane was annoyed with herself for feeling so pleased that Marcy had not been alone with Stan— at least not at the beach. But there might have been other times . . .

Greg smiled across the table at Jane. Encouraged, she smiled back, but he did not say anything that would help her enter the conversation. To hide her discomfort she took small bites of her ice cream. She could not help comparing Greg and Stan while Marcy chattered on. Greg was taller and better-looking than Stan, and there was something different about him, too. Greg knows everybody likes him, she thought, and he expects them to. He's the student-body-president-in-his-senior-year type. Yes, that was it. And Stan—Stan was every bit as friendly, but somehow he was different. Quieter, maybe. Nobody would expect him to be student-body president. He was just nice. The nicest boy she had ever met.

Jane waited for an opening in the conversation that would give her the opportunity to take part. None came. I might as well not be here, she thought unhappily, while Marcy went on about the sunburn everyone got that day at the beach and the fun they all had playing softball. And if she had been at the beach with the others, she would have been miserable trying to play softball with boys.

And then Jane began to question the success of her date. It seemed to her that she had done everything wrong and now it appeared that Stan was already part of Greg and Marcy's crowd, the crowd that belonged and that made her feel mousy and ill at ease. Sitting beside Greg, Stan seemed older and more sure of himself. He was not the studentbody president type but he was the kind of boy who would get elected to things—room representative or even president of the Hi-Y. And she was only a girl who wrote *My Experiences as a Baby Sitter* for Manuscript and didn't get elected to anything.

Stan glanced at his watch. "Well, we'd better go, Jane," he said, "if I'm going to get you home by ten-thirty."

"Oh, too bad," said Marcy, her glance lingering on Stan as if his having to take Jane home spoiled her evening. " 'By now."

Stan hurried Jane home so fast there was no chance to talk until they were standing in the dim circle cast by the Purdys' porch light. "Four seconds to spare," said Stan, and smiled down at Jane.

Jane looked at him uncertainly. "I had a wonderful time," she said hesitantly, and opened the door. Please, Stan, she thought, I like you so much. Say I'll see you again. "Well . . . good night, Stan."

"Good night, Jane," he answered. "I'll be seeing you."

Jane stepped inside the house and stood looking at Stan under the porch light. A halo of moths circled the bulb over his head. "Well, good night," she repeated, careful to keep wistfulness and disappointment out of her voice. "I'll be seeing you" could mean anything. Or nothing.

"Good night, Jane," he said again and, turning, started down the steps.

Jane closed the door behind her. Her date with Stan was over. She had had a good time in a miserable sort of way. She was proud of Stan and to be with him was a pleasure, but she had been so awkward about everything and he had been so assured, as if he were used to taking girls to the movies all the time. She wondered if he had enjoyed the evening at all. That he would be seeing her told her nothing. It could mean Stan planned to ask her for another date, or it could mean he would say, "Hi," when he happened to run into her on the street.

Jane switched off the porch light and the lamp her mother had left on in the living room, and looked out the front window into the night. If only she didn't feel so dreadfully young! She wished so much not to be fifteen—to be old enough to be casual about a boy and to order coffee instead of vanilla ice cream. Fifteen was such an uncomfortable age to be when she liked a boy like Stan, a boy who knew how to act with her parents and who was trusted with his father's car sometimes. Well, it was probably all over. Now that Stan had seen how young she was, he could not possibly be interested in another date—not when he was used to Marcy's crowd.

Something shadowy moving in the front yard caught Jane's eye. Puzzled, she peered through the darkness until she was able to separate the moving thing from the shrubs and tree shadows. It was Stan. Stan was still in the front yard! He appeared to be struggling with something in the fire-thorn bushes on the other side of the steps. The street light, obscured by trees, was so dim that she could not see what he was doing. What can he be doing, she wondered, and gasped in disbelief when Stan

moved out onto the lawn and she was able to see
him more clearly. What she saw could not really
be taking place. But there it was. Stan was wheeling
a bicycle which he had freed from the thorny shrubs.
Now he mounted it and pedaled down the street in
the direction of Poppy Lane. Jane stood staring
after him; when he turned the corner she could
hear him whistling *Love Me on Monday*. A bicycle!
Stan had ridden a bicycle over to her house.

When Jane had partially recovered from her astonishment she suddenly saw the whole evening in an
entirely different light. A boy who rode a bicycle
to a girl's house and hid it in the shrubbery while
he took her to the movies could not be so sure of
himself, after all. Probably he had to be in early
too, and had bicycled over to save time, and
had worried about the Purdys' seeing him before he had the bicycle out of sight. And when he
was out of sight he had begun to whistle *Love Me
on Monday*, the song Nibley's jukebox had played,
so he was happy when he left her. Maybe he was
even thinking about her.

A lot of things about the evening came back to
Jane—Stan's nervous look when she had opened the
front door, his crimson ears (such nice flat ears)
when he stepped on the cat's rubber mouse. Maybe
the reason she had trouble finding her left coat

sleeve was that he was not used to helping a girl on with her coat. And as for Marcy's crowd, Stan had not lived in Woodmont long enough to know who belonged and who did not. He was friendly to everyone. Well, thought Jane. Well! Things looked different now, and all because of a bicycle.

"Jane?" Mrs. Purdy's voice sounded anxious as she opened the hall door.

"Yes, Mom?" answered Jane, turning from the window.

"Did you have a good time, dear?"

"Yes, Mom," answered Jane. "A wonderful time."

Mrs. Purdy stepped into the living room in her bathrobe. "He seemed like a very nice boy. Did he ask you for another date?"

"No," answered Jane, and smiled out into the night in the direction of Poppy Lane. "No. Not yet."

CHAPTER

4

ALL day Sunday Jane drifted around the house in a happy glow, humming *Love Me on Monday* and hovering near the telephone, because she was sure Stan would call. Monday she stopped humming and hated the telephone, because she was sure he would never, never call. Tuesday he called.

"Hello, Jane? This is Stan," he said, and to Jane he spoke the most welcome words in the world.

"Hello, Stan," she answered happily.

"I have to go to work in a little while, but I wondered if I could stop by for a few minutes."

"I'm sorry, Stan," Jane was forced to say. "I was just about to leave for a baby-sitting job." But of course she could not let him get away, not after waiting two long days for his call. "Could you— could you come over some other time?" she asked.

"Do you have to go far?" Stan asked.

"About eight blocks."

"Why don't I come now and run you over to your job?" he suggested. "I have the truck."

"Oh, that would be wonderful," said Jane sincerely, because she was going to see him now instead of waiting for another call.

"See you in about two minutes," said Stan.

"Mom, Stan is going to drive me to my baby-sitting job," Jane informed her mother when she had hung up. Then, fearful that her mother might object to this short ride with a boy, she waited through an anxious moment of silence until her mother answered, "All right, dear."

Jane flew to her room, combed her hair, decided to change from her yellow dress into a dress Stan had never seen, decided against changing, because she might not have time, and wished her mother were wearing stockings. And all the while she wondered if Stan was coming to ask her for another date.

In a few minutes the red Doggie Diner truck stopped in front of the Purdys' and Stan bounded up the steps.

"Hi, Stan," Jane called through the open front door. "I'm ready. 'By, Mom."

"Hello, Stan," said Mrs. Purdy pleasantly.

Good for Mom, thought Jane; she isn't behaving badly at all, even though she isn't wearing stockings. Seated beside Stan in the Doggie Diner truck, Jane found that once more she felt shy, painfully shy. Stan seemed like a stranger, her mouth felt dry, and she couldn't think of a thing to say.

"Where to?" he wanted to know. "Sandra's again?"

"Not today, thank goodness." Jane was able to laugh naturally. "This afternoon it's Joey Dithridge." She gave an address in Bayaire Estates, the no-down-payment-to-veterans side of town, and Stan started the truck. Jane felt a thrill of pleasure just to be riding beside him. Of course, the Doggie Diner truck, with the back filled with packages of horse meat, wasn't exactly the same as a convertible, but since Stan was the driver she did not care.

"Is Joey as bad as Sandra?" Stan asked. "She's a handful."

"No, Joey's different," said Jane. "He's medium-hard to sit with, but not like Sandra. It's just that he's three years old and into everything, so he takes a lot of chasing. His mother doesn't keep anything around that he can hurt, and that helps. She's not like some mothers, who can't make their own children mind but expect a sitter to be able to. I just have to keep pulling him out of drawers and off the backs of chairs and things. Sometimes I can get him interested in trying to fill a shoe box with worms he digs out of the yard with an old tablespoon, and that keeps him busy. Or I can always read him *The Night Before Christmas*."

Stan laughed. "In August?"

"Oh, yes," answered Jane. "It's his favorite book."

Stan stopped the truck in front of the Dithridges', one of the new houses in a long row on a straight street. Few of the houses had lawns, but most of them had new shrubs too small to hide the foundations, and every house had at least one tree, two or three feet high, planted in the space that would some day be lawn. On the sidewalk in front of nearly every house was a little wagon or tricycle. Farther on down the street a bulldozer roared and a cement truck rumbled.

Stan turned to Jane and grinned at her. "I like that yellow dress on you," he said. "You were wearing it that day when you were with Sandra, and you looked cute with your hair all mussed up."

Jane felt herself blush with pleasure. Stan had remembered what she was wearing the first time they met! This was most significant. Now he would surely ask her for a date.

"Hi!" Little Joey Dithridge came running out of the house to meet Jane.

"Thanks a lot, Stan," she said, reluctantly opening the door of the truck. If they had been riding in a car, she would have waited for him to go around and open the door for her, but riding in a truck was different.

"I'll see you soon." Stan started the truck. "Don't let Joey wear you out."

"Good-by," called Jane wistfully, as Joey joyfully tackled her around the knees. "Hi, Joey."

"I'm going to chop you up in a million pieces!" cried Joey.

Jane laughed. "No, you won't," she answered, "because I'm bigger and I'll chop you up in a billion pieces first." This was the way she and Joey always greeted each other. Joey laughed delightedly while Jane absent-mindedly pried him loose from her knees. So Stan liked her in the yellow dress! But he had not asked her for another date. He had said he would see her soon. Soon. Jane did not like the word. It could mean anything—an hour or a week or a month. Men were so exasperating.

But Stan did see Jane soon. He saw her the very next day; he came by for a few minutes before he went to work and stayed long enough to drink a coke. Friday evening he telephoned to ask her to go to the movies again on Saturday. When Jane informed her mother and father that she was going to the movies with Stan again, she noticed her father raise his eyebrows ever so slightly, and an expression (could it be disapproval?) crossed her mother's face. They did not object, but Jane was left with a feeling of uneasiness. She hoped they would not start being stuffy and giving her lectures about seeing too much of Stan ("He's a nice boy, but . . ." "Really, Jane, I think you are a little young . . .") and all that sort of thing—not when everything was going so beautifully. Oh, please, please don't spoil it all, thought Jane, resolving not to mention Stan so much, even though lately it seemed as if his name was always on the tip of her tongue.

"By the way, Jane," said Mr. Purdy jovially, "I noticed a mysterious bicycle in the shrubbery that night you and Stan went to the movies. I wonder whose it was."

"Pop, please don't tease."

"Tease? Who's teasing?" Mr. Purdy asked.

"Pop, promise you won't ever mention the bicycle to Stan," Jane begged. "I'm sure he doesn't want me to know he rode it over here."

"Very mysterious," said Mr. Purdy. "Very mysterious the ways of the young."

It was not until Jane and Stan were in Nibley's after the movie that a real problem arose. This time they had a booth to themselves, near the bubbling, boiling jukebox, and Jane did not order a childish dish of ice cream. She ordered a cup of coffee.

"Do you really like coffee?" Stan asked curiously over his chocolate milk shake.

The coffee tasted bitter. Jane added more cream. "Sometimes," fibbed Jane, bravely taking another sip. She felt less sophisticated than she had hoped she would.

"I don't," said Stan. "I can't see why so many people like such bitter stuff."

"Oh, you get used to it," said Jane, trying to sound convincing. She took another cautious sip.

Someone put a dime in the jukebox, and Stan looked at Jane across the table. "Next Saturday is the last Saturday of summer vacation," he said.

"It is, isn't it?" Jane could feel that something special was coming.

"How would you like to go to the city for dinner, with two other couples, to celebrate?" he asked.

Dinner in the city! White tablecloths, courteous waiters, things cooked with mushrooms and herbs, flaming desserts! What on earth would she wear? "I would love to go," Jane told Stan, and at the same time she was sure her mother and father would never let her. But they had to, Jane decided. A date for dinner in the city was too important to miss. Jane was filled with a glorious feeling of confidence as she looked across the table at Stan. A boy did not ask a girl to go to dinner in the city unless she was somebody extra-special.

"Greg and Marcy want to go and so does Buzz Bratton, only he hasn't asked a girl yet," Stan went on.

"It sounds wonderful," said Jane, although she was disappointed that Marcy was to be included. Buzz Bratton, she had known all her life. He was a small, wiry, black-haired boy with a crew cut, and now that he was a junior in high school Jane classified him as the yell-leader type. When she was in the seventh grade and he was in the eighth he used to wait for her after school on cooking-class day—not to walk home with her, but to chase her and snatch whatever she had cooked and was taking home for her family to sample. After devouring her baked stuffed onion or chocolate cornstarch pudding, he always pretended to have terrible pains in his stomach. However, now that he was older he

might be fun on a double date, Jane conceded, if only he didn't tease. A girl shouldn't hold a baked stuffed onion against a boy forever.

"Dad said I could have the car that night," Stan continued.

At last they were going someplace in a real car, Jane thought ecstatically—or rather they were going if her mother and father weren't stuffy and old-fashioned about it. Well, if they were, she would have to talk them out of it. She would plan her campaign carefully.

"We thought it would be fun to have dinner in Chinatown. I used to eat there a lot with my folks when we lived in the city. Do you like Chinese food?"

Jane set down her empty coffee cup and hastily revised her picture of dinner in the city. "Yes, I do," she answered, because now that she had managed to get the coffee down, she was sure she would enjoy anything when she was with Stan. She tried to remember if she had ever eaten any Chinese food. Yes—once when she and her mother went shopping in the city they had ordered lunch at a department store tearoom, and chop suey had been on the menu. Or maybe it was chow mein. Anyway, something slithery that Jane did not remember clearly.

That night, after she had watched Stan take his bicycle out of its hiding place in the fire-thorn bushes, Jane lay awake, tense from coffee and excitement. Her thoughts whirled like confetti in the wind—Stan handsome in a white shirt and tie arriving in a car instead of a truck . . . riding in the front seat beside Stan . . . sitting with him in a Chinese restaurant fragrant with incense (at least she thought a Chinese restaurant would be fragrant with incense; she wasn't sure) . . . their eyes meeting across the teacups. The Chinese did drink tea. That she was sure of. How wonderful it was going to be! Now she was really grown-up, mature, sophisticated, a young woman with a dinner date. A dinner date with Stan.

Long after she should have been asleep, Jane's thoughts were interrupted by the peculiar muffled cry of a cat that has been successful in the hunt. Sir Puss had caught another gopher, Jane realized, and as she lay listening to his insistent cry she knew he would not be silent until he had received the praise that he felt was his due. Mr. Purdy raised his bedroom window, and through her own window Jane caught a glimpse of his flashlight playing on the cat. "My, that's a big one," Mr. Purdy complimented him and, satisfied, the cat was quiet.

The interruption started Jane's thoughts spinning in another direction. She had to evolve a practical plan for persuading her mother and father to let her go to the city. Sunday breakfast was the best time to bring up the matter, because it might take her all week to win the argument. She would state that she was going to the city for dinner, as if it had never occurred to her that there would be any question about her going. Then she would overcome their objections one by one. "But Mom, you said yourself he was a nice boy." "But Pop, he does drive carefully." "But Mom, of course he's a good driver, or his father wouldn't let him take the car." "But Mom . . ." "But Pop . . ." Over and over again.

On Sunday, however, Jane did not find the right moment to broach the matter to her mother and father. She waited all day, as alert as a cat at a mousehole; but late in the afternoon, when she thought the moment had come and she was about to pounce on it, friends dropped in. They were persuaded to stay for supper and then lingered until Jane had gone to bed.

On Monday Stan called to say that Buzz did not have a date, and did Jane know another girl? After thinking it over, Jane decided to ask Julie, because.

she felt guilty about having seen so little of her since meeting Stan and because Julie was also fifteen and would not make Jane feel uncomfortable. Jane waited until her mother was out of earshot to telephone Julie and extend the invitation.

"Oh, Jane! Dinner in the city—how marvelous!" Julie squealed with delight. "Mother and Dad have simply got to let me go!" Julie chattered happily on about how absolutely heavenly it would be to have a date with a boy who wasn't an old family friend, even if he was a little short, and how she was simply mad about Chinese food, especially since it wasn't fattening, and did Jane plan to wear a hat, because if she did Julie didn't know what she would do. Then, after pausing to catch her breath, she asked, "But Jane, how did you ever talk your family into letting you go?"

Jane sighed. "I haven't. That's the awful part. I haven't been able to talk to them together yet and anyway, I'm scared to bring it up."

"I know," sympathized Julie.

"If your folks will let you go," said Jane, "I'm sure mine will let me go."

"I was thinking the same thing about you," said Julie.

"Keep me posted," said Jane, not very hopefully.

"I will," agreed Julie. "And phone me the instant you talk them into it."

Tuesday Julie telephoned. "Any luck?" she asked guardedly.

"Not yet," Jane sighed. "Pop stayed in the city for dinner."

On Wednesday Julie called just before dinner. Jane knew from the sound of her voice that she did not have good news. "Tell me, Julie. What happened?" she asked.

"Wouldn't you just know?" said Julie gloomily. "They're thinking it over."

"Oh, Julie, how awful," said Jane. There was nothing worse than having parents think things over.

"Jane, you've simply got to get your folks to say you can go," Julie begged. "Then I can use that for an argument."

"I can't put it off any longer," Jane admitted. "Stan doesn't even know they haven't given me permission. He just assumed they would let me go. I guess I'll have to beard them in their dens at dinner tonight."

"Good luck," said Julie, not sounding at all hopeful.

And so that evening at the dinner table, when her father was enjoying a second helping of strawberry shortcake, Jane said casually, "Stan is taking me to the city for dinner Saturday. I think I'll wear my gray suit." Then she braced herself for the inevitable.

Mrs. Purdy set her coffee cup back on its saucer. Mr. Purdy laid down his fork. They both looked at Jane.

"Greg and Marcy are going too," said Jane chattily, as if nothing were wrong. "And Buzz Bratton will probably take Julie."

"Jane," said Mrs. Purdy, "it seems to me that you are seeing a lot of this Stan Crandall."

Here we go. This Stan Crandall again. "But Mom, you said yourself he was a nice boy." There. She had known she could get that in someplace.

"But you are only fifteen," protested Mrs. Purdy. "I don't think a bunch of fifteen-year-olds should go to the city alone at night."

Only fifteen! That old argument. Well, she wasn't going to be fifteen all her life. "I've only been to the movies with him twice and had a couple of cokes with him. I don't think that's seeing such a lot of him. Anyway, except for Julie, I'm the only one who is fifteen. The others are older. Stan must be practically seventeen."

"Now Jane, I certainly don't want you running around with an older crowd," said Mrs. Purdy.

How unreasonable could parents get, anyway? First Stan and his friends were too young. Now they were too old. "I don't think sixteen is so awfully much older than fifteen," Jane pointed out.

"Where do you plan to have dinner?" asked Mr. Purdy curiously. "It seems like a pretty expensive thing for kids that age to be doing."

"In Chinatown," answered Jane. "Stan has eaten there lots of times with his family when he lived in the city."

"Oh, Chinatown. You get a lot for your money there," said Mr. Purdy. "The boys ought to be able to fill you up for a dollar or so apiece."

Jane refrained from asking her father please not to be so crude.

"I just don't like the whole idea," said Mrs. Purdy. "How do you plan to go? On the bus?"

This was the hardest part. Her mother always got so excited at the thought of her riding in a car with a boy. "No," said Jane carefully. "Mr. Crandall is letting Stan have the car."

"Now Jane," said Mrs. Purdy sharply. "I am not going to have you running around all over the country in a car with a lot of teen-agers."

"But Mom," protested Jane. "It's less than ten miles to the city. That isn't all over the country. And Greg and Marcy and Buzz and Stan and Julie and I aren't a lot of teen-agers. Except for Stan— and you said yourself he was a nice boy—you've known all of us all our lives."

"Did Julie's mother say she could go?" Mrs. Purdy asked.

"I don't know," said Jane truthfully, for Julie's mother had not actually refused permission.

"I don't like the whole idea," said Mrs. Purdy. "You know the sort of things we read about teen-agers in the papers these days."

"Oh, Mom," said Jane impatiently, "you're acting as if we were a bunch of juvenile delinquents. As if we were all out on probation or something."

"But children your age get into such terrible scrapes," said Mrs. Purdy.

"But not teen-agers like Stan and me," Jane told her mother, ignoring Mrs. Purdy's reference to children. Surely her mother was not going to hold her personally responsible for every wild teen-age newspaper story she read. "People like Stan and me don't get into the papers. I told you before I went out with him he wasn't the type to drive around in a hot rod, throwing beer cans around. He's the kind of boy who has a purpose in life, like George. He's going to be a veterinarian when he finishes college." A purpose in life—that ought to please her mother.

"I think Jane has a point there," said Mr. Purdy. "It isn't fair to judge all teen-agers by the few we read about in the headlines."

"I suppose not," admitted Mrs. Purdy, "but it worries me just the same. I would feel a lot better if they went on the bus."

Ha! She was gaining ground. This was the first time her mother had admitted the possibility of her going at all. Jane thought quickly. "But Mom, you know how terrible the bus service is in the evening," she said. "After we got to the city we'd have to transfer twice to get to Chinatown. We'd be standing around on street corners all night waiting for buses, and Stan might not be able to get me home by ten-thirty." This was, she admitted to herself, a dangerous argument. It might lead her mother into protests against staying out till all hours. And if she weren't careful, her mother would be dragging in lots of girls. Lots of girls would be satisfied with going to the movies in Woodmont, and that sort of thing.

"I don't see why they wouldn't be safe enough in the Crandalls' car," said Mr. Purdy. "Stan has lived in the city and is used to city traffic. And he drives a truck, too, so he had to pass the test for a commercial license. He looks like a pretty steady sort of kid, and if Jane doesn't have any sense now she never will have."

"I suppose it's all right to let her go just this once," agreed Mrs. Purdy reluctantly. She turned to Jane. "But you must go straight to Chinatown and come straight home. And be home by ten-thirty."

"We will," promised Jane, and thanked her father with one grateful glance across the bowl of begonias in the center of the table. Darling Pop. He understood. Suddenly hungry because the battle had ended so much sooner than she had dared hope, Jane served herself another piece of strawberry shortcake. She really was going to the city in a car with Stan to have dinner—her first grown-up date. And it was going to be the most wonderful evening she had ever spent in her whole life!

Jane finished her shortcake and hurried to the telephone to dial Julie's number. "Julie, I can go!" she said ecstatically.

"I was just going to phone you," answered Julie, equally ecstatic. Her mother and father had finally, *finally* consented to let her go after a lot of talk about teen-agers and speeding and goodness knows what all—you know how parents are.

It did not take more than an hour on the telephone for the girls to decide they would not wear hats, because if they both went bareheaded it wouldn't matter what Marcy did about a hat; that Julie would wear her navy-blue suit, because it made her look thinner, and Jane would wear her gray suit and the white blouse that had tiny tucks down the front and really was very pretty even though it did have one of those awful round collars Mrs. Purdy always insisted on. ("But Jane, they're so becoming." "But Mom, they're so childish.") Jane would wear her black shoes that looked like pumps except they had low heels, and Julie would try to talk her mother into a new pair of shoes. Both girls would wear, or anyway carry, white gloves, because after all they were going to the city, weren't they? The city was not the same as Woodmont. They had to be well-dressed to go to the city.

"Good heavens, Jane," Mr. Purdy remarked at the end of this conversation. "You and Julie are only going about eight miles to eat some food you probably won't like, with a couple of high-school kids who are, I would like to remind you, mere mortals."

Jane smiled vaguely at her father and did not

bother to answer. For a fleeting moment she felt sorry for him—poor old Pop, with his cat and his begonias to keep him happy.

Jane spent the rest of the week in joyful anticipation. She was an extra-special girl to Stan, and if her mother and father let her go to the city with him she should have no trouble getting permission for beach picnics and swimming parties. What a wonderful summer this had turned out to be, and fall should be even better. For the first time since she entered Woodmont High she would feel that she really belonged.

Thursday Jane met Julie and although they both had cokes in their refrigerators at home, they walked to Nibley's and ordered cokes. Plain cokes, not those chocolate coke floats they used to order. This was a splurge for Julie, who had been dieting for four days and should have ordered tomato juice.

An earnest-looking boy in the front booth was holding the attention of the crowd. "And so I went up to my counselor," he was saying, "and I said, 'Why can't I know what my I.Q. is? After all, it's my I.Q.,' and he told me if I found out I had a real low I.Q. of about twenty-seven or something I might get discouraged and quit studying."

The boy paused, and the two girls exchanged a

quick glance. "I've simply got to find time to wash my hair before we go to the city for dinner with Stan and Buzz," remarked Julie, in a voice that was not exactly loud but nicely calculated to carry to the crowd around them.

"And my counselor said if I found out I was a genius I would think I was so good I would quit studying anyhow," the boy continued, but his audience was losing interest.

"I wish I had a yellow blouse," said Jane, as if she were completely unaware of the interest others were taking in their conversation. "Stan always likes me in yellow."

"So then my counselor said, 'I'll tell you one thing. Your I.Q. is over a hundred,'" the boy went on, but now no one was listening.

The faces reflected in the mirror behind the milkshake machines revealed that the girls around them were wishing they had dates for dinner in the city too, and that they were sure to spread the news to every girl in Woodmont. Jane and Julie left Nibley's feeling that they had enjoyed an unusually pleasant afternoon.

On Friday Stan came by to drive Jane to a babysitting job—an easy job this time, sitting with a baby who slept most of the time and whose mother only went out between feedings and who always left a snack for the sitter. It was really an ideal job and Jane was glad, because she did not want anything to intrude into her lovely glow of anticipation.

"I'm sure glad you can go tomorrow," said Stan, when it was time for Jane to get out of the truck.

"I'm glad too," said Jane shyly, hopping to the ground. "I know we're going to have a wonderful time."

And the next day was Saturday.

CHAPTER

5

By QUARTER to six on Saturday Jane, who had been too excited to eat lunch, was ready. She sat on the edge of the sofa in her carefully pressed suit, pulled on her white gloves, and after a few minutes pulled them off. Then she put them on again, decided they made her feel as if her hands belonged to Minnie Mouse, and peeled them off a second time. Perhaps some day she would learn to wear gloves gracefully.

Promptly at six o'clock the doorbell rang. "Be still, my heart!" Mr. Purdy laid his hand over his heart and spoke in an exaggerated whisper.

"Pop!" implored Jane, as she opened the front door.

Never had Jane seen Stan look so attractive. He had a fresh, scrubbed appearance and was wearing a gray flannel suit, a white shirt that set off his tan, and a green tie, just the right color for his greenish eyes. Jane stood smiling at him with admiration and sensed at once that something was wrong. Stan was painfully embarrassed.

"Uh . . . Jane." Stan hesitated and then went on. "At the last minute Dad had to use the car on a business trip, and Greg and Buzz couldn't get their cars either and . . . well, my cousin said I could . . . uh . . . take the Doggie Diner truck. I . . . I hope you don't mind going in the truck."

Jane was engulfed in disappointment. Driving to the city on a special date in a truck, especially the Doggie Diner truck—how perfectly awful! But the expression on Stan's face quickly made her stifle her own feelings. His eyes were pleading with her not to mind, to be a good sport about riding in the truck.

Jane was filled with sudden sympathy for Stan. She could not let him down. "Of course I don't mind," she managed to say gaily. "What difference does it make? It has four wheels and a motor, doesn't it? That's all that really counts." Her reward was Stan's smile of relief. Darling Stan. What difference did it make what they rode in, as long as they were together?

When she climbed into the front seat, Jane saw that Greg and Buzz were already sitting on cushions in the back of the truck. Buzz whistled when he saw her. "Hey, don't you look nice!"

"You're looking sharp yourself," Jane flashed back at him. It always helped a girl to have a boy whistle at her.

The first stop was Marcy's house, a new house in the hill section of Woodmont. When Marcy walked out to the truck with Greg, she stopped and laughed. "No!" she exclaimed. "We aren't really going in the Doggie Diner truck! How perfectly marvelous!"

Out of the corner of her eye Jane could see Stan's face turn red. Shut up, Marcy, she thought fiercely; can't you see Stan is embarrassed enough as it is?

"Isn't this a scream?" Marcy went on, as she climbed into the truck beside Jane. "Isn't this the funniest thing you ever heard of?"

If it were somebody else who was going to the city in the truck, Jane admitted to herself, she would think it was funny. But since it was Stan who had got them into this situation she could not laugh. She smiled reassuringly at Stan, but his eyes were on the road. Sitting beside him made Jane feel pleasantly possessive and a little important, because her date was the driver. It made up for sharing the seat with Marcy, who was wearing an expensively casual tweed suit with a plain silk blouse and pumps with real high heels. Jane began to feel that her own dainty blouse with tucks and a round collar looked like a baby dress and that her suit was too obviously her best suit. Beside Marcy she felt as prim as . . . well, as prim as Miss Muffet.

The last stop was Julie's house, because Julie lived near the entrance to the freeway. When she came out to the truck with Buzz, Jane saw that she was wearing high heels, which made her taller than Buzz, and that her hands did not look natural in her white gloves. She has the Minnie Mouse look too, thought Jane, and she's wearing a girdle because of her straight skirt. Poor Julie. Unaccustomed to her high heels, Julie turned her ankle, and Buzz caught her by the elbow.

Please, please, Julie, thought Jane, don't make fun of the truck. Don't embarrass Stan. Julie shot Jane a questioning glance. "Hi, everybody," was all she said, as she climbed into the back of the truck with Greg and Buzz. Jane relaxed. From now on, in spite of the truck, everything would be as wonderful as they had planned. Suddenly she was hungry, and she remembered that she had skipped lunch.

Jane felt excitement rising within her as the truck left Woodmont and climbed the approach to the bridge that crossed the bay. Through the sunset haze the city at the opposite end of the span looked unreal to Jane. It seemed like an imaginary city, a magic city, a city that had appeared from the mists and might disappear if she closed her eyes for a moment.

"What shall we have to eat?" Buzz asked from the back of the truck. "Shark's fins?"

"How about carp?" suggested Greg.

Leave it to Buzz to mention food right away, thought Jane, remembering the times he had robbed her of her cooking samples in the seventh grade. Then it occurred to her that goldfish were a kind of carp, but she could not believe they would really have goldfish for dinner. She pictured a platter of fried goldfish garnished with lemon and parsley. It was not an appetizing thought.

"Or fried octopuses," said Buzz.

"You mean octopi," corrected Marcy over her shoulder, and everyone laughed. Everyone but Jane. She was beginning to remember reading that the Chinese ate some strange things.

"Anyway, don't you mean squid?" asked Marcy.

"Don't forget bird's-nest soup," added Stan.

"Ugh!" This was Julie's first contribution to the conversation.

"It's all right." Greg was comforting. "They don't use any old bird's nest. They use special birds' nests."

"How about thousand-year-old eggs?" put in Buzz.

Jane, her appetite diminishing rapidly, suppressed a shudder.

"What's the matter, Jane?" Buzz asked. "Don't you like eggs that are really ripe?"

"Make mine three-minute eggs," answered Jane, who had made up her mind not to let Buzz tease her.

"Buzz, you mean hundred-year-old eggs," corrected Julie. "And anyway, they aren't really a hundred years old. I had to read a book about China for a book report, and it said the eggs were really only about a hundred days old. They just *call* them hundred-year-old eggs. And they aren't rotten. They are salted or pickled or something. Anyway, the book said they are very good."

Isn't that just dandy, thought Jane. Only a hundred days old.

"I know what," said Buzz. "Let's have flied lice."

This was too much for Jane. "They don't really eat lice, do they?" she cried in alarm.

Everyone shouted with laughter. " 'They don't really eat lice, do they?' " mimicked Buzz, and they all laughed again.

"Don't pay any attention to him," whispered Stan. "He thinks he's saying fried rice with a Chinese accent, but I have lots of Chinese friends in the city and I never heard anyone talk that way."

"Oh." Jane felt the blood rush to her face. How could she be so stupid? Determined not to be laughed at again, she took a firm grip on her sophistication.

"Which restaurant shall we go to?" Greg asked.

"How about that one on the corner up over the shop with the Chinese furniture?" suggested Marcy.

"That's a tourist trap," objected Buzz. "Let's go to a real Chinese restaurant."

"Yes, one where the Chinese eat," agreed Stan. "I know a good one at the far end of Chinatown. Hing Sun Yee's."

"Hey, I know that one." Buzz sounded enthusiastic. "I've eaten there several times. It isn't very fancy, but the food is swell."

"Let's try it," said Greg.

"Yes, let's." Jane added a small murmur to the enthusiastic agreement of the others. After all she had heard about bird's-nest soup and hundred-year-old eggs, she secretly thought a restaurant popular with tourists might have been a safer choice. Some of the talk was joking, she knew; but how much, she could not be sure.

When they reached Chinatown, Stan was unable to find a parking space in the narrow crowded streets. Around and around he drove, uphill and downhill, creeping and stopping, creeping and stopping in the heavy traffic, past a housing project, barber shops, a mortuary, laundries, chair-caning shops, around and around, up and down, creeping and stopping.

When at last Stan spotted a space in front of a hardware store, he said, "It will be a tight squeeze, but I think I can make it."

I hope so, thought Jane fervently. Backward and forward Stan maneuvered the truck, an inch at a time, it seemed to Jane, or even a half inch at a time, until he finally had it parked.

"Let's go. I'm starved," said Buzz. "Lead me to that bird's-nest soup."

Stan led the way down a dingy street unfamiliar to Jane. They passed an herb shop, its walls lined with drawers and its windows filled with glass jars displaying weird-looking specimens. What are those withered things, Jane wondered. Toads, newts, sala-

manders, pieces of unicorn horn? Don't be silly, she
told herself. They are probably just dried seaweed,
or something.

They paused to look at a Chinese grocery with its
bundles of thin beans, baskets of flat green peas, a
tank of turtles, another of gaping catfish, dishpans

full of clams and snails. I won't look, Jane told herself. I just won't look.

A neon sign above the door marked Hing Sun
Yee's restaurant. In the window was a row of ducks
that had been roasted whole and were now displayed hanging by their heads. As Stan guided Jane
into the restaurant, the man at the cash register
seized one of the ducks, tossed it onto a chopping
block, and hacked it to pieces with a cleaver. Jane
hastily looked away. The room, which had a cement
floor and a low ceiling, was filled with marble-
topped tables. Seated at several of the tables were
elderly Chinese men who were wearing hats and
eating with chopsticks.

"Hi, Tom," Stan said to the young waiter who
came forward to meet them. "How about a booth?"

"Sure," said Tom. "Golly, Stan, I haven't seen you
for a long time."

"I live in Woodmont now," Stan explained. "We
don't get over here very often."

"We'll sure miss you at school," Tom said, as he
showed them into a booth.

Jane entered first, then Stan, followed by Marcy,
who slid into a chair beside him. Jane would have
preferred to have Julie sit on the other side of Stan.
When they were all seated at the round table, Tom

handed them menus and left, pulling a red curtain across the entrance to the booth.

Buzz picked up a cruet filled with brown liquid from the center of the table. "Good old beetle juice," he remarked.

It isn't really beetle juice, Jane told herself. She spread the menu on the marble table top and looked at it in bewilderment. It was filled with Chinese characters and words that were unfamiliar to her. Chow yuke, fried won ton, polo pai gwat sounded terrible to her. From the chopping block she heard the crunch of little bones. Stop being ridiculous, she said to herself. American dishes like hush puppies or her mother's casserole, "It Smells to Heaven," would probably sound distasteful to the Chinese. It was only a question of what you were used to.

"Let's each order a dish and then pass them around," suggested Stan. "What would you like?" he asked, turning to Jane. He looked so enthusiastic that Jane longed desperately to feel the same way.

"How about some flied lice?" Buzz asked wickedly, his eye on Jane.

Determined not to let the others know how she felt, Jane made a face at Buzz and said, "I'd like chow mein."

"Oh, no," protested Marcy, swinging her blond

hair away from her face. "Only tourists eat chow mein."

I guess I said the wrong thing, thought Jane uncomfortably.

"You should get something special here." Buzz agreed with Marcy. "You can get chow mein any place."

"That's all right," said Stan. "If Jane likes chow mein, she shall have it."

Jane smiled gratefully at him. For Stan's sake she must hide her misgivings. She could not let their first big date turn into a disappointment for him.

Tom appeared with six handleless cups and a battered enamel pot filled with tea, which Stan poured while Tom wrote down the orders in Chinese characters. "Forks or chopsticks?" he asked with a grin.

"Chopsticks," the boys all said at once. Jane and Julie exchanged an anxious look before Jane bent her head to sip her tea. Good old familiar tea.

Stan held up his cup. "Here's to next semester."

"To next semester." They all raised their cups and drank the toast.

Tom set plates before them and carried in dish after dish of food—bowls of strange sauces, platters heaped with crinkled brown objects, mysterious mixtures of unknown foods. Jane, unable to identify even her own order, glanced across the table at Julie, but Julie did not appear to be worried. Everyone was looking at the bowls and platters with anticipation. Everyone but me, thought Jane miserably. The memory of the herb shop and the produce market floated through her mind. Whacking, crunching sounds came from the chopping block. Jane struggled to subdue her imagination.

"Shrimp roll!" exclaimed Julie. "I adore it. It's practically my favorite food."

"Here's your flied lice, Jane." Buzz handed her a dish.

"Thanks. I can hardly wait." Jane managed to put a note of gaiety in her voice and helped herself to one spoonful. At least she knew it was rice. That was something. As the dishes were passed around she served herself the smallest possible portions and hoped the others would not notice. One dish, especially strange-looking, made her pause, however. It was a thick red sauce in which floated pieces of onion, green pepper, and what appeared to be tiny brown hands. "What's this?" she asked lightly, as if she were merely curious.

"Sauce for the won ton," Greg explained.

"Oh," said Jane. That did not tell her much. Jane ladled a small spoonful onto her plate. Now if she only knew which was the won ton, and should she pour the sauce over it or dunk the won ton in the sauce? And what on earth could those floating things be that looked like little brown hands?

When everyone was served, Buzz picked up the cruet again and poured some of the soy sauce over his rice. "Have some beetle juice," he remarked, as he handed the cruet to Jane.

Telling herself it couldn't really be beetle juice, Jane cautiously poured two drops on her rice. Well, she thought, now I've got to start eating. She watched the others pick up their chopsticks and tried to hold hers the same way. She picked up a few grains of rice, but she could not control the bamboo sticks and the rice dribbled back to her plate. She took a firmer grip and tried to pick up a piece of green pepper from the won ton sauce. It slipped from between the sticks. Telling herself this could not be so difficult—millions of Chinese ate with chopsticks every day, didn't they—she tried again, got a tenuous hold on the pepper, and raised it from her plate toward her mouth. The chopsticks separated and the pepper went sliding down the front of her blouse into her lap.

How awful, Jane thought, as she picked up the pepper with her fingers and slipped it back onto her plate. With her paper napkin she scrubbed at the stain and succeeded only in smearing it through the sheer fabric onto her slip. Miserable, she glanced around to see if the others had noticed. Julie, who had laid down her chopsticks and was surreptitiously tugging at the top of her girdle, cast Jane a glance of sympathy, which Jane returned. Poor Julie, her girdle was cutting into her waist. Buzz and Greg were eating hungrily and Marcy, her sunbleached hair falling against one cheek, was talking to Stan as if she were alone with him.

Jane studied her plate carefully for something familiar that was not dripping with red sauce and that did not look slippery. She settled on what she decided must be the shrimp roll that Julie liked so much. It was made of shredded lettuce, shrimp, and several unknown ingredients covered with a golden crust and cut in bite-sized slices. Concentrating on the shrimp and lettuce and trying not to think what else might be in it, she slipped one chopstick through the crust, bent over her plate, and popped the bit into her mouth. Instantly she was sorry. "Oh!" she gasped as tears filled her eyes, and she clapped her napkin over her mouth. The shrimp roll was unbearably hot.

"What's the matter?" Stan turned away from Marcy.

Jane gulped and sipped her tepid tea. "I didn't know it would be so hot," she said. Because she didn't want to let Stan down, she added bravely, "It was delicious, though."

Buzz dipped into the red sauce and held up one of the little brown hands. "What do you suppose this is?" he asked.

"Sh-h," giggled Marcy. "You'll frighten Jane."

Leave it to Marcy, thought Jane bitterly. If she wasn't fooling Marcy she didn't suppose she was making the others think she was having fun, either. How awful could this evening get, anyway? Maybe some day she would look back and laugh and say, "I'll never forget that awful night a bunch of us had dinner at Hing Sun Yee's in Chinatown." But this was not some day. It was now and she was miserable. Her head was beginning to ache, she could not enjoy the food and, worst of all, she felt lonely and left out. Stan talked more to Marcy than to her. Not that she blamed him. Nobody could expect a boy to enjoy the company of a girl who hadn't learned to like Chinese food, who couldn't even pretend enthusiasm, and who spilled things all over her clothes like a two-year-old. Her first grown-up date was ruined and probably her friendship with Stan, too.

Buzz grinned at Jane. "What's the matter, aren't you hungry?" he asked.

Suddenly Jane was piqued with Buzz for teasing her about flied lice and beetle juice. Maybe Stan was losing interest in her, but she was not going to let Buzz get her down any longer. She looked him in the eye and said coolly, "It's just that your appetite is so big it makes mine look small."

Buzz seemed taken aback at his failure to get a rise out of Jane, and the others laughed.

Encouraged by Buzz's reaction, Jane went on. "After all, Buzz, if you could eat my seventh-grade cooking samples, I'm sure you could eat anything, even million-year-old eggs."

This time everyone laughed at Buzz. "O.K., Jane, you win this time," he said, in a way that made Jane wonder how he would try to tease her next.

Somehow Jane got through the rest of the meal. While the others ate heartily, she was able to pick out a few familiar bits from her plate—an almond, a flat green pea pod, a sliver of pork—and convey them unsteadily to her mouth with the chopsticks. She was glad when Tom removed their plates and set down a plate of cookies and brought a fresh pot of tea. The hot drink hurt her burned tongue, but she did not care. The meal was such a dismal failure that nothing mattered any more. There was no use even trying to pretend. She had spoiled Stan's date—the date he had meant to be so special—and he would never ask her for another. She looked sadly at him, as if he had already gone out of her life. Dear Stan, it was nice knowing you, she thought, and it was such fun for a little while until I spoiled everything.

"Hey, Jane, wake up!" Jane was nudged out of her thoughts by Buzz, who was passing her the plate of fortune cookies. "Take one," he said, "and find out all about your future." She took one and handed the plate to Stan. She should be able to eat a Chinese cookie. She had eaten them many times at birthday parties when she was a little girl.

Marcy broke open her cookie. "Listen to this. I'm going to have a career," she said. She read aloud from the slip of paper that had been inside her cookie. " 'You will be offered a high executive position with an attractive salary.' "

Stan laughed. "Marcy would rather have an attractive boss."

"I hate you, Stan," drawled Marcy, in a voice that told everyone she did not hate him at all. Jane and Julie exchanged a quick look. Marcy and her line!

"What does yours say, Julie?" Buzz asked.

Julie broke open her cookie. " 'Someone is speak-

ing well of you,'" she read, and sighed. "It's probably a dear old aunt."

"I'll bet it's that boy you met at the mountains,"
said Jane loyally. Julie had not met a boy when she
went to the mountains with her family, but it would
not hurt Buzz to think she had.

"'You will be called to fill a position of high honor
and responsibility,'" read Greg from his slip.

"Congratulations!" exclaimed Buzz. "I knew you'd
get to be student-body president some day. Hey,
listen to my fortune. Marcy isn't the only one who's
going to be rich. 'You will win prizes in contests testing your ability to answer questions.'"

"It doesn't say you'll be rich," scoffed Stan. "It
just says you'll win prizes. Probably a case of tooth
paste or a year's supply of detergent."

"And it doesn't say first prizes," Marcy pointed
out. "Maybe you'll win a pie in the face because you
don't know the answers."

"You're just jealous because you aren't quiz
kids," Buzz said smugly. "What does yours say,
Stan?"

Stan broke open his cookie and read, "'Your place
in the path of life is in the driver's seat.'"

"Right in the front seat of the Doggie Diner
truck," said Marcy, and everyone laughed.

"I don't expect to make the Doggie Diner my career in the path of life," Stan told Marcy. "Jane, it's your turn."

Hoping that her fortune would be a good omen, Jane snapped open her cookie and unfolded the slip of paper. " 'Prepare for a short journey,' " she read.

"All the way back to Woodmont," observed Marcy, and munched her cookie.

"How short can a journey get?" remarked Greg.

That's right, thought Jane. Prepare for a short journey back to Woodmont and right out of Stan's life. I'll bet Marcy can hardly wait.

"Let's prepare for Jane's short journey by getting out of here," said Stan. "We still have time to go for a walk through Chinatown."

When they left the restaurant, they found that fog had settled over the city and was swirling through the narrow streets. Foghorns were bleating and groaning down by the bay. Saddened by the sounds, Jane shivered in her light suit.

"We'll meet you at the truck in forty-five minutes," said Stan to the other couples as he put his hand on Jane's elbow. "Come on, Jane, let's go window-shopping."

Should she apologize for not enjoying the Chinese dinner, Jane wondered, as she and Stan strolled up the street together. Too dispirited to say anything at all, she walked beside Stan past the Chinese shops toward the tourist end of Chinatown. Maybe tomorrow she would be able to think what to say, but tonight she was too heartsick to do anything but wander through the fog.

"Here we are," Stan said, breaking their silence as he led Jane into a warm shop that smelled of incense. He seemed to be looking for something among the vases and bowls and embroidered slippers, but Jane had lost interest in everything but her own unhappiness. Stan selected a bamboo back-scratcher from several stuck in a brass teapot and handed the proprietor some change.

"Here," Stan said, offering the back-scratcher to Jane with a smile. "A present for you."

"For me?" exclaimed Jane in amazement, as she took the bamboo implement and stared at the little hand carved at the end of the long handle. "A back-scratcher for me?"

"Yes, for you. Buying a back-scratcher in Chinatown is practically compulsory, didn't you know? All the tourists do it."

Jane looked up at Stan and laughed, partly from amusement and partly because she was filled with a wonderful feeling of relief. Stan had bought her a back-scratcher! Maybe he wasn't disappointed in her after all.

"I think there may even be a law that says buying a back-scratcher in Chinatown is compulsory," Stan went on, and he and Jane laughed together.

They wandered out of the shop and on down the street through the swirling fog and now Jane was warmed by their laughter. In front of an ordinary American restaurant, the kind with a counter, a juke-box, and half a dozen booths, Stan turned and looked directly at Jane. "You didn't have a good time at dinner, did you?" he asked.

Hot with embarrassment, Jane looked down at the sidewalk. She did not want to answer.

"Did you?" Stan persisted.

Jane looked up at him and shook her head. She had to be honest with Stan. "It was just that it was all so strange," she said. "I never ate in a real Chinese restaurant before. It wasn't—quite what I expected."

"I'm sorry," Stan said contritely. "I should have thought. I remember I felt the same way the first time I went there."

Surprised and touched by his apology, Jane smiled at Stan. He didn't think she was a poor sport. He blamed himself for spoiling her evening, when all the time she had been worrying because she had spoiled his. "I can't say I enjoyed it, but at the same time I'm not sorry we went there," Jane told him. "I guess you would call it an—an interesting experience."

Stan no longer looked worried. "I've felt that way about things myself," he said, and glanced toward the restaurant. "I'll bet you're hungry. How about a plain old American hamburger?"

Suddenly Jane was ravenous. "I would adore a plain old American hamburger," she said joyfully, and went into the restaurant with Stan.

They sat at the counter, and after Stan had ordered a hamburger and a glass of milk for Jane, he swiveled his stool around so that he faced her. With a finger tip he touched a lock of her hair. "You have little drops of fog clinging to your hair," he told her.

"Do I?" Jane's hand flew to her fog-damp hair and she glanced at the mirror behind the counter.

"You know something?" said Stan.

"What?" asked Jane.

"You're different from most girls."

"Am I?"

"Yes. You were so swell about having to go in the truck."

"I was sort of surprised," Jane admitted, "but I didn't really mind."

"Most girls would have made me feel I'd spoiled

their evening, because riding to the city in a Doggie
Diner truck was beneath their dignity or something.
Or they would be like Marcy and make fun of it. But
with you it didn't really matter that I couldn't get
the car."

Jane looked shyly down at the counter and ran
her finger along the design in the handle of the back-
scratcher—the precious back-scratcher, her present
from Stan. "No, it really didn't," she whispered. She
picked up the hamburger the waitress set before her
and, as she bit hungrily into it, her eyes met Stan's
in the mirror. Stan was smiling at her.

CHAPTER

6

"LOVE me on Monday, but don't love me one day. Love me on Tuesday . . ." Jane sang in a throaty voice as she tossed her schoolbooks onto her bed. She pulled a comb through her hair and, smiling dreamily, paused to run a finger over the design on her back-scratcher, now tied to her mirror with a red ribbon. Then she kicked off her shoes and plopped herself cross-legged on the bed. English and French and math assignments could wait. Jane was knitting Stan a pair of Argyle socks for Christmas.

With awkward fingers she untangled the bobbins of green and yellow yarn and, after reading the directions twice to make sure, began to knit from a ball of gray wool. "Love me on Tuesday, don't make it a blues day," she hummed happily, as she thought back over the first week of school. It had been a wonderful week. All her daydreams had come true and, in the matter of locker assignments, had even been improved upon by the administration of Woodmont High. Stan's locker was almost directly across the hall from hers. This stroke of good luck was something not even Jane had dreamed of, and she marveled at it several times a day when she saw Stan across the hall. Another piece of good fortune was that Stan's history class met in the room next to her French class. They even had the same lunch period and although Stan ate with a group of boys and Jane with several girls, they usually met on the lawn toward the end of the period and walked to their lockers together.

This was enough to establish Jane as Stan's girl in the eyes of Woodmont High, and because she was Stan's girl, Jane floated through the week in an aura of joy. She was no longer Jane Purdy, onlooker. She was Jane Purdy, Stan Crandall's girl. She belonged. The other students watched her walk down the hall beside Stan and thought, Jane and Stan. . . . And she was able to say, "Stan and I. . . ." Memories floated through Jane's mind. Stan holding the handle of the drinking fountain for her. Stan sitting beside her on the front steps of the school, the golden-brown hair on his arms glinting in the sunlight. The touch of his identification bracelet against her wrist as his arm brushed hers in the crowded hall. Stan's greenish eyes smiling down at her as he leaned against her locker, or waited for her outside her French room, or stood in the same line in the cafeteria. Oh, it had been a wonderful week.

Jane paused to untangle the bobbins that dangled from her knitting, and her eye fell on the first issue of the *Woodmontonian,* which had slipped out of her notebook when she tossed her books onto the bed. Listed in a box in the center of the front page were the school social activities for the semester. Jane put down her knitting and picked up the paper. The list began with a tea to introduce the freshmen to the faculty (thank goodness, she was past *that* stage). Next was an informal dance to be held in the school gymnasium on Friday night, just one week away. This was followed by the junior-class steak bake and movie in Woodmont Park the first week in October, a show put on by all the school clubs in November, and a Christmas formal in December.

An informal dance a week away. Jane read the story in the left-hand column of the paper, which told about the dance: music by Bob Starr and his All-Stars, a girl singer who had made a record that was tenth place on the Hit Parade, the members of the ticket committee and the decorating committee. Dreamily Jane went on with her knitting, unaware that she was working yellow wool into her pattern when she should have been using green. She saw herself circling the Woodmont High gym floor in Stan's arms and she would wear . . . She did not know what she would wear, but she was sure of one thing. She had enough baby-sitting money to buy a pair of shoes with real high heels, beautiful airy shoes—heels, thin soles, and wisps of leather to hold them on her feet, shoes so light she would scarcely know she was wearing them as she whirled in Stan's arms.

Of course, Stan had not actually asked her to go to the dance yet. . . . Jane dismissed this detail from her mind. When a boy sees a girl every day and takes her to dinner in the city and buys her a back-scratcher and notices the fog on her hair, naturally he asks her to go to the first school dance. He just hadn't got around to it yet. And this time maybe he could take the family car.

Just before dinner on Saturday the telephone rang. "*Arf-arf!*" barked Mr. Purdy. Since the night Jane had ridden to the city in the Doggie Diner truck, he had taken to barking every time the telephone or doorbell rang.

"Pop! Really!" protested Jane good-naturedly, as she went hopefully to the telephone. Honestly, the things that amused her father!

It was not Stan but Julie who was calling. "Jane, guess what!" Julie was in an obvious state of excitement. "Buzz asked me to go to the dance next Friday!"

"Julie! Did he really? How perfectly wonderful!" Jane was happy for her, not only because Julie was her best friend but because now she and Stan could trade dances with Buzz and Julie and perhaps see less of Marcy and whatever boy she chose to go with. Somehow, Jane did not like to think of Stan's dancing with Marcy.

"Stan has asked you to go, hasn't he?" Julie wanted to know.

"Not exactly," said Jane cautiously. "Not yet, but I'm seeing him tonight. We're going to the movies."

"And Jane," Julie went on, too engrossed in her own anticipation to notice Jane's hesitation, "Buzz's dad says he can take the car that night!"

"What wonderful luck!" agreed Jane.

"If Stan can't get his car maybe we could double-date," Julie suggested.

"That would be fun," answered Jane, "but I hope he can get the car."

That evening on the way to the movies and afterwards at Nibley's and on the walk home, Jane waited for Stan to mention the dance. He was unusually talkative and told her about the different dogs on his route—the pair of Dalmatians that waited for him and the boxer that chased the truck so far he often had to give the dog a ride home—but he did not mention the dance. Oh, well, thought Jane, that's how men are. He's probably taking it for granted. She found it very pleasant to be taken for granted by Stan.

By Monday morning it was impossible for any student to ignore the fact that Woodmont High was having a dance on Friday night. Posters in the shape of autumn leaves and footballs appeared on every bulletin board, banners were hung across the halls, and a reminder to get your tickets now, one dollar per couple, was printed in the daily bulletin. When Stan walked across the hall to Jane's locker to say hello, she said, "The dance committee must have put in a lot of hard work over the week end to get all these posters up."

"It sure did," agreed Stan. "Well, so long. I've got to pick up a reserved book at the libe before class."

Jane stood with her hand on her locker door,

looking uncertainly after Stan as he made his way through the crowd in the direction of the library. It almost seemed as if he had been in a hurry to get away from her when she mentioned the dance. Naturally he was in a hurry, she told herself. He didn't have time to stand around talking when he had to go to the library, check out a book, and walk downstairs again before first period. Still . . .

"What are you looking so wistful about?" asked Liz Galpin, who had been assigned to share the locker with Jane. Liz was also a member of Manuscript. She submitted pieces entitled "Life and Death: a Dialogue" or simply "Hokku." A hokku was a Japanese poem that had seventeen syllables. When Jane tried to write a hokku it always turned out to have sixteen or twenty syllables, never seventeen.

"Was I looking wistful?" Jane answered lightly. I didn't know it showed, she thought. There was something about Liz, with her dark-rimmed glasses and her hair chopped off any old way, as if it didn't matter how she looked, that made Jane feel fluffy and not very bright.

"You looked positively lovelorn," said Liz as she stowed a couple of thin books, poetry probably, in their locker.

"It must be something I ate," answered Jane, trying to look bored like Marcy. She closed the locker, snapped shut the combination lock, and was about to go to her first-period study hall when she saw George, the old family friend, coming purposefully toward her.

"Hi," she said, wondering why he was taking the trouble to cross the crowded hall to speak to her.

"Hello, Jane," he said. "How about going to the dance with me Friday night?" He spoke rapidly, as if he were anxious to get the words out of the way.

Jane could feel the blood rush to her face. She had been so engrossed in Stan that it had never occurred to her anyone else might ask her to go to the dance. By this time she thought it was obvious to everyone at Woodmont High that she was Stan's girl. But apparently it was not obvious to George, who was probably so busy with his rock collection and his chemistry experiments that he hadn't noticed. That was George for you—oblivious, buried in science, with that lock of hair sticking up as usual.

What an awful situation! How perfectly awful! Jane ran one finger down the louvers on her locker and stared at the floor while she tried to think what

to say that would not hurt George's feelings, yet would leave her free to go to the dance with Stan. She had to choose her words with care. Going to the dance with George was out of the question. Loping around the gym trying to appear two inches shorter than she was, when she had dreamed of whirling in Stan's arms in her first high heels! It was impossible.

If she said she already had a date with Stan she wouldn't be telling the truth and George might know it. If she said she was busy Friday evening and then George took another girl to the dance and she turned up with Stan—well, that wouldn't do either. But she couldn't just stand there. She had to say something. "I—I'm sorry, George," she said at last. "I already have a date for Friday night." And she told herself she did—almost.

"Well, O.K. Some other time maybe." George's face was as flushed with embarrassment as Jane's.

He knows, thought Jane miserably. George had guessed that she didn't want to go with him and that she didn't really have a date. He might be oblivious about a lot of things, but he wasn't stupid.

They stood facing one another, Jane ashamed to have hurt George's feelings and George embarrassed to have his feelings hurt, uncertain of what to say next, until the sound of the first bell clanging through the hall rescued them.

"See you around," muttered George, and disappeared into the stream of students moving toward their classrooms.

Well, I don't care, thought Jane defiantly. I do have a date—sort of. And anyway, she had always suspected George's mother made him take her out, because she was an old friend of the family; his mother probably told him she was a sweet, sensible girl. But Jane did care. Because she had hurt the feelings of someone she liked, she felt uneasy and uncomfortable all the rest of the day. On the way home from school she walked past the shoe store without stopping to search the windows for the dancing shoes she dreamed about—the delicate shoes with heels, soles, and mere wisps of leather to hold them to her feet. Darn Stan anyway.

By Tuesday morning Jane was cheerful again. This was the day Stan would mention the dance. He had just forgotten—men were so absent-minded about such things—and had been carrying the tickets in his wallet all the time.

As usual he crossed the hall to her locker and said, "Hi, Jane."

"Hi," she said, and waited.

"Old Hargrave is really piling it on in math," he said. "I thought I was going to be up all night on his assignment."

Plainly Stan was not thinking about the dance and yet Jane did not see how he could forget it, when the whole school was plastered with banners and posters and cardboard autumn leaves.

Later in the morning a girl in Jane's algebra class remarked wistfully, "I suppose you're going to the dance with Stan."

Jane smiled and said nothing. A smile could mean anything.

"Of course you're going to the dance with Stan," said another girl, in the cafeteria during lunch period.

"Could be," said Jane. "I hope they're serving lemon pie today."

"You're sure lucky," answered the girl. "I wish a new boy would turn up for me."

Jane realized the situation was getting complicated. She could not honestly say she was going to the dance with Stan, and neither could she say she was not going with him. Her pride would not let her admit to anyone that she had not been asked. It would be all over school in half an hour. Everyone would talk and wonder. The boys would think she wasn't any fun on a date and the girls would start inviting Stan to parties and asking him to help them with their math. And what would she be doing? Drinking cokes with the girls on Saturday nights.

It was while she was playing volley ball during her gym class that Jane made up her mind that she could not stand this uncertainty any longer. A few minutes before, while she was changing into her shirt and shorts in the locker room, two girls had asked her what she was going to wear Friday night. Waiting her turn to serve, Jane decided that when Stan walked down the hall with her between sixth and seventh periods she would bring up the dance once more and find out for certain whether she had a date or not. She was sure she did—well, pretty sure—but she wanted to hear Stan say so himself. Satisfied that she had at least made a decision, Jane gave the volley ball a vicious whack that sent it out of bounds.

That afternoon when Stan met Jane outside her French class she said gaily, *"Bonjour."*

Stan grinned at her. *"Onjourbay,"* he answered. "French pig Latin. How's that for class?"

Jane laughed, but her thoughts were fixed on bringing up the subject of the dance. Her mouth was dry, and all the gay, casual remarks she had composed during her French class had slipped away from her. If this continued much longer she was sure to flunk everything. Only a few minutes ago she had not bothered to look up *colère* in the vocabulary and had translated *"Il était emporté par sa colère"* as "He was dragged away by his collar," when it should have been "He was carried away by his anger." The laughter of the class still rang in her ears.

Silently the two made their way through the stream of students toward Jane's English classroom. I've got to say something, Jane thought wildly. Something light, something casual, something that would let her know for sure and yet not reveal to Stan how important this was to her.

When they reached the door of Room 214, Jane turned to Stan. This was the moment. Somehow, words came out of her mouth, and they were not at all the words she had meant to speak. "George asked me to go to the dance Friday, but I said I already had a date," she blurted out.

An expression—could it be relief?—crossed Stan's face. "Hey, that's swell!" Stan was enthusiastic about something; just what, Jane was not sure. She stared at him, shocked by his reaction.

"If you have a date we can trade dances," Stan went on.

"But I don't," Jane cried out in spite of herself. "I thought—"

The bell clanging through the hall stopped Jane from saying any more, but she could not help giving Stan one stricken look. His expression changed from enthusiasm to bewilderment, embarrassment, and, worst of all—how could she bear it?—pity. Silently Jane fled into Room 214, and Miss Locke, her English teacher, closed the door behind her.

The efforts of Miss Locke to teach clear thinking in English composition were wasted on Jane during the next hour. Squinting modifiers, dangling participles—who cared? All she could think about was herself and Stan. Now it was all so painfully clear. Now, when it was too late to undo what she had done. Stan had asked another girl (What girl? Who could she be?) to go to the dance, when she had assumed he would ask her. And she had let him know she expected him to ask her, and now he felt sorry for her. Never in her life had Jane felt so hurt, so humiliated.

Of course Stan had a right to ask anyone he pleased to the dance. But she had thought . . . she had wanted . . . she had been so sure. He was

everything she liked in a boy. Oh, how could Miss
Locke stand there and go on about squinting modifiers? How could she care? The irony of it all, having to sit through Miss Locke's lesson in clear thinking after she had been so dumb! Stan was so nice
to be with and she had been so sure . . . But she
had no right to be sure. She knew that now. If
only she had known it before she spoke to Stan.
Stan, who now felt sorry for her, poor little Jane
Purdy, the girl who got her hopes up, just because
he had had a few dates with her and had bought
her a back-scratcher. A back-scratcher! How silly
it seemed now. How could she have taken it so seriously? A back-scratcher!

But even though Stan had asked some other girl
to go to the dance, even though he felt sorry for
her, Jane could not dislike Stan. It wasn't his fault
she was so stupid. She could never, never face him
again, but she still liked him. She would avoid him
in the hall, keep her books in Julie's locker, forget
him if she could. A few dates, and one wonderful
week at school, and now she was no longer Jane
Purdy, Stan's girl, a girl who belonged. She was
plain Jane Purdy, a nice girl but nobody special.
It was all over.

Now if she were the kind of girl Marcy was,

nothing like this would ever happen. If she were like Marcy, Stan would want to take her to the dance and would have asked her for a date way ahead to be sure no other boy would ask her first. And then the thought came to Jane that Stan might be taking Marcy to the dance. She remembered the way they had talked together in the Chinese restaurant. But no, he couldn't be taking Marcy. She would have heard about it before now—unless everyone was trying to keep it from her so her feelings wouldn't be hurt.

Jane stared blankly at the blackboard while Miss Locke wrote with squeaking chalk, "Some members of the class I know are not paying attention." Miss Locke always liked to relate her examples to the experience of her students. Several girls laughed politely.

"Jane," said Miss Locke, pointing to the sentence with the chalk, "can you tell us what is wrong with this sentence?"

Jane forced her eyes to focus on the blackboard. The words were meaningless. "I'm sorry, Miss Locke," she said. "I guess I wasn't paying attention." This brought a loud laugh from several boys in the back of the room and a titter from the rest of the class.

"Elizabeth, will you tell Jane what is wrong with the sentence?" asked Miss Locke.

" 'I know' squints," answered Liz promptly. "The sentence should read, 'I know some members of the class are not paying attention' or 'Some members of the class are not paying attention, I know.' "

Jane tried to look as if she were absorbing this bit of knowledge, but all the time she was thinking desperately, Will I be so dumb about boys when I am sixteen? Will I still be so dumb?

CHAPTER

7

WHEN the bell finally brought to a close the period that she should have devoted to clear thinking in English composition, Jane knew that she could not face Stan. She dawdled over her books at her desk and then, with her back turned toward the door, paused by the blackboard to ask Miss Locke some hastily composed questions about the next day's assignment. On Tuesday Stan had to leave school in a hurry to start his Doggie Diner route. When five minutes had clicked by on the electric clock, she was sure that Stan was gone and that she was safe.

Abruptly Jane thanked Miss Locke and fled down the hall to Julie's locker. "Julie, something awful has happened. I'll tell you on the way home. May

I keep my books in your locker?" The whispered words came out in a rush.

Julie looked at her in surprise. "Why, sure. You can use my locker any time. You know the combination." She lowered her voice to a whisper. "What happened?"

"I can't tell you here," said Jane. "Julie, do me a favor. Go to my locker and get out all my books."

"All right. If you want me to." Julie looked mystified, but she did as Jane asked. Jane selected the books she needed for her homework, stored the rest in Julie's locker, and hurried out of the building with her friend.

"Quick, tell me," begged Julie. "I can't stand the suspense any longer."

Miserably Jane poured out the story.

Julie was silent while she considered the implications of Jane's problem. "How ghastly!" she said at last. "How perfectly ghastly!"

"Yes," agreed Jane unhappily. "I don't know what to do. At least I didn't come right out and tell anybody he was taking me to the dance."

"I wonder who he is taking," mused Julie.

"I don't know," said Jane. "The way things get around school you'd think I'd have heard by now. And what I can't understand is why he's taking someone else. We'd been getting along so well and having such fun together. And he took me to the city and—and everything." Her voice trailed off as she remembered the way Stan had looked at her when he ordered the hamburger for her in Chinatown.

"Maybe he has to take the boss's daughter, or something," suggested Julie.

"No, that isn't it," said Jane gloomily. "His cousin owns the Doggie Diner and if he has a daughter she's probably about two years old."

"Maybe he's taking his sister." This was far-fetched, but Julie was trying to be comforting.

"No, one is too old and the other is too young. Anyway, Stan isn't the type to take his sister to a dance."

The two girls walked in silence, Jane lost in humiliation and Julie quiet out of sympathy for her friend. When they reached Julie's house, Julie said, "Come on in for a coke. Maybe we can think of somehing."

"No, thanks. Not today," answered Jane, and hesitated. "Julie, do you think . . . Stan could be taking Marcy?"

Julie looked serious. "I don't know. I hadn't

thought of that, but it's a possibility. She talked to him a lot that night in Chinatown."

"Do you suppose you could sort of ask around and find out who she's going with?" This was a favor Jane did not like to ask, even from Julie, but she felt she had to find out. "But don't let anybody know I want to know," she cautioned.

"Sure, Jane, I'll try to find out and let you know. And say, I just had an idea. Buzz might know somebody who needs a date," said Julie. "Maybe he could arrange something for you."

"No, it wouldn't be the same," said Jane. She could not let it get around school that Buzz was trying to dig up a date for poor little Jane Purdy, the girl Stan Crandall used to go with. Maybe she wasn't one of *the* crowd, but she still wasn't the kind of girl who had to have dates dug up for her. Besides, if she couldn't go to the dance with Stan, she didn't want to go with anyone.

"No, I suppose it wouldn't be the same," agreed Julie.

Feeling more lonely than ever, Jane hurried home to the privacy of her own room. She threw her books on the bed, untied the ribbon that held her back-scratcher to the edge of her mirror, and flung the piece of carved wood into her wastebasket.

She stared at it lying among the lipstick-smeared Kleenex and, after a moment of hesitation, took it out again and hid it at the back of a drawer under a pile of sweaters. Then she sat down on her bed and yanked the needles out of the Argyle sock she had been knitting. It was not very good knitting, anyway. The sock was grubby from being raveled and reknit so many times to correct mistakes and, no matter how often Jane read the directions, the yellow stripes that ran across the green diamonds refused to go straight. Jane found a gloomy satisfaction in jerking out the stitches. There, she thought, when the last stitch was unraveled. There goes Stan out of my life. It was all over and done with, and all there was for her to do was to forget him.

But the next day Jane found it was not easy to forget someone she had to work so hard to avoid. She had to get to her classes early and by devious instead of direct routes to keep from running into Stan. At noon she did not go to the cafeteria but sat instead on the steps of the gym and nibbled at a sandwich and an apple from home. She found, too, that she not only had to avoid Stan, but everyone else as well. She could not face the questions the other girls might ask her about the dance or their speculations when they heard she had not been asked by Stan. It was a lonely week. And as the week wore on, the silence of the Purdy telephone told her that Stan was avoiding her too. In a miserable sort of way she was glad. She never wanted to see him or talk to him again. Never. Especially if he was taking Marcy to the dance.

On Friday evening, while Jane was picking at her dinner, the telephone rang.

"*Arf-arf!*" barked Mr. Purdy.

"Pop!" pleaded Jane in real anguish as she left the table. Out of the corner of her eye she saw her mother frown ever so slightly and shake her head at her father. Mr. Purdy looked surprised and then indicated by his expression that he understood something was wrong.

So Mom has guessed, thought Jane, as she picked up the receiver. Now her family and her school and probably all of Woodmont knew that something was wrong between her and Stan. As she had expected, the call was from Julie.

"Did you find out?" Jane asked in a dull voice.

"Yes, finally," answered Julie. "I had a hard time, because I didn't like to come right out and ask anybody. You know. So I sort of had to go around with my ear to the ground. And then I happened to be walking past the drugstore and I heard a girl say something about Marcy and I slowed down—"

"Julie, just tell me. Is Stan taking Marcy?" Jane begged.

"No," said Julie. "Marcy is going with that cute boy in the school-bus crowd, the one that broke up with that girl who wears the tight skirts—"

"I know the one," said Jane. So it wasn't Marcy. That was something.

"That was only half of what I called about," Julie continued. "Mrs. Lashbrook called for a sitter for Nadine this evening. It's awfully short notice, but I wondered if you would want the job."

Since I'm not doing anything else—Jane finished the sentence silently. Julie might as well have said it right out loud. "I guess so," she said halfheartedly. Nadine, an eleven-year-old bookworm, was no trouble to sit with. "What time?"

"Mr. Lashbrook will pick you up at seven," Julie told her.

"O.K.," said Jane. She hesitated before adding, "Have a good time tonight, Julie. And Julie, call me in the morning and tell me about . . . everything."

"Sure," agreed Julie, and the sympathy in her voice was genuine. "I'll call you the first thing and . . . let you know."

Numb with misery, Jane assembled a stack of textbooks to take to the Lashbrooks' for the evening. Their house was quiet, Nadine would be buried in a book, and this would be a good chance to do a lot of studying and try to make up for the poor grades she had earned so far in the semester. She would put Stan and dates out of her mind and devote her time to her studies. No more C's or even B's for her. From now on she would get straight A's. She would be known throughout Woodmont High as Jane Purdy, the brain. Her name would be engraved on the silver scholarship cup in the trophy case at school. She would write intellectual essays for Manuscript like Liz Galpin, instead of childish articles entitled "Springtime in Yosemite National Park" or "My Experiences as a Baby Sitter." She might even submit a series of hokkus if she could get them to come out in seventeen syllables. Or sonnets might be better. Fourteen lines of poetry would give her more scope than seventeen syllables. If a new boy came to Woodmont High he would wonder who this attractive Jane Purdy was who made such wonderful grades. And everyone would say, That is Jane, our top student, straight A plusses, who has such a brilliant career ahead of her that she can't waste her time on boys. When she finished high school she would have a selection of scholarships to choose from. She would go to one of those Eastern women's colleges. . . .

Jane recalled her English II teacher, who once said sarcastically, when Jane had failed to look up *albeit* in the dictionary during the study of *As You Like It*, "Jane Purdy, have you no intellectual curiosity?" Well, she may not have had any intellectual curiosity in English II, but she did now.

By the time Jane arrived at the Lashbrooks' she was filled with a comforting feeling of martyrdom. The Lashbrooks were among her favorite baby-sitting customers. They always came home before midnight, they always had the right change to pay her, and they lived in a gracious old redwood house set in a grove of redwood trees in the hills. The wood-paneled living room, fragrant with eucalyptus wood burning in the stone fireplace, was inviting, and Jane looked around the room with pleasure. She liked the worn Oriental rugs, the comfortable chairs slip-covered in faded linen, the mellow furniture waxed until it glowed and flickered in reflected light from the fire. Tonight there was a brass bowl of apples on the coffee table, and the open curtains framed a view through the redwood trees of Wood-mont below and the bay and the city in the distance.

Nadine, a pale, spindling child, was curled up in a chair with a book. "Hello, Jane," she said, barely lifting her eyes from *The Pinto Stallion Revolts Again* long enough to peer at her sitter through her glasses. From time to time she sniffed. Nadine was allergic to cats and house dust, and although the Lashbrooks did not keep a cat, no one had ever figured out what to do about house dust.

"We should be home by eleven. The number is beside the telephone in case you want us," said Mrs. Lashbrook. Noticing Jane's pile of books, she added, "You may use Mr. Lashbrook's desk if you wish," and cleared a pile of papers out of the way. "Good night, girls. Go to bed at nine, won't you, Nadine?"

"Yes," said Nadine, turning a page and reading avidly.

Jane sat down at the big desk that faced the room and the view, and briskly prepared to study. She opened her notebook, got out several sheets of paper, and pulled her English book out of the stack of texts. Brilliant students did not waste time. Then she read the assignment. "Rewrite a scene from *Julius Caesar* in modern English." Feeling pleasantly intellectual to be spending part of her evening with Shakespeare, Jane flipped through the book until she found the play.

Nadine gave a loud sniff, rose from her chair, and without raising her eyes from her book, walked across the room, took an apple from the bowl on the coffee table, returned to her chair, and curled up again.

You'd think she'd trip over something, thought Jane, and turned to Shakespeare. Nadine gave a loud sniff and crunched into the apple.

Jane read, "ACT One. Scene One. Rome. A street. Enter Flavius, Marullus, and certain Commoners." There didn't seem to be anything to change about that. It was modern enough. She read on. "*Flavius.* Hence! home, you idle creatures, get you home! Is this a holiday?" Jane considered this. Because she was full of intellectual curiosity this evening, she consulted the cast of characters to see who this Flavius was. He was a tribune. Some sort of old Roman army officer, she thought, although today a tribune sounded more like a newspaper.

Nadine sniffed again, chewed noisily, and stopped abruptly.

Jane waited. Well, go on and chew, she thought. Finish the bite. Nadine turned a page and, except for the snapping of the fire, the room was silent. Suddenly she began to chew vigorously once more.

She must have come to an exciting part of the

story, Jane thought. Now to get back to Shakespeare. "Hence! home, you idle creatures" in modern English? Jane stared out the window at the lights on the bridges, strung like two golden necklaces across the bay. After a moment's thought she wrote down, "*Flavius.* Scram!" She looked critically at her work. This was not right. This did not fit into the picture of herself as a brilliant student. Miss Locke had said modern English, not slang.

Nadine had eaten the skin off the apple and was now gnawing her way around the core in a series of rapid nibbles without pausing to take the apple away from her mouth. Nibble, nibble, nibble, sniff. Silence.

Well, go on, thought Jane, distracted from *Julius Caesar.* Go on, chew it. Nadine prolonged the silence and suddenly began to eat again. Nibble, nibble, nibble , sniff. Jane relaxed. She crossed out "Scram" and wrote down, "*Flavius.* Go home." Somehow that was not the effect she wanted to achieve, either. This old tribune Flavius should be more forceful. He shouldn't sound as if he were ordering a dog out of a begonia bed. No, this was not the sort of thing a brilliant student would write. However, if Flavius could sort of orate instead of just yelling, "Go home," it might sound more in-

tellectual. Jane wondered if Miss Locke would object to the addition of directions. "*Flavius* (orating).
Go home." Most likely Miss Locke would not approve. She would want her students to think of a
forceful phrase that would convey the meaning
without directions. That was Miss Locke for you.

The nibbles grew smaller and faster as Nadine
turned the apple core in her fingers. She'll be eating
the whole thing, seeds and all, if she doesn't look at
it once in a while, thought Jane, as she looked up
from *Julius Caesar*. Through the window she noticed
soft fingers of fog slipping across the bay. She found
herself thinking of Stan and the night in the city
when he had touched her fog-damp hair and smiled
at her. And now he was dancing with another girl,
someone he liked better than Jane. Who could she
be, Jane wondered. Someone from one of his classes,
or a girl who lived near him? And would he touch
her hair and smile down at her, too? But she must
not think about it. Resolutely Jane turned back to
her work and studied the next phrase, "you idle
creatures." Now what did that mean? Were these
men lazy or were they unemployed?

Somewhere in the house a clock struck nine.
Nadine stood up and tossed her apple core into

the fireplace. "Good night," she said and, still reading, walked out of the room.

"Good night, Nadine," answered Jane, marveling that the girl did not bump into the furniture.

The eucalyptus log in the fireplace burned through and sank into a pile of coals. A chill and a silence, magnified by the hum of the refrigerator in the kitchen, settled over the house. This was the lonely hour of baby-sitting, when the house was still and the minutes began to drag. Two more hours. Jane sat staring at the first scene of *Julius Caesar* until the sound of the furnace turning itself on made her start. Quietly she closed her book. She did not want to be a brilliant student. She did not want to be intellectually curious. She wanted to be Stan's girl, dancing with him in the gymnasium of Woodmont High.

Jane walked to the window and stood looking out over the lights of the town at the fog that billowed over the bay, blotting out the bridges and the city. The sound of a car driving up the road only made the house seem lonelier. In the distance the foghorns had begun their melancholy chorus. *Yoo-hoo* boomed a horn far away. *Yoo-hoo. Come back* moaned another near the bridge. *Come back.*

Jane pressed her forehead against the cool glass. The dance had started and Stan was dancing with the other girl, the girl he had asked because he did not want to take Jane. And when the girl singer who had made the record that was tenth place on the Hit Parade began to sing, everyone would stop dancing and gather round the bandstand. Stan and the girl would stand close together and Stan would put his arm around the girl. . . .

Tomorrow Jane would know who the girl was. Julie would tell her, but she might never know why

Stan had invited the girl to go to the dance. The humiliation that Jane had felt turned to something else—grief perhaps, or regret. Regret that she had not known how to act with a boy, regret that she had not been wiser. Perhaps next year when she was sixteen . . .

The creeping fingers of fog began to blot out the lights of Woodmont below. *Come back, come back* moaned the foghorn, only to be mocked in the distance. *Yoo-hoo, yoo-hoo.*

Ten years from now I'll look back on this night and laugh, Jane thought. But she knew in her heart it was not true. In ten years she might look back, but she would not laugh, not even then. This night was too painful to laugh about ever. Jane knew that. Slowly two tears brimmed her eyes and slid down her cheeks.

Come back, pleaded one foghorn. *Yoo-hoo,* mocked the other.

CHAPTER

8

SATURDAY morning, soon after breakfast, Julie phoned.

"Hi," said Jane, as cheerfully as she could. "Did you have a good time last night?"

"Wonderful," answered Julie. "The music was good and Buzz is a smooth dancer, although I do wish he was a little bit taller."

"I'm glad you had a good time," said Jane as she kicked off her loafers. There was a moment of silence. Both girls hesitated to bring up the real reason for this telephone call, Jane because she dreaded finding out the name of the other girl, and Julie because she knew the whole incident was distressing to her friend.

Jane was first to break the silence. "Who was she?" she asked bluntly.

"A girl from the city."

"Oh." Jane had never considered the possibility of Stan's having a girl in the city.

"She was sort of an old family friend," Julie went on. "Anyway, she came over to Woodmont with Stan's dad after work and had dinner with his family before the dance."

Jane felt a little better. She would not have to face Stan's other girl at school. Maybe Stan's father had made him take her to the dance because she was an old family friend. Maybe the girl was long and lanky and stepped all over Stan's toes. Maybe she even had pimples.

"Stan called her Bitsy," said Julie.

"Bitsy?" Jane thought she had misunderstood. "Don't you mean Betsy?"

"No. Bitsy. Everybody calls her Bitsy, because she is such a little bitsy thing."

Jane detected more than a trace of cattiness in Julie's voice as her friend continued. "You know the type. She had to wear real high heels, because she is so little. The type that makes the other girls feel big and awkward. Especially me. She made me feel all wool and a yard wide as if I should be running around with a hockey stick instead of dancing."

"What did she look like?" Jane persisted. She had to know all the details, no matter how disturbing they might be. And so far they were very disturbing indeed.

A gusty sigh from Julie came over the telephone. "Well . . . I hate to say it, but she was perfectly darling."

That, thought Jane, is that. Even if she was an old family friend, Stan's father did not make him take her to the dance. If she was perfectly darling, Stan took her because he wanted to. Stan's darling little Bitsy.

Julie sighed again. "She was real smooth and she had one of those sleek new haircuts." Jane resolved to stop snipping off her own hair with the manicure scissors. "And most of the girls were wearing full skirts," said Julie, "but not Bitsy. She wore a dress with a straight skirt. You know, simple and sort of elegant, like you see in the shop windows in the city."

"Yes, I know," agreed Jane. "The kind that even if we had the money our mothers would say we couldn't buy because they were too sophisticated for us."

"Exactly."

"And I suppose she has a terrible time finding

anything to wear in her size, because she is so little." Jane found a certain relish in being catty herself.

"How did you guess?" Julie sounded surprised. "That's exactly what she said when we were putting on fresh lipstick during intermission."

Jane had to know everything. "Was she nice?"

"Yes, she really was," said Julie regretfully. "She was friendly with everyone. Everybody liked her, and the fellows really went for her."

"Oh." Jane felt this was the end. She did not have a chance with a smooth girl—a little bitsy smooth girl—from the city. A girl who was not only smooth, but a girl everyone liked. Probably the only reason Stan had taken Jane out at all was that she was handy. Good old Jane, always available for a date when Bitsy wasn't around. She brought herself up sharply. What was she thinking about anyway? This was not the end. The end had come that day outside her English class over a week ago, when she had put Stan out of her life forever.

"Jane, are you still there?" Julie asked.

"Yes. I was just thinking," answered Jane. "I suppose you traded dances?"

"Yes, and Stan is a wonderful dancer, in case that's what you're wondering."

"Yes, I was wondering," Jane admitted.

At that moment the doorbell rang.

"I've got to hang up," said Jane hastily, as she slid her feet into her loafers. "There's somebody at the door and Mom's downtown."

"Probably the Fuller brush man," said Julie. " 'By."

Tucking in her shirttail with one hand, Jane opened the front door. Stan was standing on the front porch.

An electric feeling flashed through Jane, the same sensation she had felt the first time she had picked up the telephone and found that Stan, the strange boy who delivered horse meat, was on the line. She stood staring at him, and although she was unable to think of anything to say, she was aware that he was wearing a fresh white T shirt and sharply creased sun tans and that his identification bracelet was still on his wrist. At least he didn't give his bracelet to Bitsy, thought Jane; not that it means anything to me.

"Hello, Jane," said Stan, without smiling. "I tried to call you this morning, but your line was busy."

Jane felt her cheeks begin to burn, as all the hurt and humiliation of the last two weeks came back to her. And after the description of smooth little Bitsy she had heard from Julie, she felt awkward and untidy in her jeans and plaid shirt with her hair carelessly combed. "Hello, Stan," she managed to say, brushing aside a feeling of annoyance that a girl she had not even met could make her feel this way.

"Could you come for a ride with me?" Stan asked. "I—I want to show you something."

Jane tried to collect her thoughts. Stan needn't think he could treat her the way he did and then come around any old time and expect her to go out with him on a moment's notice. She wasn't going to be good old handy Jane Purdy. He needn't think he could take her for granted. She forgot that only the week before she had found it pleasant to be taken for granted by Stan. "I'm sorry," she said coolly. "I have a baby-sitting engagement at eleven."

Stan looked at his watch. "It's only ten-fifteen. Come for a ride and I'll drop you off. Please, Jane I—I've got to talk to you."

Of course I won't go, thought Jane. Then she wavered. For a moment she was undecided, but only for a moment. Curiosity won out. She had to find out what Stan wanted to show her and what he had to talk about. She would ride with him this once, but never again. She would be cool and aloof the whole time. Not that she would let him know her feelings were hurt. Nothing like that. Just . . . well, cool and aloof. "All right," she said in a polite, impersonal tone. "Just a minute."

Jane scribbled a note for her mother and jerked a comb through her hair. She did not bother to change her clothes, because she had found that jeans were practical to wear when sitting with little children. What difference did it make what she had on? Stan liked girls with sleek haircuts, who wore sophisticated clothes. Besides, it was all over between them and had been for over a week.

"Where's the truck?" Jane asked, as she and Stan started down the steps. The only car in sight was a blue coupé with the top down, which was parked in front of the house next door.

"We're not going in the truck," said Stan. "We're going in my car."

"Your car!" Jane was so surprised she could not believe Stan meant what he said. He must be joking.

"That's right. My car. There it is," said Stan proudly, pointing to the blue coupé. "I wanted to surprise you."

"Why, Stan!" Jane, forgetting to be cool and aloof,

was astonished and delighted all at the same time. "You mean it's your very own?"

"It sure is. I bought it with my Doggie Diner money and the money I saved from the paper route I had in the city." Then he added apologetically, "Of course, it isn't exactly new, and my cousin and I had to do a lot of work on it to get it to go, but it works all right now. And I have to leave the top down, because it's sort of ragged, but I hope to get a new top before the rainy season."

"Why, Stan, how marvelous! How perfectly marvelous!" Jane stood admiring the car, and the thought flashed through her mind that now Stan would no longer have to hide his bicycle in the firethorn bushes. The car was a model-A Ford and, in the strictest definition of the word, a convertible. That is, it had a folding top. Or, to be more accurate, what was left of the top folded. The seat was neatly covered with an army blanket and the trim, which had very few dents, was polished until it twinkled in the sunlight. The fresh blue paint, which Jane felt was in quiet good taste and which had only a few streaks, gleamed. There was not a speck of dust on the car anywhere.

"Like it?" asked Stan.

"It's perfect," said Jane, and meant it. The car

was neither a jalopy nor a hot rod. It looked plain and serviceable, exactly right for riding around Woodmont.

"I knew you'd like it," said Stan. "Some girls might think it was old and funny, but I knew you wouldn't."

"I think it's neat-looking," commented Jane.

"So do I." Stan held the door open for Jane. "Hop in and let's go for a ride."

Jane stepped onto the high running board and sat down on the army blanket. It seemed strange to be sitting up so high, and she found it much pleasanter than sitting in a more modern car. The view was better. The car started easily. Jane shifted her position on the seat, because she was sitting on a broken spring, and rode in silent admiration. Somehow, Woodmont looked different when seen from a boy's own car. The air seemed clearer and the trees stood out more sharply against the sky line. A wisp of hair blew across her eyes, and Jane brushed it away with the same gesture Marcy used when she rode in Greg's father's convertible. This must be the way Marcy felt.

"I—I wanted you to be the first girl to ride in it," Stan said.

"Did you really? Oh, Stan!" They drove past a

girl who had been in Jane's math class and who was now walking toward the library with an armload of books.

"Hello there," called Jane. Poor girl, going to the library on such a beautiful morning!

"Hi," the girl answered, and looked wistfully at Stan and his car.

They drove into Woodmont Park, where Stan stopped under some bay trees by the stream. "I didn't use my car last night, because I wanted you to be the first to ride in it," he said, turning to Jane. "I took Dad's car instead."

Last night. The humiliation Jane had felt for the past week came rushing back. She could not look at Stan. "I hope you had a good time," she said stiffly, picking up a dry bay leaf that had drifted onto the seat between them, and twirling it around in her fingers.

"I guess I should have explained it all to you ahead of time," said Stan miserably.

"You don't have to explain anything to me." This time Jane was cool and aloof. She looked away from Stan and crumpled the bay leaf to release its fragrance. "If you wanted to take another girl, there was no reason why you shouldn't."

"But I didn't want to," said Stan.

Oh, Stan, thought Jane, please don't try to make me believe your father made you take Bitsy because she is an old family friend.

"I mean, I didn't want to take her after I met you," Stan went on. "I used to take Bitsy out once in a while when I lived in the city. Her folks are friends of my folks and I sort of liked her. Anyway, just before we moved over here I told her I would have her over for the first school dance. I know it was a dumb thing to do, but after I had done it I couldn't very well break the date, especially since Mom and Dad knew about it. You know how families are."

Joy surged through Jane. So that was the reason Stan had not asked her to go to the dance! She should have known he would have a perfectly good explanation. He wanted to take her, but he had to keep a date he had made before he knew her. It was as simple as that, and she was still Stan's girl. But even so, Jane found she could not forget her unhappiness of the past week.

"I would rather have taken you," Stan told her. "Honest. I'm sorry I couldn't. I sure felt awful that day in the hall at school. I felt so awful I couldn't even call you up or anything."

"It's quite all right," Jane said stiffly. "I hope you had a good time," she repeated.

"Oh, it was all right." Stan showed no enthusiasm. "But Bitsy is too short and she got lipstick on my coat and she wore a dumb dress with a narrow skirt and I had to take short steps all evening."

Well! thought Jane. It just goes to show that boys don't look at things the way girls do. Here I was feeling awkward and unsophisticated beside this Bitsy, the smooth girl from the city.

"She's not like you," said Stan. "She laughed at my job. She kept laughing and saying, 'Imagine delivering horse meat to *dogs!*' all evening. Maybe it does seem funny to some people, but I like dogs and I like my job."

Poor Stan, thought Jane tenderly; he sounds so hurt. How thoughtless of Bitsy to make fun of his job.

A car drove past the spot where Jane and Stan were sitting. Jane began to feel uneasy. She did not want it to get around town, and back to her mother and father, that she and Stan had been seen parked in a car. Not even in broad daylight. Her mother would have enough to say about Stan's having a car of his own, even though it could not possibly be called a hot rod, without bringing up the question of parking.

Jane turned to Stan and smiled. "I know what," she said. "Let's go show Julie your car."

"You're not mad?" he asked, looking down at her.

Jane knew that her answer was important to Stan. "No, Stan," she said honestly. "I'm not mad at you." But she could not tell him that even though she was not angry, the hurt of the last week was still with her. She was ashamed to admit it.

"Sure?" Stan asked.

"Sure."

"O.K.," said Stan, eager to show off his car to someone else. "Let's go!"

They drove out of the park and down the hill toward Julie's house. The car made loud, popping noises as it went downhill. "It's just the carburetor," explained Stan. "Most cars make that noise going down a steep hill."

Jane brushed her hair out of her eyes with her new Marcy gesture. "Oh," she said, resolving to look up "carburetor" in the dictionary when she got home. Every car had a carburetor, she knew, and she had a vague idea that a carburetor in a car was something like an appendix in a human being, but this was the first time she had met the word in conversation. If Stan wanted to talk about a

carburetor, she wanted to find out exactly what it was.

When Stan stopped his car by the curb in front of Julie's house, Jane reached over to the center of the steering wheel and sounded the horn twice, long and loud. Julie and then Buzz appeared at the window. They smiled and waved and in a moment came running down the front steps.

"Say, that's all right!" Buzz stood back to admire the Ford. "She sure looks a lot better than when you got her. Neat but not gaudy."

"You mean me or the car?" Jane glanced sidelong at Buzz, the way Marcy so often looked at boys.

"The car, of course," bantered Buzz. "Anybody can find a girl."

"Stan, do you mean this car is yours, your very own?" Julie asked.

"That's right," said Stan proudly. "I bought it last month, but I had to do a lot of work on it before I could use it."

Julie stepped up on the running board and leaned over to examine the dashboard. "And it runs and everything?" she demanded incredulously.

"It sure does," said Stan. "A model-A is a little

noisier than the cars they make now, but it runs like a top."

"What's this?" Julie asked, pointing to a cap on the hood in front of the windshield.

"That's the top of the gas tank," Stan explained.

"In front?" asked Jane.

"On this model," said Stan.

Buzz opened one side of the hood and bent over to examine the engine. Stan got out of the car and leaned over beside him.

With the two boys half-hidden under the hood, Jane and Julie looked at each other and, without uttering a word, carried on a conversation. Jane's look told Julie that everything was all right. She now understood about Stan and the dance, she was happy to see him again, and she was thrilled about his car. Julie's look told Jane that she was so glad Jane and Stan had things straightened out and that she was both surprised and excited that Buzz had come over to see her so soon after the dance. Both girls silently expressed to each other a feeling of great satisfaction at the way everything had turned out.

"Stan painted his car himself," said Jane aloud.

"Did he really?" Julie stepped back to admire the paint job.

The two boys came out from under the hood

of the car. "I painted it with a powder puff," said Stan.

"A powder puff!" laughed Jane. "Stan, not really!"

"Sure," said Stan. "There's a kind of plastic paint for cars, that you put on with a powder puff. You just wipe it on. Of course, I did get a few streaks, and a little dust got in it. And when I tried to paint it in the garage under an elecric light, a few moths got into the paint on the hood. See, that's what made these spots."

"It looks marvelous," said Julie. "The spots hardly show, and nobody would ever dream you did it with a powder puff."

"Look, Julie, it has an old-fashioned rumble seat," Buzz pointed out. "That's for you and me to ride in."

"A real rumble seat!" exclaimed Julie. "I've always wanted to ride in one. Mother used to ride in one when she was a girl and she's often said what fun it was."

Stan got into the car and put his foot on the starter. "We'd better be on our way if I'm going to get Jane to her baby-sitting job on time."

Buzz stepped up on the running board beside Jane to look at the inside of the car, and as he stood there he looked down at Jane. Then he said, "Jane, for someone who used to be a scrawny kid who was a terrible cook, you've turned out to be a mighty Purdy girl."

Jane felt pleased and a little embarrassed by this remark. Buzz was teasing, she knew, but at the same time she was sure he really thought she was pretty. Not knowing how to answer him, she flashed him her new Marcy look.

"A pun is the lowest form of humor," observed Julie.

Buzz continued to look down at Jane. Then he reached into his pocket and pulled out a fifty-cent piece, which he tossed into the air and deftly caught. "Stan, I'll give you fifty cents to let me kiss your girl," he said.

Jane looked at Buzz in astonishment and afterwards she was shocked by her own sudden behavior. Still feeling like Marcy, she met his challenge. She smiled at him, closed her eyes, and lifted her lips. Buzz leaned over and kissed her lightly on the mouth.

Oh, thought Jane, as his lips touched hers, what have I done? She felt her face flush scarlet as she opened her eyes and saw Buzz, grinning cockily, flip the fifty-cent piece across her lap to Stan, who caught it automatically.

Confused and ashamed, Jane looked down at her hands. She could not think what to do or say. She did not want to look at Buzz and she could not look at Stan. No one spoke.

Unsmiling, Stan kicked the starter button, and the motor roared. As the car began to move, Jane glimpsed Buzz still grinning wickedly at her and, beside him, Julie looking dejectedly after the car, the gaiety she had shown a few minutes before gone out of her. Now I've gone and hurt Julie's feelings, on top of everything else, thought Jane, and I didn't mean to.

"Where to?" asked Stan.

Jane gave him an address in Bayaire Estates. "I'm sorry, Stan," she said timidly. "Really I am."

"That's O.K.," said Stan briefly, his eyes on the road.

"I guess I just had a silly impulse. I didn't mean to—to do what I did."

"Forget it," said Stan.

He really was angry, Jane realized, and trying to explain wasn't going to help. She could not tell him that she had let Buzz kiss her because she was trying to act like Marcy. It wasn't the sort of thing a boy would understand.

Stan drove on in silence until they came to a bridge that crossed a narrow arm of the bay. In the middle of the bridge Stan stopped his car. Jane put her hand over her eyes to shade them from the brilliant sunlight. "Why are we stopping?" she asked.

Stan did not answer. With one quick motion he shied Buzz's half dollar across the railing of the bridge and out over the bay. It flashed in the sunlight above the water for an instant before it hit the surface with a plop and sank from sight. "That takes care of that," Stan said.

"Why, Stan . . ." Jane was startled by his gesture. He's hurt, she thought suddenly. I should have known. Stan was angry, because he was hurt. And with a flash of insight she realized that was the real reason she had let Buzz kiss her. She wanted Stan to feel some of the hurt she had felt. Now she was sorry and ashamed.

When Stan stopped his car in front of the house where Jane was to baby-sit, he glanced at his watch. "I got you here two minutes late," he said. "I'm sorry."

We seem to be spending the whole morning apologizing to each other, Jane thought, as she got out of the car. He's sorry about the dance. I'm sorry I let Buzz kiss me. He's sorry, because he got me here late. "That's all right, Stan," she said, and looked directly at him. "Are you still mad at me?"

"No," he said with a weak smile.

"I'm glad, because I really am sorry," said Jane, and smiled at him. "Good-by for now."

"So long, Jane," he said, without looking at her.

He looks pale under his tan, Jane observed. Actually pale. He must really be upset. She wanted to reassure him, to tell him not to be hurt—that she liked him better than any boy she had ever known—but there was no time to talk. Stan was already driving away.

"Stan!" she called urgently above the noise of the model-A engine. "Stan, phone me this afternoon!"

She could not hear his answer but it did not matter. A boy who turned pale beneath his tan when another boy kissed her really cared, and a boy who really cared would call. Darling Stan. She was sorry for what she had done, and she could hardly wait for the telephone to ring.

CHAPTER
9

Althouch baby-sitting with Patsy Scruggs was hard work, Jane was always glad when Mrs. Scruggs, the youngest of her customers, called her. Jane felt that the pleasant home the Scruggs had created with ingenuity and not much money was the sort of home she would like to have some day in the shadowy future when she was married. But first she would go to college and have a career. Just what career, she did not know—an airline stewardess, or a writer of advertising copy for a big department store, or perhaps a job at the American embassy in Paris— something like the girls in the pages of *Mademoiselle*, who always managed to be clever about clothes and to be seen in interesting places with men who had crew cuts.

While little Patsy was engrossed in moving three

dolls, a set of blocks, a floppy bear, two old aluminum pans, and a frozen orange-juice can out of her doll buggy and into first one home-upholstered chair and then another, Jane, her thoughts full of Stan, sat smiling dreamily at a framed photograph of Mrs. Scruggs, looking young and radiant in her wedding gown. Darling Stan, who was sure to call soon—probably before he started his Doggie Diner route. Stan, who had really wanted to take her to the dance, Stan, who wanted her to be the first girl to ride in his car, Stan, who really cared . . .

Jane let her gaze drift around the room at the odds and ends of furniture, the unbleached muslin curtains at the windows, the bright unframed prints on the wall, the bookcase made of boards set on stacks of bricks, the worn copy of Dr. Benjamin Spock's *Pocket Book of Baby and Child Care*. Mrs. Stanley Crandall . . . Jane Purdy Crandall . . . Stan Crandall, Jr. . . . .

Patsy, chubby in her corduroy overalls stuffed with diapers and a pair of plastic pants, toddled across the room and plumped her floppy bear and the orange-juice can into Jane's lap.

"Thank you, Patsy," murmured Jane, and wondered what was showing at the Woodmont Theater that evening. Or maybe Stan wouldn't ask her to go to the movies this time. Maybe they would just ride around in his car and then go to Nibley's for a milk shake. Patsy, delighted with her game, laughed and made trip after trip to Jane's lap with pans, blocks, and dolls. "Thank you, Patsy," said Jane politely each time.

Then the telephone rang. Stan! Jane dumped Patsy's toys to the floor and flew to the kitchen, where she had to throw her shoulder against the door to open it. Doors so often stuck in Bayaire Estates. How thoughtful of Stan to call so soon! He must have remembered he had not mentioned a date for that evening and telephoned the minute he reached home. Jane picked up the receiver. "Hello," she said eagerly.

"Hello, Jane." It was Mrs. Scruggs. Jane not only felt let down. She also felt foolish, because of the way she must have sounded when she answered the telephone.

"I'm calling from the dentist's office," said Mrs. Scruggs. "I forgot to tell you that when you get Patsy's lunch she likes her milk heated."

"Yes, Mrs. Scruggs," answered Jane. Oh, why couldn't it have been Stan who had called?

"She doesn't like it cold," continued Mrs. Scruggs, "and she doesn't like it hot, either."

Hurry, Mrs. Scruggs, thought Jane. Stan may be trying to get the line.

"Just heat it enough to take the chill off," said Patsy's mother. "I don't like to chill her little stomach with milk right out of the refrigerator."

"Of course not, Mrs. Scruggs." Hurry and hang up, please!

"But be careful not to get it too hot," said Mrs. Scruggs. "I wouldn't want her to burn her tongue. And when you heat it, be sure you turn the handle of the pan so she can't pull it off the stove."

"I'll be careful," promised Jane.

"And she likes her applesauce in the dish with the bunnies on the bottom," Mrs. Scruggs went on.

"I'll find it," said Jane.

"I guess that's all," said Mrs. Scruggs, and finally left the line free for Stan.

Because it was time to fix Patsy's lunch, Jane decided to move the little girl into the kitchen with her. She did not like to leave Patsy in the living room alone, because she was never sure what mischief her small mind might devise. "Come on, Patsy," she coaxed. "Let's go into the kitchen and fix some nice lunch."

Agreeably Patsy pushed her doll buggy into the kitchen and removed from it a box, which she dumped onto the floor. Spools of all sizes rolled across the linoleum.

"Patsy, you're not much help," remarked Jane as she looked around the kitchen. Mrs. Scruggs had done everything possible to make the room child-proof. The handles of the gas stove had been removed and set out of reach of little hands. Yardsticks had been run through the rows of drawer pulls so that no drawer could be opened without first pulling out a yardstick. The lower cupboards and the refrigerator door were tied shut with lengths of clothesline rope.

Patsy threw a spool across the kitchen, and Jane sighed. It was here that she had to prepare lunch. "Patsy, how would you like to sit in your high chair while I fix you some nice lunch?" At least she would be near the telephone while she worked.

"No!" said Patsy stubbornly, and hurled another spool across the kitchen.

Jane realized she had made a mistake. She should have told Patsy, not asked her. Oh, well, what difference did it make whether Patsy was underfoot or in her high chair? She could watch the little girl while she waited for Stan's call. Jane untied the refrigerator door and removed, according to Mrs. Scruggs' instructions, the milk, some cooked green beans, a bowl containing chopped liver and bacon, some applesauce, and some cheese for her own sandwich. Then she tied the door shut again.

Next Jane untied a cupboard to look for pans, but the cupboard was full of platters and casseroles. She tied it shut again and untied another cupboard, from which she removed two small pans for heating the meat and the vegetable. She tied it shut, remembered she must heat the milk, untied it, removed another pan, and tied it shut again.

Patsy rolled some spools across the floor. Stepping carefully, Jane carried the pans to the stove. Then she examined the knobs that had been removed and fitted them into place on the front of the stove. She stepped back across the kitchen and pulled a yardstick out of a row of deep drawers. The first metal-lined drawer was filled with flour, the second contained sugar, and in the third she found a loaf of bread, which she took out and placed on the draining board. Then she remembered that the butter was still in the refrigerator, so she untied the door, took out the butter, and tied the door again.

The telephone rang. Stan! cried Jane's heart, as she stepped on a spool, caught herself on the edge of the draining board, and picked up the receiver. "Hello?" she said, cautiously this time.

"Oh, hello, Marilyn," said a woman's voice. "I just wanted to tell you I went downtown this morning, and Penney's is having the most wonderful sale of children's corduroy overalls. You know—the kind with snaps. These were so cute, because the knees were padded and quilted in designs like ducks and kittens, and when I saw them I thought, I must call Marilyn, because I'm sure she'll want to buy some for Patsy."

"Excuse me," said Jane, her voice heavy with disappointment. "This is not Mrs. Scruggs. This is her sitter."

"Oh. Excuse *me*," apologized the woman. "Isn't that funny? I could have sworn it was Marilyn Scruggs who answered."

"Could I take a message?" asked Jane, wilted because the call was not from Stan. By now he had started the Doggie Diner route, but he could easily telephone from a drugstore between stops.

"No, thanks," said the woman. "I'll call back."

Once more the line was free for Stan. Jane heard the sound of a drawer opening behind her and turned just in time to see Patsy fill both hands with sugar and fling it onto the kitchen floor. She bubbled forth a laugh of sheer delight as she slid her little feet across the floor through the gritty sugar.

"Patsy!" cried Jane, and then told herself she might as well save her breath. It was her own fault. She should have remembered to replace the yardstick and she should not have turned her back for one instant. She would not think about the telephone any more. Then it would be sure to ring.

Somehow, Jane managed to pick up the spools, sweep up the sugar, prepare Patsy's lunch, install her in her high chair, and get her started eating, partly with a spoon and partly with her fingers. With one hand Jane ate a cheese sandwich and drank a glass of milk and with the other she assisted Patsy in finding her mouth, and all the time she wondered where Stan was on his route. The Doberman's house? The boxer's house? Or had he reached the gray poodle's house yet?

"Blah, blah, black sheep," said Patsy, dribbling applesauce down her chin.

"Have you any wool?" prompted Jane.

Patsy squished applesauce around in her mouth and studied Jane. "No," she answered, and Jane laughed.

When Jane finished her own lunch she used both hands to help Patsy get the applesauce into her mouth and find the bunnies in the bottom of her dish. She was about to wipe the little girl's face

with a damp washcloth and find a rag for mopping
up the food spilled on the floor when the telephone
rang again. This time it *had* to be Stan. The third
time was the charm. Jane snatched up the telephone
and said breathlessly, "Hello?"

"Hello, Jane," said Mrs. Scruggs. "I'm just leaving
the dentist's office and I'll be home in about fifteen
minutes. Is everything all right?"

"Everything's fine, Mrs. Scruggs," answered Jane,
disappointed a third time. "Patsy has just finished
her lunch."

"I want to talk," cried Patsy from her high chair.

"Let her say hello," said Mrs. Scruggs. "She loves
to talk on the telephone."

With a sigh, Jane plucked the chubby little girl
from her high chair and carried her to the telephone.
"Say hello to Mommy," she directed.

Patsy grasped the telephone with both hands. "I'm
fine," she shouted into the mouthpiece, before her
mother had time to speak to her. "I'm fine."

It took Jane several minutes to separate Patsy
from the telephone—the minutes, she was sure, in
which Stan was trying to reach her. She dampened
the washcloth again under the faucet, and while
she wiped applesauce from Patsy's face and from
the telephone she decided Stan might not want to

call her at a stranger's house. Perhaps he was waiting until later in the afternoon, when he was sure
she would be at home.

It was not long before the front door opened and
Mrs. Scruggs came in. "Hello, Jane," she said,
snatching Patsy into her arms. "How's Mommy's
'ittle s'eetheart?" she cried. "How's Mommy's 'ittle
s'eetheart? Have you been a good girl while Mommy
was away?"

Patsy laughed and buried her face in her mother's
neck. Mrs. Scruggs set the little girl down and
reached for her purse. Jane glanced at her watch
and saw that she had been sitting only an hour and
a half. It had seemed longer. Mrs. Scruggs handed
Jane seventy-five cents and Jane thanked her. The
Scruggs, Jane knew, did not have much money for
baby sitters.

"Mrs. Scruggs, if anyone telephones for me, would
you say I'll be home in about five minutes?" Jane
asked.

"Of course, Jane." Mrs. Scruggs smiled under-
standingly. "Especially if someone is a boy."

Jane left as quickly as she could and all but ran
home, because she did not want to be away from a
telephone an instant longer than necessary. When
she entered her own house she found her mother

telephoning her grocery list. "A quart of mayon-naise . . . a large bottle of vanilla . . . a box of Kleenex . . . oh, all right, send me two . . . a large box of oatmeal . . . yes, the quick-cooking kind . . ."

Hurry, Mom, thought Jane. Stan may be trying to call me between deliveries this very instant. He won't have much time.

"Do you have any nice cross-rib roasts?" Mrs. Purdy went on. "Good. Send me one about four, no, about five pounds . . . and a pound of lean bacon. . . . Let me see. Yes, I think that's all for today."

Thank goodness, thought Jane, as her mother hung up. Now Stan could reach her.

"Hello, Jane," said Mrs. Purdy, her hand still on the telephone. "I know I forgot something. What could it be?"

"I don't know, Mom. It sounded as if you or-dered everything," answered Jane, wishing her mother would get away from the telephone.

"Oh, I know." Jane's mother dialed a number, as if she had nothing to do the rest of the day. "Hello, this is Mrs. Purdy again. I'm sorry, but I forgot the most important item on my list. A pound of lamb liver for the cat . . . yes, that's right, we can't forget him. He's the most important member of the family. At least that's what he thinks." She laughed comfortably before she hung up.

It's about time, thought Jane. Now maybe Stan can reach me. She went into her room and pulled her back-scratcher out from under the pile of sweaters in the drawer and tied it to the edge of her mirror once more. She changed into her yellow cotton dress, in case Stan dropped by instead of telephoning, and tried brushing her hair down close to her head to see how she would look with a sleek new haircut. Awful, she decided. Sort of forlorn and underfed. She fluffed up her hair again and renewed her lipstick, carefully outlining her mouth with the lipstick brush. Then she got out her paper sack of yarn and cast on seventy-six stitches to start an Argyle sock.

"Jane, would you go out and move the hose?" Mrs. Purdy asked. "It's been running on the fuchsias long enough."

"O.K.," said Jane. She left the front door open, in case the telephone should ring, and ran down the front steps. She turned off the water, moved the sprinkler to another corner of the lawn, turned on the water, and ran back into the house. The telephone had not rung.

As the afternoon wore on, Jane began to feel that something must be wrong. Stan had been delayed on his route. He had had a flat tire. Or, as sometimes happened, the boxer had followed the truck so far he had been obliged to return the dog to its home and tie it up. Or maybe the telephone was out of order. Or the other party on their line was talking. Quietly Jane slipped to the telephone and slid the receiver off the hook. The dial tone buzzed busily in her ear. With a sigh, she replaced the receiver. She wished the line had been out of order. Then she would know why Stan had not called. I guess a watched telephone never rings, she thought gloomily, as she went back to her knitting. Doubt began to creep into her mind. Maybe she had misunderstood. She had not actually heard Stan say he would telephone. Perhaps she had made him so angry he would never call her again. Perhaps— but she could not bring herself to believe it.

At a quarter to five the telephone rang, startling Jane so that she dropped six stitches and tripped on the edge of the rug before she could answer it. "Hello?" She tried to keep eagerness out of her voice.

"I have good news for you!" exclaimed a man's voice enthusiastically.

Jane was surprised. Good news for her? Who could be calling with good news for her?

"You have been chosen to receive one of our special gift offers of one nine-by-twelve tinted photograph with any order of ten dollars or more at Sherwood's Photography Studio!" The voice bubbled with enthusiasm.

"No, thank you. I'm not interested," said Jane dully, and hung up. He has good news for me, she thought ironically. That's what *he* thinks. The only good news she wanted was Stan's call. The minutes began to drag.

By five-thirty Jane knew that Stan had finished his route long ago and was home by now. She had to face the unpleasant truth. Stan was not going to telephone. She could make excuses no longer. She felt tired, let down, worn out by anticipation. Wearily she set the table for her mother, her thoughts still filled with Stan. The happiness she had felt earlier in the day was gone, replaced by doubt and confusion. She laid a fresh napkin at each place. She must have been mistaken about Stan's set look, the pallor beneath his tan. He had not been hurt at all. He was angry and disgusted with her for having acted like a silly, impetuous fifteen-year-old. And she did not blame him one bit. He had been so sorry about the dance and had wanted her to be the first girl to ride in his car, and then she had acted that way. How dumb can I get, she asked herself bitterly, just exactly how dumb?

Jane ate her dinner in silence. Sir Puss, who had dry adobe mud clinging to his paws, walked with a clicking sound across the bare floor between the living-room and dining-room rugs.

"That cat makes entirely too much noise pussy-footing around this house," said Mr. Purdy.

Jane responded to her father's joke with a wan smile.

Mr. Purdy tried again. "Well, I hear the horse-meat king came to call this morning," he said jovially.

"Pop, please!" implored Jane. "Mom, would you excuse me? I really don't care for any dessert."

"Yes, of course, Jane," said Mrs. Purdy.

"*Now* what's wrong with her?" Jane heard her father ask as she fled the room.

"The same old thing," answered Mrs. Purdy. "Love."

You'd think people who had been young once would be more understanding, Jane thought, as she sat down on her bed and picked up her knitting.

Slowly she pulled out the needles and one by one began to undo the stitches she had knit that afternoon. Apathetically she wound the frayed yarn into a ball. She did not know what to do now.

Jane wondered what she would do about Stan if she were some other girl. If she were the kind of girl who went to school with her hair in pin curls, she would probably telephone the disc jockey at Station KWOO and ask him to play *Love Me on Monday* to Stan from Jane. If she were intellectual like Liz, she would probably say that dancing and riding around in a model-A Ford were boring or middlebrow or something, and spend the evening writing hokkus for Manuscript. Or if she were the earnest type, she would write a letter to Teen Corner in the newspaper. The letter would begin, "Dear Ann Benedict, I wonder if you could help me solve a problem. Recently I met a boy . . ." If she were the cashmere-sweater type, like Marcy, she would date several other boys and forget Stan.

But Jane was not any of these girls. She was Jane Purdy, an ordinary girl who was no type at all. She was neither earnest nor intellectual, and she certainly wasn't the kind of girl the boys flocked around. She was just a girl who liked to have a good time, who made reasonably good grades at school, and who still liked a boy who had once liked her. There was nothing wrong with that.

All right, then why didn't she act that way, Jane asked herself, instead of trying to toss her hair around like Marcy the minute she got to ride in a boy's car with the top down. If she had not been trying to act like Marcy, she would never have closed her eyes and lifted her lips for Buzz to kiss.

Jane sat toying with the ball of yarn and thinking about Marcy. Why, she did not even like the girl. Not really. She did not like girls who acted bored and who made other girls feel uncomfortable. She liked girls who were friendly and interested in others. Then why, Jane asked herself, did she try to act like someone she did not like? Maybe she didn't have a lot of sun streaks in her hair or a drawer full of cashmere sweaters, but a nice boy like Stan had liked her once and Buzz had wanted to kiss her, so she was certainly as attractive as most girls at school. All she lacked was confidence. She didn't know why she hadn't thought of it before.

From now on, Jane resolved, she would be Jane Purdy and nobody else. She would stop feeling like Miss Muffet around Marcy and she would no longer feel fluffy and not very bright when she talked to Liz. From now on she would be confident. When she saw Stan she would act glad to see him, because no matter what had happened that was the way Jane Purdy felt. After all, Stan had liked her when she was baby-sitting with Sandra and when she walked through Chinatown with him, and she had been herself both those times. Maybe if she continued to be herself, Stan would like her again. And if he didn't, there was nothing she could do about it. Jane was filled with a wonderful feeling of relief at having made this decision. That was that. Period.

Jane tossed the ball of yarn onto her bed and, humming the Woodmont High victory song, went into the living room, where she dropped into the nearest chair. "Hi," she said amiably to her father and mother.

"Welcome," said Mr. Purdy over his evening paper. "Have you decided to join the family once more?"

"Oh, Pop, don't be silly," said Jane.

"I thought you were going out with the horse-meat king."

"Not tonight," said Jane casually, and picked up a magazine. "I guess the horse-meat king is doing something else." The telephone rang, but she made no move to answer it. She was not expecting any calls, and she found it restful after the day she had spent.

"You get it, Jane," said Mrs. Purdy.

"O.K.," answered Jane, and walked leisurely into the hall to pick up the receiver.

"Hello. Jane?" Julie's excited voice sounded muffled and far away.

"Julie, where are you?" Jane asked. "You sound as if you were at the bottom of a well, or something."

"In the hall closet at Greg's."

"In the hall closet? What on earth for?" Jane demanded. "And what are you doing at Greg's in the first place?"

"Buzz brought me over, and we're listening to records with a bunch of kids. Their telephone has a long cord, and I just had to talk to you where nobody could hear me, so I took it into the hall closet," Julie explained. Then she said something Jane could not understand.

"Julie, I can't hear you," complained Jane.

"It's dark in here and a coat or something fell down on me," Julie told her.

Jane had something she was anxious to get off her mind. "Julie, I am terribly sorry about—what I did this morning. You know what. I can't talk much now," she said, aware of her parents in the next room.

"That's strange," Jane heard her father say. "Usually she is good for a couple of hours."

"It's all right, Jane," said Julie. "I mean, after all, Buzz asked me for a date tonight, and that's what counts. But that isn't what I called about. Jane, did anybody tell you about Stan?" Julie sounded eager and excited, as if she had important news.

Stan! What could have happened to Stan? "No. Nobody called. Is something wrong?" Jane asked anxiously.

"Late this afternoon he was rushed to the hospital and had his appendix out!" Obviously Julie relished breaking this news.

"In the hospital?" Jane was stunned. Stan in the hospital? He couldn't be. Not Stan. But he must be, if Julie said so. "Is he all right?" she asked at last.

"Yes. Buzz talked to his mother a little while ago, and she said everything was fine," answered Julie.

"Oh. That's good!" Jane's mind was not really on what she was saying. She was seeing everything in a new light. This was the reason Stan had not called! An appendix, of all things! He must have been pale under his tan that morning, not because he was angry, not because he was hurt, but because he had a pain in his appendix!

"Look, I've got to go now," said Julie. "It's hot in here and the others might miss me."

"Thanks for calling," said Jane absently. "Have fun." She sat staring at the cover of the telephone book. Stan in the hospital. Stan, pale and still in a narrow white bed, stuff dripping out of a bottle into a vein in his arm, nurses hovering over him, taking his temperature, feeling his pulse . . .

And how, Jane asked herself, does Jane Purdy, the confident Jane Purdy, behave when the boy she likes, who is angry with her (she *thought*—now she wasn't sure), is in the hospital with his appendix out?

CHAPTER

10

For the next three days Jane wondered what she should do about Stan. She looked over the get-well cards in Woodmont's stationery store, but neither the sentimental cards adorned with roses and violets nor the cards printed with elephants or kittens and silly verses seemed exactly right for a special boy. She considered sending Stan a note and even wrote on her best letter paper, "Dear Stan, I am sorry to hear about your operation. I hope you get well soon." Then she sat nibbling the end of her fountain pen. She could not think of another thing to say.

Jane reread what she had written. It would be the right message, she decided, to put on a card enclosed with a gift. But what gift could a girl send to a boy who had had his appendix out? A book, perhaps, but she did not know what Stan

liked to read. She did not want to send something
he would not enjoy and then have him feel he had
to read it just to be polite. Besides, she did not know
how to get a book to a boy in a hospital. She did
not want to visit him, because he would probably
be surrounded by his mother and father and sisters
and a few aunts and uncles and cousins, and he
would have to introduce her to everyone and that
would be embarrassing, especially if he was angry
with her.

Flowers? Jane chewed the end of her pen and
considered this idea. She could go to the flower
shop, select some flowers, write a few words on
a card, and ask the florist to deliver her gift for
her. Stan would know she was sorry about his bad
luck and they would not have to meet in case he
didn't want to see her. But flowers to a boy? Well,
why not? Anyone in a hospital ought to enjoy receiving flowers. The more Jane considered sending
flowers—masculine flowers, of course—to Stan, the
better she liked the idea. It would be a friendly but
not overeager thing to do. And she had resolved to
act like Jane Purdy and nobody else, hadn't she?
No matter how Stan felt toward her, she was truly
sorry to hear that he was in the hospital and she

really did hope he would get well soon. Well, all right then. She would send Stan some flowers.

But a hint of doubt still lingered in Jane's mind, because she had never known a girl who liked a boy who had his appendix out, and so she had no precedent to follow. Jane did not like to ask her mother's advice about anything, because she almost never liked the advice her mother gave, but this time she felt she had to consult someone.

Jane found her mother reading a magazine in a deck chair in the back yard. Sir Puss, who always sought the most fragrant spot, was sunning himself in the middle of the herb garden. "Mom," she said, eyeing with disapproval her mother's bare legs, "do you think it would be all right if I sent Stan some flowers at the hospital?"

Mrs. Purdy looked up from her magazine. "Why, I think it would be a very nice thing to do. The begonias are about gone, but there are some pretty chrysanthemums on the other side of the garage."

"I'll go look at them," said Jane noncommittally.

"If you want to pick some I could drive you over to the hospital," suggested Mrs. Purdy. "It's too late for visiting hours, but you could leave them at the desk and a nurse would take them to Stan."

"Not right now," murmured Jane vaguely, as she

walked around the garage on the pretense of examining her father's chrysanthemums. Imagine her mother thinking she could just go out in the yard and pick a bunch of flowers and take them to Stan at the hospital! If that wasn't just like Mom. She probably expected her to wrap the home-grown flowers in a newspaper or in a piece of waxed paper from the roll in the kitchen and then walk into the lobby of the Cronk Memorial Hospital with a bouquet that looked too loving-hands-at-home for words. The nurses would probably laugh at her. And what did Mom expect her to use for a card? A piece of notepaper? That was the trouble with Mom. She meant well, but she just didn't understand.

Jane lifted the head of one of her father's chrysanthemums, a great spidery blossom in a delicate shade of pink. It was fragile and lovely, but honestly, what was Mom thinking of? Pink flowers for Stan! A boy should have masculine flowers, like geraniums or something. No, not geraniums. They were too common. But some kind of masculine flower.

The conversation with her mother had cleared up one point for Jane, however. It was perfectly proper for a girl to send flowers to a boy who was in the hospital. Tomorrow, after school, she would walk confidently into De Luca's Flower Shop next door to Nibley's, select some masculine flowers, write her message on a proper florist's card, and have Mr. De Luca deliver the bouquet to the Cronk Memorial Hospital. What could be simpler?

Twenty-four hours later Jane, who had never before sent flowers to anyone, paused in front of De Luca's Flower Shop. One window displayed a bouquet of white stock and chrysanthemums suitable for a wedding. The other was filled with philodendron, its split leaves the size of dinner plates, climbing a moss-covered stick. Confidently Jane opened the door and stepped into the cool shop.

"May I help you?" asked Mr. De Luca, who was wearing a green smock.

"Yes, please." Jane glanced around at the displays of vases, figurines, and potted plants. "I want to send some flowers to someone in the hospital."

"We have some nice yellow roses," said the florist, reaching into the refrigerator at the back of the shop and producing a container of roses. "We can give you a nice arrangement of a dozen and a half roses tied with yellow satin ribbon and set in a round glass bowl for five dollars."

Dubiously Jane looked at the roses. They were too pretty. It was difficult to believe that such perfect blooms had once been attached to bushes with roots growing in soil and manure. No, hothouse roses with a satin ribbon were not right for Stan, Jane decided. "I don't think that is exactly what I had in mind," she told the florist.

"We have some nice chrysanthemums today," suggested Mr. De Luca, pointing to a container of tousle-headed blooms, the kind Jane hoped to wear to a football game some day when she was in college.

"No, I don't think so," said Jane.

"Or how about these?" asked the florist, pointing to some spidery pink chrysanthemums.

Jane felt that these blooms were not nearly so pretty as those in her own back yard. "Well . . . no, I guess not." She was beginning to be embarrassed. By now Mr. De Luca must be impatient with her.

"Are the flowers for a new mother?" asked the florist. "Perhaps if I had some idea . . ."

"Oh, no," said Jane hastily. "They are for a—a man."

"I see." Mr. De Luca's voice was grave, as if he realized the importance of the occasion. "A young man?"

"Sort of. I wanted something more . . . well, something more masculine."

"Yes, of course," agreed Mr. De Luca. "Let me see," he muttered to himself. "masculine flowers."

Jane began to feel uncomfortable. She had not realized it would be so difficult to select flowers.

"Would a nice dish garden do?" the florist asked helpfully. "We have some made up with ivy, variegated peperomia, and white-veined fittonia."

Jane, used to the lovely flowers her father grew in their yard, decided that plants without blossoms did not appeal to her. "No, I want to send flowers," she insisted, wishing she was not so much trouble to wait on.

"I have it!" exclaimed the florist. "How about glads?" He reached into the refrigerator and brought out a couple of stalks of pink gladiolas and held them up for Jane's inspection. "Nothing sissy about glads, is there?"

Jane scrutinized the blossoms on the long straight stems. They were pink, but not a delicate, feminine pink. They were more of a flaming sunset pink. Yes, Jane decided, gladiolas could probably be called masculine flowers.

"With a few delphiniums and some ferns they make a nice arrangement," said Mr. De Luca hopefully. "I can give you a dozen glads, half a dozen delphiniums, and throw in some ferns for three dollars and a half."

"All right. I'll take them," agreed Jane, glad to

have made a decision at last. She dug into her coin purse for some of her baby-sitting money, which she handed across the counter. "And would you please send them to the Cronk Memorial Hospital?"

"I'm sorry, miss," said the florist. "We don't deliver under five dollars."

"Oh." Jane was taken aback by this news. Still, it was only about four blocks to the hospital, and she could easily walk over with the flowers and leave them at the information desk to be sent up to Stan's room, the way her mother had suggested. The flowers would be wrapped in proper green florist's paper and would not have the loving-hands-at-home look of flowers picked in the garden and wrapped in waxed paper, so she would have no reason to feel ashamed of them. "I'll take them anyway," said Jane. "I can carry them over to the hospital."

"You can be writing a card if you like," suggested Mr. De Luca. "I'll have the flowers ready for you in a few minutes."

Jane sat down at the desk in the corner of the shop and chose a plain white card. She wrote, "Dear Stan, I am sorry to hear about your operation. I hope you get well soon. Jane." Then she carefully wrote *Stanley Crandall* on an envelope and was

about to put the card inside when she realized her
message was all wrong. It was too stiff and prim, too
Miss Muffetish. She tore the card into bits and
dropped them into the wastebasket. On a second
card she wrote, "Sorry to hear about your bad luck.
Hope you get well soon. Jane." That was better. It
was friendly and casual and not so prim.

"Here we are," announced Mr. De Luca.

Jane turned from the desk to look and it occurred
to her that it was a good thing she was sitting down.
Otherwise, the shock of seeing her flowers might
have been too much for her. They were not dis-
creetly wrapped in green paper, as she had anticipated. The flaming sunset gladiolas, the intense blue
delphiniums, and the ferns were arranged in a foil-
covered container ornamented with a blue ribbon.
The stalks of flowers stuck out like the spikes on
the crown of the Statue of Liberty, and the spaces
between were filled with asparagus fern. The whole
lurid thing was at least three feet across.

"Made up real nice, didn't it?" Mr. De Luca adjusted a fern and stood back to admire his work.

"Uh . . . yes," answered Jane. Now what was
she going to do? She couldn't tell the florist she
had changed her mind after she had paid him and
he had gone to all that work and looked so pleased

with what he had done. For a frantic moment Jane considered rushing out of the shop, never to return. She couldn't do that either, and she did not know what she could do except deliver the monstrous bouquet. Good old Jane Purdy, she thought grimly. She means well, but she always manages to do the wrong thing. She has a real talent for it.

Since she had made up her mind to be herself and since she was the kind of person who always did the wrong thing, Jane decided she might as well make the best of it and start out by delivering the flowers to Stan. That was exactly what she would do. She would see this thing through if it was the last thing she did. Jane felt a kind of triumph at this decision. What if she did run into someone who knew her? What if the kids from school did tease her? She would find an answer for them. A little confidence was all she needed.

"Is something wrong?" asked Mr. De Luca. "You don't like it?"

"It's very pretty," answered Jane faintly. And it *was* pretty in a gaudy way. The blossoms were fresh, the blue bow was jaunty, the colors harmonized. It was just that it was so big. Jane told herself she might as well get started. She couldn't just sit there all day. In spite of her decision she rose reluctantly and lifted her flowers from the counter. "Thank you for—for arranging the flowers," she said as she peered through the foliage at Mr. De Luca.

"Here, let me open the door for you," said the florist. The bouquet was too wide for the door, so Jane walked sideways out of the shop.

Jane had to pass Nibley's on her way to Cronk Memorial Hospital and, as she had expected, a gang from Woodmont High was congregated in front of the entrance. A gang of boys, she gathered from their voices. And this time she was not going to let anybody tease her, she told herself severely. She would show them. She would remember she was Jane Purdy and no one else. Maybe she was doing the wrong thing, but that was the way she was.

"Hey, look what's coming!" she heard a boy's voice exclaim, and there was a hoot of laughter from the crowd.

"What is it?" asked another boy.

"It has a skirt and legs and feet. It must be half human," said another boy.

"Yes, and the legs aren't bad." Jane recognized Buzz's voice. She had tried to avoid Buzz since he had kissed her, but this time she didn't care if he did see her. Ha, she'd show him. That wolf, junior grade.

Jane lowered her bouquet and peeped over the blossoms. "Hi," she said.

Buzz grinned at her, that annoying grin he had flashed at her since the morning he had kissed her. Jane felt her face flush in spite of herself. "What do you think you're doing, hiding behind that?" Buzz asked.

"I'm taking this to Stan, at the hospital," Jane said coolly. "Is that all right with you?"

"You call that thing a bouquet?" asked Buzz.

"No, I don't call it a bouquet," Jane answered pertly. "I call it a camouflage."

This time everyone laughed at Buzz. Score one for me, thought Jane. The door of Nibley's opened and Marcy, followed by Greg, walked out.

Jane did not wait for Marcy to make her feel like Miss Muffet. "Hi, Marcy," she said. "Look at the flowers I'm taking to Stan. Did you ever see anything so enormous in all your life?"

"Wow!" exclaimed Greg with a friendly laugh. "I'll bet he'll be surprised."

Jane giggled. "Not half as much as I was when I saw it."

"You mean you're taking Stan flowers after he took someone else to the dance?" asked Marcy.

Meow to you, too, Marcy, thought Jane, but she said, "Why not? He could hardly break a date he had made before he met me, could he?"

Marcy looked surprised. "No, I suppose not," she had to admit.

Score two for me, thought Jane, and said sweetly, "Stan told me all about it."

"Oh," said Marcy.

That takes care of that, thought Jane. Good-by, Miss Muffet. Good-by forever. "And now if you gentlemen will step aside, I'll be on my way," she said to the crowd of boys.

The boys parted, and Jane saw Julie and Liz approaching Nibley's. "Jane!" cried Julie in horror. "Are you . . . you're not—"

"Yes," answered Jane calmly. "I am."

"Why didn't you have them delivered?" whispered Julie, when she had reached Jane's side.

"Because they won't deliver anything under five dollars," said Jane, "and being me, I didn't find it out until it was too late."

"Don't you want me to go with you?" asked Julie.

"No, thank you, Julie," answered Jane. Actually, Jane would have been grateful for her friend's company, but she had made up her mind to see this thing through and she was going to see it through without any help from anyone. "I can peek through this, you know. I don't need someone to guide me. But thanks anyway for the moral support."

"It's a pretty bouquet," said Julie, "even if it is sort of big."

"You know, you remind me of Birnam wood," remarked Liz.

"What's Birnam wood?" Jane wanted to know.

"Haven't you read *Macbeth?*" Liz sounded superior.

Jane stood her ground and refused to let Liz make her feel fluffy and not very bright. "No, I've only had *As You Like It* and *Julius Caesar*," she answered, and it occurred to her that high school students, except intellectuals like Liz, always said they had had Shakespeare's plays instead of saying they had studied them.

"You'll get *Macbeth* next year," explained Greg, making Shakespeare sound like the measles. "This bunch of soldiers broke off a lot of boughs and branches and stuff in a place called Birnam wood and held them up in front of them for camouflage and crept up on Macbeth's castle. It looked like the wood was advancing."

Jane laughed. "That's me. I'm creeping up on Cronk Memorial Hospital."

"Say, I'll walk over with you," offered a boy in a second-year letter man's sweater.

"No, thank you," said Jane, and smiled at the crowd. " 'By now."

"Funny I've never noticed her before," she heard the letter man remark as she left.

A delicious feeling of satisfaction flowed through Jane as she proceeded behind her flowers toward the hospital. She had been herself, Jane Purdy, and no one else. It hadn't been easy, but it had worked!

People turned to stare at her, cars tooted at her, but Jane did not care. She only smiled and went on her way, past the shops, down a shaded street, and up the steps of the Cronk Memorial Hospital.

Inside, everyone — doctors, nurses, visitors — stopped to stare at Jane and to smile as if highly amused. Her ordeal was nearly ended. Jane propelled her bouquet across the lobby to the information desk where, free of it at last, she set the bouquet on the counter. "I would like to leave this for Stanley Crandall," she said.

The attendant, obviously trying to suppress a smile, flipped through a file of cards. "I'm sorry, but Mr. Crandall was discharged this morning," she informed Jane.

"So soon?" asked Jane in dismay.

"Yes, we don't keep them long nowadays," explained the attendant, glancing at the card again. "You can reach him at 17 Poppy Lane."

Jane's confidence wavered. "17 Poppy Lane," she repeatedly blankly. That was only three blocks away. There was nothing to do now but go ahead and deliver the flowers to his house. If she didn't, Stan was sure to hear about them from the crowd at school and wonder why he had never received them. Stifling a sudden desire to giggle, she picked

up her flowers once more. Here goes Birnam wood
again, she thought, and advanced behind her bouquet across the lobby, out of the hospital, and down
the street toward Poppy Lane.

When Jane reached Stan's block, a stocky little
girl about eight years old, who had been roller-
skating aimlessly up and down the sidewalk, darted
up to Jane. "What are you carrying that for?" she
demanded.

"Because," answered Jane.

"Because why?" persisted the girl.

"I'm taking them to a sick friend," Jane told the
child.

"My brother had his appendix out. He just came

home from the hospital today," the girl informed Jane.

Jane lowered her bouquet for a better look at this child, who had brown pigtails, a dirty face, and Stan's gray-green eyes.

"Say!" exclaimed Stan's little sister. "I'll bet you're taking all those flowers to my brother!"

Jane felt she might as well admit it. "Yes," she said. "I am."

The child's face lit up with excitement. "Gee!" she exclaimed, and darted off, her skates going *ching-chung* against the cement. At number seventeen, she turned and clomped up the steps. "Hey, Mom," she yelled, as she threw open the front door. "Come quick! Somebody's bringing flowers to Stan, and it's a girl!"

Jane squelched an urge to fling her flowers into the gutter and run. It was too late for that. With her cheeks flaming, she marched bravely up the steps of Stan's house and reached the front door just as Mrs. Crandall appeared. There she was, face to face with Stan's mother. From behind her floral screen Jane wanted to faint, disappear in a puff of smoke, drop dead, anything to get out of this awful situation. Instead she stared, as if stricken, over the spikes of gladiolas at this unknown person, Stan's mother.

Mrs. Crandall, a comfortable-looking woman, smiled reassuringly at Jane. "What lovely flowers!" she exclaimed. "And how thoughtful of you to bring them to Stan."

"I—I meant him to have them at the hospital," said Jane shyly. "I didn't know he would leave so soon."

"They don't keep patients long in hospitals after an operation these days," explained Mrs. Crandall. "Here, let me take the flowers."

Gratefully Jane surrendered her burden.

"Stan is taking a nap right now," Mrs. Crandall went on, as if receiving a gaudy floral piece from a strange girl were not at all unusual, "but won't you come in?"

"Well, no—thank you," said Jane uncertainly. "I think I had better be going home. My—my mother is expecting me."

Mrs. Crandall smiled warmly at Jane across the flowers. "You must be Jane Purdy," she said.

"Yes, I am," Jane admitted, and wondered what Stan had said about her to his family.

"Stan has spoken of you so often," said Mrs. Crandall. "You must come over and have dinner with us sometime."

"I—I would love to," stammered Jane, pleased and embarrassed by this unexpected invitation. She only hoped that Stan would be pleased too.

"Boy, does Stan like you!" the little sister informed Jane. "He always shines his shoes for about an hour before he goes to see you!"

"Mitzi!" exclaimed Mrs. Crandall with a laugh.

"Well, he does," persisted Mitzi. "He says—"

"Mitzi!" Mrs. Crandall's voice held a warning.

Jane felt her face flush even redder. "Tell Stan everybody misses him at school," she said, and turned to leave.

"Thank you so much for the flowers, Jane," said Mrs. Crandall. "It was thoughtful of you to bring them to Stan, and I know he'll be pleased."

"I hope so," said Jane, more at ease with this pleasant woman, who looked as if she understood how difficult it was to be fifteen. "Good-by, Mrs. Crandall."

"Good-by, Jane."

"Good-by," called Mitzi, as Jane walked down the steps. "Golly, Mom, did you ever see such a *big* bunch of flowers?"

Jane walked sedately down the street and around

the corner from Poppy Lane, but she did not feel
at all sedate. She wanted to run and skip and shout.
Her ordeal was over. She had not acted like Miss
Muffet when the gang from school had tried to
tease her. Mrs. Crandall had been friendly and had
not laughed at her and, best of all, she had learned
that Stan liked her enough to talk about her to his
family. Maybe she had, in her usual way, done all
the wrong things, but everything had turned out
all right. Maybe that was the way things were when
a girl was fifteen. And Stan shined his shoes before
he came to see her. His sister said so. Darling Stan
in his shiny shoes!

"Hi, Mom," Jane greeted her mother cheerfully,
as she walked into the house.

Mrs. Purdy looked up from sewing and smiled.
"Did you have a good day?"

"M-m-m. Good and bad. Mostly good, though."
Jane lifted Sir Puss from the chair in which he was
napping and buried her face in his tabby fur. "How's
the old pussy cat?" she asked him. "Hm-m? How's
the old pussy cat today?"

Sir Puss struggled free and leaped to the floor,
where he glared at Jane and then began meticulously to wash himself, as if the touch of her hands
had soiled him. "You're a spoiled old thing," Jane

told him, as the telephone rang. "I'll get it, Mom," she said, and went into the hall. "Hello?" She spoke blithely, for once not caring who was on the line.

"Hi there." It was Stan.

"Oh—hello," answered Jane eagerly. It was so good to hear his voice once more.

"I want to thank you for the flowers," said Stan. "They're sure pretty."

"I'm glad you like them," answered Jane. "I wasn't sure whether you would or not. The bouquet turned out to be bigger than I expected."

"Hold the line a minute, will you?" Stan asked, and Jane heard him say, "Beat it, Mitzi, will you? Can't a fellow have a little privacy once in a while in his own home?" Then he continued, "I just wish I'd been awake when you came over. I told Mom she should have called me. I'm sure sorry I couldn't phone you last Saturday."

"That's all right," said Jane and then added guardedly, because her mother was in the next room, "I thought you might be mad at me because of what happened that morning. You know. In front of Julie's house."

"I guess I was sort of mad at first." Stan's voice was also guarded, and Jane knew that his mother and Mitzi were near. "But that was just because—well, because I wished it was me instead of Buzz."

"Oh." It was all Jane could say, and even though she was alone in the hall she could feel herself blush with pleasure.

"Would you mind?" Stan's voice was almost a whisper.

"No." Jane could barely whisper back, she felt so stifled by emotion.

Then Stan spoke in a normal voice. "I'll be back at school in time for the steak bake and movie at Woodmont Park. Is it a date?"

"Yes, it is," answered Jane. "I'm glad you'll be well in time."

"I'll call you before then," promised Stan. "I'll call you often."

When Stan had hung up, Jane sat motionless, smiling dreamily at the telephone. Stan wanted to kiss her! She glanced at the calendar that hung above the telephone and saw that the steak bake was two weeks away. Two long weeks! How could she live that long?

CHAPTER
11

THE next two weeks passed quickly for Jane. It did not take long for the story of her walk behind the screen of gladiolas and delphiniums to spread through Woodmont High. Everyone laughed at the story, but the laughter was friendly. And all because I kept my head up during the whole awful thing, Jane thought, and if I had walked down the street cringing with embarrassment, everyone would be making fun of me now. Instead, boys she did not know, even seniors, grinned at her as they passed her in the corridor and called out, "Hi there! Picked any petunias lately?" or "How are things in Birnam wood?" Girls said, "How did you *ever* do it? Didn't you just about *die* of embarrassment?" The gossip column of the *Woodmontonian* printed an item that asked, "What sophomore was seen hiding behind a

floral duck blind on her way to visit what junior at
Cronk Memorial Hospital?" Even the faculty must
have heard the story, because the football coach
and the physics teacher smiled at Jane as she walked
down the hall.

Best of all, Stan telephoned every day at four
o'clock, and Jane spent a happy hour on the telephone saying nothing in particular, just talking to
Stan. She longed for the day when she could see
him again, free from the listening ears of her mother
and his little sister. She turned over in her mind
what Stan had said about wishing he had been the
one to kiss her, not Buzz, and she wondered if he
would remember on the night of the steak bake.
Perhaps he would ask her to walk under the trees
along the stream. . . .

It seemed no time at all until that evening arrived
and Jane was actually alone with Stan, riding toward
Woodmont Park with him in his blue car. He was
even better-looking than she had remembered. His
profile was clean-cut and his skin a scrubbed golden
tan. The evening was warm, and he was wearing
a white shirt with the sleeves rolled up, revealing
his identification bracelet on his strong right wrist—
a bracelet that he might some day ask her to wear.
Jane glanced down at his shoes. Even by the dim

light of the dashboard she could see that they had been polished until they gleamed. Jane smiled secretly to herself and felt some of her old shyness return. She had been at ease talking to Stan over the telephone, but now that she was beside him she could think of nothing to say.

Stan took his eyes off the road long enough to glance down at Jane. "This beats walking, doesn't it?" he remarked. "Or riding in the Doggie Diner truck."

Jane laughed. "It certainly does."

"You know something?" said Stan. "The first time I took you out, Dad said I had to be in by ten-thirty. He wouldn't let me take the car, either. I was worried about how I was going to take you to the movies and get you home and still get home myself. I knew Dad wouldn't care if I came in five or ten minutes late, but it was cutting things pretty close. So I took a chance and rode over to your house on my bike. I rode past on the other side of the street first to see if anyone was looking, and when I didn't see anyone I hid my bike in your shrubbery. I was sure scared somebody would look out the window and see me. I didn't want you to think I was just a kid who rode around on a bike."

Jane smiled to herself before she answered demurely, "I knew about the bike. After I turned out the light that evening I saw you pull it out of the shrubbery and ride it down the street."

"You did!" Stan was astonished. "You knew and you never mentioned it?"

"I didn't say anything, because I knew if you hid your bicycle in the shrubbery you didn't want me to know about it," Jane explained. "I was glad you rode it over to my house, because then I was pretty sure you weren't too grown-up to like me. You seemed so much older at first."

"Well, for Pete's sake!" Stan laughed. "And here I was feeling so awkward and thought you had so much poise!"

"You know," said Jane thoughtfully, when they had finished laughing, "it's funny about bicycles. I never ride mine any more. For some reason, when you're in high school it won't do to be seen riding a bicycle because you need it to get someplace, but it's all right to ride one for fun if you don't really need to. Like going on a picnic or something."

"That's right," agreed Stan. "That's exactly how it is." They smiled at each other, pleased to have shared this understanding. Jane was sorry they were going to the steak bake. It was so wonderful to be with Stan once more. She wanted to ride on and on through the warm fall evening.

Stan parked his car at the edge of Woodmont Park and went around to help Jane out. A noisy crowd was gathered under the lights around the barbecue pits, and the smell of cooking steak mingled with the fragrance of the bay and redwood trees. "I'm starved," said Stan. "Come on, let's join the others."

"Hello, Jane." "Hi, Stan, glad to see you back." "Hi there, Jane." "Stan, you're looking swell." The crowd welcomed them.

"Hi, everybody," said Stan, while Jane smiled happily beside him. Not many sophomores had dates for the junior-class steak bake.

Mr. Degenkalb, a history teacher who was the harried class adviser, was herding the crowd into line beside the barbecue pits where the steaks were sizzling on grates over open fires. Greg and another boy were turning the steaks with pitchforks. Jane and Stan took their place in line and picked up knives and forks and paper plates. Someone served them scalloped potatoes that had been cooked in the school cafeteria and rushed to the park; someone else put steak on their plates.

"Hi, you two," said Buzz, who was serving salad. "I'm on garbage detail."

"Looks to me like you're serving salad," remarked Stan, as Jane held out her plate.

"You know how salad turns into garbage when it's been sitting around a couple of hours," said Buzz. "That's why I'm on garbage detail." He ladled some limp greens onto Stan's plate. "Have some tossed green salad. Take it and toss it into the trash can."

"Buzz, you're awful," laughed Jane.

"Come on, Jane," whispered Stan. "Let's not sit at the tables with the others. Let's go over by the stream."

Jane's smile was her answer. Now she knew that Stan wanted to be alone with her as much as she wanted to be alone with him. Carrying their paper plates of food, they walked through the carpet of wood sorrel that grew along the bank of the stream and found two rocks near the trickle of water. It was a perfect spot to be with Stan. There was even a full moon rising through the bay trees. Jane sat down on her rock with a sigh of pleasure. It was a beautiful, romantic moonlit night. Perhaps after Stan had eaten his steak he would turn to her and look deep into her eyes. . . .

"This stream doesn't have much water in it, but at least it's wet," observed Stan, settling himself on his rock.

"It's the only stream I know of around here that has any water at all this time of year," said Jane, as she eyed her steak. It was large and thin and overhung the edges of the paper plate. It did not look like any cut of meat her mother had ever ordered from Jake's Market. Jane set her plate on her knees and took a bite of cold scalloped potato. Perhaps if she ate her potatoes first there would be more room for the steak on her plate. She sampled the salad. Buzz was right.

Here goes, thought Jane, and sawed at her steak with her cafeteria knife. Nothing happened to the steak, but the pressure of the knife bent the paper plate. Gingerly she tried another side of the steak. This time she succeeded in separating a morsel of meat, which she put into her mouth. That was her mistake. She chewed and chewed and chewed. From the tables by the barbecue pits she could hear laughter and chatter from the crowd, snatches of song, cries of "Speech!" She was missing the fun, but she didn't care. She was alone with Stan. Alone and chewing.

Stan, too, was occupied with chewing. He gulped,

and turned to Jane. "It sure is a beautiful night, isn't it?" he asked softly, and looked into her eyes.

Jane stopped chewing. She hadn't expected this from Stan so soon, before he had finished his steak.

"Isn't it, Jane?" he asked, as if her answer were important to him.

Jane gulped and swallowed her meat whole. "Yes, it is," she said nervously. The moment was so terribly important. "It's—it's a good cat-fight night."

Stan looked so startled that Jane immediately regretted the words that had slipped out. "I mean, that's something we always say at home when there's a full moon," she said, and wished she hadn't. Now she had to go on and explain why the Purdys said a moonlit night was a good cat-fight night. "When Sir Puss was younger he always got into fights when there was a full moon. Now he goes out and hunts mostly. You know how it is. A good cat-fight night is a sort of family phrase." *Oh*, she thought, why do I have to babble on this way? Stan was looking into my eyes and now I've spoiled everything.

"Sure, I know," said Stan, applying his knife to his steak. "At our house we always call a clear windy day a good drying day. Where we lived in the city there was so much fog Mom always had a hard time getting the washing dry, and almost every morning she would look out the window and say hopefully, 'Maybe today will be a good drying day.' "

I guess that ought to take care of the weather for a while, thought Jane, and attacked her steak once more. As she sawed away, she glanced at Stan to see how he was managing and found him watching to see how she was cutting her meat. All at once the humor of the situation struck Jane and she began to giggle.

Stan relaxed and laughed. "Why don't we just pick it up and gnaw?" he suggested.

"I don't know how else we can manage," agreed Jane, and took her cold steak in both hands. She was careful to tear off a small bite in case Stan should look into her eyes again. Resolutely she and Stan chewed.

"At least tonight we know we're eating meat," said Jane. "That night we had dinner in Chinatown I didn't know what anything was. We had just walked past one of those herb shops that has all those weird-looking things in the window and a grocery store that had a tub full of snails, and my imagination went to work. And I wanted to be so sophisticated, too."

Stan laughed. "I knew you weren't having a good time, but I didn't know it was that bad."

Jane chewed thoughtfully. She really had changed since that night in Chinatown. Tonight, only a month instead of ten years later, she could look back on that dinner at Hing Sun Yee's and not only laugh, but admit to Stan she had tried to be sophisticated. And the first time she had a date with Stan she had been so nervous she could scarcely eat a dish of vanilla ice cream, and now look at her. Here she was, sitting on a rock holding a tough piece of meat in her hands and gnawing at it—and laughing about it.

"Look at the lovebirds over there by the stream," Jane heard someone on the nearby path say. She winced, and hoped Stan had not heard. He appeared to be concentrating on chewing. Jane considered the size of her meat and the time it took to chew each bite. At this rate, if they were going to finish their steaks they would have to take them along to the movie.

"I give up," said Stan at last, setting his plate on a rock and wiping his hands on his paper napkin. "This is too tough for human consumption. It's tougher than Doggie Diner meat."

"It certainly is," agreed Jane, as she searched for her paper napkin. She could not find it, so she set her plate aside and surreptitiously wiped her fingers on the edge of her slip. When she looked at Stan he was rubbing one finger back and forth over the name plate on his identification bracelet.

"Jane . . ." Stan looked into her eyes.

Jane felt her heart begin to pound. Nervously she moistened her lips.

"*There* you are!" shouted a voice behind them. It was Buzz, with Julie beside him. "What are you trying to do? Hide? We've looked all over for you."

"Hi," said Stan, with no enthusiasm at all.

Jane flashed her best friend a Julie-how-could-you look, which Julie returned with an I-know-but-what-could-I-do expression.

Buzz sprang onto a rock and with a sweeping gesture of his right hand proclaimed, "What is this atomic age we live in? May we by simply touching a button or turning a knob—"

"This isn't your public-speaking class," interrupted Stan.

"No, but it's a good place to practice," said Buzz, in his ordinary voice, before he continued eloquently, "How can we prepare ourselves for what lies ahead?"

"Come on, Buzz," said Julie. "We can prepare ourselves for the movie by finding seats."

Buzz ignored her. "Today's generation can be the

salvation of tomorrow," he announced, with a sweep of his hand.

Darn Buzz, anyway, thought Jane. He's doing this on purpose, because he knows Stan and I want to be alone.

Stan glowered at Buzz. "Come on, Jane, let's find a trash can for the remains."

" 'Four score and seven years ago—' " said Buzz. "What's the matter, Stan? Don't you like my public speaking?"

"No, I don't," said Stan.

"I'm cut to the quick," said Buzz cheerfully. "Mr. Chairman, members of the faculty, and fellow students. I stand here before you today to ask you to consider the merits of adopting a twelve-month school year for Woodmont High School."

Jane gave Julie a do-something-quick look.

Julie flashed Jane an I'll-do-the-best-I-can look. "Come on, Buzz," she said. "The movie is about to start. Let's go and find good seats before they're all taken."

"Let it start," said Buzz. "I found out what it's going to be."

"What?" Julie asked.

"The John Quincy Adams Story," said Buzz.

Julie groaned. "Not really! Why did they have to go and choose something like that?"

"Probably because it is pure, high-minded, and educational," answered Buzz.

"Come on, Jane," whispered Stan. "Let's ditch the movie and go for a ride."

"O.K." Jane's answer was eager. She could not bear the thought of sitting through a movie, any movie, on such a beautiful night. Not when she could be riding under the stars with Stan.

"Good idea, Stan," said Buzz heartily. "Julie and I have been wondering when you were going to ask us to go for a ride in that rumble seat."

"I didn't," said Stan flatly. "Come on, Jane. Let's go."

Jane clambered up the bank beside Stan and dropped her paper plate into a trash can. Buzz and Julie followed close behind, and Jane hoped that she and Stan would be able to shake them. The junior class, unaware that it was about to see *The John Quincy Adams Story*, was assembling on the benches in front of a motion picture screen.

Mr. Degenkalb, still looking harried, was rounding up the stray members of the class. "Well, Stan, you're not trying to run out on us, are you?" he asked jovially.

"Well, uh—" said Stan.

"Come on, there are plenty of good seats left," said Mr. Degenkalb, and herded Jane and Stan toward the benches. Out of the corner of her eye Jane noticed Buzz seize Julie by the arm and hurry her out of the park. From the sidewalk he grinned, and waved at Jane and Stan. That Buzz! thought Jane bitterly.

"Let's sit in the last row," whispered Stan. "Then we can slip out as soon as they turn off the park lights and the movie starts." They found seats on the end of a bench in the very last row, back under the redwood trees, and sat down, confident that they could get away soon. One by one, the park lights blinked out and Jane sat poised on the edge of the bench ready to flee with Stan to the privacy of his car.

"Say, Stan," whispered Mr. Degenkalb, "would you mind moving over?"

Jane and Stan exchanged one stricken look. Silently they moved over, and Mr. Degenkalb sat down beside Stan. Jane leaned back on the bench. There was no chance of getting away now. They were trapped. Trapped for all six or eight or maybe even ten reels of *The John Quincy Adams Story*. I can't stand it, thought Jane. I simply cannot stand it. An entire evening wasted, an evening that she wanted to spend riding through the moonlight with Stan, the evening she had waited for so long. For days she had dreamed of this date. . . . Well, here they were. Trapped with Mr. Degenkalb and John Quincy Adams.

The title of the movie flashed on the screen and the junior class groaned. John Quincy Adams, secretary of state, and John Quincy Adams, sixth president of the United States, moved before Jane's eyes, but all she noticed were the magnified shadows of moths that flew between the projection machine and the screen. The junior class applauded wildly for the moths. The bench grew harder by the minute. Even the rocks by the stream had seemed softer. Two by two, the members of the junior class slipped off the benches and, crouching low beneath the light of the projector, fled from the park.

Jane looked wistfully after these students, these fortunate escapees, who were dispersing to Nibley's or the Woodmont Theater, where a good movie was playing, or to their cars, and thought longingly of the front seat of Stan's car. If they could only get away they could drive up in the hills, where the night would be aromatic with the scent of eucalyptus trees. She would feel the wind in her hair and when they came to Lookout Point . . .

Jane stole a glance at Stan. He was looking straight ahead and his expression was serious, as if he were absorbed in the activities of John Quincy Adams as secretary of state.

And when they came to Lookout Point, Jane's thought ran on, Stan would park the car so it faced the view of the bay and the city, and he would turn off the ignition and turn to her in the moonlight and say . . .

There was no use thinking about it, Jane told herself. Not when they were practically surrounded by Mr. Degenkalb. But she did not know what else she could think about. Certainly not John Quincy Adams, not on a night like this. Everything had looked so hopeful when she and Stan were sitting on the rocks by the stream, but life never turned out the way she planned. Oh well, there would be other dates of course, but it would have been so nice if . . .

Jane felt Stan's hand brush hers, but when she looked up at him in the flickering light he was staring straight ahead. She was surprised to feel his hand on her arm and still more surprised—almost unbelieving—to see his fingers unclasp his identification bracelet and remove it from his arm. Silently he fumbled with the bracelet and slipped it around her right wrist. With a tiny click he snapped the clasp shut. Jane gave a gasp of astonishment and turned questioningly to Stan. She was wearing his identification bracelet! The silver links on her wrist were still warm from his arm.

Stan leaned toward Jane. "O.K.?" he whispered.

"Yes," she whispered back and smiled radiantly at Stan, at John Quincy Adams, at the backs of the rapidly diminishing junior class. She really was wearing Stan's bracelet on her arm, something she had scarcely allowed herself to think about—at least not often; it would be so far in the future, if it happened at all. And now it had happened, months before she had dreamed it could. Jane's wrist felt small and feminine in the circle of heavy silver links. Tenderly she caressed the letters of Stan's name with her finger tips. Stanley Crandall. The nicest boy in the whole world.

After that it seemed only a few minutes until the movie ended and the lights in the park went on "Well, Stan," said Mr. Degenkalb, "it was a pretty good movie, wasn't it?"

Dreamily Jane wondered how Stan would answer. He laughed easily and said, "Especially the parts played by moths." Then he took Jane by the hand—something he had never done before. "Come on, let's get out of here," he said, and pulled her through the crowd to his car.

Finally after hours—no, days—of waiting, Jane was alone with Stan. She climbed up into the seat and looked at her watch by moonlight. "Stan," she wailed, when she saw the time. "It's twenty-five minutes past ten. I have to go home." Only five minutes left to be with Stan. This was the way things always turned out for her.

Stan started the car and headed toward Blossom Street. "Jane," he said urgently, above the sound of the model-A motor, "you know what it means to wear a fellow's bracelet?"

"Yes," answered Jane breathlessly.

"It means you're going steady."

"I know." Jane touched the bracelet.

"You really want to?"

"Yes, Stan. I really want to."

Stan stopped the car in front of Jane's house. "I wish it wasn't so late," he said, and ran around the car to open the door for her. He took her hand in his as they went up the walk together. Halfway to the house Stan stopped and turned to Jane. He put his hands on her shoulders and drew her toward him. "I'm glad we're going steady," he whispered.

"So am I." In spite of the reassuring weight of his bracelet on her wrist, Jane suddenly felt shy. It seemed strange to be so close to Stan, to feel his crisp clean shirt against her cheek. She could not look up at him. Gently Stan lifted her face to his. "You're my girl," he whispered.

At that moment they both heard the strange, muted cry of a cat that has successfully stalked a gopher. Jane stiffened. Sir Puss appeared from the shrubbery and tossed his catch into the air so that it landed with a thud at Jane's feet. Crying insistently, the cat hovered over his prey. He would, she knew, cry until he was praised.

Jane felt Stan start to pull away from her. Then he hesitated and quickly bent his face to hers. Their noses bumped, but their lips met tenderly, clumsily, one side of his mouth against one side of hers. Jane had not known a boy's lips could be so soft. Stan's first kiss—it was a moment to cherish.

Persistently Sir Puss cried over his gopher. A window flew open, and Jane stepped away from Stan. The beam of a flashlight played over the yard and settled on the cat and his catch. "My, that's a big one!" said Mr. Purdy, still half asleep. The cat, satisfied that his good work had been recognized, silently picked up his gopher and disappeared into the bushes. "Why, hello there, Jane." Mr. Purdy sounded bewildered. "You home already?"

"Yes, Pop," answered Jane. First the cat, now her father!

"Well, I guess I'd better be going," said Stan awkwardly.

"Good night, Stan," said Jane softly. "I had a wonderful time."

Stan started down the walk toward his car. "Good night, Stan," called Mr. Purdy.

"Good night, sir," Stan called back. "I'll see you tomorrow, Jane."

Smiling to herself, Jane turned and walked toward the house. She was Stan's girl. That was all that really mattered.

BEVERLY CLEARY was born in a small town in Oregon, where she lived until she reached school age. At that time her family moved to Portland (the scene of her previous books), where she spent her grammar and high-school years. After graduating from the University of California at Berkeley, she entered the School of Librarianship at the University of Washington in Seattle, specializing in library work with children. In 1939 she became Children's Librarian in Yakima, Washington.

In 1940 she married Clarence T. Cleary, and they moved to Oakland, California. During World War II Mrs. Cleary was Post Librarian at the Oakland Army Hospital. The Clearys now live in Berkeley. They are the parents of twins, a boy and a girl.

The Luckiest Girl

BEVERLY CLEARY

The Luckiest Girl

MORROW JUNIOR BOOKS

New York

24   25   26   27   28   29   30

The Luckiest Girl

Chapter 1

One Saturday morning early in September Shelley Latham sat at the breakfast table with her mother and father. Her mother was reading the women's page of the morning paper while her father read the editorial section. There were dahlias in the center of the table and linen mats under each plate; the electric coffeepot gleamed in a ray of morning sunlight. It was a peaceful scene, apparently no different from any other Saturday morning breakfast at the Lathams', but this morning there was a difference, invisible but real. This morning Shelley was plotting.

Outside Shelley heard the rasp of a dry leaf scudding along the driveway. The sound meant the season was changing, and she intended to make her life change with it. That was what made the start of a new high-school year exciting—the possibility t this time things could be different. New school clothes, a change of locker partners, a new boy across the aisle in English class, even the autumn air, crisp and shining—all these could make a big difference in a girl's life.

And Shelley had made up her mind that this year, her junior year, there was going to be a difference. For one thing, she was no longer going to go steady with Jack. How she would break off she did not know, but it would be soon, this very day perhaps.

But before she could do anything about Jack, Shelley had another problem to settle and the time to do it was now. She looked at her mother, who was innocently eating a soft-boiled egg, and made up her mind to be firm from the very start.

"Shelley, here's an advertisement for a school dress that would be pretty on you," remarked the unsuspecting Mrs. Latham. "A blue wool-and-rabbit hair with a full skirt."

Shelley was not going to lose sight of her goal. Anyway, she did not want a dress like that for school. She preferred sweaters and skirts such as all the other girls wore. "Mother, I am going downtown this afternoon to buy my slicker," Shelley stated. It was always best to be definite about a controversial subject and to introduce it when her father was present. "School starts Tuesday and I might need it," she explained logically, although her reason for wanting the slicker was not logical at all. She did not know

why she wanted a slicker. She only knew that owning one was important and somehow might help
make her year different.

"Oh, Shelley, you don't really want one of those
awful slickers," remarked Mrs. Latham as she used
her napkin to wipe up some pollen that had fallen
from the dahlias to the gleaming surface of the
mahogany table.

Shelley could not help smiling, because this was
exactly what she had expected her mother to say.
I'll put it on my list, she thought. If she ever had a
sixteen-year-old daughter who wanted a slicker, she
would not refer to it as "one of those awful slickers."

Shelley's list, now imaginary, had begun when she
was twelve, going-on-thirteen. At that time she had
printed on the outside of an envelope: "To be read
by me if I ever have a twelve-year-old daughter."
On a sheet of paper she had written:

"1. I will let her read in bed all she wants without
telling her she will ruin her eyes.

"2. I will not tell my friends embarrassing things
that happen to her and laugh.

"3. I will not hang crummy old paper chains on
the Christmas tree just because she made them
when she was a little girl."

A year later Shelley, touched that her mother had
treasured the faded paper chains because she had

once worked so hard to make them with colored paper and library paste, crossed the third item off the list. A few months ago when she had been going steady with Jack for some time, she had written in its place: "3. I will not show her baby pictures to boys who come to see her." And soon after that Shelley decided the list was childish and tore it up. But the habit persisted, the list becoming imaginary and the items half-forgotten as soon as Shelley noted them.

The conversation about the purchase of the slicker was postponed by a letter that dropped through the slot in the front door and slid across the polished floor. Shelley picked up the letter and glanced at the return address, 613 N. Mirage Avenue, San Sebastian, California—an address that never failed to delight her. She always wondered if there was a South Mirage, too, and if both parts of the avenue might not someday disappear because they were named for something that was not real at all, but only an illusion of the eye. "It's from your college roommate," she said, as she handed the letter to her mother.

Mrs. Latham tore open the envelope and began to read. "Honestly, if that isn't just like Mavis," she remarked after a moment, as she paused to fill her cup from the electric coffeepot.

"What's like Mavis?" asked Shelley, who had always been interested in her mother's former roommate. Mavis, Shelley remembered her mother's telling her, had brought a mounted deer head—the head of a six-point buck—to school to decorate their small room in the dormitory of the teachers' college.

"Listen to this," said Mrs. Latham, and began to read. " 'Why don't you send Shelley down here for the winter? We have an excellent high school in San Sebastian and classes do not start until the day after Admission Day. We have plenty of room and it might be fun for her to spend a winter in California. I know we would enjoy having her and I am sure that another girl in the house would be a good experience for Katie, who has reached a difficult age.' " Mrs. Latham put down the letter. "That's just like Mavis—always suggesting something impractical on the spur of the moment. As if we could pack Shelley up and send her over a thousand miles away on a few days' notice!"

Of course she could never pack up and go to school over a thousand miles away. Shelley felt there was no point in even discussing it. She would finish high school and go to the University just like everyone else. Anyway, she did not want to be a good experience for a girl who had reached a difficult age, even though she was curious to know what a difficult age for a girl like Katie would be. Six years before, Tom and Mavis Michie with their children, Luke and Katie, had visited the Lathams for three days during the Rose Festival. Shelley had been expected to entertain Katie, but after half a day she had looked forward to the younger girl's departure. Katie had also been at a difficult stage six years ago.

"What's Admission Day?" Shelley asked idly.

"I don't know," answered Mrs. Latham, returning the letter to the envelope, because she was equally sure there was no reason to discuss Shelley's going to California. "I suppose it is some California holiday."

"Admission Day is the ninth of September, the day California was admitted to the Union," explained Shelley's father, looking up from the editorials. Mr. Latham had a way of knowing the answers to unexpected questions.

What a nice thing to celebrate, thought Shelley, wondering why Oregon did not have a similar holiday. Perhaps it was because California's history of Spanish settlers, earthquakes, and the gold rush had always seemed so much more colorful than Oregon's traditional history of hardy pioneers toiling with their hands to the plow.

"What else does Mavis say?" asked Shelley's father.

"Tom expects to have more students in his math class this year and hopes to coach a winning basketball team," answered Mrs. Latham. "They had a record crop from their orange grove last winter. Luke has managed to get hold of an old wreck of a motorcycle that he hopes to get into working order

—Mavis says she would be worried except that it is so dilapidated that she is sure it never will run—and Katie is doing very well with her piano lessons if only she would practice."

"A motorcycle! It doesn't seem possible that Luke is that old," observed Mr. Latham. "Let's see, how old was he that time they visited us?"

"Katie was seven, Luke was nine, and I was ten, so that makes Katie thirteen and Luke fifteen," answered Shelley. "I'll never forget how I was supposed to entertain Katie and how awful she was. She tried to chin herself on the towel racks in the bathroom and pulled them right out of the wall."

"And Shelley," said Mrs. Latham, laughing, "do you remember how your father was fit to be tied when she used his favorite pipe to blow soap bubbles?"

Shelley giggled. "And he didn't say a thing, but the way he *looked* . . . ." Shelley and her mother went off into a gale of laughter.

"Luke was easy enough to entertain. I remember he spent all his time tinkering with an old alarm clock, but Katie certainly was a handful." Mrs. Latham laid the letter beside the place mat in front of her and took a sip of coffee.

Because the conversation about the Michies seemed to be over, Shelley felt this was the moment to mention the slicker once more. "Mother, I'll have to go downtown this afternoon to buy my slicker," she stated a second time, trying not to sound anxious. "The stores will be closed Monday because of Labor Day and school starts Tuesday."

"Shelley, I saw the prettiest raincoat the other day," said Mrs. Latham. "It was pink with a black velveteen collar and had a little hat with a velveteen button on top—"

"Pink!" exclaimed Shelley with distaste. "But Mother, I don't want a pink raincoat with a velveteen collar. You *know* I want a plain ordinary everyday yellow slicker and a plain ordinary everyday hat to match."

"And to look just like that boy on the label of a can of sardines," Mrs. Latham told her daughter. "Shelley dear, yellow is not becoming to you, and the girls who wear those slickers always look so sloppy."

"But Mother, if I wore a pink raincoat with a velveteen collar to school everyone would think I was too dressed up or something," said Shelley stubbornly. "I want a slicker."

"Oh, Shelley," said Mrs. Latham impatiently. "Do you want to be one of a bunch of sheep?"

"Yes," answered Shelley flatly.

Mr. Latham looked up from his paper, glanced at Shelley and then at his wife, frowned, and resumed his reading.

"Those slickers get so dirty and there is no way to clean them. And they get torn and shabby in no time at all," Mrs. Latham pointed out. "They really aren't practical."

"But a slicker isn't—well, *mellow* until it gets dirty," Shelley tried to explain.

Mrs. Latham laughed. "Shelley, I don't know where you girls get such ideas."

"I don't care, Mother," said Shelley, resenting her mother's amusement. "It's what all the girls wear and it's what I want. And besides, it's my own money."

"Oh, well, there is really no hurry," said Mrs. Latham lightly, as she rose to clear the table. "We've had such a wet summer we're bound to have some nice weather this fall."

The trouble with Mother, thought Shelley, as she carried her plate into the kitchen and dropped a scrap of toast into the Disposall, is that she doesn't understand. And the importance of a slicker was so hard to explain. A dirty yellow slicker, mended with adhesive tape and covered with names in ink— the right names, of course—was the smartest thing a girl could wear to school. It showed a girl was . . . well, Shelley was not quite sure what wearing a shabby slicker showed. It was one of those things that was difficult to put into words, but it was *important*. Couldn't her mother see that?

"Is Jack coming over this evening?" Mrs. Latham asked, pointedly changing the subject while she and Shelley washed and wiped the breakfast dishes.

"I suppose so," said Shelley, deciding to let the question of the slicker drop for the time being. "He always does. At least, I am expecting him to phone after a while." And ask if anything exciting had happened, even though she had seen him only the night before. Jack always asked if anything exciting had happened just as he always said *Gesundheit* if she sneezed. Always. If she sneezed twice, he said *Gesundheit* twice. Not that Shelley sneezed any more than anyone else. It was just that she had seen so much of Jack that she felt she knew what he was going to say before he said it.

"He's such a nice boy," said Mrs. Latham comfortably. "I never worry when you are out with Jack."

"I know." There was wistfulness in Shelley's voice, not because she wanted to worry her mother, but because she was so tired of Jack.

Jack was not the first boy Shelley had known. First there had been Peter, who had taken her to the Girls' League Show at school and to a movie. There had been nothing wrong with Peter, really, but both he and Shelley were so uncertain and had such difficulty finding anything to talk about that they could not feel comfortable in one another's company.

Next came Roger, from Shelley's Latin class, who took her to her first school dance. Shelley liked Roger even if he did have large ears and wore glasses. He solved the problem of dancing by repeating a set pattern of steps he had learned in his dancing class. Since the pattern did not vary, Shelley quickly learned to do a reverse version of his steps instead of trying to follow—something that she could not do very well. Then Roger suggested that they speak as much as possible in Latin. Shelley thought this was fun as well as a solution to the problem of something to talk about. She used her ingenuity and limited Latin to make such remarks as "The floor of the gymnasium is divided into three parts." When another couple bumped into them, she produced two complete sentences: "The boy and girl are not our friends. They are bad." She and Roger both thought this extremely funny.

When Mrs. Latham asked Shelley about the dance, Shelley described her evening. Mrs. Latham smiled and said, "I'm glad you had a good time, dear." Then she said thoughtfully, "Isn't it too bad you don't have some really nice-looking boy to take you to school affairs?"

Not long after that Shelley came home from school one warm afternoon when the front door was open and heard her mother talking to a friend on the telephone. "Yes, Shelley seemed to have a good time at the dance," Mrs. Latham was saying. "It was her first dance, you know, but I could hardly keep my face straight when she was telling me about it. She and Roger spoke *Latin*—can you imagine, at a *dance?* . . . I don't know exactly what they found to say, but Shelley did mention that she said, 'The floor of the gymnasium is divided into three parts,' the way Caesar said all Gaul is divided into three parts, and she seemed quite proud of it." Mrs. Latham shared a laugh with her friend before she continued, "Poor child. He is so homely. I do wish—"

Shelley's rickety confidence collapsed. Her evening with Roger now seemed ridiculous, laid waste, as the old Romans would have said, by her mother's account to a friend. But Mother did not mean me to hear, Shelley tried to tell herself, and she would have been dreadfully upset if she knew I had overheard the conversation. But Shelley could not, no matter how hard she tried, escape the fact that she *had* overheard and that her feelings had been hurt. After that she saw Roger through her mother's eyes, as a homely, rather ridiculous boy.

Jack was next. Shelley had liked Jack the first time he asked her for a date and her mother liked him too. Shelley liked him the second and the third time she went out with him, but by the fourth date, when everyone assumed they were going steady, Shelley found she did not like Jack nearly so much as she thought she had. And then it was too late. Now she wished some other girl would have to listen to him say, "Penny for your thoughts," every time there was a lull in the conversation.

"So many girls don't have anybody," Mrs. Latham was saying as she rinsed the electric coffeepot, "but you have a good-looking boy with nice manners who comes from a good family."

For the first time that morning Shelley faltered in her determination. Her mother was right. So many girls stayed home on Saturday night and pretended to have fun playing records or looking at television. So many girls tried to make one date sound like half-a-dozen when they talked to one another at school. Lots of girls would be eager to go out with Jack. Even Rosemary, her best friend. Everybody said that Shelley was so lucky to have such a nice boy to take her places, that she and Jack made a cute couple (cute couple—she detested the phrase!) . . . and where would she find another boy to take his place? All the boys a girl would like to know were either going steady or they were the exasperating kind who were more interested in sports or studies than dates.

"I'm going to cut some roses for the table," said Mrs. Latham, removing her apron. "Maybe you would like to arrange them."

"All right, Mother," agreed Shelley, who enjoyed flower arranging. She went into her room and began to make her bed. She tossed her pillows onto a chair and smoothed the sheets, and while she worked she carried on a mental conversation. Good-by, Jack . . . no, I'm not mad at you—I'm just not going out with you any more. In her imagination, while she pulled up the soft blue blankets, Jack answered,

But golly, Shelley . . . . Jack always said, But golly, Shelley, when she said something that worried him. Then she would say—what? I'm sorry, Jack, but you bore me stiff? No, a girl could not say that to a boy who had, in his own way, tried to give her a good time. Shelley pulled up the quilted chintz spread. There must be a way out. There had to be and soon, too. If she were seen with Jack during the first few days of school, everyone would assume she did not want to go out with any other boy and then her junior year would be just like her sophomore year—a series of Saturday nights each like the one before and the one that lay ahead.

"Here are the roses," Mrs. Latham called out from the kitchen.

"All right, Mother." Shelley went into the kitchen, where she found a tangle of roses on the draining board. She began to strip the lower leaves from the stems and drop them into the Disposall. The roses were among the last that would bloom that season and the colors, pink and red, yellow and white, showed that her mother had cut most of the blooms from the bushes to have enough for the table. Because she had so many colors to work with, Shelley decided to make a bouquet rather than a formal arrangement. She found a blue bowl and a frog in the cupboard and was sorting out the roses with the longest stems for the center of the bouquet when the doorbell rang.

"It must be the parcel service," remarked Mrs. Latham and went to the door. She returned in a moment with a suit box, which she laid on the draining board while she snipped the cord with her garden shears. She removed the lid, pushed aside the tissue paper, and lifted out a pink raincoat with a black velveteen collar.

"Mother!" cried Shelley in dismay.

"A surprise for you," announced Mrs. Latham gaily.

"But Mother—" protested Shelley.

"Now Shelley," said Mrs. Latham comfortably, "be sensible."

"I don't want to be sensible," cried Shelley. "I want a yellow slicker. You knew I wanted a slicker. I saved my money for it."

"But Shelley, this will be so becoming to you," said Mrs. Latham. "You look so sweet in pink."

Shelley enunciated with exaggerated distinctness. "Mother, I do not want to look sweet." Sweet! How old did her mother think she was, anyway? Six instead of sixteen?

"Now Shelley," said Mrs. Latham in what Shelley recognized as her subject-is-closed voice, "I don't want my daughter wearing a sloppy old slicker. Your father will pay for this and you can use your money for something else. A pretty new skirt perhaps."

But Shelley was not willing to let the subject be

closed. She did not want a pretty skirt. She wanted a yellow slicker. An ugly yellow slicker. A slicker patched with adhesive tape. Rebellion mounted within her. She was being silly and childish and she knew it, but she had her heart set on that slicker, she had saved her money, and her mother had no right—

Shelley was frightened. What if she did not find the courage to tell Jack she did not want to go out with him again? And what if she wore the pink raincoat her mother had selected? Then nothing would be different after all. She felt cornered, desperate. Then, feeling as if she had been building up to this moment for a long time, Shelley knew she had to do something that very instant to relieve her feelings. She looked wildly around the kitchen, snatched the roses from the draining board, and ignoring the thorns that scratched her hands, she stuffed the blooms into the Disposall, turned on the water, flipped the switch that started the motor and stood with her back to her mother, her fingers gripping the edge of the sink, and listened with savage pleasure while the angry jaws of the Disposall chewed the roses, petals, leaves, and stems to bits.

When the last shred of the roses was noisily ground up and washed away, Shelley stopped the motor and turned off the water. Then, taking a deep breath, she whirled around and faced her mother.

This time it was Mrs. Latham who was angry.

Angry and shocked. "Shelley Latham!" she exclaimed. "Roses in the Disposall!"

Shelley looked defiant—more defiant than she felt, because she, too, was shocked at what she had done.

"Really, Shelley—" began Mrs. Latham and stopped. She did not know what to say.

Shelley remained silent. They faced one another, mother and daughter, one puzzled and hurt, the other stubborn and rebellious.

"What's going on here anyway?" asked Shelley's father, entering from the living room, the morning paper still in his hand.

"Shelley threw the roses into the Disposall," answered Mrs. Latham. "Perfectly good roses that I had just cut."

Shelley thought her father looked as if he were trying not to smile. I suppose it is funny, putting roses into the Disposall, she thought suddenly—funny to someone else. But she could not feel that there was anything funny about what she had done. She only knew that, for some reason she did not understand, she felt better because she had stuffed those roses into the Disposall, as if she had ground up some of her exasperation along with the petals. But this was something she did not know how to explain to her father.

"Shelley, sometimes I think I don't understand you any more," said Mrs. Latham with a sigh.

This did not surprise Shelley, who sometimes felt

she no longer understood herself. "I just . . ." Shelley hesitated, not knowing how to justify her behavior to her father. "I guess . . . it is just that when I am bad I am horrid."

"I was only trying to do something for her own good," Mrs. Latham explained to Mr. Latham, "and suddenly she seized perfectly good roses, probably the last of the season, and stuffed them into the Disposall. *Destroyed* them. I can't understand it."

"But I don't want something done for my own good," protested Shelley. "That's the whole point."

"What was the argument about?" asked Mr. Latham. "I wasn't listening to this particular one."

"My slicker. Mother knew I had saved my money for a slicker," explained Shelley, "and she went and bought me a raincoat I didn't want."

"But that is no reason to grind up roses." Mrs. Latham leaned wearily back against the draining board. "Shelley, sometimes I don't know what to do with you."

Shelley stared at the ceiling. "Let me buy the slicker," was what she wanted to say, but instead she was surprised to hear her own voice telling her mother, "Send me to California."

"Now, Shelley," said Mrs. Latham, relenting. "Don't dramatize so. What you did was wrong, but we certainly don't intend to—to banish you over a few roses."

"But I want to go," answered Shelley, and knew

as she spoke that she meant what she said. Even though it meant living in the same house with Katie, she wanted to go to California.

"But that is out of the question," protested Mrs. Latham. "As if we could send you all the way to California."

"Why is it impossible?" Mr. Latham asked. "A girl has to leave home sometime."

"Of course," agreed Mrs. Latham, "but there is plenty of time for that when she is ready for college. After all, Shelley is only sixteen and young for her age at that." Mrs. Latham acted as if there was nothing more to say on the subject. Briskly she set the blue bowl and the frog back in the cupboard and shut the door.

"Leaving home and having the opportunity to make a few mistakes is a good way for a girl to grow up," persisted Mr. Latham. "And this looks like a splendid opportunity for a girl who has never been more than a couple of hundred miles from home."

Shelley carefully examined a scratch on her forefinger. It was difficult to believe that her father could be serious, but it would be exciting to spend a winter in California, to wear a dirty old slicker if she felt like it, to go to a different school, and see some of the country, and meet new people—and not go out with Jack. Let Rosemary or some other girl have him. She wouldn't care, not when she was in California. What was it like down there in California, where history was so colorful and oranges came from trees instead of bins at the supermarket?

"Send our little girl so far away to live with someone else's family?" Mrs. Latham's voice expressed disbelief. "You can't really mean it."

Mr. Latham continued as if his wife had not spoken. "After all, Shelley is an only child and the experience of living with a larger family should be good for her."

Shelley considered this. She had always liked being an only child and had felt sorry for some of her friends who sometimes had to go without new clothes because of the expense of keeping an older brother or sister in college, or who had to baby-sit with younger brothers or sisters. It did not matter. Even if she had to baby-sit with Katie, she still wanted to go to California.

"But I couldn't bear to let her go so far," said Shelley's mother.

"I think she should go," Mr. Latham stated flatly.

"Daddy!" cried Shelley, while Mrs. Latham looked at her husband in silence.

"She may not have another chance like this." Mr. Latham went on as if Shelley was not listening. "When she is ready for college we won't be able to send her any farther than the state university, and going to school a hundred miles from home with the same crowd she knew in high school and coming home for all the holidays is really not leaving home.

I think nine months away from home with a family with other children would be a valuable experience."

Shelley's parents were talking about her as if she were not present, the way they must talk about her when she heard their voices, low and earnest, after she had gone to bed.

"But California—" protested Mrs. Latham. "How would she get to San Sebastian?"

"Fly," answered Mr. Latham.

"But she would have to change planes," Mrs. Latham pointed out.

"She has to change buses when she goes downtown," said Mr. Latham.

"Please, Mother, I *want* to go," insisted Shelley. "It's only for a school year and not a whole year. And I would write every week. And it isn't as though I were going out into the world to—to seek my fortune. I'll be living with a family, a family you know, and I would be back next June. Please, Mother! Daddy, make her let me go!"

"Shelley is right," agreed Mr. Latham. "It isn't as if she were going to live with strangers."

"Yes, Mother," Shelley persisted. "And I have my school clothes all ready and all I would have to do is pack and have my records transferred and a few things like that. Say I can go. Please say I can go!"

"I seem to be overruled," said Mrs. Latham, admitting defeat with a rueful smile.

"Mother!" cried Shelley joyfully, and at the same

time she was deeply touched by her mother's smile, which showed so plainly how much it hurt her mother to let her go.

"I hope this is the right decision," said Mrs. Latham, still turning the whole discussion over in her mind. "Nine whole months. If only California were not so far away—"

"Oh, Mother, everything will be all right," Shelley insisted, anxious to reassure her mother. "I know it will be all right. Everything is going to be wonderful!"

Slowly Mrs. Latham folded the tissue paper over the raincoat and replaced the lid on the box. "How much a lovely raincoat like this would have meant to me when I was sixteen," she remarked sadly. "I was sixteen during the Depression and I wanted a raincoat more than anything in the world. I had to carry a shabby old cotton umbrella to school and I was so ashamed of it."

Shelley was silent. It hurt her to see her mother look so sad. She wanted to say, But this is not the Depression and I don't want a raincoat, but she could not say it. She could not say to her mother. I am not you. I am me.

The ring of the telephone interrupted Shelley's thoughts. "It's Jack," she remarked as she picked up the receiver.

"Hi, Shelley," said the familiar voice. "Has anything exciting happened?"

"Yes!" answered Shelley, for once glad that Jack had asked that question. She was eager to tell her news to someone, to make sure it was really true. The rest, she knew, was going to be easy. All she had to do was say good-by. And in California, she was sure, she would find the boy she had always wanted to meet.

Chapter 2

As the plane began to lose altitude to land at the Vincente Municipal Airport, the landing field nearest San Sebastian, Shelley fastened her seat belt with trembling fingers. It was ridiculous for her fingers to behave that way. She was eager to begin her new life. Of course she was. It was just that everything had happened so fast and the world seen from the air was such a strange place, like a giant relief map. Cars were ants on ribbon highways and farms were old-fashioned crazy quilts. Lakes were puddles, trees on the mountains had toothpick trunks, and finally in California so much of the map was flat and brown with dust-colored hills like miniature circus tents. It did not seem real at all.

The plane landed on the runway with a gentle bounce and as it taxied toward the airport building that a moment ago had looked like a shoe box, all

Shelley could think of was that now she could unpin the ten-dollar bill that her mother had insisted she pin to her slip in case she lost her purse when she changed planes. Shelley had not wanted to pin that bill to her slip—at sixteen she was certainly old enough to hang onto her purse—and she had started to protest but had thought better of it. Talking about the ten-dollar bill and what she should do if she lost her money had helped fill those last awkward minutes at the airport this morning, when she was about to leave home for the first time in her life and suddenly discovered she did not know what to say to her mother and father. And what was even more surprising, her mother and father did not seem to know what to say to her. Oh, they said the expected things like Be careful of strangers, and Study hard, and Don't forget to write, but Shelley knew that these remarks were only meant to fill up the long minutes until her plane was announced.

Shelley unfastened the seat belt and remembered how surprised she had been to learn that at sixteen there were so many things a girl could not say to her mother and father—things like I'm both glad and sorry to be leaving, and I really do feel dreadful about grinding up those roses in the Disposall, and Please don't look so sad behind your smiles—nine months isn't forever and I'll write often.

The heat, as Shelley stepped through the door of the plane, was like the blast of a hair-dryer against her face. She walked down the steps and as soon as she stepped onto the concrete, the door was shut behind her, the steps were rolled away, and the plane, her last link with everything she had known, was heading down the runway once more. I'll pretend I'm a stranger in a foreign land, Shelley told herself, and tried to feel a little braver. Somehow her legs carried her through the gate toward a woman with curly hair touched with gray whom she recognized as Mavis.

"Shelley!" cried Mavis Michie. "How wonderful to see you after all these years! We're so glad to have you!"

"I'm glad to be here." Shelley smiled shakily. "Mother sends her love."

Mavis led the way to a battered station wagon. As they left the Vincente airport and headed toward San Sebastian, Shelley settled back for her first look at California from the ground. In that spot California was flat and brown, shimmering in the heat, and not at all what Shelley had expected, although exactly what she had expected she did not know. Something lush and tropical, perhaps.

Mavis pointed to a row of towering trees and identified them as eucalyptus. Shelley noticed that their smooth trunks were shedding their bark in long, ragged strips. She had never seen a tree shed bark before and had, in fact, been told that a tree could not live without bark. Apparently things were different in California. In the distance, against the mountains they were approaching, was a row of palm trees, the first Shelley had ever seen. They looked to her like a row of shabby feather dusters balanced on their handles. Then the station wagon rattled across a bridge and Shelley was shocked at what she saw below. *There was no water in the river bed.* Never in her whole life had Shelley seen a river without water.

Next the station wagon passed a stretch of orange trees. A grove, thought Shelley, and not an orchard. How tidy it looked. The trees were round, with branches so low they touched the ground. The green oranges looked as if they might have been hung among the leaves for decoration. Even the soil beneath the trees was arranged in neat furrows.

"What are those round metal things between the trees?" asked Shelley.

"Smudge pots," answered Mavis. "If there is danger of frost the pots, which are filled with oil, are lighted to keep the oranges from being frostbitten."

"You mean they heat up the *outdoors?*" Shelley asked incredulously.

Mavis laughed. "Enough to save the crop."

Then Shelley saw a startling billboard that announced in big red letters, "Rain for Rent." Shelley could not believe what she read until a closer view revealed the words, "Farm sprinkler systems for rent or sale." The next sign that attracted her attention was painted orange with black letters that proclaimed, "Giant Orange 300 yards." Now I know exactly how Alice in Wonderland felt when she fell down the rabbit hole, thought Shelley, as she watched to see what a Giant Orange might be. It was a roadside stand shaped like an orange, which bore the sign, "Fresh tree-ripened orange juice. Foot-long hot dogs."

Shelley felt reassured as they entered the town of San Sebastian. She saw much that was familiar—a J. C. Penney store, Shell and Standard service stations just like those at home, a theater advertising a movie she had seen only last week. It was the setting for the familiar that was strange to her—the dry heat, the palms, the orange trees and, everywhere, dusty geraniums actually growing outdoors in the ground.

After they passed through the business district, the orange trees became more numerous and the Spanish houses with tile roofs gave way to ranch houses. "Here we are," said Mavis suddenly, turning into a driveway beside a high privet hedge.

Here I am, Shelley's thought echoed, as she stepped out of the station wagon and through the opening in the hedge. To her surprise she found herself facing a very old two-story clapboard house. It was painted gray with green shutters and in the center of the front door, which was beneath a vine covered with magenta blossoms, was an old-fash-

ioned doorbell such as Shelley had not seen since she
had visited a great-aunt when she was a little girl.
It was a doorbell with a handle to twirl instead of a
button to push. *And I thought everything in California was modern,* Shelley marveled.

"Welcome to our house," said Mavis. "I know you
want to change into something cooler. You must be
dreadfully warm in a suit." She led Shelley into the
house and up a flight of creaky stairs. "And here is
your room. The bathroom is at the end of the hall."
Mavis smiled and patted Shelley's shoulder. "It's all
so strange the first time away from home, isn't it?
Come on down when you have freshened up. Supper
will be ready in a little while and you can meet the
rest of the family then."

Grateful for a moment alone, Shelley sat down on
the bed, which was covered with an India print
spread, and looked around the long, narrow room.
Because of the low, sloping ceiling, the sills of the
windows were only a few inches from the floor. The
windows looked out on a tangle of vines and treetops.
Between the windows was a desk, painted black,
and on the desk a pair of old flatirons, gilded and
obviously intended to be used for book ends. At the
end of the room between two closets was an old-
fashioned dresser waiting for her lipstick and bobby
pins. On the wall over the bed were two unframed
Japanese prints. Opposite the windows were two
doors that led into the hall (that was odd—two

doors into the hall) and between them was her trunk, waiting to be unpacked. Shelley, who all her life had slept in a square room with one door, framed pictures, and windows a conventional distance from the floor, felt even more strongly that she had fallen down a rabbit hole into a new life.

Quickly she slipped out of her suit and into a cotton dress that she had brought in her overnight bag in case her trunk had not arrived. She ran a comb through her hair before she walked down the hall to the bathroom, which was like no bathroom she had ever seen before. Because of its size, she guessed that it had once been a bedroom. The windows, curtained in red-and-yellow calico, looked out upon a row of eucalyptus trees and, beyond them, an orange grove. Around the bathroom were seven towel racks, each labeled with a name printed on adhesive tape—Mavis, Tom, Katie, Luke, Shelley, Mother, Guests. Whose mother, Shelley wondered as she washed her hands and dried them on a towel from her rack. The rough white towel had the words "Santa Theresa Union High School" printed on a green stripe down the center, and as Shelley examined the bathroom more closely she saw that all the towels were white, with the name of a school printed or stitched on them. This seemed peculiar and she felt a moment of longing for the white bathroom at home with its fluffy pink towels carefully selected to match the tile. She was relieved, though, to see the names *Mavis* and *Tom*, for that was how she thought of Mr. and Mrs. Michie. Obviously they thought of themselves that way too.

Then, noticing the open lid of the hamper, Shelley closed it without thinking, because she had been brought up always to close drawers and cupboard doors. She was startled when this brought forth an indignant meow from inside the hamper. She lifted the lid and looked in at a small gray cat, the color of the shadow of a cat, blinking at her in annoyance from a heap of bath towels. "Oh—I'm sorry," apologized Shelley, and left the lid open. Obviously this family cared more for the comfort of the cat than the tidiness of the bathroom. For the first time since she stepped off the plane, Shelley's face relaxed into a smile.

Shelley was about to leave the bathroom when a commotion below led her back to the window. A tall man in a sweat shirt was bending low over the handle bars of a bicycle as he rode along the row of eucalyptus trees and disappeared around the corner of the house. He was followed by a shouting boy and girl, also on bicycles, and a large, barking police dog. They must be Tom and Katie and Luke, Shelley realized as she listened to their laughter and shouting from the other side of the house. Californians and their outdoor living!

Timidly Shelley left the bathroom and descended the stairs, hesitating a moment to look at the living room. It, too, was an unusually long, narrow room. There was a quaint old fireplace, and on its mantel an old walnut clock with a cupid painted on the glass was ticking. On either side of the fireplace bookshelves reached to the ceiling. The chairs and couches wore bright print slip covers. At the far end of the living room was a pair of doors, each topped by a glass transom. From the other side of these doors Shelley heard the rattle of dishes. The least she could do was offer to set the table, so she walked the length of the living room and tried one of the doors. It was locked.

"Come around through the dining room, Shelley," Mavis called through the door.

Shelley walked through the dining room (no one she knew at home had linoleum and painted furniture in the dining room) and into the kitchen, where she found Mavis shredding salad greens into a wooden bowl. "Shelley, would you mind doing this while I put the fake Stroganoff together?" she asked. "The rice is already cooking."

"I'd be glad to," said Shelley, wondering what fake Stroganoff could be. If things were reversed and someone had come to Shelley's home from California, her mother would have had a special dinner with fried chicken, home-made rolls and angel food cake with orange icing, all of them genuine, none of them fake.

Outside, the trio on bicycles and the barking dog tore past.

"Anything to amuse the dog," observed Mavis. "They'll all be in shortly and you can meet them."

Shelley felt a little hurt by the casualness of this family toward herself, a guest who had traveled so far. At her own home she would not have been allowed to ride around the house on a bicycle when a guest had arrived. She must remember she was a stranger in a foreign land, she told herself sternly, and she must accept the customs of the natives. They were probably right—after all, she was to be a member of the family for the winter and there was no reason why she should be treated like company.

"I'd better explain about those doors that don't open," Mavis said, as she sliced onions into melted butter in an earthenware casserole. "You see, this house was once a boardinghouse in the center of town. When it was to be torn down to make way for a filling station, Tom had a chance to buy it for practically nothing. We had it moved up here and knocked out a lot of partitions—the rooms had been very small—and that is why we have so many long, narrow rooms and why you have two doors in your bedroom. We didn't know what to do about those doors at the end of the living room, so we just left them where they were. We can't open them, because we have the refrigerator against one and some cupboards against the other."

"It—it's very nice," said Shelley, aware that "nice" was not the word she wanted to use. She did **not** know the exact word to describe it—shabby and comfortable and like no house she had ever seen before. No one at home lived in a converted boardinghouse. No one at home left the hamper open for the convenience of the cat.

Mavis took three packages of frozen sirloin tips out of the refrigerator, tore them open, and added their contents to the onion and butter in the casserole which she put into the oven. "There," she said. "Now all I have to do is add sour cream at the last minute."

The back door opened and the rest of the family burst into the kitchen. "Well, look who's arrived!" Tom exclaimed, and gave Shelley a hearty hug before he held her off to look at her. "Shelley, it's good to have you here!"

"Hello, Shelley," said Luke, with a smile that was shy but friendly.

"Hi," said Katie, taking in Shelley's shoes and dress and hair.

So this was the girl for whom she was to be a good experience. Uncomfortable under her scrutiny, Shelley managed to smile, uncertain what to say to three strangers at the same time. They all looked tan and healthy and there was a look of the out of doors about them. Tom and Luke she liked at once, because she felt they liked her, but Katie she was not so sure about. Perhaps this sturdy thirteen-year-old was not pleased to have another girl in the house being a good experience for her.

"Go on, all of you, and wash up for supper," ordered Mavis. "It's such a warm day we'll eat out under the pergola."

Pergola was such an old-fashioned word. Shelley had thought everyone in California had a patio.

"Katie, you slice the French bread and carry it out to the table," directed Mavis.

As she opened the breadbox, Katie heaved a noisy, exhausted sigh, as if slicing bread were a terrible chore.

"It's just a phase," said Mavis grimly.

"Mommy, do you have to go around saying everything I do is just a phase all the time?" asked Katie.

Mavis laughed. "I certainly hope it is just a phase," she said. "I would hate to think that some of your behavior was permanent."

Katie picked a leaf of curly chicory out of the salad, held it up beside her face as if it were a lock of hair, and remarked, "I wish I had curly hair."

Mavis stirred sour cream into the bubbling casserole before she ladled the Stroganoff over rice. The meal was served on trays and Shelley noticed that there was a fresh cloth napkin on each tray. She would have expected such a casual family to use paper napkins.

The Michies carried their trays out through the

dining room to a table under the pergola, which Shelley saw was a sort of arbor supported by pillars and covered with vines. As she joined the family at the long table she was aware of a lovely fragrance. "Why, there are lemons growing on that tree and blossoms, too!" she exclaimed, when she had discovered the source of the fragrance. Real lemons growing in the garden!

Everyone laughed. "Haven't you ever seen lemons before?" asked Katie.

"Not growing," answered Shelley. "Why, there are green lemons and ripe lemons and blossoms on the tree all at the same time!" Nature in California must be in a state of utter confusion to produce such a tree as this.

While the others were discussing lemons, Katie left the table and walked across the yard to a tree with a gnarled trunk and slender gray foliage. She picked something, which she laid on the table in front of Shelley. "We have olives growing in the yard, too," she said.

"Fresh olives right off the tree!" marveled Shelley. How kind of Katie to offer her one. "I simply adore olives."

"Oh, Shelley—" began Mavis.

It was too late. Shelley bit eagerly into the olive. The taste was so bitter and so terrible that she could not believe it. She sat shocked, not knowing what to do.

Katie went into a fit of giggles.

"Oh, Shelley, I am so sorry," said Mavis. "I tried to warn you."

Shelley swallowed and gulped from her water glass while Katie continued to giggle.

Then Tom spoke. "Katie, that was not a nice thing to do. I think you should apologize to Shelley."

Katie tried to look repentant but did not succeed. "I'm sorry," she said, giggling, "but you looked so surprised when you bit into the olive."

Shelley was so embarrassed she did not know how to answer. Apparently Katie had made her the victim of a practical joke. And just when she was beginning to feel at ease, too.

"All olives are bitter until they have been cured," Tom explained. "Katie was counting on your not knowing that."

"She certainly caught me," said Shelley, managing to smile to show she was a good sport, even though she did not feel like one. If this was part of Katie's difficult age, she did not like to think what the rest of the winter could be like. "It tasted so awful I don't see how anyone ever thought of eating them in the first place."

"You know, that is exactly what I have always wondered," said Katie, smiling warmly at Shelley for the first time, as if now they had something in common. "Well, I guess I had better go do my practicing."

"Mother, she's just trying to get out of the dishes," protested Luke. "She always gets out of the dishes."

"I have to practice, don't I?" asked Katie virtuously, as she rose from the table.

"Yes, you do," agreed Mavis, "but that doesn't mean you get out of the dishes."

Katie heaved a sigh that showed she was exhausted, abused, and misunderstood by her family. Then she disappeared into the house, and chords crashed out of the piano in the living room.

When Katie settled down to play, Shelley thought she played surprisingly well for a girl of thirteen. The music she recognized as Liszt's *Second Hungarian Rhapsody* but while she listened, the rhapsody turned suddenly and logically into *Pop Goes the Weasel.*

"Katie!" yelled Tom, in a voice that would have carried across a gymnasium full of shouting boys.

The music stopped. "But Daddy," protested Katie. "It fits there. See, the music goes like this"—she demonstrated with a few notes—"and then it just naturally wants to turn into *Pop Goes the Weasel.* Like this."

"You stick to the notes as they are written," ordered Tom.

Mavis sighed. "She has talent, but she simply doesn't care."

Katie finished playing *Pop Goes the Weasel.* The

rest of the family continued to sit under the pergola while darkness fell.

Shelley peered at her watch. "It is getting dark awfully early," she observed.

"That's because you are farther south. A thousand miles makes a big difference in the time darkness falls," Tom explained.

Why, I knew that, Shelley thought suddenly, but the information had never seemed real before, any more than igloos or the international date line or a lot of other things in schoolbooks seemed real. Until now this had been a fact to be learned, stored away, and pulled out again to be put down on a test paper if that question happened to be asked. Now she had really traveled, had seen before her eyes the things she had learned about in school.

Suddenly Tom rose to his feet. "There's a full moon," he announced. "Let's do the washing."

For a moment Shelley thought she must have misunderstood, but Mavis said matter-of-factly, "That's a wonderful idea. I'll gather up the laundry."

Shelley was not sure how she should react, so she offered to wash the dishes. Willing dishwashers, she knew, were always welcome. When in doubt, wash the dishes should be a good rule to follow when living in a strange household.

The Michies carried their trays into the kitchen, where Shelley began to scrape and stack the plates. From the sink she could look into the laundry, a room with a sloping roof that looked as if it had been added to the house as an afterthought. The room was equipped with an automatic washing machine, a pair of laundry tubs, an old washing machine with a wringer, two ironing boards, and a mangle so large it must have belonged to a professional laundry at one time. On the wall over the mangle was the mounted head of a deer with several old hats hung jauntily on its antlers.

While Shelley washed and wiped the dishes, Mavis sorted piles of towels, sheets, and clothing. Luke loaded the automatic washer while Tom put colored clothing through the second washing machine. They all appeared to be enjoying themselves. From the living room came the first notes of the rhapsody.

"Katie's starting that piece again just to get out of helping," remarked Luke.

Beneath her feet Shelley could feel the old house shake from the vibration of the automatic washer. A frightened mouse ran out from under a cupboard and stared at Shelley, with its whiskers quivering, before it disappeared under the refrigerator. Shelley, who had never lived in a house with mice before, did not feel surprised. A little gray mouse seemed a perfectly natural member of this household.

When Shelley had wrung out the dishcloth and hung it over the faucet, she went into the laundry. "May I help?" she asked.

"You're just in time," answered Tom, piling clean wet clothes into a clothesbasket on a child's wagon. "You and Luke can start hanging these out."

Luke pulled the wagon out into the back yard under the clotheslines. Shelley followed, thinking how strange it was to be living in the same house with a boy so near her own age and how much stranger to be hanging out laundry with him. She picked up a clothespin and began to pin a towel to the line. The moonlight, even filtered through the eucalyptus trees, was so bright that she could read the words "Vincente Junior College," printed in a green stripe down the center of the towel. The eucalyptus trees gave off a medicinal odor something like cough drops, which mingled with the sweetness of the lemon blossoms.

"I understand you are working on a motorcycle," said Shelley, wanting to start a conversation with this quiet boy.

"Yes." Luke sounded pleased at her interest. "It keeps me broke buying parts, but I think I can get it running sometime."

"Won't it worry your mother to have you riding around on a motorcycle?" Shelley asked.

"I guess so." Luke sounded discouraged, as if he had been losing an argument for a long time.

Shelley wished she had not mentioned his mother.

Tom, followed by Mavis, carried out a second basket of laundry, which they began to hang. Shelley, who had a towel with "St. Joseph's High School" stitched in one corner, remarked, "You certainly have a lot of towels."

Mavis laughed. "I suppose our towels look odd to you. You see, visiting teams playing at the high school bring their own towels with them and they usually leave one or two behind. Tom started bringing them home when he discovered the janitors only threw them away. Tom never wants anything to be wasted."

"We use towels for everything—dusting, mopping up whatever gets spilled, wiping the dog's muddy feet," said Tom.

The moon, rising above the eucalyptus trees, shone even brighter. I wonder where the moon is in the sky at home, Shelley wondered, as she picked up another towel and clothespin; but no matter where it was, she was sure that no one else was hanging out a washing by its light. It seemed too bad when she thought about it. It was such a lovely way to hang out a washing. Shelley pulled the last towel out of the basket, and as she pinned it to the line she decided that if it were not for Katie, she would like living here. So far she enjoyed the customs of the natives. Tom was friendly, Mavis comfortable, Luke shy and quiet, but Katie . . . Shelley could not bring herself to like Katie wholeheartedly. And she not only had nine months of Katie's company ahead of her, but she was supposed to be a good experience for her, which probably meant to be a good example.

From inside the house came the frisking notes of *Pop Goes the Weasel.*

"Katie!" shouted Tom. *Pop Goes the Weasel* turned into the rhapsody.

Later that evening after she had unpacked her trunk and taken her turn at the towel-filled bathroom, Shelley was sitting on her bed in her pajamas, putting her hair up in pin curls. The edge of the India print spread was not even hemmed, she noticed. She was thinking that at home everything was hemmed when she heard a knock on her door.

"Come in," she said.

Katie entered. She was wearing a full red-and-white printed skirt and a white blouse with little buttons like strawberries down the front. In her hand she carried a half-eaten banana. She twirled around so that the skirt stood out. "See my dress for the first day of school!" she said, and her face shone with pleasure. "Mommy bought it for me and I wasn't even hounding her." She sank down on the bed beside Shelley and took a big bite of banana. "You know something?" she said, sounding wistful even though her mouth was full. "I wish my hair looked nice like yours."

"Why, thank you," answered Shelley, pleased by this compliment.

"Do you have a permanent?" asked Katie.

"No, my hair is curly if I coax it," replied Shelley. "It may take a lot of coaxing here, because the air is so dry."

"Do you have lots of boy friends at home?" asked Katie bluntly.

"Not lots." Katie's admiration made her feel attractive and popular, a pleasant feeling for any girl to experience.

"I wish Mommy would let me have a permanent," said Katie wistfully, running her hand through her straight dark hair. "Pamela—she's my best friend—has permanents all the time. If I ever have a daughter my age I'll let her have all the permanents she wants."

That sounds familiar, thought Shelley with a twinge of amusement. She wondered if Katie kept a list.

"Katie!" Tom's voice rang out. "Bedtime!"

"Yes, Daddy," answered Katie in her exhausted voice. She stuffed the rest of the banana into her mouth. " 'Night, Shelley," she said, her voice muffled. "And I really am sorry about the olive. I just couldn't resist it."

"Oh, well, I guess everyone has to be a greenhorn or tenderfoot or something sometime," answered Shelley, this time forgiving Katie. When Katie had gone, she turned off the light and slipped into bed. She lay enjoying the fragrance of the lemon blossoms below her window and listening to the strange night sounds—the rustle of eucalyptus leaves, the dry rattle of palm fronds, the sound of tires on the road, the friendly creaks of an old house settling for the night, and in the distance the blat-blat of a diesel train. Where were the lonesome whistles, the a-hooey, a-hooey of song writers, Shelley wondered. Nobody wrote songs about the blat-blat of a diesel train, but then it wasn't a lonely sound.

Shelley smiled in the darkness, her uneasiness about living with a strange family now completely banished. The only thing wrong with Katie was her age. She was thirteen years old. Now that Shelley understood this, she knew that everything was going to be all right after all. She was going to like living in a house with a cat in a hamper and mice in the kitchen and a family that hung out the washing by the light of the moon.

But tomorrow was the first day of school . . . .

Chapter 3

The morning heat made Shelley languid, and feeling as if she were moving in slow motion, she walked down the creaking stairs to join the family for breakfast.

"But Mommy, Pamela's mother lets her stay up to watch the Hit Parade," Katie was saying. "I don't see why I can't."

"Good morning, Shelley!" Tom's voice would have carried across a basketball court. "You're just in time to help bring in the washing."

Shelley smiled. At home washing was hung out in the morning, not brought in.

"Go on, Katie, help Luke and Shelley," said Mavis, who was standing over a skillet of bacon while Tom supervised the toast he was making under the broiler.

"Well, I don't care," said Katie, as the three went out into the back yard. "I don't see why I never get to do the things Pamela and the other girls get to do."

"Pamela is a creep," said Luke concisely.

"She is not!" retorted Katie. "She's smooth." Katie unpinned a sheet and stuffed it into the laundry basket. "Pamela lives in a ranch house with two bathrooms."

"She's still a creep," said Luke.

Shelley enjoyed the feel of the rough clean towels that shone so dazzlingly in the morning sun. As she folded them she looked around the yard by daylight. The house, she now discovered, was set in the middle of a large piece of property—how large she could not guess. Perhaps it was an acre. At least it was the size of eight or ten city lots at home. The yard was a pleasant tangle of trees, shrubs, and vines, most of them strange to Shelley. A double garage with a room above it—Mavis's studio, Shelley learned later, where she had her potter's wheel—stood at the back of the property and in the garage Shelley could see Luke's motorcycle. Both tires were flat, one fender was missing, and it looked so battered she wondered how he ever expected to get it to run.

At the side of the house under the eucalyptus trees that bordered the driveway was a child's slide. In front of the slide, near the end of a single rope suspended from the top of one of the trees, dangled a ring, the kind children swung on in parks. Katie dropped a sheet into the clothesbasket and walked over to the rope. She took the end of it in her hand, climbed the slide, grasped the ring, and swung out over the road with her hair and skirt flying.

"Hey, you're supposed to be helping!" yelled Luke.

"I have to wait till it stops, don't I?" answered Katie. Gradually the rope stopped swinging and Katie dropped to the ground.

"Breakfast!" called Tom.

After breakfast Tom was the first member of the family to leave for school with his lunch in a paper bag. Then Luke, with his paper bag, left earlier than was really necessary and Shelley suspected he did not want to be seen walking to school with her. It was funny how much younger a fifteen-year-old boy could be than a sixteen-year-old girl. Then Pamela appeared at the kitchen door and Shelley could see what Katie meant about Pamela's being smooth. She was small and trim. She made Katie, in her full red-and-white skirt, look brown and sturdy but awkward in a nice way, like a teddy bear in a dirndl. The two younger girls set off in the direction of the junior high school.

It was Shelley's turn to go forth with her brown paper bag in hand.

"Don't worry about a thing," advised Mavis with a smile. "I'm sure you'll make a lot of friends."

Shelley did not like her feelings to show so plainly

to Mavis. "I'm not worried," she answered lightly and untruthfully.

As Shelley walked to school she thought nervously of new girls who had transferred to her high school at home—the homesick girl from the South whose honey-thick accent had so amused the class the first day of school that the girl had looked as if she were about to cry. And a girl who was so determined to establish herself with the right crowd that she made a nuisance of herself with those who were popular, snubbed those who were not popular, and succeeded only in making herself lonely and unhappy. And that new girl who was so anxious to be noticed that she took off her shoes the minute school was out and walked barefooted to the bus, explaining that she simply hated wearing shoes. Everyone had laughed good-naturedly at this and the crisp autumn days soon put an end to her pose.

Naturally I'm not going to do any of those silly things, Shelley told herself, as she walked along the road through the orange groves. She would be extra-cautious about everything she said until she had made some friends. And she would make friends. Of course she would. Everyone had friends.

But Shelley felt less brave as she approached San Sebastian Union High School, a tan stucco building with a missionlike tower in the center and a row of scraggly palm trees across the front. The lawn was colorful with the gay cotton dresses of the girls, so different from the girls at home, who would be wearing their newest sweaters and skirts. Shelley was aware of the curious stares of the other students as she walked up the front steps of the school. Everyone was so tanned that Shelley felt pale—it had been a wet summer at home. There was something else different, too. The students seemed older, and then Shelley remembered that there were no freshmen here. The ninth grade attended junior high school. Among the tan faces there was not a single face that Shelley had ever seen before and yet somewhere among them were her companions for the next nine months. She made her way through the crowds of students busy renewing acquaintances after their summer vacation to the office, where she found— thank goodness!—that her records had arrived from her school at home, and where she was assigned to a registration room.

It was on her way to this room that Shelley first saw the boy. He was standing in the hall talking with a group of boys and Shelley knew at once that this was the boy she wanted to meet. She did not know why, but there was something about him that she liked at once. He was tall, with fair hair bleached by the sun, and he was deeply tanned except for a red patch on his nose where the tan had peeled off. It was not just his looks that attracted Shelley. It was something else about him. Perhaps it was the way he stood, which seemed almost graceful, or perhaps it was a sort of dignity about him. Shelley did not know. She only knew that here was a boy she wanted to meet and at the moment there was nothing she could do about it. A girl could not go up to a boy in the hall, tap him on the arm, and say, "Excuse me. I want to meet you."

Reluctantly Shelley walked away from the boy, located her registration room, and slid into the first vacant seat she saw. Chattering stopped for a moment as students glanced at the new girl. She stared at her hands, clasped on the desk in front of her. She wanted to begin to make friends but she did not know how to start.

Someone tapped Shelley on the shoulder and she found herself looking at a dark-haired boy with lively brown eyes who was sitting across the aisle.

"Don't tell me," he said as if he were cautioning her. "I have it—your last name begins with L."

"Why, yes," she admitted. "But how did you know?"

"I'm psychic," he said modestly.

"Don't let him kid you," said someone behind Shelley. "We are grouped alphabetically. This room is L's, M's, N's, and a couple of stray O's. He's just lucky he chose the right letter."

"She didn't take my hint," observed the brown-eyed boy.

"What hint?" asked Shelley.

"All right, I'll say it right out loud," answered the boy. "What's your name?"

Shelley could not help laughing at having missed something so obvious. "Shelley Latham," she replied. "I'm spending the winter with the Michies."

"You mean Slats Michie, the basketball coach?" asked the boy.

"Why, yes," answered Shelley, "only I didn't know he was called Slats."

Everyone was interested. "He's a swell guy," said a boy.

"You're sure lucky," remarked a tall girl, "living in the same house with the basketball coach."

Why, it's going to be easy, thought Shelley. All she had to do was say she was spending the winter with the coach's family and everyone was interested. She wondered why she had not thought of this before. "What's your name?" she asked the brown-eyed boy.

"Hartley Lathrop," he answered as a teacher entered the room.

The teacher read the names on the role and asked the students to take seats in alphabetical order. Shelley found herself sitting in front of Hartley.

"Latham, Lathrop," he whispered. "I'll always sit behind you."

Unconsciously Shelley put her hand to the back of her hair to make sure it was in order.

"Your hair looks fine," he whispered, making Shelley feel extremely foolish.

It seemed to Shelley that she spent the rest of the day hunting for her classrooms and trying to make a few faces in this building full of strangers seem familiar. Students were friendly and interested in the new girl but Shelley could not feel that she belonged. Even the sight of Hartley would have helped, but he was not in any of her classes. Latin, English, physical education, lunch period. While Shelley ate her sandwiches on the lawn, she was included in the conversation of a group of girls. She tried to remember if she had seen any of them during the morning but she was not sure. When their conversation turned to their summer vacations, Shelley felt like an outsider, a paleface among the natives.

After lunch period came that part of the day set aside for activities. The morning bulletin had said that class meetings would be held at this time, so Shelley made her way alone to the study hall on the second floor, where her class, the Low Elevens, was meeting. Even being a member of the Low Elevens seemed odd. At home she would have been called a Fifth-termer. Shelley slipped into a seat near the door. At home she would have known everyone in her class and would not have this left-out feeling. At home Jack would probably be sitting beside her. What was she thinking about anyway? She didn't want Jack to sit beside her. She wanted to be in San Sebastian, didn't she? All right then. All she needed was a little time.

And then Shelley saw the face that she knew she would not forget. It was the face of the boy she had seen in the hall that morning. Now he was leaning against the window sill, talking to two other boys. She wondered if the three of them might be on the basketball team, because they were all tall and athletic-looking. A girl spoke to him and the boy flashed her a shy, lopsided grin that made Shelley skip a breath, even though the grin was not meant for her.

"Will the meeting please come to order?" It was Hartley Lathrop who spoke from the front of the room.

Shelley forced herself not to stare at the tall boy by the window.

"We will dispense with the reading of the minutes," announced Hartley, "because this is our first meeting and we don't have any." This brought loud applause from the boys in the class.

"Our first problem is to raise some money for our class fund," Hartley went on, "and since we have always done it by selling something on the front lawn at noon and since we have permission from the office to sell something a week from Monday, does anyone have any suggestions as to what we should sell?"

"I nominate Sno-cones," someone called out.

"No! No!" protested several voices all at once. "Everybody sells Sno-cones."

"Order!" shouted Hartley. "Sno-cones have been nominated and if everyone will please be quiet we will have some more nominations and then take a vote."

"Dixie cups!" someone called from the back of the room.

Shelley glanced at the boy by the window. She could not take much interest in the class meeting, because she felt like an observer instead of a participant. At home all the classes would have raised money at the annual Spring Festival in the park next to the school. First there would be the crowning of the queen. Every year Shelley's mother remarked, "Shelley, wouldn't it be fun if you were chosen queen of the Spring Festival when you are a senior? You are just as pretty as any of the girls." And every year her mother was puzzled when Shelley answered, "It takes more than being pretty and anyway, I don't want to be Festival queen." After the queen was crowned, the girls' gym classes would wind the Maypole. It would be a lovely spring day— unless it rained and the whole thing was moved into the gymnasium. Each class and club would have a booth and there would be nail-driving booths and candied-apple booths and phonograph-record-breaking booths, and all the kids from the elementary school would come running when their school was out and feel grown-up to be mingling with high-school students. Shelley remembered one time when she was working in a booth . . . .

Suddenly, almost without thinking, Shelley stood up to make a nomination.

Hartley recognized her and grinned. "Miss Shelley Latham wishes to speak."

Everyone—even the boy by the window—knew her name now. Shelley moistened her lips and spoke. "I nominate doughnut holes."

For a fraction of a second the room was silent and Shelley had a panicky feeling that she had made some terrible mistake. Then the room was filled with a shout of laughter. Shelley felt her face turn crimson as she stood there, too paralyzed by surprise to sit down. They were laughing at her. These horrible Low Elevens, as they called themselves, were laughing at her. The whole horrible roomful. She hated them! Every single one of them. Out of the corner of her eye she caught a glimpse of the boy by the window looking at her and laughing with the rest of the class. The boy she wanted to meet.

"Order! Order!" shouted Hartley, and when the room finally quieted down, he said, "Thanks for the joke, Shelley. Any more nominations?"

"But I'm not being funny," Shelley cried out in dismay. "I meant it."

The president of the Low Elevens looked puzzled.

"How can we sell something that doesn't exist?" he asked.

"But they do exist," protested Shelley, and all at once the whole situation was clear to her. The students of San Sebastian High did not know about doughnut holes. Maybe the town was too small to have a doughnut shop. Of course. Why, they must have thought she was talking like a character out of *Alice in Wonderland*.

Shelley had to raise her voice to speak above the babble in the room. "I don't mean the actual hole in the doughnut," she explained. "I mean the dough that is cut out of the doughnut to make the hole. At home the doughnut shop cooked them along with the doughnuts."

"You mean we could really buy doughnut holes?" asked Hartley.

"Yes," answered Shelley. "We sold them at the school I came from. Two for a nickel, and they were very popular."

"Doughnut holes have been nominated!" announced Hartley.

"I move the nominations be closed!" shouted half-a-dozen students.

"I second it!" everyone seemed to say at once.

Doughnut holes were chosen unanimously and one of the girls volunteered to make all the arrangements with a doughnut shop in Vincente. Shelley felt the crimson of her embarrassment turn to a flush of pleasure as everyone smiled at her, the new girl with the good idea. Now she belonged.

When the bell rang and the meeting was adjourned, Hartley sought out Shelley, who was finding it very pleasant to feel like a member of the class. "Thanks for the swell idea," he said. "I didn't know there were any new ideas for selling things left. Where are you headed for?"

Shelley consulted her schedule. "Biology lab. Room 211. I guess everyone thought I was crazy at first, but I thought every town had a doughnut shop."

Hartley grinned at her. "What we needed was some new blood around here."

"That's me," answered Shelley. "A regular transfusion."

"Maybe you and I should drive down to Vincente sometime to sample the doughnut holes," said Hartley.

"Maybe," answered Shelley, smiling. He had said maybe and she did not want to be any more definite than he. Even so, she felt heady with success. She had walked right into a new school and had made herself a part of the class the very first day. And now the president of the class was walking down the hall with her and she almost had a date with him.

"Here's where I'm going. Chemistry. Right next door to biology," said Hartley.

" 'By," said Shelley with a smile. Hartley had not really made a date but she was not worried. Latham, Lathrop. She would see him often. If only he were the tall boy with the sunburned nose . . . .

Shelley entered the biology laboratory, a room that was so hot she felt stifled. The study of a laboratory science, one of the requirements for college entrance, was to be a new experience for her. She sat down at one of four vacant chairs at a table which was covered with a film of dust that had been partially erased by the arms and notebooks of a previous class. The room was on the west side of the building and the shades were drawn almost to the sills to keep out the afternoon sun.

A girl, tiny and as alert-looking as a sparrow, sat in the chair opposite Shelley. "Hello," she said with a friendly smile. "That was a wonderful idea you had about doughnut holes." Then before Shelley could answer she called to someone behind Shelley, "Hi, Phil! Here's a chair."

Shelley turned and saw two boys. One was tall and heavy and one of the healthiest-looking boys Shelley had ever seen. He looked as if he ate steak three times a day. The other was the boy with the sunburned nose.

"Hi, Jeannie," they both said. The heavy boy sat in the chair beside Jeannie and the other boy sat beside Shelley. From the look of disappointment on

Jeannie's face, Shelley knew that this boy must be Philip.

Shelley smiled at Philip, who glanced down at the table top for an instant before he flashed her the shy, lopsided grin that made Shelley skip a breath for the second time that day. He was perfect, she decided instantly, and glanced away, realizing that Jeannie's sharp eyes had missed neither her smile nor Philip's grin. Philip. Shelley was intensely aware of him even though she dared not look at him.

A man stepped behind a counter at the front of the room and addressed the class. "If you will do me the honor of giving me your attention—"

Oh, dear, a man teacher, thought Shelley. They were always harder than women teachers, especially when they were the sarcastic type.

"I will pass around this diagram of the tables. Sign your names in the appropriate spaces," continued the teacher, whose name was Mr. Ericson.

Why, that means we will have these seats for the whole semester, thought Shelley. She would sit beside Philip for a whole term. What luck. What glorious luck! She glanced quickly at Philip, hoping that Jeannie would not notice. What a nice-looking boy he was. And that sunburned patch on his nose— there was something so—so touching about it.

Shelley forced her attention back to her teacher, who was saying, "Biology is, as I hope you already know, the science of living things. . . ."

Of course I know, thought Shelley, drowsy in the heat. Her thoughts drifted. Dear Mother and Daddy, she mentally wrote. Today was the first day of school. I liked all of my teachers except my biology teacher and I am not sure about him. The nicest boy named Philip sits next to me in biology. He is very good-looking. . . .

Shelley wondered what Philip's last name was and where he lived. And wouldn't it be wonderful if he really was on the basketball team and she got to wear his letter man's sweater (did boys let girls wear their sweaters down here the way they did at home?) and everybody thought how lucky she was. Dear Rosemary, Shelley began another mental letter. Today I met the most wonderful boy. He sits next to me in biology lab and he has the nicest grin. You would be simply mad about him. . . .

Shelley came out of her daydream long enough to sign the seat chart and to learn from it that the other girl at the table was Jeanne Jones, the boy who looked as if he lived on steak was Frisbie Gerard, and Philip's last name was Blanton. Philip Blanton. And he was going to sit beside her for an eighty-minute period for a whole semester. If only the room were not so oppressively warm. . . .

Shelley propped her chin on her fist and stared dreamily out the window, below the partially drawn shade, at the top of a palm tree. An honest-to-goodness palm tree in San Sebastian, California. Why, the closest she had ever been to a palm tree was in church on Palm Sunday when she had been given a bit of dried palm leaf. This was a real live palm tree. Shelley knew it was real, but she had difficulty making it seem real because here nothing seemed very real. It was all so unreal and so perfect—living on North Mirage Avenue, the wonderful Michies who hung out the washing by the light of the moon, the enthusiasm of her class at her suggestion of a doughnut-hole sale, Philip beside her in biology lab for a whole semester. Philip, who was the kind of boy every girl dreamed of meeting. It was all like a happy dream and this was going to be a wonderful year, she knew. Her world was full of sunshine and friendly people and nothing could possibly happen to spoil it. Shelley was sure of that.

Chapter 4

Drowsy in the new climate, Shelley felt as if she were drifting through her first week in San Sebastian in a beautiful dream of sunny days, blue skies, and strange faces—faces that grew less strange as each day passed. It was a happy week. Everyone was friendly and with the exception of the sarcastic Mr. Ericson, Shelley liked her teachers. She found it pleasant to study at the black desk with the gilded flatirons for book ends and to know that Luke and Katie were studying at the dining-room table downstairs. Luke asked her help with his Latin and Shelley enjoyed helping him find the main verb in sentences similar to those she had translated the year before. Katie would drop into her room to tell her about her struggles with a book report. ("The teacher says we have to tell something about the author and I don't know anything about the author.

Do you think it would be all right if I just made something up?")

And then there were letters from home. "Shelley dear," wrote her mother. "The house has seemed so quiet since you left. Every time the telephone rings I expect it to be a call for you. We miss you but are so happy you are enjoying . . . ." "Dear Shell," wrote Rosemary. "Having fun lolling about under the palm trees? Guess what? Jack walked home from school with me today, not that I think you'd care. I'm just reporting the facts, ma'am. Anyway, he talked mostly about you. . . ." "Dear Shelley," wrote Jack. "Holly cow! School doesn't seem the same with you way off down there." Shelley giggled. Holly cow! Poor Jack. It seemed as if she had known him a long, long time ago.

However, there was one thing about her first week of school that bothered Shelley. That was Philip. He always greeted her with his shy grin and although he sat beside her for the eighty minutes of biology laboratory, he did not offer to start a conversation. Shelley purposely left her notebook in her locker so that she could ask to borrow paper from him. This would give her two opportunities to talk to Philip because, of course, she would have to return the paper. He loaned her the paper but somehow this did not lead to the conversation she had planned. Instead, Philip talked across the table to

Frisbie while Jeannie's smile showed she had missed nothing.

"Say, Friz," Philip said before class, toward the end of the week. "Do you think we can get that topsoil moved on Saturday?"

"Sure," answered Frisbie. "If we start early enough."

"What do you mean, move topsoil?" asked Shelley. After all, sitting there at the same table she couldn't help overhearing the conversation, could she? And it didn't hurt to be friendly, did it?

"One of our neighbors who is going to put in a back lawn had a load of topsoil dumped on his driveway and Phil and I are going to move it for him," answered Frisbie. "We have formed a company. Blanton and Gerard, Contractors If the Job Isn't Too Hard. You know, pick-and-shovel work, tree cutting, wood splitting. Things that take brawn but not brains."

Shelley laughed. "Where is the topsoil you are going to move?" she asked Philip directly.

"Up the street a few blocks," he answered pleasantly, and opened his textbook.

Jeannie smiled wickedly across the table at Shelley.

Darn him, anyway, thought Shelley. What was the matter with him, acting like a yup-and-nope character in a western. She did not think he was unfriendly. He was only shy, and it was going to be up to her to find a way to make him less shy.

Mr. Ericson called the class to order and Shelley languidly opened her book. It must be difficult for a boy to be as shy as Philip. He probably felt uncomfortable around girls. Well, she would go right on being friendly toward him and maybe he would stop her in the hall sometime when Jeannie and Frisbie weren't around to hear what he said. He would look down at her with that shy grin of his and turn red and look embarrassed and say, "Shelley, I—I wondered if you were doing anything Saturday night." And she would smile to put him at his ease and say gently, "Why, no, Philip, I'm not. . . ."

"When Shelley Latham decides to join the class," said Mr. Ericson, "we shall begin."

The class laughed and Shelley felt herself blushing. If only she were not stuck with this man for a biology teacher when everything else in San Sebastian was so pleasant. Oh, well. . . . The lab was so hot in the afternoon sun. It was so hard to concentrate. Shelley's mind drifted again, this time to all the cool things she could think of—maidenhair fern growing along the streams in the woods, trilliums blooming through the last crusts of melting snow in the mountains, dark caves hollowed in the cliffs at the bottom of a waterfall where she had stood and watched the rainbows in the thundering curtain of

water between her and the sunshine. Cold, cold
water. . . .

That evening Shelley was introduced to another
Michie custom. Because Mavis bought groceries for
the whole week on Friday, supper on Thursday was
always made up of the accumulation of leftovers—
the one helping of beef Stroganoff, the last of the
spaghetti, the one tomato, the heel of the roast.
Mavis also served a platter of scrambled eggs "to
fill in the cracks."

Halfway through the meal Shelley turned to Tom
and asked, "Is there a boy on the basketball team
named Philip Blanton?"

"Well, Shelley," answered Tom with a quizzical
smile. "You, too?"

"I'll say he's on the basketball team," said Luke
enthusiastically. "Last year he was just about the
best forward in the whole county, is all. And he
was only a sophomore."

"And all the girls are mad about him," added
Katie with equal enthusiasm, "but he never bothers
with any of them."

"I just wondered," said Shelley hastily, helping
herself to three tablespoons of creamed tuna fish
that had been served in a custard cup. "He sits next
to me in biology and he is so tall I thought he must
be on the basketball team."

"He is, Shelley. He is," said Tom.

"You're sure lucky to get to sit next to him," said Katie. "Do you think he'll ask you for a date?"

"Oh, Katie, don't be silly," said Shelley with a forced laugh. Katie was always so blunt.

"It would be just wonderful if he would," said Katie wistfully.

"He won't," said Luke flatly. "He isn't going to waste his time on girls."

Oh, is that so, thought Shelley, even though she was afraid Luke might be right. Philip was not like a lot of athletes, the chesty kind who lounged around on the front steps at school and gave the girls they bothered to speak to that you-lucky-girl look, as if the girl should feel honored to be noticed by someone with a block letter on his sweater. Philip was pleasant and courteous to everyone, but in a reserved way. It wouldn't hurt to encourage a boy who was shy, would it?

"Katie dear, clear the table," said Mavis. Katie sighed wearily while Mavis said, "For dessert we have leftover devil's food cake, macaroons, one serving of vanilla ice cream, two servings of chocolate ice cream, and frozen pineapple. I have to get rid of it so I can defrost tonight."

"Did Katie bake the cake?" asked Luke.

"Yes, I did," said Katie, lifting a plate as if it were very, very heavy.

"Did you bake it from mix or from scratch?" Luke wanted to know.

"From cake mix," said Katie. "It won't poison you. Besides, lots of boys would be glad to have a sister who baked cake."

Shelley nibbled at a macaroon and wondered how she could help Philip overcome his shyness as far as she was concerned.

Shelley was glad when Friday afternoon arrived. The days were so warm she found it increasingly difficult to stay awake in class, particularly in the biology laboratory. It was so hard to be alert when all she wanted to do was put her head down on the table and take a nap. When it came time to go to the office of the school paper to pick up her copy of the *Bastion,* she was tempted not to bother. She had to force herself to take the extra steps and when she presented her student-body card, she accepted the paper without much interest. As she walked toward her locker she glanced at the paper and saw that it contained the usual articles found in the first issue of a school paper—a welcome from the principal, a welcome from the student-body president, a picture of the captain of the football team, an editorial about not throwing lunch sacks on the lawn.

Then halfway down a column called "The Roving Reporter" a name leaped out at Shelley. Her drowsiness disappeared as she read with wide-awake interest. "Looking forward to next winter's basketball season is Phil Blanton, San Sebastian's right forward. Draping his six-foot frame over a garbage can by the gym, Phil revealed that he believes San Sebastian stands a good chance of trouncing Vincente when basketball season rolls around. In the meantime he expects to keep busy with the firm of Blanton and Gerard, Contractors If the Job Isn't Too Hard. When your reporter queried Phil about his interest in girls, he answered, 'Girls? Never heard of them.' However, his partner, Friz Gerard, who was draped over the next garbage can, was heard to comment, 'Except when they come from up North and take biology.' "

Why, that's me. Shelley quickly reread the paragraph. " 'Except when they come from up North and take biology.' " The words could mean only one thing—Frisbie knew that Philip liked her. And since Frisbie was Philip's best friend and business partner, who could know him better? There it was in black and white for the whole school to see. Philip liked her.

Blessings on thee, Frisbie Gerard, thought Shelley, and her footsteps were light as she walked out of the building and through the orange groves. When she reached her room she lay down on her India print spread (at home she would have been expected to turn the spread back) and held the paper up over her head to read the words of the Roving Reporter a third time. And a fourth. Surely these were the most interesting words ever printed and surely they would give Philip the push he needed.

It occurred to Shelley that this was the first Friday night in a long time that she did not have the prospect of a date for the week end. At home she would have seen Jack whether she wanted to or not. Now she felt pleasantly carefree. Jack was over a thousand miles away, she had no date, and anything might happen. Maybe when Philip read the interview in the paper he would get up his courage to telephone. Maybe this very evening.

Later, when supper was over and Shelley and Luke had washed the dishes while Katie fed Sarge, the dog, and Smoky, the cat, Mavis remarked, "I don't know where this week has gone. I sprinkled the clothes but I haven't had a minute to do any ironing."

"Let's do it now," said Tom promptly. "Come on, everybody, we're going to iron."

Amused, Shelley followed the family into the laundry, where Tom lit the gas that heated the old-fashioned mangle and Mavis prepared to iron at the ironing board.

"Shelley, you take the other ironing board," directed Tom. "Katie, you and Luke feed the flat things into the mangle while I run it."

Obediently Shelley plugged in the iron and selected a sport shirt while Mavis started to iron one of Katie's blouses. Tom operated the lever that raised the top of the mangle. "Now!" he ordered, and simultaneously he and his two children fed napkins into the mangle. This was the secret of the fresh napkins at each meal. Tom brought the top down on the heated cylinder and the napkins rolled in and came out ironed. They ran the napkins through to fold them, laid them aside, and reached for more unironed linen. "Now!" Tom ordered, and the operation was repeated.

Why, ironing is fun, marveled Shelley, running her iron in and out around the buttons on the sport shirt and feeling a little like a child who has finally been asked to the party. Once the telephone rang, and Shelley started. At home Friday-night calls were almost always for her. This one was not. She finished ironing the shirt and hung it from the top of the door on a hanger. As she turned back to the ironing board she noticed the head of the six-point buck. "Is that the deer's head Mother says you took to college with you?" she asked Mavis.

"Yes, it is," answered Mavis, and laughed. "Your poor mother. I'm afraid I was a terrible trial to her."

"Why?" asked Shelley, finding it difficult to imagine Mavis a trial to anyone.

"I was so untidy and our room in the dormitory was so small," explained Mavis. "I used to hang my one hat and my scarves on the antlers, because they were so handy, and every week your mother would take them down just before room inspection.

She was so fastidious—she always looked as if she had just stepped out of a shower into freshly ironed clothes."

Shelley smiled, thinking that her mother still looked that way. Maybe that was why she had not wanted Shelley to wear a dirty slicker. She wanted Shelley to look the way she had looked when she was a girl. The words that Shelley had not spoken the day she threw the roses into the Disposall came back to her now. But Mother, I am not you. I am me.

"But Mommy, why did you take a deer's head away to school?" asked Katie, from the mangle.

Mavis laughed. "Why does a girl that age do anything? A boy I thought was perfectly wonderful shot the deer and had the head mounted for me, and naturally I couldn't bear to leave such a precious gift at home."

"And you've kept it all these years?" exclaimed Shelley, and realized at once that her reference to all these years was scarcely tactful.

Mavis burst out laughing. "It isn't easy to get rid of the mounted head of a six-point buck."

"Were you madly in love?" asked Katie.

"Girls in their teens always fancy themselves in love with the wrong boy," said Mavis, smiling. "However, this boy came to visit me at school, took one look at Shelley's mother, and lost interest in me."

"He did?" Shelley was amazed at this glimpse of her mother's girlhood. "But didn't you mind?"

"A little at first," admitted Mavis, "but I think I was really relieved to get rid of him, because he wanted me to hunt jack rabbits with him. Anyway, he helped make up for your mother's disappointment that week end."

"What sort of disappointment?" asked Shelley curiously.

"She didn't get elected Soph Doll," said Mavis. "That is what we called the queen of the sophomore ball."

"Soph Doll!" repeated Shelley in astonishment. *Mother* wanted to be Soph Doll?

"Yes, and it was a shame she didn't win," said Mavis. "She was the prettiest of the candidates but lost out through some sort of campus politics."

Shelley was incredulous. Mother wanting to be elected Soph Doll of all things. Of course, she was pretty for an older woman, but she was—well, a housewife. She had been ever since Shelley had known her. Before that she had been a teacher and before that—apparently she had been a girl who hoped to be Soph Doll. For Shelley this was an entirely new picture of her mother and as she ironed another sport shirt she found herself feeling sorry that her mother had not been elected to rule over a sophomore ball a long time ago.

"And you know," Mavis continued, "I've always

felt I should have turned the deer's head over to your mother along with the boy. The Great White Hunter, we called him."

In the front of the house the doorbell twirled. "You get it, Katie," directed Tom, opening the mangle once more.

Katie returned in a moment, her eyes sparkling. "Someone to see you, Shelley," she announced.

"Me?" asked Shelley, as excitement shot through her. Philip! The story in the paper had given him the push he needed.

It was Hartley Lathrop who entered the laundry behind Katie. "Hi, Shelley," said Hartley. "Good evening, Mrs. Michie and Mr. Michie."

"Why, Hartley!" In her surprise Shelley set the iron down flat.

"I know you weren't expecting me," apologized Hartley, "but at the last minute I got the car. When I tried to phone, the line was busy so I thought I'd take a chance. You can throw me out if you want to."

"Why—" Shelley was not sure what to say. She only hoped that her disappointment did not show. A scorched smell rose from her ironing board and she hastily lifted the iron.

"Not a chance," said Tom. "We're starting sheets and can use another hand around here."

"Sure," said Hartley, pulling a sheet out of the laundry basket. He and Luke folded it in half the

long way while Tom and Katie folded a second
sheet. They laid the ends on the roller. "Now!" said
Tom. The mangle closed and the sheets rolled
through.

Shelley wondered what Hartley would think. She
could not picture any of the boys she knew at home
helping with the ironing, any more than she could
picture her mother or father asking them to help.
Hartley seemed to be enjoying himself so Shelley
went on with her task.

"I promised Shelley a trip to Vincente to sample
doughnut holes," Hartley explained, as he picked
up another sheet.

"You two run along," said Mavis. "The rest of us
can finish."

"No hurry," said Hartley, folding the sheet. When
the last sheet and shirt and dirndl had been ironed,
he turned to Shelley. "Shall we go?" he asked.

"Yes." Shelley felt a little shy under the interested
scrutiny of Katie.

"Thanks for the help, Hartley," said Tom.

"And do come over sometime when we aren't
ironing," said Mavis. "We won't always put Shelley's guests to work."

Shelley enjoyed the drive through the warm evening. The stars seemed lower than the stars at home.
Once there was a hint of moisture in the air as they
passed a grove that had been irrigated that day.
As they turned a corner the headlights caught for

an instant a graceful tree with foliage that trailed
in the breeze. "What was that feathery tree?" she
asked.

"A pepper tree," answered Hartley.

"Oh, of course. The tree with the pink berries,"
said Shelley. "Mavis sent us some at Christmas once
when I was in grade school and I took some to
school to show the class. I felt so important."

Vincente looked very much like San Sebastian,
though a little larger perhaps, and farther from the
mountains. The doughnut shop, which was near the
Orange Belt College, was filled with students who
had stopped in on their way from the library. They
made Shelley feel young and inexperienced, but
Hartley was at ease. He guided her past a rack displaying every kind of doughnut—plain, sugar-coated,
chocolate-frosted, nut-covered—into a booth, where
he ordered doughnut holes and milk shakes. Then
he smiled across the table at Shelley, who was enjoying the cinnamon and nutmeg fragrance of the
shop. "Your hair looks nice in front, too," he said.

Shelley laughed and to change the subject said,
"I hope you didn't mind helping with the ironing
tonight."

"Not a bit. It was fun," answered Hartley. "The
Michies made me feel like part of the family."

"I know," said Shelley. "They made me feel that
way the minute I arrived. I was so scared. I had

never been away from home before except for two weeks at camp once."

"Do you like California, Shelley?" Hartley asked seriously.

"I do now," said Shelley. "At first everything looked so flat and dry and there wasn't any water in the river bed. A river with no water—I had never seen anything like that before."

"Don't worry," said Hartley. "There will be water this winter."

"It seems hard to believe," said Shelley. "At first all I could think was that I had to spend the winter in this place. I had heard so much about California I guess I expected to step across the border into the tropics." Shelley munched a doughnut hole thoughtfully before she said, "And you know, now that I'm used to it, it really is beautiful. I love it. Oranges and olives really growing on trees, and down the street from our house there is a tree with pomegranates growing on it. Real pomegranates!"

"You make them sound like something special," said Hartley. "I've seen pomegranates around here ever since we came to California when I was about three years old, and I never thought much about them."

"They remind me of a story I used to read when I was a little girl," said Shelley, thinking that Hartley had a nice face. Not as nice as Philip's, with his sunburned nose, but nice in a different way. Thinner, more sensitive, the kind of face that in the movies belonged to the man who didn't get the girl but you sort of wished he had.

"What was the story?" asked Hartley.

"I used to like fairy tales," said Shelley, "and this was a myth about Persephone, who was snatched away by Pluto to the lower world, and while she was there she ate six pomegranate seeds and that is why we have six months of summer and six months of winter."

Hartley looked at her so steadily that Shelley was embarrassed. How silly to be sitting here talking about fairy tales. She did not know what had come over her. She would never have thought of telling Jack such a thing. They were both silent a moment, and out of habit Shelley opened her mouth to say something. Then she closed it and was silent.

"You started to say something," Hartley reminded her.

Shelley looked down at the table. "Not really."

"Yes, you did," Hartley insisted.

Shelley laughed nervously. "I don't really know what I was going to say. Just anything, I guess. A boy I—I used to know always said, 'Penny for your thoughts' when there was a silence and I guess I fell into the habit of saying anything that popped into my mind to keep him from saying it."

"Didn't you like the boy?" Hartley asked curiously.

For the first time since she had left home, Shelley stopped to think about Jack. She found that being a thousand miles away gave her a new perspective. "Yes," she said thoughtfully, "I liked him. He was really an awfully nice fellow, but you know how it is. You go out with a boy three or four times and everybody assumes you are going steady. I guess we just ran out of things to talk about." As she spoke Shelley knew that although she was tired of Jack, she was also grateful to him. He had taken her to school dances and the movies and different places to eat so that she had learned how a girl should act and could sit here with Hartley without worrying about her behavior.

Shelley stirred her milk shake with her straw. She had not meant to confide in Hartley but, for a boy, she found him surprisingly easy to talk to. And the thought crossed her mind that if he had been Philip she would have been more cautious in expressing disapproval of going steady. It was funny how a girl would behave one way with one boy and an entirely different way with another boy.

Feeling that she had let the conversation become too personal, Shelley said, "I like school, too, and next semester I get to take journalism. I've wanted to take journalism ever since I entered high school."

"I'm going to take it too," said Hartley. "I want to go to Stanford and it would help the family a lot if I could get a scholarship. And to get a scholarship you have to take part in activities. I figured that if I worked on the school paper I would get credit for an activity and an English course at the same time."

"That's a good idea," said Shelley, admiring Hartley's ability to plan ahead. They sat in silence, each thinking about individual plans for the future.

"I think doughnut holes taste better than doughnuts," said Hartley. "Maybe it is because they were your idea."

Shelley wrinkled her nose at Hartley. "I think we had better go," she said, glancing at her watch. "I'm not sure what time the Michies expect me to be in." And the funny part of it was that since no one had mentioned when she should come home, she was anxious to return early.

They said little on the way home. Hartley parked the car outside the privet hedge and walked Shelley to the door, which she found was unlocked. She opened it and Hartley stepped into the front hall with her. A lamp was shining in the living room, but Shelley was not sure whether she should ask Hartley to sit down or not.

"I won't stay," Hartley said, as if in answer to her thoughts.

"I had a good time." Shelley meant it, even though she would have preferred spending the evening with Philip.

"I like you, Shelley," said Hartley directly "You

make me feel as if I were seeing things around me for the first time. Like pepper trees. And that pomegranate tree. I've seen it all my life and never thought anything about it except when I was a kid and we used to snitch pomegranates at Halloween. But you make it seem as if having a pomegranate tree growing down the street is something special."

Shelley smiled, not knowing quite how to answer. A girl always enjoyed hearing a boy say he liked her. Before she could think of an answer, she began to have an uneasy feeling that she and Hartley were being watched. She glanced up over Hartley's shoulder, and there in the transom over the unused door at the end of the living room was the face of Katie, beaming down at her like a Cheshire cat.

Why, she must be crouched on top of the refrigerator, thought Shelley in astonishment, and at the same time she noticed that the transom had been opened.

"Uh . . ." said Shelley, ill at ease under the interested eye of Katie. "Well, uh . . . thank you, Hartley. I had a good time."

"Shelley, I . . ." Hartley began.

"Good night, Hartley," said Shelley firmly and with what she knew was false brightness. Darn Katie anyway. Little snoop.

"Good night, Shelley," said Hartley, looking puzzled and a little hurt.

"See you at school," said Shelley, realizing that

the pleasant evening was ending on an awkward note. "You know, Latham, Lathrop."

"We can't miss, can we?" answered Hartley. "Good night, Shelley."

Even if Hartley was not Philip, Shelley did not want him to go away with his feelings hurt. She glanced at the transom and saw that Katie was still watching with avid interest. She could not think of a thing to say so she said, "Good night, Hartley."

As Shelley closed the door she heard the thump of Katie jumping to the floor. Wait till I get hold of her, thought Shelley. Just wait. If Katie thought she was going to let her get away with spying on her just so she could tease . . . .

Shelley did not have to wait. Katie appeared in the living room in her pajamas. "Shelley, he said he *liked* you!" she exclaimed. "Aren't you simply thrilled to *pieces?*"

"Why, yes, I am pleased," Shelley admitted cautiously. Katie's reaction was not at all what she expected.

Katie looked at Shelley with admiration shining from her face. "It must be wonderful to have a boy say he likes you!"

Shelley did not have the heart to scold.

"I know I shouldn't have watched," said Katie, with disarming frankness, "but I just had to so if a boy ever asks me to go out I will know what to do." She paused and sighed gustily. "But I don't suppose a boy ever will ask me."

"Oh, I wouldn't say that," said Shelley, wondering if Katie would crouch on the refrigerator if Philip ever brought her home.

"What would you have done if he had tried to kiss you?" Katie asked bluntly.

Shelley made a face at Katie and put her hand on the banister rail. "I don't know—he didn't try," she said, and ran up the stairs.

Chapter 5

The next week, at school, Hartley was still friendly toward Shelley but there was a restraint in his behavior that was new. Shelley was sorry, but she did not know how to tell him about Katie's watching them say good night. A girl on top of the refrigerator was such an improbable thing to try to explain. Everything about Shelley's new life was so fresh and so exciting that she did not let her thoughts linger on anything or anybody—except Philip—very long.

Every day she found something new to like about San Sebastian Union High School. It seemed so much more friendly than the school she had attended at home and, because it was smaller, everyone knew everyone else. Shelley and Jeannie soon became friends. Jeannie was different from any girl Shelley had ever known. She was so small and quick and eager and yet beneath her eagerness she seemed wistful, as if she were waiting for something to happen and was afraid it might not.

The girls usually ate their lunches together on the lawn under a palm tree. "I think it is fun to bring a lunch when everyone does," confided Shelley one day. "It makes every lunch period seem like a picnic."

"I would like to go to a school that had a cafeteria," said Jeannie. "If all the tuna-fish sandwiches I have eaten since kindergarten were laid end to end, they would reach farther than I care to think about."

"At home the students who brought bag lunches were embarrassed, because they had to eat them in the cafeteria along with those who could buy lunches. This way is more fun."

Jeannie smiled at Shelley. "You have fun in the funniest ways. I guess that's why I like you."

The rooting section at the football games was a happy surprise to Shelley too. Any girl who wore a white blouse could sit in the rooting section. The girls who forgot to wear white blouses on game days ran out to the gym and pulled on their gym blouses over whatever they happened to be wearing. This made Shelley's new school perfect. "I've always wanted to sit in a rooting section," she confessed to Jeannie.

"Don't all schools do it this way?" asked Jeannie.

"No, they don't. At home one girl was chosen from each room," Shelley explained. "The trouble with you, Jeannie, is that you just don't appreciate San Sebastian."

Even a football game seemed like an entirely new experience for Shelley. The rooting section of the home team courteously faced the sun, allowing the visitors the scant shade of their own shadows. Shelley licked a Popsicle and acquired a sunburn while she cheered for her team. At home she would have worn her raincoat and tried to warm her hands on a soggy hot dog while she wished that she were part of the rooting section.

And then there was the *Bastion,* so different from her school paper at home, which mentioned the names of the same students over and over as if, by writing the names of these popular students, the reporters hoped that they, too, would become popular. Shelley's name had always appeared in the honor roll and once it had appeared in the gossip column when she and Jack began going steady, but never had she been interviewed.

That was why she was so pleased when a boy stopped by her locker one afternoon and said, "Hi, Shelley. I'm the Roving Reporter this week and I am interviewing new students. Can you spare a couple of minutes?"

"Hello, Rover," said Shelley, flattered that she had been chosen. "I'd be delighted."

"R-ruf!" answered the boy. "Tell me, as a new student, what do you think of San Sebastian High?"

"I think it is marvelous," answered Shelley. "Everyone is so friendly."

"What specifically do you like about the place?" the reporter wanted to know.

Shelley knew from reading the paper that a serious answer was not expected of her. The sight of her locker gave her an idea—not a very good idea, but all she could think of at the moment. "I like the cunning little lockers arranged in two tiers in the halls," she answered. "Where I came from we had to have long lockers to hold our slickers and boots."

"Boots!" exclaimed the boy. "Then it isn't true that the entire population of the state of Oregon is born with webfeet?"

"Of course we have webfeet," answered Shelley. "We just keep them dry, is all."

The boy made notes on a pad of paper. "Is there anything else you like about San Sebastian High?"

"Lots of things," answered Shelley, stumped for the right sort of answer.

"Such as?" prompted the boy.

The only Roving Reporter interview that Shelley could recall very clearly was the interview in which Philip, or rather Frisbie, had referred to her. This gave her an idea. "Specifically, I like basketball players who take biology," she answered with unaccustomed daring.

"Basketball players, biology," muttered the reporter, and flashed a grin at Shelley. "Thanks a lot. That should fill up my space."

"You're welcome," answered Shelley with a smile, and turned to her locker. Had she done the right thing, she wondered. Maybe Philip wouldn't like a girl who practically threw herself at him in the school paper. Maybe he would be embarrassed. But what was a girl supposed to do when a boy was shy? She had to do something and there was a chance this might work.

"Hi, Shelley," said Hartley unexpectedly. "You look as if you thought something exciting was about to happen."

"In San Sebastian, who knows?" said Shelley. Hartley grinned and walked on down the hall, and Shelley watched until he turned the corner. Sometime she must find a way to explain about Katie on the refrigerator. . . .

Half hoping the reporter would not use her statement, Shelley nervously awaited the next issue of the *Bastion*. When she received her copy she turned with trembling hands to the Roving Reporter column. There it was, her name in print. Her eye skimmed through the paragraph. She was almost afraid to look at the last sentence. " 'I like basketball players who take biology,' confessed this pert L-11 miss."

Her remark had been printed and there was nothing she could do about it now. Seeing the words in black and white made Shelley regret her statement to the reporter. She had been too bold, she was sure. And what would Tom and Mavis think when they read the paper? And what if Mavis happened to mention the story when she wrote to Shelley's mother—or even send her the clipping? Well, anyway, Shelley told herself ruefully, it had seemed like a good idea at the time.

When the next biology period arrived, Shelley dreaded facing Philip. She lingered at her locker as long as she dared, hoping that if she entered the room just as the class started she could avoid talking to Philip a little longer. Unfortunately Shelley underestimated the time it would take her to reach the laboratory.

Mr. Ericson had already begun to talk when she entered the room. He was silent as he looked directly at Shelley, who was trying to slip inconspicuously into her chair. Then he said to the class, "May I introduce the late Shelley Latham?"

Shelley's face was crimson and she did not move her eyes from the initials inked on the cover of the notebook she had laid on the table in front of her. The late Shelley Latham! Why did Mr. Ericson have to be so sarcastic all the time anyway? She was so annoyed with her teacher that for once she did not feel drowsy in the afternoon heat.

"Hi, Webfoot," whispered Philip, under cover of the laughter of the class.

Shelley did not dare look at Philip. She could not risk any more of Mr. Ericson's sarcasm. The next seventy-nine minutes of laboratory were difficult for Shelley. She tried to give the appearance of concentrating on algae and fungi so that she would not attract Mr. Ericson's attention. Actually, she was considering the implications of the words, "Hi, Webfoot." For one thing, they told her that Philip had read the interview. But Webfoot? Did Philip, like Mr. Ericson, mean to be sarcastic? No, she was sure he did not. He had sounded as if he were teasing in a friendly way.

Shelley clamped a slide under her microscope and prepared to draw a picture of a protococcus. Philip would never be sarcastic like Mr. Ericson. She turned the knob that adjusted the microscope and peered through the finder with her right eye until the one-celled plant came into focus. Then she looked through the microscope with her left eye and at the same time tried to look at her paper with her right eye. Mr. Ericson said that was the proper way to use a microscope, but Shelley felt as if her eyes were going off in different directions. To rest them she let both eyes stray to Philip.

"Shelley," said Mr. Ericson, "can you tell us how fission plants differ from thallus plants?"

"Um . . ." said Shelley, taken by surprise. "A fission plant . . . I'm sorry. I don't know."

"Philip?" asked Mr. Ericson.

"No, sir," answered Philip. "I don't know."

Jeannie knew. Quick, bright-eyed Jeannie always knew the answers.

Somehow Shelley got through the rest of the laboratory period. As she put away her microscope and closed her notebook, Philip turned to her with his lopsided grin and said, "So long, Webfoot." As usual, he left the room with Frisbie.

"Aren't boys maddening?" asked Jeannie sympathetically.

"Yes," agreed Shelley, and decided she had better forget about Philip before she became the laughingstock of the whole school—if she was not already. She was ashamed of what she had done. When Philip was interviewed he had not said he liked her. Frisbie had said it for him, perhaps meaning it as a joke which she had been foolish enough to take seriously because she had wanted it to be true. She had been so sure that life in San Sebastian was going to be perfect and now she had made a mess of everything.

That afternoon after school Shelley wrote a long letter to her mother and father, telling them about her studies and the success of the doughnut-hole sale and the fun she was having with the Michies.

When she had sealed the letter she started a second letter. "Dear Rosemary, San Sebastian is simply perfect! And guess what? Remember that cute boy I told you about who sits next to me in biology? Well, now he calls me Webfoot! How's that for a nickname?" Shelley did not really feel the enthusiasm she was displaying in her letter, but she felt that since she had written so much about Philip in a previous letter to her best friend, she should mention him again. Webfoot was really not a promising nickname. A boy who liked a girl a lot would not call her Webfoot. Because Philip was important to her, she did not even think of him as Phil. He was Philip, and if she were important to him he would call her Shelley. Webfoot was a nickname for a girl who was a pal. Well, she didn't want to be a pal to Philip. She might as well forget him as she had decided once before that afternoon. Slowly Shelley tore the letter to bits and sprinkled the pieces into the wastebasket.

At supper that evening Katie announced, "Shelley was interviewed in the *Bastion*. I was looking at Luke's paper and I saw the interview."

"Oh, that silly thing," said Shelley hastily. She was not anxious to have Tom's and Mavis's attention called to her bad judgment. Mavis might even feel she had to speak to Shelley about it.

"Shelley said she liked basketball players who take biology," persisted Katie. "And they put it in the paper. And you know what? Philip Blanton plays basketball and takes biology!"

Shelley felt herself blushing. She was thoroughly ashamed of the example she had set Katie. She glanced at Tom and Mavis, who did not seem particularly concerned with the turn of the conversation. Mavis, with two children of her own, could not concern herself with Shelley's small problems. It was different at home, where Shelley's mother had only one child to think about. "Katie, I shouldn't have said what I did," said Shelley. "It was a stupid thing to do and I'm sorry I said it and I'm sorry they printed it."

"Just the same," said Katie dreamily, "I hope I get interviewed for the paper when I get to high school."

Tom turned to his son. "Well, Luke, what's this I hear about your having trouble in English?" he asked.

"It isn't fair!" Luke burst out. "Other kids don't have dads who teach at the same school they go to and hear every single little old thing that happens!"

"What did happen?" asked Tom.

Luke scowled at his plate.

"Yes, Luke, tell us," Mavis urged.

"Aw . . . the teacher wrote a bunch of sentences on the blackboard before class and then during class she went right down the row and asked each of us to read a sentence aloud and put the punctuation in," Luke explained. "When I came to my sentence I didn't want to do it, is all," said Luke.

"Why not?" asked Mavis. "Didn't you know how to punctuate it?"

"Sure I did," answered Luke, "but I knew if I read it all the kids would laugh. They laughed anyway."

"What was the sentence?" Tom asked jovially. "You can tell us. You're among friends."

Luke spoke rapidly, and without expression. " 'Mother,' I cried, 'they've crowned me Queen of the May.' "

Shelley could not help it. A shout of laughter escaped her along with the laughter of the rest of the family.

"See?" said Luke bitterly. "What did I tell you?"

The family made an effort to control its amusement. "Did you finally read it?" asked Mavis.

"She made me," said Luke. "And then she said I got it right except that if I had been crowned Queen of the May I would be excited and so it should be Queen of the May exclamation point. Boy, that really slayed the class."

Poor Luke. Shelley sympathized with him even though she could scarcely keep from laughing. She remembered how she had felt that afternoon when she was called "the late Shelley Latham."

"Luke, do the best work you can and try to be patient with your English teacher," said Mavis gently. "She obviously doesn't have a sense of humor and that is something she can't help."

"Mother, they've crowned me Queen of the May exclamation point!" said Katie dramatically.

"Now, Katie," warned Tom, "Luke has had enough trouble with that sentence."

"You know what we had to cook in cooking class today?" asked Katie. "Mush and breakfast cocoa." She made an expressive gagging noise. "And right after lunch, too."

Shelley studied the faces around her. The interview no longer seemed so important. This was one of the things she enjoyed most about living with a larger family. When she became absorbed in a problem, someone else came along with another problem and somehow her difficulty lost its importance. At home all her problems were the center of interest.

Saturday morning after breakfast Tom and Luke went out to work in the grove. Mavis went to her studio over the garage and Shelley decided to run the vacuum cleaner in her room. She even moved the bed and was cleaning in the corner when Katie burst into the room.

"Hi," said Shelley, switching off the vacuum cleaner.

"Shelley!" exclaimed Katie, who was plainly trying to suppress great excitement. "Come down the road with me. I want to show you something."

"What do you want to show me?" asked Shelley.

"It's a surprise," said Katie. "Shelley, you've got to come!"

"All right," agreed Shelley, to please Katie. "How far down the road?"

"Not very far," said Katie. "Get a bicycle and come on."

The two girls, accompanied by Sarge, bicycled down the road that bordered the grove and as they pedaled, Katie chattered. "I can hardly wait until tonight," she confided. "The dancing class that meets at school once a month is having a hat dance."

"A hat dance?" asked Shelley. "I thought a hat dance was a Mexican folk dance where the man throws his hat on the floor and stamps his feet around it."

Katie giggled. "Not this kind. It is our regular dancing class, only everybody is supposed to concoct some sort of château to wear and there will be prizes for the best ones," answered Katie.

Shelley found this statement puzzling. "Oh, you mean chapeau," she said, when she had figured out Katie's meaning.

"Well, anyway, a crazy hat," said Katie. "Mine is a secret. Wait till you see it. I know it will win a prize."

"Is there some special boy you like?" asked Shelley.

"Could be," answered Katie mysteriously.

The two girls approached a house that was protected by a windbreak of eucalyptus trees and as they came near the trees, Shelley heard the sound of sawing.

"Look!" cried Katie triumphantly. "Up there in the wild blue yonder!"

Against the blue sky fifty feet above the ground and half-hidden by leaves was Philip. He was leaning away from the tree, his body supported by a lineman's belt buckled around the trunk, his spiked heels digging into the wood. For a moment Shelley stood staring up, motionless in surprise, before she collected her thoughts and decided to leave quickly before Philip saw her.

From another treetop Frisbie's voice called out, "Hey, Phil! Here's the late Miss Latham!"

Philip stopped sawing at a branch and called down, "Hi, Webfoot!"

"Hi." Shelley had to answer, but she was sure that Philip would think she had found out where he was working and had deliberately ridden out to see him. She realized now, when it was too late, that she should have insisted upon Katie's telling her what the surprise was. Now, after that silly interview in the paper, Philip would think she was as persistent as—as a bloodhound. Not only had she tracked him down, now she had him treed. Well, she had no intention of sitting there baying at him. "Come on, Katie, let's go," she whispered.

"No, let's watch," begged Katie.

"Katie, please!" Shelley's whisper was urgent. Just wait till she got Katie alone! There were a few things she was going to explain to her.

Philip wiped the dust and sweat from his forehead with the back of his hand and went on sawing. The branch broke through and came crashing to the ground in a cloud of dust and a flutter of dry leaves. The sudden loss of the branch made the treetop spring back and forth and in spite of herself Shelley watched, fascinated. Philip looked so tall and strong up there in the swaying treetop.

"Katie," Shelley whispered, turning her bicycle around. "You can stay if you want to, but I'm leaving."

"But you said you liked him." Katie sounded hurt.

"Katie, you don't understand." Shelley mounted her bicycle. "I'll explain later."

"Hey, Webfoot," Frisbie called from a treetop. "Stick around. Phil wants to talk to you."

"Aw, shut up, Friz," Shelley heard Philip say in an undertone.

"Go on, ask her," said Frisbie.

"Sorry, Friz," Shelley called. "I have things to do." She gave what she hoped was a jaunty wave and started down the road.

"Shelley, wait!" Philip yelled, loud enough for the whole countryside to hear. "I want to talk to you."

This from shy Philip? Shelley hesitated. stopped,

and looked back up at Philip, who was working his way down the tree trunk. He had called her Shelley so perhaps he meant what he said. She felt confused and, under Katie's interested eye, uncomfortable. Darn Katie, anyway.

"You heard the boy," shouted Frisbie from his treetop.

"You keep out of this, Friz," said Philip, unfastening the belt and jumping to the ground.

Shelley hesitated. After the way she had behaved she did not want to appear to pounce on him. On the other hand, she really did want to talk to him —terribly. Philip approached her, and even though he was dirty and sweaty he looked clean and healthy underneath the dirt and more wonderful than any boy Shelley had ever known.

"Shelley, may I come over this evening?" he asked.

When Shelley did not answer immediately, Katie whispered, "Go on. Say yes."

Shelley did not dare hesitate any longer, because there was no telling what Katie would take into her head to say or do. "Yes, I would love to have you come over," Shelley answered.

"Swell," said Philip. "I'll be over about eight."

"I'll see you then," answered Shelley, and pedaled down the road. She did not want to linger and appear too anxious, especially when she was so excited that her hands would have trembled if she had not been gripping the handle bars so tightly. She finally had a date with Philip.

Katie rode along beside her. "I knew he would ask you for a date," she said happily. "I just knew it."

"Katie—" began Shelley, and stopped because she did not know what to say. It was difficult to scold someone who was so happy for her and she did not know how to explain to Katie that although she was delighted to have a date with Philip, she felt she had done all the wrong things. After all, she was supposed to be a good experience for a girl who had reached a difficult age. She did not want Katie to think a girl should advertise in the school paper that she liked a boy and then go out and tree him. She should try to set the younger girl a good example and so far she had done a poor job. "Katie, it is nice of you to want me to have a date with Philip," she said tactfully, "but I am afraid he will think I chased him, especially after that awful interview I gave the school paper."

"But it worked," Katie pointed out.

"I know," admitted Shelley, thinking that this was what made it so difficult to explain. "But a girl really shouldn't run after a boy—at least not so he knows she is running after him."

"I suppose not," said Katie thoughtfully, as they turned into the Michies' driveway, "but just the same, I'm glad he's coming over to see you. Aren't you terribly excited? I would be."

Shelley laughed. "Yes, I'm excited," she admitted, in a voice much calmer than the feelings behind it. At the same time she wondered how she was going to keep Katie off the top of the refrigerator.

Chapter 6

That evening, as soon as the dishes were washed, Shelley ran upstairs to wash her face and change into a fresh cotton dress, one that she had not worn to school. She brushed her hair, applied her lipstick with care, and because this was such a special occasion, dusted powder across her nose. Glancing at her watch, she was disappointed to find she still had an entire hour to wait before Philip would ring the doorbell. One long hour. She could write to her mother and father, but she felt too excited to sit down with pen and paper. She twirled around to see how far her skirt would stand out. This made it necessary to comb her hair all over again, a task that used up only a few seconds of the hour. She sat carefully on her bed so that she would not wrinkle her skirt. Fifty-three minutes to Philip. Fifty-three crawling minutes. How could she ever live fifty-three minutes?

"Mom! Dad! Shelley!" yelled Katie from the living room. "Come and see my hat for the hat dance!"

Shelley, glad of a way to use up part of the fifty-three minutes, went downstairs to see the hat that Katie had spent the afternoon creating in secrecy in the laundry.

Now Katie stood admiring herself in the mirror in the front hall. Upside down on her head was a hollowed-out head of curly chicory so large it covered almost all of her hair. Fastened here and there to the lettuce, were radishes and green onions. Sticking out of the back like two enormous hatpins were a wooden salad fork and spoon. The whole creation was anchored by two green ribbons tied under Katie's chin. "I'm a tossed green salad!" she announced.

Tom and Mavis shouted with laughter and Shelley thought Katie looked like a robust sprite. Luke, sitting in an easy chair with a pile of science-fiction magazines on the floor beside him, groaned and said, "Oh, for dumb!"

"Katie, that is priceless," said Mavis. "How did you ever think of such a thing?"

"I've always thought this kind of lettuce looked like curly green hair," said Katie.

"Mom, you don't mean you are going to let her go out in that thing, do you?" demanded Luke.

"Of course," answered Mavis. "I think it is fetching."

"Well, I think it looks dumb," said Luke. "Do we have to eat it after she gets through wearing it?"

"No, you don't," said Katie. "I bought the lettuce and radishes and onions with my own money. I didn't get them out of the salad things in the refrigerator."

"Come on, green salad," said Mavis, picking up the car keys from the mantel. "You don't want to be late."

"Have fun and I hope you get lots of dances with the right boy," said Shelley sincerely. If it hadn't been for Katie, she might not be waiting for Philip this very minute.

"He can graze on her hat while they dance," remarked Luke, from behind his magazines.

"Oh, be quiet," said Katie cheerfully, as she went out the front door. She was too happy to be annoyed by anything her brother said.

Shelley rather envied Katie her puppyish excitement. She was excited too, but at sixteen a girl had learned to be more cautious about letting her feelings show until she knew for sure that a boy really liked her.

"Now, Luke," said Mavis. "Shelley is to have the living room this evening if she wants it."

"O.K.," said Luke without looking up.

Shelley smiled to herself. Not only was Philip coming to see her, she was going to have the living room all to herself when he came. This time she would not have to cringe inside, the way she always had when she introduced a boy to her mother and father and could feel them looking him over, wondering what his family was like and what his father did and what time he would bring her home. This time was going to be different.

Shelley was restless when Mavis and Katie had gone. Tom went outdoors and she was left alone with Luke. She glanced at the clock and wandered around the room, reading titles in the bookcase, picking up magazines and laying them down again. She wondered if Philip would walk or come in a car and what they would do when he arrived. Making a date with Katie present was not very satisfactory, because a boy naturally would not like to discuss the details with a younger girl hanging on every word he said. Whatever they did, she wanted more than anything for him to have a good time so that he would ask her out again and then again. It would be such fun to have dates with a boy all the girls wanted to know and especially during basketball season. She would go to all the games and when Philip scored everyone sitting near her would look at her and think, There's Phil Blanton's girl, and she would go on cheering just as if she wasn't aware that everyone was looking at her. . . .

Shelley hummed to herself, nibbled at a hangnail, sat down. She wished Luke would hurry up and leave the room. It was not like him to spend the evening reading when he could be working on his motorcycle. And she still had Katie to worry about. If Katie came home and climbed up on the refrigerator again, perhaps she should look her straight in the eye through the glass in the transom and say, "Well, if it isn't Katie!" Maybe that would embarrass her enough to make her scramble down. There were, Shelley decided, a number of advantages to being an only child, after all. She hoped that Tom would not suddenly announce that this was a good night to wash or iron. It would never do to ask a star basketball player to help with the Michies' laundry.

Shelley looked at her watch again, stood up, read a few more titles in the bookcase, wandered across the room, and picked up one of Luke's science-fiction magazines.

"Luke, why do you read this stuff anyway?" Shelley asked, hoping to draw his attention from the story so that he might think about leaving.

"Because I like it," answered Luke, not looking up from his magazine.

Because she had to do something to fill the dragging minutes, Shelley read a few sentences to herself, giggled, and began to read aloud with exaggerated expression. " 'The sun beat down on the asteroid. Sweat stood out on the lean jaws of Brad Conway as he stared at the dials of the transmutor. In thirty seconds . . . in twenty seconds . . . in—' "

"Aw, cut it out," said Luke, looking up at last.

Amused that she had finally caught Luke's attention, Shelley dropped the magazine and picked up another, which she opened at random and began to read. " 'The spaceship left the planet and was only thirty light years into the galaxy when Captain Rowley felt the controlcomp go dead in his hands. Automatically he glanced earthside in the telescan—' "

The magazine was snatched from Shelley's hands. "You cut that out!" ordered Luke, so fiercely that Shelley was taken aback. These stories, which were funny to her, were not funny to him.

"I guess I was just surprised to see you reading, is all," Shelley faltered. "You're usually working on your motorcycle."

"Aw, Mom's right," said Luke morosely. "I'll never get it to run."

So that was what was bothering Luke. He was discouraged about his motorcycle. "Yes, you will," said Shelley, wanting him to succeed. "I know you will get it to run sometime."

The twirl of the doorbell was so startling to Shelley that she felt as if everything inside her had stopped. Philip! He had come and now she felt completely unprepared. Nervously she ran her hand over her hair and smoothed her skirt. What on earth would she say? She moistened her lips and with a hand chilled by nervousness, opened the door. Philip really was standing on the doorstep.

"Hello, Shelley," he said.

"Hello, Philip," answered Shelley. "Won't you come in?"

As Philip stepped through the door, Shelley saw that Luke had disappeared with his magazines. Uncertainly she asked Philip to sit down. She sat down on the opposite end of the couch. She found she could not look directly at him and so, instead, she stared at the toe of her shoe as if it were some strange new object she had never seen before. It was ridiculous to feel so embarrassed, she knew. and for a moment she could not understand why she felt that way. A first date was usually a little awkward but not this awkward, although, of course, none of her other first dates had been with Philip Blanton. Then Shelley realized she felt awkward because she was alone with him. Always before, the first moments had been spent introducing the new boy to her mother and father. She had never enjoyed the introductions, but at least introducing a boy had given her something definite to do for those first few moments. Now she was face to face with Philip, alone and on her own. She almost wished Tom would appear and say it was a good night to iron and why didn't they all pitch in and help?

Bravely Shelley looked at Philip and was rewarded by the lopsided grin. Encouraged, she said, "I was certainly surprised to see you up in that tree when Katie asked me to go bicycling this morning." That would show him that she had not intended to track him down.

"You saw the firm of Blanton and Gerard, Contractors, at work," said Philip. "We were cutting some of the branches before they got big enough to overhang the house. Eucalyptus is brittle in hot weather and sometimes the branches fall."

"Aren't you scared to climb such a high tree?" asked Shelley.

"No," said Philip. "I like it. I feel so sort of— well, I don't know—free, I guess, when I am up there."

"Do you get many jobs cutting branches?" asked Shelley, who until now had known only boys who earned money mowing lawns or washing cars.

"Some," answered Philip. "Friz and I cut trees, too, if they aren't too big. His dad lets us use his chain saw and we cut them up into fireplace lengths and then split them. You have to split eucalyptus wood as soon as it is cut or it gets too hard."

"You do?" said Shelley, admiring Philip and thinking that the sunburn on his nose the first day of school must have come from splitting wood under the California sun.

Conversation died. Philip and Shelley both looked down, looked at one another, and looked away, embarrassed that their eyes had met. For the first time Shelley noticed that the old clock on the mantel had an unusually loud tick.

Shelley could think of no way to revive the conversation. She had to do something, but what? The television set was not working and the Michies had not bothered to have it repaired. They did not have a record collection. Feeding a boy was always acceptable, but it was too early in the evening. Maybe she should suggest making fudge, the way teen pages in magazines recommended girls should entertain boys. They would have to wait for the fudge to cool and that would take time. But somehow Shelley did not feel she could ask a star basketball player to step into the kitchen to whip up a batch of fudge the minute he entered the house. Lots of boys she had known at home would make fun of a girl if she made such a suggestion. They would laugh about it by the lockers in the halls at school. Shelley did not really think that Philip, who was so reserved and had such nice manners, was that unkind but she did not want to suggest something he would merely be polite about. She wanted him to enjoy himself because she wanted him to come back. Why, *why* hadn't she thought of this problem before he came? *Tick, tick, tick* went the clock relentlessly. She had wasted the whole afternoon floating around in a happy glow wondering what she should wear, when she should have been planning something to do. *Tick, tick, tick.* Precious minutes were slipping away.

Shelley was actually relieved when the front door opened, Mavis entered, and she was no longer alone with Philip.

"Good evening, Mrs. Michie," said Philip, rising to his feet.

"Hello, Philip," said Mavis. "Shelley, I'm going out to my studio to work until I pick up Katie at eight-thirty. And by the way, there is a table tennis set in the bottom drawer in the dining room. It fits on the dining-room table."

Saved, thought Shelley, saved from the awful ticking of that clock. "Would you like to play table tennis?" she asked Philip.

Finding the set and clamping the net to the painted table gave them something to do, and while they worked Shelley thought of the mahogany dining table at home and how carefully her mother always wiped up the pollen that fell on its polished surface from the flowers in the centerpiece. They could never have played ping-pong on that table.

Shelley and Philip selected paddles and began to warm up with a few practice strokes. Philip served to Shelley, who missed. She had to get down on her hands and knees to retrieve the ball from underneath the table and as she got up, she bumped her head. She hit the ball back to Philip but it missed the table. Philip caught it easily in his hand and quickly served it back to Shelley. This time she managed to hit the ball into the net. Philip expertly scooped it up with his paddle and hit it toward Shelley once more.

This time I'm going to do it right, thought Shelley with determination, and swatted the ball as hard as she could. It flew across the net, hit the table, bounced up against the ceiling, dropped to the floor, and rolled into the kitchen, where Philip had to lie on his stomach on the floor to retrieve it from under the refrigerator.

Shelley laughed nervously. A star athlete, and she was pitting her skill against him. Shelley Latham, the girl who took physical education only because it was required.

Philip served to Shelley a ball so gentle that she was able to return it. "Let's start playing," he suggested, and served another easy ball for Shelley to return.

The restrained game continued, the ball bouncing gently back and forth across the net. Twice Shelley missed and had to chase the ball into the hall and once she overshot the table with her serve and Philip had to poke the ball out from under a chair with his paddle. Shelley was filled with humiliation. The county's star basketball player playing a ladylike game for her sake, letting her win points. He must be bored stiff.

The game finally ended with Philip winning, 21-18. "Your serve," he said, starting another game.

Grimly Shelley applied her paddle to the ball. Philip was being nice to her, but nice was not what she wanted him to be. Not in this way. She wanted him to have fun. *Plonk, plonk* went the ball on the dining-room table. This was like asking an All-American quarterback to enter a hopscotch contest. Shelley stole a glance at her watch. Katie would be home before long, and that was another problem. There was no telling what Katie would do or say except that whatever it was, it would be enthusiastic and most likely all wrong. Katie would probably walk in wearing her lettuce hair and say, right out loud, "That's not a very exciting game you are playing."

Plonk, plonk, plonk. Somehow Shelley got through the second game, and smiled brightly at Philip in an effort to make him think she had enjoyed herself. She felt hot and flushed while he did not look as if he had been exercising at all.

Philip laid his paddle on the table. "I don't have the car," he said, "but if you don't mind walking we could go downtown for something to eat."

"That would be fun," said Shelley, who felt that anything would be better than batting that plonking little ball back and forth. After they had put away the net and paddles, Shelley led the way out the back door toward the garage. "I had better tell someone where I am going," she explained. They found Tom working on the engine of the station wagon, which was parked under a light on the front of the garage. "We're going to walk downtown for something to eat," said Shelley.

"Hello, Phil," said Tom. "Why don't you take our old tandem instead of walking?"

Shelley was aghast. A tandem *bicycle?* Only the Michies would own such a thing.

"Sounds like fun," said Philip. "How about it, Shelley?"

"Why . . . yes, it does sound like fun," Shelley agreed, with as much enthusiasm as she could muster. From one set of muscles to another, she thought. At least Philip was getting exercise even if he wasn't having any fun.

But riding the tandem was surprisingly easy. Shelley felt almost as if they were floating as they rode past the orange groves and down San Sebastian's wide main street. The night was soft and fragrant. Cars full of high-school students were cruising up and down the street, the boys and girls apparently having nothing better to do than ride around seeing what everyone else was doing. They tooted and yelled at one another and when they saw Philip and Shelley, they sang out, "On a bicycle built for two." It was a small-town Saturday night, a new experience for Shelley. Philip seemed to be enjoying himself. Shelley marveled that she was riding down the main street on a tandem behind the straight, slim back of Philip Blanton, the shy boy whom all the girls wanted to date.

And to Shelley, the most wonderful part of it was that such an experience could never have happened at home. Nobody she knew owned a tandem, and even if someone did, she could not imagine two high-school students riding it in the evening on a date. Anyway, at this time of year it would probably be raining and if she went out with a boy who did not have a car, she would have to wear galoshes. Free of galoshes, Shelley felt light as air as she coasted through the night, and as she coasted she made a resolution. Never in the state of California, no matter how hard it rained, if it ever did rain, would she wear galoshes. Never.

Downtown, Shelley was surprised by the crowds of people walking up and down the sidewalks and by the number of cars looking for parking places. She had forgotten that in San Sebastian stores were open on Saturday night. Philip and Shelley parked the bicycle in the rack in front of a small restaurant and soda fountain called the Chicken Coop. The place was crowded and the jukebox was blaring. Another couple was leaving so they were fortunate to get a booth beside the jukebox near the front door. As they sat down at the table, littered with empty milk-shake glasses, crumpled napkins, and paper coverings from straws, Shelley looked around her. The walls were papered with a design of mother hens each leading four chicks and repeated all the way around the restaurant; the hens and chicks appeared to be marching in endless processions, around and around. Planting boxes were filled with artificial plants and behind the counter a pair of metal arms revolved continually in a plastic vat of orange juice. In the next booth a weary mother tried to appease two tired children with ice-cream sodas.

"What will you have?" asked Philip above the noise.

"A chocolate malt," answered Shelley. It was then that Shelley saw Katie and her mother sitting on stools eating ice-cream sodas. Katie was slowly spooning the ice cream out of the bottom of her soda. Dejection showed in the way she sat on the stool, the way she put the spoon in her mouth and pulled it out again half-full of ice cream. Mavis was looking at Katie with a mixture of sympathy and irritation and Shelley knew she wanted to say, "Katie, don't eat your ice cream that way," but because of Katie's mood she was restraining herself.

So Katie had not had a good time at the dancing class she had looked forward to with such eagerness. Shelley was sorry. She had really wanted Katie to have a good time, because she liked Katie and because she was grateful to her for her own date with Philip.

A waitress appeared to clear off the table and take Shelley's and Philip's orders. "Two chocolate malts and a grilled peanut-butter sandwich," said Philip.

"A grilled *peanut-butter* sandwich!" Shelley could not help exclaiming. She had never heard of such a thing.

"I'm hungry," explained Philip.

When the waitress had gone, Shelley raised her voice above the noise and said, "I was surprised when you came down from the top of that tree to ask me for a date." The record on the jukebox ended suddenly and Shelley found herself speaking the last words for everybody to hear.

Philip flashed his wonderful grin. "Maybe I should have swung from branch to branch yelling my bull-ape cry like Tarzan."

Shelley giggled. "That really would have surprised me." Shelley saw Mavis pay for the sodas and leave the counter with Katie. "Hi," Shelley called out, when they reached the door.

"Oh, hello there," said Mavis, as Philip rose awkwardly to his feet behind the table.

"Hi," said Katie without expression. Whatever was wrong must be very wrong indeed, if Katie could not look admiringly at Philip.

Mavis lowered her voice. "We needed a little something to cheer us up," she said as they went out the door.

"What's the matter?" asked Philip as he sat down and picked up his grilled peanut-butter sandwich.

"It's Katie," said Shelley. "Something awful must have happened at her dancing class."

"Kids that age—" said Philip, leaving his remark unfinished as if whatever he had in mind was such common knowledge that he did not need to say it. The mechanical arm of the jukebox picked another record out of the stack, dropped it into place, and the voices of a quartet boomed forth.

The door opened. "Hey, Wilma," a man startled Shelley by yelling to the waitress. "Charlie been in yet?"

"Nope. Not yet," the waitress yelled back.

Philip, used to the ways of a small town, did not appear to notice the interruption. "I wanted to ask you for a date sooner," he confessed, in the lull between records on the jukebox, "but I—I couldn't."

Puzzled, Shelley wanted to ask what had prevented him, but she felt that she should not pry. Perhaps he meant that he did not have the courage, although he did not seem excessively shy, since he had asked her for a date in front of Katie. Some boys would not have done that. "I hope you didn't mind what I said to the Roving Reporter," she said, not really wanting to bring up the matter, but feeling that she must because she still felt guilty about it.

"Oh, that," said Philip, and laughed. "I hope you didn't mind what Friz said about you."

The sound of a slap and the wail of a child came from the next booth. "Charlene, I *told* you not to put sugar cubes in your soda without taking the wrappers off." The woman's voice was tired and sharp. "Just for that I'm not going to buy you no water pistol."

Shelley lowered her eyes and pulled the wrapper off the straw the waitress had laid in front of her. "No. I—I was pleased by what Friz said," she admitted, and stirred the milk shake with her straw. The jukebox blared again, making conversation across the table almost impossible. Well, anyway I am with him, thought Shelley, wishing she could put a nickel in the jukebox and buy five cents' worth of silence. If only they could talk she might find some sign that he was having a good time—or not having a good time. It was the suspense of not knowing that was so hard to bear.

When Philip pulled the tandem out of the rack and they started home, Shelley discovered why riding downtown had been so easy. It had been downhill all the way, because San Sebastian was built on the gentle slope at the foot of the mountains. And now the way home was uphill. Shelley pushed harder on the pedals, because it did not seem fair to let Philip do all the work. The street was steeper than it looked.

"This is the widest main street I have ever seen," said Shelley, managing not to puff.

"The men who planned San Sebastian way back planned it that way so they could turn a span of eight mules," explained Philip, with no sign of a puff.

"Oh," said Shelley, tempted to let her aching legs coast around with the pedals. "That's interesting." The slope seemed to grow steeper with every turn of the pedals.

When Philip stood up on the pedals to exert more pressure on them, Shelley listened for some sign that he, too, was out of breath. His wind was excellent. A line of verse that she had read someplace a long time ago pushed its way into Shelley's thoughts. She could not recall it exactly, but it was something about, "Does the road go uphill all the way? Yes, to the very end." It was a perfect description of San Sebastian's main street.

Shelley gathered all the breath she could spare and said, "It's such a beautiful night." She hoped that from then on her silence would be taken for a rapt appreciation of the stars shining down on San Sebastian.

Fortunately the road was level when they turned off the main street, and Shelley partially caught her breath before they turned into the Michies' driveway. While they parked the tandem in the garage and walked around to the front door, Shelley wondered uneasily what Katie was doing. She opened the front door, and before she turned to face Philip she glanced at the transom at the end of the living room. Katie was not in sight. "Well . . . good night, Philip," Shelley said uncertainly. A first good night was so terribly important. It could mean the beginning of so many things or it could mean—good night.

Philip smiled down at Shelley. "You're a good sport," he said.

Encouraged, Shelley said, "I'm not much of a ping-pong player, but I had fun anyway."

"So did I," said Philip. "Say, Shelley, I was wondering—would you like to go to Vincente to the movies next week end?"

"I'd love to, Philip," said Shelley happily. So he had had a good time after all! The suspense had ended. Now she knew.

"Swell," said Philip. "I'll see you at school. Good night."

"Good night, Philip." Shelley silently closed the door. Philip Blanton had asked her for another date! The polite table-tennis game, the puffing ride home seemed unimportant. He liked her, she liked him, and Katie had not been on top of the refrigerator. Shelley climbed the creaking stairs as quietly as she could and at the door of her room she hesitated. A strip of light shone beneath the door of Katie's room across the hall. Shelley waited a moment and then tapped on the door of Katie's room with one fingernail.

"Come in," answered Katie in a dull voice, and Shelley entered. Katie was leaning on her dresser, her chin propped on her fists, staring at herself in the mirror. Her mouth was heavily made up with dark lipstick.

"I suppose you had fun," said Katie in the same dull voice.

"A wonderful time." Shelley tried not to smile at the sight of Katie's mouth. Although she knew the answer, she asked, "Did you?"

"No," said Katie flatly.

"What went wrong?" asked Shelley.

"Everything," answered Katie, turning away from the mirror. "Just everything."

"Didn't the right boy dance with you?" asked Shelley.

"Dance with me!" exclaimed Katie. "He wasn't even there. Practically no boys came except some whose mothers made them come and you know that type."

"Yes, I know," said Shelley. "But why didn't the boys come? They usually turn up."

"They didn't want to make hats," said Katie. "They said it was too much bother. You know how boys are."

"Yes," agreed Shelley, sorry for her. "But didn't you win a prize for your hat?"

"No," said Katie. "Pamela did, though. She said she was going to make a hat out of a bird cage and instead she turned up in a straw hat with a little palm tree and a monkey on it. When she wound up the monkey it played a drum."

"I'm sure your hat was more becoming." Shelley tried to be comforting.

Katie sighed gustily. "What difference did it make, when I had to dance with girls? Do you think that this lipstick, not that Mommy would ever let me wear it, makes me look sophisticated?"

Shelley managed not to smile. "Well—not sophisticated exactly."

"It's just hopeless," said Katie. "I'm nothing but a wholesome outdoor type. The type that has to lead when there aren't enough boys to dance with. And it is horrible to be thirteen."

"Cheer up, Katie," Shelley said. "You won't stay thirteen all your life. After all, I was thirteen once."

"I guess that's right," said Katie, brightening. "But you don't know how lucky you are to be sixteen."

"Am I?" asked Shelley dreamily. "Well, good night, Katie." She went to her room and, without turning on the light, stood at the window looking out into the soft, dark night. She recalled how she had felt at thirteen. Nothing had seemed right. The girls were taller than the boys and at dancing class, even when there were enough boys to go around, the girls had really led, because the boys all seemed too confused to learn the steps. And clothes had never fitted properly. And at thirteen there never seemed to be anything to do, because at thirteen a girl is too old for toys and not old enough for dates. Now that she looked back on that age, Shelley knew that she was glad to be through with it, to have said good-by to so many things.

Shelley smiled in the darkness. Katie was right. She was lucky to be sixteen. She was the luckiest girl in San Sebastian, because she was sixteen and Philip Blanton liked her. Shelley was filled with a wonderful feeling of excitement as if something was about to happen, something more wonderful than anything that had ever happened before. Something magic.

Chapter 7

After Shelley's first date with Philip, each day seemed more golden and more spellbound. The sun shone and the sky was clear. The oranges were ripening. Violets and iris bloomed in November, Shelley discovered, and felt sorry for these poor confused California flowers that did not know they were supposed to bloom in the spring.

The leggy plants beside the back door put forth scarlet leaves and Shelley saw that these plants which she had thought so ugly were poinsettias. Poinsettias higher than her head! Until now she had seen them only in pots and thought that was the way they always grew.

At the same time the spreading gray-green tree that overhung the two-story garage began to burst with buds, clusters of tiny greenish-yellow balls, and Shelley discovered that this was an acacia tree. At home acacia blossoms were bought in bunches at the florist shop and she had supposed that an acacia was a small bush. As Shelley stood under the poinsettias and looked up at the acacia tree, she felt like Alice in Wonderland after she had drunk from the bottle labeled *Drink Me* and found everything the wrong size because she was shrinking. Yes, San Sebastian was a magic place.

And the most magic thing about Shelley's new life was Philip. Whenever he saw her at school he smiled his slow grin, detached himself from the group of boys he was talking to, and came to smile down at her and say a few words while the other girls watched enviously. On Friday afternoons he had a way of seeming suddenly to remember that the next day was Saturday and of asking her for a date just when, after an agony of anticipation, she was sure he had forgotten. Sometimes they went to the movies and sometimes they played table tennis on the dining-room table. Although it was Philip whom she liked, and not ping-pong, Shelley found her game improving. Philip showed no interest in any other girl and Shelley, busy with her life at the Michies', was not interested in any other boy. She was completely happy.

Hartley, of course, Shelley saw every day, because he sat behind her in her registration room. Although their relationship had never been quite comfortable since they had said good night under the interested eye of Katie, he was always fun to talk to. Hartley was—well, good old Hartley.

One afternoon in biology lab, while Shelley and Jeannie and the two boys who sat beside them were getting their microscopes out of the cupboards and opening their notebooks, Jeannie said, "I'm in charge of decorating the gym for the barn dance. I hereby appoint the three of you to be on the committee. If we round up a bunch of others it shouldn't be too much work."

"I'd love to," said Shelley. This was one of the things she liked best about San Sebastian High. The chairman of a committee was formally appointed, but after that arrangements for school activities were casual and usually resulted in anyone's taking part who wanted to.

"You've talked me into it," Frisbie told Jeannie, "if you'll go to the dance with me."

"Of course," agreed Jeannie. "Why else would I ask you to be on the committee?"

"I thought maybe you wanted me for my muscles," said Frisbie, "to lift bales of hay or something."

"Maybe the four of us could double date," suggested Philip, his eyes on the rubber band he was playing with.

"I think that would be fun," said Shelley, delighted that for once Philip was asking her ahead of time.

"Well, what do you know!" exclaimed Frisbie. "Phil is finally going to break down and go to a school dance. After all these years."

"Aw—" muttered Philip.

Shelley could not help smiling to herself. It was nice to know she was to be the first girl Philip took to a school dance. It made her feel special.

"Does anybody know where we can borrow any authentic old wagon wheels?" asked Jeannie.

"There's one leaning against the front of practically every ranch house in town," said Frisbie. "Phil and I can probably round up a few."

Mr. Ericson interrupted the conversation. "If the cozy coterie at the table by the door will adjourn, we shall turn to the topic of the day—osmosis. Jeanne, will you please define osmosis?"

"Osmosis is the movement of molecules of water and dissolved substances through semipermeable membranes," answered Jeannie promptly.

For this she had Shelley's admiration. Shelley was sure that Jeannie's mind had been entirely on the dance. That was where Shelley's mind had been. Fortunately Mr. Ericson had not asked her the question.

The afternoon of the barn dance Philip came to pick up Shelley in his father's car. In the back seat was a pair of wagon wheels, each labeled with the name of its owner.

"One of those wagon wheels is Pamela's mother's,"

said Katie, as she looked admiringly at Philip's green sweater with the yellow block S and the yellow stripe on the left sleeve. Katie always managed to be on hand when Philip arrived and Shelley enjoyed showing him off. "You'd better take good care of it. Pamela's mother had to look all over before she found it in an antique shop. They are awfully hard to find."

"Don't worry," said Shelley. "We'll take good care of the rare old antique."

As they drove to school, Shelley noticed that the sky was more cloudy than she had ever before seen it in San Sebastian. There had been a shower or two since she had come to California and once it had rained hard in the night, but this was the first time that she had seen threatening rain clouds. She did not know why she was surprised. It was really winter, although to her, because there had been no autumn leaves and no frost, it did not feel like winter. It did not seem like any season at all and the brooding clouds seemed out of place in the sky.

The clouds did produce rain, though, and suddenly. Large drops spattered flatly against the car and all at once rain was being dumped on San Sebastian. The windshield wipers wagged furiously and then more slowly, as if the weight of the unexpected rain was too much for them.

Shelley rolled the window down a few inches. "M-m-m," she breathed. "Smell the rain and feel the wonderful damp air. I feel as if I were absorbing it like a sponge." Now her hair would curl without so much coaxing.

Philip laughed. "Maybe you'll begin to swell up," he said, as he parked the car near the gym under a pepper tree that made a lacy green curtain, shutting them off from the street. He turned off the windshield wipers. Rain beat down on the car and flowed down the windshield, blurring the outside world.

"Hi, Webfoot," Philip drawled, turning toward her.

"Hi." Shelley half-whispered the syllable. They were so alone and Philip was so close. She was aware of him, clean and tan in his letter man's sweater, as she never had been before. She was aware of the rough wool of his sweater and the stripe on his sleeve just five stitches wide, the texture of the block S like thousands of tiny French knots, the clean white T shirt, the golden tan of his skin, that tiny mole just below his left ear lobe. . . . Shelley did not know why, but she felt frightened.

Philip took Shelley's hand in his. His hand was thin and hard, the way a boy's hand should be. "Shelley—" he began, and stopped.

Shelley managed to raise her eyes to his. She knew with a panicky feeling that he was about to kiss her.

Philip, lowering his eyes in his shy way, looked down at her hand in his. "Nothing," he said quietly. Slowly he released her hand. The moment was over.

Shelley realized she had been holding her breath and tried to let it out quietly so it would not sound like a sigh. Enclosed in the car, even with the rain beating on the roof, she was sure he could hear her breathe and perhaps hear her heart beat. She struggled to swallow without sounding as if she were gulping. It was funny how being alone with a boy and close to him could be so exciting and at the same time so embarrassing.

"Maybe we better run for it," she said reluctantly. "I mean—we can't just sit here all afternoon, can we?"

"Maybe we better." There was reluctance in Philip's voice, too.

"It's awfully wet out." A silly thing to say, with the gutter running like a river.

"Yes. . . ." Philip was looking at her. She could feel it. "It's pretty wet."

All right. They agreed it was wet.

"Here." Philip pulled off his sweater. "You'd better wear my sweater or you'll get soaked. That sweater of yours is pretty thin."

"But what about you? You'll get wet." Philip's sweater was a temptation to Shelley.

"If I get too wet I have a sweat shirt in my locker

in the gym." Philip draped his sweater around Shelley's shoulders.

"In that case, all right." Shelley slid her arms into the too-big sleeves, which made her feel fragile, like someone who needed to be protected from the elements. The wool, which was rough against her skin, smelled pleasantly of Philip.

Another couple ran past the car toward the gym. They were wearing slickers, and soldier hats folded out of newspaper. The girl, who carried her shoes in her hand, was barefooted.

"Wait till I get the wagon wheels out," said Philip, as he ducked out of the car.

Shelley followed him. The rain was cold against her face and legs but she did not care. She took one of the wagon wheels from Philip and together they raced, rolling the wheels like hoops ahead of them. They arrived at the door of the gym wet and laughing. Inside, the committee and Mr. Lutz, the teacher of commercial subjects and sponsor of the dance, were hard at work.

"Hi, there," called Jeannie. "Trickle in and go to work. We're leaning the wagon wheels around the bandstand."

Shelley ran her finger through her damp hair and looked around. Wires had been strung from one end of the gym to the other, and over the wires hung yards of blue cloth that hid the ceiling and hung down over the windows. Although the cloth did not succeed in looking like the sky, at least it diminished the gymnasium look, particularly in the dim light produced by the spotlights. Sheets of brown paper had been tacked up at the end of the gym, where members of the art class were painting barn scenes with poster paint.

A girl who was painting a row of cheerful, smiling cows stood back to look at her work. "Talk about contented cows," she said admiringly.

"They may be contented," said Frisbie, from the top of a stepladder where he was adjusting a spot- light, "but they are knock-kneed."

"It's the effect that counts," answered the girl.

Leaving a trail of wet footprints behind them, Shelley and Philip rolled their wagon wheels to the bandstand, where Jeannie and two other girls were making a scarecrow.

"I'm going to change into my sweat shirt," said Philip, and went off to the locker room.

Shelley was pleasantly aware that the other girls were looking at her in Philip's sweater with the sleeves pushed up above her elbows so they would stay up. Although it was not the custom in San Sebastian for a girl to wear a letter man's sweater (Shelley had found that out the first week of school), still there was something special about a boy's even lending a girl his sweater with a block letter—especially when the boy was Philip.

Philip came running out of the locker room in his

sweat shirt, dribbling an imaginary basketball. He stopped, caught it, and made what was obviously a difficult shot.

A cheer went up from the committee.

"Isn't that sweater awfully damp to be wearing around?" asked one of the girls, whose name was Arlene. She was in Shelley's English class and was the kind of girl who enjoyed catching the teacher in mistakes.

"Not especially," answered Shelley lightly. She did not mind the girl's jealousy a bit. Not one little bit. She went to work pinning a pair of garden gloves to the scarecrow's sleeves.

"Hey, Friz," yelled one of the boys. "You're giving us too much light."

"I'll fix it," Frisbie yelled back.

"Now wait a minute," said Mr. Lutz, coming over to Frisbie's stepladder. "What we need is more light, not less."

Voices rose in protest. "Aw, Mr. Lutz, nobody wants to dance around in broad daylight!" "Aw, Mr. Lutz, that's no fun." "Be a sport and let us dim them some more."

"I'm prepared to be scientific about this." Mr. Lutz pulled from his pocket a light meter, the kind amateur photographers use, and held it up toward the spotlight. "Sorry," he said, squinting at the red indicator on the meter, "but the light meter has to read one foot-candle for each spotlight. It's a rule."

Then he grinned. "I have to keep one step ahead of you kids." The boys grumbled good-naturedly and went back to work.

The afternoon went quickly for Shelley. Reluctantly she took off Philip's sweater, but not before she was sure everyone had seen her wearing it. It was such wonderful fun to be part of behind-the-scenes. This had never happened to her at home. She enjoyed every minute of the committee's clowning. One of the boys caught Arlene and put a dab of red poster paint on the tip of her nose while she squealed, "Let go! You're hurting me!" and everyone knew Arlene enjoyed it. And when it came time to sprinkle the special powder for dance floors on the floor of the gymnasium, Shelley joined the others in running and sliding. What fun she would have writing home about this! Dear Rosemary, she would write. I had the craziest afternoon. We were having a barn dance at school and Philip and I were on the committee. . . . Dear Mother and Daddy, This afternoon Philip and I helped decorate for the barn dance at school. He is such a nice boy. I know you would like him a lot. . . .

Finally, when the work was done and Mr. Lutz was off someplace seeing that the stepladders were put back where they belonged, Jeannie looked around thoughtfully. "I wish we had some hay," she remarked to Philip and Frisbie. "It doesn't seem like a real barn dance without a few bales of hay."

"That's easy," answered Frisbie. "I know where we can get some. You know that place up near the mountains that has the horses? I know the man who owns it."

"I never thought of that," said Jeannie. "Could you really get some?"

"Sure, if Phil will help," answered Frisbie. "We can load it into the station wagon and get it here in plenty of time. Phil and I will drive out and get the hay and pick you girls up half an hour early. That will give us time to bring the hay in before the crowd arrives."

Mr. Lutz began to turn out the lights in the gym, and the few committee members left straggled toward the door. "Shelley, you look as if you thought something exciting was about to happen," remarked Jeannie, as she and Shelley paused in the doorway of the gym and looked out into the rain, which was now falling steadily.

"I'm going to the dance tonight," Shelley answered, remembering that Hartley had once made the same observation about her.

Jeannie looked curiously at her. "And you feel that a school dance is something to get excited about?" asked Jeannie.

"Of course," said Shelley. "Aren't you excited?"

"I suppose so." Jeannie sounded doubtful.

"But Jeannie, what is a dance for if it isn't fun and excitement?" Shelley wanted to know. To her a dance was an occasion, something to anticipate. She reminded herself that she was going with Philip and Jeannie was going with Frisbie, and that might make a difference.

Jeannie did not answer, because Philip and Frisbie joined the two girls and together they ran out through the rain to their cars.

The rain continued to fall and was still falling at seven-thirty, when Philip was to call for Shelley. She had, with concealed reluctance, returned his sweater to him when he had brought her home that afternoon. Now, when Philip twirled the doorbell, she realized she had to wear some kind of wrap. "Let him in, Katie, will you?" she called down the stairs. She always enjoyed showing Philip off to Katie, who quite plainly agreed that he was the most wonderful boy in San Sebastian.

Shelley snatched from her closet shelf a box that she had stuffed into her trunk unopened when she had packed and which had remained like that on her closet shelf since she had come to California. From the box she pulled the pink raincoat with the velveteen collar and the little hat with the black velveteen button on top. Oh, well, she thought and slipped the raincoat on over her blouse and full cotton skirt. She put on the hat and patted the button on top while she looked at herself in the mirror. It really was a pretty raincoat.

Shelley drew the line, however, at galoshes. She

had vowed she would never wear galoshes in California, and she would not. But Shelley, she could almost hear her mother say, you'll get your feet wet and you'll ruin your shoes. But Mother, she could hear herself answer, I'm in California now and I'm not going to wear galoshes. I'll run quickly through the rain, but I won't wear galoshes.

Philip was wearing jeans and a blue plaid shirt under his letter man's sweater. "Hey, look at the glamorous raincoat," he said when he saw her.

At the foot of the stairs Shelley twirled around for his inspection before they ran out through the rain to the station wagon. They slid into the second seat in front of two bales of hay.

"Whew! It smells dusty in here," remarked Shelley.

"What a pretty raincoat," remarked Jeannie from the front seat beside Frisbie. "Is that what they wear up North?"

"Some people," answered Shelley, remembering the front steps of school crowded with girls in slickers. She discovered the price tag still dangling from one sleeve. Carefully she untied it and put it in her pocket. It was an expensive raincoat, more expensive than her family could really afford. She was sorry she had behaved the way she had.

"We'd better not let the hay get wet," said Frisbie. "Remember that hay Mr. Ericson soaked in water?"

"And we looked at a drop of the water under the microscope," added Jeannie. "It was swimming with all sorts of squirmy little things."

When they reached the gym they all climbed out of the station wagon. "Look!" exclaimed Jeannie, pointing. "I see a couple of stars over there. Maybe it is going to clear up after all."

As Philip and Frisbie dragged one of the bales of hay out of the station wagon and carried it up the steps of the gym, Frisbie sang, " 'Lift that barge, tote that bale,' " in his deepest voice. He pounded on the door and the janitor, who was turning on the lights, let them in. "Where do you want the hay, Jeannie?" Frisbie asked, while the janitor, protector of the gymnasium floor, eyed their wet feet with disapproval.

"Down at the end of the gym," directed Jeannie. "Did you bring some pliers?"

"Sure did," said Frisbie, pulling them out of his hip pocket and snapping the wire around the hay.

Jeannie and Shelley scattered the hay across the end of the gym while the boys carried in the second bale. By the time that bale was scattered, the orchestra had assembled, unpacked their instruments, and were blowing a few experimental notes.

Frisbie grabbed Jeannie and danced her around, singing at the top of his voice, " 'I want a buddy, not a sweetheart.' " They were an odd-looking couple. Frisbie was so big and Jeannie was so small.

Philip put his arm around Shelley, still in her raincoat, and began to dance with her to the tootling of the band. Shelley laughed and thought how different she would have felt at home. At home she would probably have slunk off to the checkroom the very first thing to get rid of the raincoat before anyone saw it. Here she did not care who saw it. That's funny, she thought. I wonder why.

The door of the gym opened and Mr. Lutz entered with a man in the uniform of the San Sebastian fire department. They stood looking around at the decorations. Then the man from the fire department saw the hay. "Has that hay been fireproofed?" he asked.

The two couples stopped dancing. "Why—no," confessed Jeannie, because she was chairman of the decorating committee.

"Where did it come from?" asked Mr. Lutz.

"We brought it, sir," said Philip.

"Who gave you permission?" demanded Mr. Lutz.

"Nobody," admitted Frisbie. "We didn't know we needed permission."

"It didn't seem like a barn dance without hay," explained Jeannie.

"So we drove up toward the mountains and got a couple of bales," continued Frisbie.

"Sorry," said the man from the fire department. "You'll have to get it out of here. It's a fire hazard."

"But nobody smokes at a school dance," protested Frisbie.

"That doesn't matter," said the man from the fire department. "It's still a fire hazard. You can't leave it here."

By this time couples were arriving and gathering around to see what the discussion was about.

"But what will we do with it?" asked Jeannie. There was a lot of hay in two bales.

"Take it out to the incinerator and burn it," said Mr. Lutz. "Every bit of it."

"In the rain?" asked Frisbie.

Mr. Lutz grinned. "You got it here in the rain, didn't you? And anyway, the rain has just about stopped."

Frisbie and Jeannie groaned. The orchestra began to play and couples began to dance. "Now," said Mr. Lutz sternly. "I thought I had managed to stay one step ahead of you kids, but you put one over on me this time."

Shelley joined the others in gathering up armfuls of hay. " 'Lift that barge, tote that bale,' " Frisbie sang, and the other three joined in as they trooped toward the door of the gym. The rest of the crowd stopped dancing and began to clap hands to the rhythm of the song. The orchestra stopped what they had been playing and one by one the instruments took up the tune. The two couples, with their arms full of hay, splashed through puddles under the clearing sky and, while the fire inspector watched, threw the hay into the yawning cement mouth of the incinerator. They returned to the gym for a second load and then another and another. Everyone saw Shelley in her pink raincoat and the hat with the velveteen button on top, but she did not care. She thought the whole incident was funny, just one of those wonderful crazy things.

As Shelley made her way out the door of the gym with her last armful of hay, she found herself face to face with Hartley, who was entering with a girl from her English class. For some reason Shelley was startled. She had not expected to see Hartley at the dance and certainly not with that girl.

"Well, hello there," said Hartley.

"Hello," answered Shelley uncertainly. If Hartley wanted to bring that girl from her English class to the dance, there was no reason why he shouldn't, was there? Hartley and his date went on into the gym and Shelley went on out to the incinerator, trailing wisps of hay behind her.

The fire inspector had touched a match to the hay, which was burning merrily. "Too bad we don't have some marshmallows," said Frisbie, brushing hay from the sleeves of his sweater.

Philip stood close to Shelley and as she watched the sparks fly up and disappear into the night, she laughed from sheer happiness. Shelley felt Jeannie looking at her and knew that Jeannie was probably thinking wistfully that Shelley had fun in strange ways. Shelley did not care. Since she had come to San Sebastian everything had been fun, surprising and exciting. Even wearing the raincoat that had once caused her to stuff roses into the Disposall now seemed part of a delightful adventure. It almost seemed like magic, the way her feelings had changed.

And all at once Shelley understood why she was having such a good time in a raincoat she had once said she would never wear. When a girl comes to a school and makes a name for herself with a good idea and is interviewed for the school paper and liked by a boy all the other girls like—a boy who wanted to kiss her and who lets her wear his letter man's sweater while she decorates for a dance, it doesn't matter what kind of raincoat she wears. Any kind will do.

Chapter 8

When Christmas vacation arrived Shelley was surprised to learn that in California spruce and pines and even hemlocks were used for Christmas trees. She had always thought Christmas trees were Douglas fir, or they were not Christmas trees. She was even more surprised at the Michies' admiration for what was to her the ordinary holly wreath that her mother sent. They hung it on the front door and everyone who entered the house exclaimed, "Real English holly!" as if it were something rare and beautiful.

The days went quickly. There was shopping to do and packages to mail. Shelley helped Katie make a gathered skirt and spent hours watching Mavis at the potter's wheel in her studio. The spinning clay beneath her fingers was like a living thing. Shelley was fascinated. She experimented with a simple bowl and made up her mind that someday she would have a potter's wheel too.

There was a wonderful Christmas box from home, full of all the things a girl would like to receive— a new sweater and a matching skirt, a pretty scarf, two frilly slips, a bottle of perfume, a purse with a crisp five-dollar bill inside. Shelley could tell that her mother had found a lot of pleasure in packing that box. Christmas afternoon there was a long-distance call from home. Shelley was excited and a little sad to talk to her mother and father so far away.

And then New Year's Eve came. The Michies celebrated by inviting all the neighbors, young and old, for a buffet supper. Babies were bedded down, toddlers ran around in their sleepers, and grand-parents were given the most comfortable chairs. Philip came too. He joined the crowd in making paper hats out of the crepe paper Mavis had sup-plied because she found paper hats for a crowd cost too much and decided it would be more fun and much less expensive if everyone made his own. Philip's hat looked something like a football hel-met and a little like a baby's bonnet. Shelley thought it was the nicest party she had ever attended.

There was New Year's Day to be spent picking up after the party, and then vacation was over and it was time for school again. One damp day Shel-ley and Jeannie were eating their lunches in the study hall. From the window Shelley could see the top of an acacia tree in full bloom, each panicle a burst of fluffy balls of pure yellow. The blossoms were the essence of yellow and Shelley knew that whenever she thought of the color she would remember this sight—the soft blue-green foliage bending under the weight of raindrops and the sharp, clear yellow of the blossoms that somehow never looked wet no matter how hard it rained.

"Starry-eyed Shelley," remarked Jeannie.

"Am I starry-eyed?" asked Shelley, surprised.

"All the time," said Jeannie positively.

"If I am I guess it is because everything is so new and exciting down here," said Shelley, "but I don't really think I am starry-eyed."

"How you can find a dull little town like San Sebastian exciting is a mystery to me," said Jeannie, stuffing the waxed paper wrapping from her sandwich into her brown paper bag. "I can't wait to leave it and go out into the world and find some excitement."

"Isn't that funny?" remarked Shelley. "I won't even let myself think about the time I have to leave it."

"You don't know how lucky you are," said Jeannie. "I would give anything to go to a big city high school and live in a town where there is something to do on Saturday night besides riding up and down the main street tooting at everyone else riding up and down the main street." She paused and wadded the brown paper bag into a tight ball. "I'm tired of living in a town where everyone knows everyone else's business, and I'm tired of living in a little house practically hidden by a clump of dusty pampas grass, and I'm tired of scorching-hot summers. Why, my family took a trip to Oregon once, and do you know what we saw? In downtown Portland on several street corners there were drinking fountains—each one was really four fountains made out of bronze or something—and the water ran *all the time!* There weren't even any handles so you could turn the water off."

Shelley laughed. "Why, that's true. I've seen those drinking fountains hundreds of times and I never thought a thing about them."

"I thought they were the most wonderful sight I had ever seen," said Jeannie. "All that lovely cold water."

Both girls were silent. Jeannie was occupied with her own rebellious thoughts. Shelley was thinking that this was the end of the semester. Half her precious months were already gone. "Report cards today," she remarked. "I wonder what the verdicts will be."

Jeannie did not appear to hear her. "Anyway," she remarked as they prepared to leave the study hall, "I'm not so sure it is San Sebastian that makes you starry-eyed." This time it was Shelley who did not appear to hear.

After the last class the students returned to their registration rooms to receive their report cards. When Shelley's grades were handed to her in a white envelope with her name typed in one corner, she accepted them with a nice feeling of accomplishment. One semester was behind her, another was about to begin. One by one she pulled out the cards for her different courses. A in English. A in Latin. Shelley always got A's in Latin, a language that she enjoyed because it seemed to her like a complicated puzzle. B in history. She had expected this—she was good at remembering dates, but this teacher had a way of wanting to know why historical events had taken place rather than when. Never mind, she would do better next semester. B minus in physical education. Field sports in this heat —she was lucky to get a B minus! D in biology.

Biology, D. It couldn't be! Shelley had never received a D in her life. Of course she realized she wasn't exactly at the head of the class, but D—why, Mr. Ericson could not do that to her. She wouldn't make the honor roll. She had to have a B average to get into college. She simply could not get a D; that was all there was to it.

Shelley turned around to speak to Hartley, because she had to confide in someone and she was sure he would understand.

"Shelley, is something wrong?" he asked, when he saw her face.

"Mr. Ericson gave me a D in biology," she said. "I can't understand it. I've never had a D in my life."

Hartley's expression showed genuine concern. "Maybe there is a mistake someplace. Why don't you go talk to him?"

Yes, there must be a mistake someplace. There had to be. "Maybe he accidentally wrote someone else's grade on my card," Shelley said to Hartley. "You are right. I'll go talk to him."

"Good luck," said Hartley.

It was nice to know a boy who understood that grades were important. As Shelley walked toward the biology laboratory she began to have some misgivings. There had been that C on her first report card, but she had not been too worried about it because it was not a semester grade. And maybe her drawings of some of the things they had examined through a microscope weren't exactly works of art, but they weren't supposed to be, were they? This was biology, not art. And there was the time she had forgotten to draw the nucleus in the pleurococcus—that was the day Philip had asked her to go to the barn dance and naturally she had a lot of distracting things to think about. But a D! Shelley Latham did not get D's.

Shelley entered the biology room, where she pretended to look at some exhibits until the room was clear of students and she could speak to Mr. Ericson alone. "Mr. Ericson," she said tentatively as she approached his desk, where he was busy with some papers.

"Yes, Shelley," he said, looking up from his work.

"I think there might be a mistake on my report card," Shelley said nervously, because she was always ill at ease with Mr. Ericson. "I—I have a D in biology."

"There is no mistake," answered Mr. Ericson. "You earned that D fair and square."

Shelley felt her face turn red. "But I've never had a D in my life," she protested.

Mr. Ericson leaned back in his chair and smiled sardonically. "You have now."

"But Mr. Ericson," said Shelley desperately. "I want to go to college—"

"Why?" interrupted Mr. Ericson.

Shelley paused. Why did she want to go to college? No one had ever asked her this question before and she felt confused. She could not tell this man she wanted to go to college because all the girls she knew were planning to go or because her parents had told her she should go. Those were not the real reasons. "Because I want to have a career," she said lamely, although this was not the right answer.

"Oh, you do," said Mr. Ericson. "What sort of career?"

"I—I don't know. I mean, I haven't made up my mind yet." Shelley felt more and more uncomfortable with Mr. Ericson looking at her as if he expected her to explain herself concisely in outline form on a moment's notice. She decided to try changing the subject. "To go to college I have to maintain a B average," she said. "I just can't get D's."

"Then I would suggest that you stop doing D work," said Mr. Ericson.

Shelley found that there was not one thing that she could say. She was filled with anger and humiliation.

"Perhaps the seating arrangement for the semester was unfortunate," said Mr. Ericson.

Shelley looked sharply at her biology teacher. Was he referring to Philip? The gleam of amusement in his keen blue eyes told her that he was. "The seating arrangement had nothing to do with it," she said, with all the haughtiness she could manage.

"You know, I would not be doing you a favor if I gave you a B for D work in high school," Mr. Ericson said. "You will have to take a laboratory science in college, too, and if you do poor work, it is better to find out about it now while there is still time to do something about it than to wait until you are in college."

Probably this was true, but the way Shelley felt toward Mr. Ericson, she did not want to admit that anything he said was right. D—and this was only the first semester. She had months ahead of her of drawing crawly things under a microscope and dissecting the worm and the frog and the crayfish that came in the second semester. And all under the sardonic eye of Mr. Ericson, because in a school of this size there was only one biology teacher. Now she wouldn't dare even look at Philip during the whole eighty minutes of the period.

"I'll make a bargain with you," said Mr. Ericson. "If you turn in B work the second semester, I'll give you a C for the whole year."

"I'll do B work," promised Shelley and thought, If it kills me.

"Good," said Mr. Ericson, as if the subject were closed.

"Thank you, Mr. Ericson," Shelley said stiffly, and left the room. *Oh*, she thought as she left the building, that man! Who did he think he was, anyway? As if Philip had anything to do with this. Well, she would show him!

But gradually, as she walked down the road, Shelley's explosive mood spent itself. She felt ashamed because she had done poor work and embarrassed because Mr. Ericson had noticed her preoccupation with Philip. New feelings began to replace her anger.

The trouble with me, Shelley thought, is that I don't really have any brains. In elementary school she had kept her handwriting neat, her papers unsmudged, and her two-finger margins straight, so her teachers approved of her and gave her good grades. In high school, too, she was neat, prompt, and conscientious and so her teachers liked her. But brains, no. Giving good grades to Shelley Latham was just a habit with her teachers at home. Probably she didn't deserve them at all. But even while she railed at herself, Shelley knew that what she was telling herself was not true. Being conscientious had helped, of course, but she had always been a good student and had enjoyed most of her studies. Even in the subjects she had not enjoyed, her pride had kept her near the top of the class. That this was her first experience with a laboratory science was no excuse. Perhaps if Philip had not sat beside her . . . .

Shelley turned into the opening in the privet hedge. And the worst of it was, Tom or Mavis would have to sign her report card and know about the D. It seemed as if there was to be no end to her humiliation. If only she hadn't taken biology. Maybe chemistry would have been better. But then Philip would not have been in her class and she might not have known him. Besides, chemistry smelled so awful. Now, knowing that Mr. Ericson's

eagle eye was upon her, she wouldn't dare look at
Philip. Old Eagle Eye Ericson. She had promised
him B work and now she would have to study like
a fiend at a subject she hated. She thought she hated
it, but actually until today she had not thought much
about the subject one way or another. She had been
too busy thinking about Philip.

Shelley entered the house, tossed her books on a
couch in the living room, and flopped down beside
them. She sat brooding about the D. Dear Mother
and Daddy, she would have to write. Today was re-
port-card day and I was unpleasantly surprised to
get a D in biology. I thought I had studied . . . .

Before Shelley could compose the letter, Katie
burst through the front door. At first glance Shelley
was shocked at the sight of her, and then she saw
that Katie was smeared with lipstick. There were
daubs of lipstick on her arms, smears of lipstick on
her cheeks, and smudges of lipstick on her blouse,
but her expression was radiant.

"Katie!" exclaimed Shelley. "What happened to
you?"

Katie dropped into an armchair. "Well," she began, "Pamela and I were walking home from school.
We were walking along just minding our own business and not doing a *thing,* when Pamela took a
lipstick out of her purse to show me. It's a new
shade called Lucky in Love and I think it's yummy.
I don't see why Mommy won't let me wear lipstick

for dress-up. She never lets me do *anything*. Anyway, Joe and Rudy came along and they asked Pamela if they could see her lipstick. Pamela gave it to them, never dreaming what they were going to do." Katie paused for breath. "And do you know what those crazy boys did?"

"I can guess," said Shelley.

"They started smearing us with lipstick," Katie continued with relish. "It was simply *awful*. They got lipstick all over us. And then I grabbed it away from Rudy and rubbed it all over his face." Katie sat smiling at this happy memory before she said regretfully, "I guess I better go wash it off before Mommy sees me. You know how she is."

Shelley recalled her own thirteen-year-old adventures walking home from school—the rain hat grabbed and thrown up into a tree, the scarf snatched and tied around the neck of a passing dog. "You like Rudy, don't you?" asked Shelley.

"Yes," admitted Katie frankly. "I have a terrible crush on him."

"What's he like?"

"Simply divine," said Katie, getting up to admire her smudges in the hall mirror. "Taller than I am, if you count the way his hair sort of sticks up." She started up the stairs. "Promise not to tell what I said about Rudy."

"I promise." After this interruption Shelley felt more cheerful. Watching Katie go through a phase she herself had outgrown always made Shelley feel serene and experienced, capable of meeting any situation that might arise in the course of growing up. She picked up her books and went to her room, where she looked through the second half of her biology book to see what lay ahead of her during the second semester.

When Shelley came downstairs sometime later she found Tom studying Luke's report cards while Luke, his face smudged with grease from his motorcycle, sat staring moodily out the window. "Luke, this doesn't make sense," Tom was saying. "An A in Latin and a C minus in English."

Luke was silent.

"You must have some explanation." Tom waited expectantly. "I am glad you earned an A in Latin, but how do you explain your grade in English?"

Luke looked unhappy. "Aw, Dad, you know how English is. All that stuff about sentence structure and having to read *Idylls of the King*."

"Sentence structure!" exclaimed Tom. "You complain about sentence structure in English and then get an A in Latin, which is much more complicated. Ablative absolute and *hic, haec, hoc*—Latin is much more difficult."

"Aw, Dad, don't you understand?" Luke asked. "I *like* my Latin teacher."

Shelley sympathized with Luke's problem. The next semester would be so much easier if she liked

Mr. Ericson. Postponing the moment when she must confess her D, Shelley went into the dining room to set the table while Mavis prepared supper. When Tom finished discussing Luke's report card, he went into the kitchen and helped himself to an olive that Mavis was about to stir into a tamale pie.

Katie came thumping down the stairs and appeared in the kitchen. Her face was rosy from its recent scrubbing. "Dad, do you know what?" she asked, with an air of suppressed excitement. "Pamela said her father said if we divided up our orange grove and this property into lots and sold them we would be *rich.*"

"Oh, he did," answered Tom dryly. "And what would we do with our riches?"

"Pamela says we could build a new house," said Katie. "A ranch house."

Oh, no, thought Shelley, forgetting her own problem for the moment. Not give up this comfortable, creaky old house and live in a house just like anyone else's.

"For the information of Pamela and her father, not that it is any of their business," began Tom, "it just so happens that I don't want to live in a new house. I like this house just as it is, slanting floors, too many doors, creaking stairs, and all. I like having my own trees around me, and room for the dog to run, and a place for your mother's studio, and extra bedrooms for Shelley and your grandmother and anyone else we want to visit us."

"Yes, that is nice," agreed Katie, and added wistfully, "but Pamela's house has wall-to-wall carpeting and all the furniture is Early American."

"Goodness!" exclaimed Mavis. "I wouldn't have wall-to-wall carpeting. I don't like to run the vacuum cleaner that much. And we have some Early American furniture. The secretary and those two little tables in the living room came from your grandmother's family home in New England and are very, very old."

"Oh, Mommy," said Katie impatiently. "I don't mean that kind of Early American. I mean *new* Early American like you buy in a store."

Mavis began to laugh. "Katie, you funny little girl. I think you see too much of Pamela."

Katie was injured. "I am not a funny little girl," she said, with her most dignified air. "I don't know why you always have to say things like that. Or why you have to criticize my friends all the time. Pamela is—"

"Katie," said Tom sternly. "You aren't by any chance trying to avoid the subject of report cards?"

Katie's dignity wilted. "Oh, all right," she said. "I got a C in cooking. But it really wasn't my fault at all. The teacher just doesn't like me. She picks on me."

"Poor kid," said Tom jovially.

"Daddy, do you always have to make fun of me?" asked Katie.

Tom ignored her question. "Perhaps you would do better in cooking if you had a little more practice at home."

"I do cook at home," said Katie. "I baked a cake yesterday."

"I mean cook from the basic raw materials, not from a mix in a package," said Tom. "How about cooking some of the things you cook at school?"

"You mean like white sauce and mush?" asked Katie, and made a gagging noise.

"I'm game," said Tom. "Anything to raise your grade in cooking."

Shelley decided this was the time to speak. "I guess this must be the season for poor grades," she said with a nervous laugh. "I got a D in biology, but Mr. Ericson says if I get a B the second semester he will give me a C for the whole year."

"You see, Daddy?" Katie sounded triumphant. "I'm not the only one."

"Oh, Shelley, what a shame," said Mavis sympathetically. "But I am sure that if you apply yourself you won't have any trouble raising the grade. After all, with a subject like biology, all you really have to do is go to work and learn it."

Why, that's so, thought Shelley. She had never thought of it that way. She made up her mind that she would do exactly that—go to work and learn it.

"A D is worse than a C," observed Katie virtuously.

Shelley made a face at her. "But it isn't going to stay a D," she reminded Katie.

"That reminds me," remarked Tom, picking another olive out of the tamale pie.

"Tom!" objected Mavis. "There won't be any olives left if you keep this up."

"This is the last one," promised Tom. "I was just going to say that I lost a star basketball player today."

"What happened?" asked Mavis.

"Phil Blanton flunked biology," said Tom. "His father had told him that if he didn't keep his grades up he couldn't play basketball and so—no more basketball for Phil."

Shelley felt her face turn scarlet.

"He sits beside Shelley in biology," Katie lost no time in pointing out.

There was nothing Shelley could say. She looked into a cupboard so that she could turn her back to Tom and Mavis. Memories of biology came rushing back to her—the day Mr. Ericson stopped lecturing until she and Philip stopped whispering. The day they had made the date for the barn dance. Her D was bad enough, but an F! An F was really something to be ashamed of. And now Philip not only could not play on the team, the whole school would know he had flunked biology. The whole school already knew that she sat at the same table with him and everyone would blame her because he had flunked. The star of the team! The forward Tom had been counting on. All that was bad enough, but an F on Philip's record was far worse, because it might keep him from getting into college. Maybe she had ruined his whole career, even his whole life.

Shelley wondered what Philip would think of her now. If they had not been so aware of one another in class, if they had both worked harder . . . . Then Shelley remembered that Philip had not asked to see her this week end.

Chapter 9

Friday evening Shelley tried to forget Philip while she dutifully studied biology. Because the new semester did not begin until Monday, she was studying when she did not actually have an assignment. She wished Mr. Ericson could see her now, her head bent over her textbook, and on Friday night, too. She could not forget Philip, however, and he occupied her thoughts while her eyes slid over the sentences in the biology book.

Time dragged on Saturday morning and Shelley made it drag even more by dawdling over the breakfast dishes. She wondered what Philip was doing. Perhaps he was out working someplace and thinking bitter thoughts about her, the girl who had caused him to flunk. She began to dread Monday and the moment when they would inevitably meet in the hall at school. Maybe he would look at her and glance away as if he did not even know her. Everyone would talk about them over sandwiches at noon. And with the basketball season about to start, too. She could never face going to the games and having the whole student body whisper and point her out as the girl who made the star forward flunk off the team.

Shelley swished her hands back and forth in the dishwater to stir up more suds. She dreaded seeing Philip but at the same time she longed to see him. If she could only tell him how sorry she was and tell him about her D, he would understand.

Katie entered the kitchen and said enthusiastically, "I just saw an idea for a cute cake in a magazine."

In spite of her preoccupation with Philip, Shelley managed to laugh.

"Well, it *is* a cute cake. You take a package of cake mix"—Katie found a package in the cupboard —"and you bake it in two oblong pans. Then you cut one half in two the long way to make rabbit ears, and you frost the whole thing and sprinkle it with coconut and use jelly beans for the eyes and nose, and when you get through you have a cake that looks like a rabbit." Katie dumped the mix into a bowl, found two eggs in the refrigerator, carefully separated them and added the yolks to the mix along with the milk. The whites of the eggs she poured into the cat's dish. "Here, kitty, kitty," she called, and Smoky came running to lick up the egg. "I'll hide part of the cake from Luke so you and Philip can have some when he comes over tonight."

"Thank you, Katie," said Shelley, "but Philip isn't coming over tonight."

"Why?" demanded Katie, looking up from the batter she was about to beat.

"He just isn't," answered Shelley, running more hot water into the dishwater.

"Did you have a quarrel?" asked Katie, her eyes alight at this interesting possibility. "Did you tell him you never wanted to see him again?"

"No. Nothing like that." Shelley was hard pressed for an explanation. "He—well, he has something else to do." That was true enough, and she hoped the answer would satisfy Katie's curiosity for the time being.

Katie was busy reading the directions on the cake-mix box. "Wouldn't you know?" she exclaimed. "I needed those egg whites for the frosting." She took two more eggs out of the refrigerator, separated them, and gave the yolks to the cat. "Don't tell Daddy," she said. "You know how he is about wasting food." She beat her cake batter, counting under her breath, and when she finished, she said, "Pamela thinks Philip is the handsomest boy in school. I think so, too, but I thought Hartley was sort of nice that night he helped with the ironing."

"He is nice," said Shelley, as she emptied the dishpan. "I see him a lot at school, but—well, it is just different with Philip." The ringing of the telephone startled Shelley so she dropped the dishcloth. Sometimes the ring of a telephone could be such a hopeful sound.

Katie set down her bowl and went into the dining room to answer. "Yes, just a minute," she said. "It's for you, Shelley."

Shelley caught her breath. Philip? Her eyes must have asked the question.

"I think it's that big old Frisbie," whispered Katie.

Oh. Frisbie. Why should he telephone her? Shelley hoped he did not think that just because Philip was through with her that he could ask her for a date. After all, he was Philip's best friend. Shelley picked up the telephone but did not answer at once. She was looking at the San Sebastian telephone book. It was a mere pamphlet compared to the telephone book at home. "Hello?" she said in an impersonal voice.

"Hello, Shelley," said Philip.

"Philip!" Shelley's heart beat fast. "I thought—"

"I had Friz make the call because I didn't know who would answer and I didn't feel like talking to the coach," Philip explained. "Look, Friz and I have a job splitting some eucalyptus wood down the road from the Michies' and I wondered if you could come by. I—I want to talk to you."

"Why—" Shelley hesitated, trying to think. Maybe

she should insist on his coming to the house. Still, he did have a job to do and she could understand how he might not want to talk to Tom right now. "All right," she agreed happily, because Philip did not sound angry or even bitter. He sounded anxious. Perhaps he thought she would think he was blaming her for his F and wanted her to know he didn't feel that way at all. Whatever it was he wanted to talk about, everything was going to be all right.

"You know the place," said Philip. "Where I told you we took down the tree last week."

"Yes, I'll be there in a little while," answered Shelley. Philip was not angry with her. He wanted to see her right away. He couldn't even wait until this evening.

"Katie, be an angel and dry the dishes," said Shelley, when she had replaced the receiver.

"Sure," said Katie. "Are you going out with Frisbie?"

"No, with Philip." Shelley could not keep the lilt out of her voice. She ran up to her room to comb her hair and then left by the front door to avoid any more questions from Katie. She hurried down the road, following the sound of metal ringing against metal, until she saw Philip and Frisbie. Then she walked more slowly so she would not appear too eager.

When Philip saw her he leaned his maul against a section of a eucalyptus tree, dropped his wedges on the ground, and came to meet her. They stood facing one another under the arching fronds of a low palm tree beside some neglected-looking geraniums. Philip's face was dirty and he wiped the sweat from his forehead with the sleeve of his sweat shirt.

"Hi," he said, looking serious. "I suppose you heard I can't play basketball because I flunked biology?"

"Well—yes, I did," Shelley admitted. "I feel awful about it. As if it were partly my fault."

"Aw, Shelley, don't feel that way," pleaded Philip. "It wasn't your fault."

"I—I got a D," Shelley confessed reluctantly.

"Did you?" remarked Philip. "Well, that's better than flunking."

Shelley was surprised that he did not show more concern. Of course a D was better than an F, but it still was nothing to be so casual about. "But now I can't be on the honor roll," she said.

"I wouldn't know. I've never been on it," was Philip's offhand answer. He picked up a eucalyptus bud that lay in the road and pegged it at a telephone pole. "I'll miss playing on the team," he remarked.

"I know," said Shelley sympathetically, "but what about college? Will this keep you from getting in?"

"Maybe," answered Philip, pegging another eucalyptus bud at an orange tree. "But I don't care."

"Don't care!" Shelley was shocked. "You mean you don't care whether or not you go to college?"

"I don't even want to go," answered Philip.

"You don't want to go to college?" Shelley could scarcely believe it. It was true that she could not explain to Mr. Ericson why she wanted to go to college, but at the same time she was sure college was important. "But I thought everyone wanted to go to college."

"I don't," answered Philip. "Everyone wants me to go—Mom and Dad think just because they went to the university I should go, too, but I don't want to go. They're pretty disappointed in me, I guess, and I feel awful about it because they are really swell."

"But—why don't you want to go to college?" asked Shelley.

"Because I don't like to study," answered Philip. "I feel all cooped up sitting at a desk with a pile of books. I like to be outdoors doing things—things like cutting trees. Dad wants me to be a lawyer or something and I'm not cut out for it."

"But you can't cut trees all your life," Shelley protested.

"Why can't I?" asked Philip. "Lots of men earn their livings cutting trees and clearing land, especially now that there is so much building going on. Of course I'm not sure that's what I want to do, but it is one thing I could do."

Shelley was silent. She broke off a sprig of geranium still damp from yesterday's rain and carefully pulled the dead blossoms from the cluster. Philip earning his living cutting trees—this did not fit in with her picture of him at all. The fairy-tale phrase, "poor woodcutter," popped into her mind. How silly, she thought. Nobody was a poor woodcutter in this day and age. She felt sorry for Philip. It must be hard for a boy to study when he disliked studying. And he was going to miss so much.

"If it weren't for the team and Dad's feeling so bad, I wouldn't even care about flunking," said Philip moodily. "That and one other thing."

"What is that?" asked Shelley.

Philip picked up another eucalyptus bud and took careful aim at a dove on a telephone wire. He missed but the dove flew away. "Shelley—I feel terrible about this," he said, looking down at her. "Dad says I can't have any more dates until I bring my grades up."

Shelley stared at Philip, not quite believing what he said. Then, embarrassed, she began to pluck the fresh petals from the geranium one by one. He loves me, he loves me not. He loves me, he loves me not. She could not keep the words from running through her mind.

"Dad is pretty strict," explained Philip. "That's why I couldn't often ask you for a date ahead of time. If he thought I hadn't studied enough during the week, he wouldn't let me go out on week ends."

So Philip had not been so casual after all. And now she was being given notice. Shelley did not know what to say. What could she say—thanks, it's been nice knowing you and now I'll run along? And what would her mother think when she found a boy was not allowed to go out with her?

"I'm sure sorry, Shelley," said Philip. "I feel terrible about it."

"I—I guess you can't help it." Shelley's fingers continued to pluck at the geranium. He loves me, he loves me not. One more petal. He loves me. She threw the empty stem to the ground.

"You're not angry?" Philip sounded anxious.

"No, I'm not angry," answered Shelley. What was there to be angry about?

"Swell," said Philip. "I knew you'd understand. I'll really work to bring my grades up."

"You do that, Philip." Shelley found she felt completely blank, as if she did not have any emotions. "Well, I guess I'd better go now."

Suddenly Philip took her hand. "You're awfully nice, Shelley."

Shelley smiled faintly. "Thank you, Philip. Good luck. I'll miss you in class next semester."

"Oh, I'll be there," said Philip. "They are letting me take the second semester and then I have to repeat the first semester next year."

"Oh," was all Shelley said. This was worse. To

sit beside Philip another semester when he could not come to see her and the whole school would know about it. . . . Feeling as if she were walking in her sleep, Shelley turned and left. She walked slowly past the grove and through the privet hedge and into the house. She climbed the creaking stairs and sat down on her unhemmed bedspread. She felt numb, but beneath the numbness was hurt pride. It hurt to have a boy tell her he was not allowed to go out with her. And it was going to hurt even more to have the whole school know she wanted to go out with him when he was not allowed to go out with her. And then there were the letters filled with references to Philip that she had written to her mother and to Rosemary. It had been such a joy to write his name.

Shelley sat listening to the whir of a lawn mower down the road. Now there was no longer any reason to write Philip's name at all. He was not allowed to go out with her and there was nothing she could do about it. San Sebastian was not a magic place. She could not perform some task that would break a magic spell and free him. And his father was not an ogre. He was a man who wanted his son to do well in school.

Shelley felt sorry for Philip. It would almost be easier if he were the kind of boy who would rebel, but he wasn't. He would do the best he could in that reserved way of his, trying to please his father and knowing in the long run he wouldn't. It must be hard for him to study when he didn't like studying. She was sorry, too, because he did not want to go to college. There was no reason why everyone should go to college, but for herself, she knew that her life would be more interesting if she did go. That was what she should have told Mr. Ericson. But Philip was not the kind of boy who wanted to go. . . .

Shelley buried her face in her bedspread. She was suddenly and desperately homesick. She was homesick for her mother and father and for Rosemary. She was homesick for the soft Oregon rain and the feel of dampness against her cheeks when she walked home from school. She was homesick for definite seasons, autumn leaves in fall and iris and violets that understood they should bloom when spring had come. She was homesick for fir trees in the park and sea gulls wheeling over the school lawn when there was a storm at sea. She was homesick for the mahogany dining-room table and fluffy pink bath towels. She was homesick for those drinking fountains that were never turned off.

Outside, the eucalyptus leaves rustled in the breeze and from down the road the sound of the lawn mower continued. There was something wrong about that sound and at first Shelley could not think what it was. Then she knew. It was a lawn mower in winter. At home the sound of the first lawn mower meant that spring had come, even though no one wrote poetry about it. Now Shelley listened to the lawn mower and thought about the four long months that were still ahead of her in this strange country. From now until the first week in June. She did not know how she could face them without Philip.

Chapter 10

In her homesickness Shelley saw San Sebastian through different eyes. The tan stucco high school with its imitation mission tower seemed ugly when compared to her red-brick school at home. And palm trees—how could she ever have thought those trees with their ragged dirty petticoats of dead fronds were exciting to behold? She began to recall the little things she had missed in California, really crisp eating apples and the cozy feeling of being in a warm bed when sleet was slatting against the windows.

Even enrolling in Journalism 1, a class Shelley had looked forward to since she started high school, did not help. She found the subject interesting and she enjoyed being in the same class with Hartley, but her enthusiasm was gone. Biology lab was every bit as difficult as she had expected it to be. She felt humiliated. The other members of the class exchanged knowing glances, the way she had known they would. She appreciated Jeannie's silent sympathy, but she found being in a situation that called for sympathy hard to take. Frisbie's knowing smile was downright irritating.

But Philip—it was the presence of Philip himself that was hardest to bear. He still talked to her in his shy and courteous way but there was a difference now, as if he, too, knew that things could never be the same. The sight of him working so doggedly over his dissecting pan and notebook was painful to Shelley. What kind of person was she, anyhow, to grind up roses at home and then come down here and cause Philip so much unhappiness? When the class came to the worm-dissecting assignment, Shelley asked herself what was the one thing in the world she least wanted to do. The answer was easy. Cutting up a worm in San Sebastian, California, under the sharp eyes of Mr. Ericson beside a boy who was not allowed to go out with her.

Shelley mentioned Oregon so often that Frisbie said, "If you like it up there so much, why don't you go back?" And once when Shelley started to say, "In Oregon we always—" someone interrupted by saying, "We will now pause while Shelley delivers a commercial." After that Shelley was miserable in silence. She couldn't go back now. At home the second semester was well under way and she would be behind in her classes if she transferred now. Besides, her father had told her that if she came to California, he expected her to stay for the whole school year.

The weather grew colder. Snow fell in the mountains, and the sight of the green trees loaded with golden oranges against a background of snow-topped mountains almost raised Shelley's spirits. Then she found that San Sebastian paid a price for this beauty.

At eight o'clock in the evening the Michies turned on the radio to listen anxiously to the frost warnings. Tom went out in the night to check the temperature in the grove. Later he called Luke out of bed to help light the smudge pots. Shelley was awakened by the smell of oily smoke and a sound like the roar of airplane propellers. When she got up to close her bedroom window she saw flames shooting up from the smudge pots throughout the groves and knew that the wind machines were fanning heated air through the trees. It was an eerie and beautiful sight, like nothing Shelley had ever seen before. These Californians, who thought they could heat up all out of doors! What was she doing here, anyway?

In the morning Tom and Luke came in red-eyed, washed but not clean. They had stopped to try to scrub off the greasy smoke in the showers at the gym. but smudge did not wash off easily. Their eyes were rimmed with black, and when Shelley went to school she saw that many of the boys had the same washed-but-not-clean look. As the day wore on, heads began to nod over books and drop down on folded arms. Shelley noticed Mr. Ericson smiling sympathetically at Frisbie sleeping in biology lab. She had not known her teacher was that human.

The next days were anxious ones. Tom and Luke were grimy and tired. Mavis was worried. "We have a tiger by the tail," she told Shelley. "Once we start smudging we can't stop until the cold spell breaks. If it should be a long one it can eat up all the profit from the oranges."

The smudging continued for three nights before the temperature rose and the Michie household returned to normal. Shelley then felt it worthwhile to wash the smudge out of her hair. She had never been inconvenienced by a crop before. Things like that did not happen in the city, thank goodness.

One day while Shelley was trying to make herself eat a sandwich, Jeannie suddenly asked, "You are really in love with him, aren't you?"

"In love?" repeated Shelley, surprised. Love was such a big word, almost too big to talk about. "Why, I suppose . . . I always think of love as something that comes later."

Jeannie did not say anything. She just looked at Shelley with her sharp, bright eyes. A few days later she said, "Let's go to the basketball game together."

Shelley had been dreading the basketball season. "Well . . . no, Jeannie," she answered vaguely. "You'd better not count on me. I doubt if I can make it."

"If you say so." Jeannie's glance was sharp and penetrating.

Shelley was so homesick she even wrote to Jack, whose last unanswered letter had lain on her desk for over two months. Her letter was short—she was really not eager to communicate with Jack. It was just that he was someone at home. Letters to her mother were more difficult. In each one she carefully managed to include some reference to Philip so that her mother would not wonder what had happened to him and start asking awkward questions that might force Shelley to confess that Philip was not allowed to take her out.

Then came the night of the first basketball game with Santa Theresa, the night Philip could not play. Shelley had made up her mind that she could not face this game. She had to go to school but she did not have to attend a basketball game. She felt so miserable she thought perhaps she was coming down with a cold.

Tom left the house early that evening. Shelley went up to her room to study. Her head felt heavy and when she swallowed, she was pretty sure her throat was scratchy or was going to be. She heard some of Luke's friends stop for him on the way to the game. Soon Mavis and Katie would be gone and she would have the whole house to herself. She was so miserable she felt as if in complete solitude she would dissolve into a puddle of tears.

Shelley sat huddled at her desk when Katie knocked and entered. "Hi," said Shelley forlornly. She knew that Katie would not mention Philip, because she had not spoken his name since the day he told Shelley he could not see her. This was so unlike Katie that Shelley was sure Mavis had taken her aside and told her to say nothing about Philip.

"Come on, go to the game with Mommy and me," Katie pleaded.

"No, thanks, Katie," said Shelley with a wan smile. "I really don't feel like it."

Mavis appeared in the doorway behind Katie. "Come on, Shelley," she urged.

Shelley smiled and shook her head.

"It will be lots more fun if you come," begged Katie.

Shelley was touched as she always was by Katie's eagerness for her company, but she still shook her head.

"Come on, Shelley. You'll feel better if you go." There was quiet insistence in Mavis's voice.

Shelley was, after all, a guest in the Michies' house and Mavis was the coach's wife. Shelley had an obligation to please whether she felt like it or not. "All right," she agreed, trying to conceal her reluctance as she pulled her coat out of the closet.

The gymnasium where the two teams were already warming up was bedlam. Pairs of yell leaders from both schools were leading yells that seemed to Shelley to reverberate from the walls and ceiling. Santa Theresa had brought along an electric megaphone that added to the din.

Mavis led the way to the section of seats across the aisle from the coach's bench, where room was soon found for the family of the popular coach. "Thank goodness, San Sebastian is expected to win," she remarked, as they sat down on the bench.

Shelley supposed she should have worn a white blouse and sat in the rooting section behind the team, but she was too dispirited to care. She did not feel like mingling with the other students and wondering what they were thinking of her.

The referee blew his whistle and tossed the ball into the air to start the game. It was at that moment that Shelley saw Philip, sitting on the end of the players' bench farthest from her. He was wearing his letter man's sweater, the sweater that would not have a second stripe added to the sleeve at the end of the year. His feet were spread apart, his hands were in his pockets, and he was leaning forward, tense, following the ball as if he were playing the game himself. Shelley was surprised to see him, although she realized she should not have been.

A boy like Philip would care about the game even though he was not allowed to play.

San Sebastian scored. Santa Theresa scored through the basket at the end of the gym where Shelley and Philip had scattered hay a long time ago. "Take it away! Take it away!" chanted the San Sebastian rooting section. "Score! Score!" yelled the opposing section, the rooters making their voices swoop up on each word. The leader with the electric megaphone was carried away by the sound of his own voice electrically magnified until it seemed to Shelley to fill the entire gymnasium with sound waves so vibrant they were almost visible.

San Sebastian scored twice. Philip could not sit still on the bench and when he sprang up for a better view, Shelley wished desperately for her school to win to make up for Philip's not being allowed to play. Katie jumped up and down and screamed. Santa Theresa made three baskets in a row. A San Sebastian player fell and hurt his knee. Time out. Philip sat down on the bench sideways, facing the player beside him, talking earnestly.

The playing started again. The referee's whistle shrilled. There was a foul against Santa Theresa. "Score! Score!" swooped the electrically led rooting section. "Take it away! Take it away!" screamed San Sebastian. Santa Theresa scored. The ball was in the hands of a San Sebastian player, who was dribbling it down the length of the gym. Philip was on his feet again. The ball teetered maddeningly on the edge of the basket, wobbled, and fell through. The electric megaphone seemed to be ringing inside Shelley's head. Katie beat her arm in excitement. More shouts, more feet pounding on the floor, more arms waving, the referee's whistle and, somehow, Santa Theresa was ahead by four points at the half.

Girl yell leaders took over the floor with their giant pompons of colored crepe paper, green and yellow for San Sebastian, purple and white for Santa Theresa. They performed their stylized dances, shaking their pompons to the right and to the left while Philip sat with his hands clasped between his knees.

"I do so hope Tom wins his first game," said Mavis, "but now I am not so sure."

"He's got to win," said Katie.

The pompon girls left the floor and the janitor came out with a push broom to sweep up the scraps of crepe paper left behind. This time, when play was resumed, San Sebastian was trying for the basket through which Philip had shot an imaginary ball when he and Shelley were decorating for the barn dance. That bittersweet memory. San Sebastian scored three times in succession and the rooting section was in a frenzy. Then suddenly in front of Shelley there was a tangle of sinewy legs and sweating bodies. She and Katie had to throw up their arms in front of their faces to avoid being struck by the ball.

Shelley knew then that Philip must have seen her, and after that she would not let herself look in his direction. She wondered what he was thinking about her, if indeed he bothered to think about her at all. It would be so much easier if they had quarreled or he had met a girl he liked better or she had met another boy. Then she would have had some idea of how to behave, because she knew how other girls had acted (and perhaps should not have acted) in those more ordinary situations.

The rest of the game for Shelley was a noisy blur of knees, elbows, and a bouncing, flying ball. And then it was over and San Sebastian had lost. Mavis was quiet. Katie drooped. Shelley had a glimpse of Philip talking to one of the players on his way to the locker room. He looked serious and from the gestures he was making with his hands, he seemed to be re-enacting one of the plays.

And it was all Shelley's fault. Things might have been different if Philip could have played. Now all she wanted to do was to leave the gymnasium without meeting him. This should not be hard to do. Philip, she was sure, would not want to meet her.

Shelley followed Mavis and Katie through the straggling crowd that had cheered for the losing team. At the end of the gym, under the basket that San Sebastian's ball had too often failed to go through, Shelley felt a hand on her shoulder. It was a boy's hand, and the feel of it made her start. She looked back and found herself looking into Hartley's dark eyes.

Hartley smiled at her, a sympathetic smile. "Don't feel that way," he said. "It's only a game, you know."

"I know, but—" was all Shelley could say.

"I know," answered Hartley, and Shelley knew that he did know. He patted her shoulder and with an encouraging smile, disappeared into the crowd.

Shelley found she felt a little better. Somehow, Hartley's pat on the shoulder had helped, because it showed he understood how she felt. She thought of the evening he had helped with the Michies' ironing and had taken her to Vincente. She had really enjoyed that evening, but of course that was a long time ago.

Chapter 11

It was the mail that brought about a change in Shelley's feelings. On this particular delivery the mailman left in the Michie mailbox two letters for Shelley and a package for Katie. All three were to prove important to Shelley.

Shelley returned from school one afternoon to find Mavis reading a book with Smoky curled up in her lap and Sarge lying on the rug at her feet. "How did biology go today?" Mavis asked, looking up from her book.

"Ugh. We dissected a crayfish," answered Shelley and then added thoughtfully, "but you know, dissecting is rather interesting. A worm has five pairs of hearts. I didn't know that until I dissected one."

"There are a couple of letters for you," said Mavis.

Shelley knew. She had spotted them on the mantel the moment she entered the room. Never had

mail seemed so precious, and the most precious letters of all came in the square white envelopes addressed in her mother's neat handwriting and the
pale-blue envelopes that displayed the handwriting
Rosemary was experimenting with this year, a back-
hand with little circles instead of dots over the *i*'s.
Rosemary was always experimenting with something—nail polish, hair styles, personalities.

Now Shelley picked up the two letters, and as
she did so she noticed beside them the package addressed to Katie. Sitting on the couch she weighed
the two letters on her finger tips before she decided
to open Rosemary's first. It was written on notebook
paper and many of the words were underlined.

"Dear Shelley," it began. "I'm writing in study
period as usual—I have so much to do I'm simply
frantic, to put it mildly. Anyway, you're sure lucky
to be way down there in sunny California practically *surrounded* by handsome basketball players."
(How am I ever going to explain Philip away, Shelley wondered. Of course she could not admit Philip
was not allowed to go out with her, not after the
way she had described him to Rosemary.) "Jack
turns up once in a while to take me to the movies
or something. But don't worry. We are Just Pals and
I am keeping him safe from Other Women until you
come back in case you still want him. I think he's
sort of cute, though. Right after you left he took
me to this movie that was made in Italy where

everybody kept saying *a rivederci* (I guess that's how you spell it) instead of good-by and now Jack says it too. Don't worry—as I said before, we are Just Pals, but the way things are around here a boy in the hand is worth two in the bush or any old port in a storm or something like that. Anyway, it is beginning to snow here, not that a little snow would interest anyone who spends all her time lolling about under a palm tree—"

Shelley giggled and dropped the letter into her lap. If Rosemary could know what San Sebastian was like during smudging! Then Shelley picked up the letter and reread it thoughtfully. She had half hoped Rosemary would like Jack so much she would want to go steady with him. Apparently this was not going to happen. And now Jack was saying *a rivederci*. Well, as Rosemary said, probably a boy in the hand was worth two in the bush. Rosemary was always so practical about these things.

Shelley tore open her mother's letter, which had come by airmail, and, as always happened when she opened a letter from her mother, the guilty memory of the morning she threw the roses in the Disposall crossed her mind. "Shelley dear," the letter began. "I am so glad biology is going smoothly for you this semester. Philip sounds like a very nice boy and it must be pleasant to have him sitting beside you a second semester. Mavis writes that his family is very well liked in San Sebastian. I hope, dear, that you will remember that living in a small town is quite different from living in the city and that everyone will notice everything you do. I am sure Philip is a very nice boy and I know I can trust you not to lose your head—"

Shelley stopped reading. Lose her head! As if she had a chance! Honestly. I'll put it on my list, she thought. If I ever have a daughter my age I will not talk about her losing her head. And if her daughter went away to school, she would not write for references on every boy she happened to go out with. What did her mother think she was—a child? Shelley did considerable mental sputtering before she went on reading. "By the way, whatever happened to the boy named Hartley, whom you mentioned when you first went to California? It has begun to snow here and by tomorrow your father will probably have to shovel the driveway before he can get the car out. It seems only yesterday that I used to bundle you into your snow suit and red mittens so you could run out to catch the first snowflakes."

Shelley folded the letter and returned it to its envelope. Poor Mother, she thought, she really does miss me even if I was so awful about the raincoat that day. She sounded lonely. But even if she was lonely, Shelley wished she would not write to Mavis for references and talk about Shelley's losing her head.

Shelley looked across the room at Mavis and was

grateful to her. Mavis had simply written a nice letter answering her old friend's inquiries about Philip and had said nothing about his not coming to see Shelley any more. She had not mentioned the matter to Shelley, either, although Shelley was sure she knew all about it, and for this Shelley was also grateful.

And the worst of it was, Shelley did not know how she was going to explain Philip away in her letters. She had mentioned him often and enthusiastically, because she knew her mother wanted her to have a good time. When she had reluctantly confessed her D she had not mentioned Philip at all, because she did not think her mother would approve of a boy who flunked. Shelley did not want to confess the real reason she was not going out with Philip. After all, she had her pride. Maybe she should start making casual references to other boys in her letters. Her mother had already inquired about Hartley. Now that he was in her journalism class, she saw him more often and it would be easy enough to say something about him in her letters home.

Katie came in through the front door and flung her books on a chair. "A package from Nana!" she exclaimed, when she saw the package on the mantel. "Loot!"

"Katie, what an expression!" said Mavis with a

laugh. "What would your grandmother think if she could hear you?"

Eagerly Katie pulled the string off the package, threw the brown paper on the floor, and opened the box. Shelley saw the pleasure on her face fade to disappointment and then to dislike.

"What's the matter?" asked Mavis.

"It's a sweater," answered Katie in a flat voice.

"Just what you've been wanting," said Mavis. "Let's see it."

Katie held up the sweater briefly and then dropped it back into its box.

"Why, it's a lovely sweater," said Mavis.

Shelley agreed. The sweater was a delicate apricot color becoming to Katie. It was knit of soft yarn with a double row of cable stitch down the front. "You're certainly lucky," observed Shelley. "It's just right to wear with your brown skirt."

Katie looked obstinate.

"Katie, you're acting as if you don't like the sweater," said Mavis.

"I won't wear it!" Katie was so vehement that even Sarge lifted his nose from his paws to look at her.

"Katie!" exclaimed Mavis. "Of course you'll wear it."

"No, I won't," said Katie, "and nobody can make me!"

Inwardly Shelley was embarrassed. This all

sounded much too familiar. She and her mother had said these same words so many times.

Mavis began to sound impatient. "Now why on earth should you refuse to wear a beautiful sweater like this?"

Katie stared at the floor. "It's hand-knit," she said finally. "With *cable* stitch." She made cable stitch sound like something peculiarly loathsome.

Mavis could not help laughing. "Katie, how ridiculous," she said. "That makes the sweater all the more lovely."

"I'm *not* ridiculous," said Katie resentfully. "I don't see why you have to go around saying I am ridiculous all the time."

Mavis ignored this outburst. "Katie, you couldn't go into a store and buy a sweater as lovely as this," she pointed out.

"I don't want to go into a store and buy a sweater like this," said Katie stubbornly.

Mavis's controlled patience reminded Shelley of her own mother. "But dear," said Mavis, "why don't you want to wear a hand-knit sweater?"

"Nobody wears hand-knit sweaters," said Katie. "The kids would make fun of me."

"No, they wouldn't," contradicted Mavis gently.

And they probably would, too, thought Shelley, remembering how her classmates had behaved about any unusual clothing when she was Katie's age. If they did not openly make fun of her, they would somehow make her feel as if there were something odd about her appearance.

"What kind of sweater would you prefer?" asked Mavis curiously.

"A plain old Orlon sweater from Penney's," said Katie emphatically. "The kind the rest of the kids wear."

"Oh, Katie!" Mavis's exclamation was a mixture of amusement, impatience, and irritation.

"Mother, you just don't understand," protested Katie.

"That seems to be a favorite phrase of yours," commented Mavis.

"Well, you *don't* understand," said Katie, "and I am *not* going to wear the sweater!"

"Of course you'll wear the sweater," said Mavis firmly. "You have been needing a sweater and now you have one, a very becoming one. And what is more, your grandmother is coming to visit us in a few weeks and I shall expect you to behave yourself."

"I'll freeze to death first." Katie thrust up her chin and stared out the window.

Shelley tried not to smile. She knew Katie was thinking, I'll freeze to death and then you'll be sorry.

"That would be pretty hard to do in San Sebastian," remarked Mavis drily.

"Oh, Mother!" Katie was angry. "Why do you al-

ways have to go and say things like that? Why can't
you ever *understand?*"

"I don't know," said Mavis wearily. "But I do understand one thing. You are going to wear that
sweater and no more nonsense. You know what your
father would say."

Katie was silent as a variety of emotions passed
over her face. Anger, stubbornness, the brink of
tears. Finally she settled on haughtiness. "All right,
I'll wear the old sweater," she said coldly, as she
pulled it out of its box and jammed her arms into
the sleeves. "Come on, Sarge, let's go."

The dog rose from the rug, shook himself, and
trotted over to the door. Katie paused dramatically
with her hand on the doorknob. "Why do *I* have to
have a grandmother who knits?" she asked rhetori-
cally before she flounced out, slamming the door behind her.

Poor Katie. Shelley's impulse was to run after her
and say, It's all right about the sweater—really it is.
All Katie needed was to feel that she was as attractive as Pamela, and to have Rudy dance with her
at dancing class, and then it wouldn't matter what
kind of sweater she wore. But it would not do any
good to tell Katie this. She would not believe it until she found out for herself, just as Shelley had to
learn about the raincoat for herself.

Mavis sank back into her chair with a sigh. "Well,
I hope slamming the door makes her feel better."

"It probably does," said Shelley. "Where does her grandmother live?"

"Up in Carmel-by-the-sea," answered Mavis. "She has a little house that she lives in during the winter and rents out during the tourist season while she visits her children or travels. She expects to come down early this year, because she has it rented for the entire season to an elderly couple from the Valley who want to escape the heat."

The house was quiet without Katie clumping up and down the stairs. In the distance, through the grove, Sarge's barks could be heard. There seemed to be nothing for Shelley to add to the conversation. "Well, back to the salt mines," she remarked, and carried her books up to her room.

Shelley spent the rest of the afternoon reading the next chapter in her biology book, with frequent pauses when she propped her chin on her fist, stared out the window, and composed letters to her mother and to Rosemary. Dear Mother and Daddy, I can't magine how I happened not to mention Hartley ately. Just a lapse of memory, I guess. He is in ny journalism class and I see him all the time. More than I see Philip, really. . . . Dear Rosemary, Where on *earth* did you ever get the idea I was practically surrounded by basketball players? I may know one or two but I also know an interesting journalism student. I may have mentioned him before. His name is Hartley Lathrop and he . . . .

And he what, Shelley asked herself. It was not going to be easy to give the impression that Hartley was important to her if she saw him only in the classroom. It would be a good idea, even fun, to see him outside the classroom, but she did not see how this could ever happen. If only she had explained her peculiar behavior the time he said good night to her, things might be different now.

Shelley stared out the window and turned over in her mind the one date she had shared with Hartley. From the garage came a feeble pop-pop-popping sound from Luke's motorcycle. Sarge's bark in the distance reminded Shelley of Katie, and as she listened she wondered what Katie was going to do about the sweater. She would not wear it to school. Shelley was sure of that. Not a girl like Katie.

It was almost suppertime before Katie appeared. She came through the back door into the kitchen, where Shelley was helping Mavis prepare the meal. "Mommy!" cried Katie. "Just look what happened."

The front of the sweater was covered with muddy streaks and a large raveled hole was torn in one side, revealing more muddy streaks on the white blouse she was wearing under the sweater.

"Katie, I'm surprised at you," said Mavis coldly.

"But Mommy," protested Katie with conspicuous innocence, "I couldn't help it. I was running along with Sarge in the grove and I picked up a stick for him to fetch and before I could throw it, he jumped up on me and tore my sweater. Honest, Mommy, it all happened so fast I didn't even know what was happening."

Shelley watched fascinated. Surely Mavis would not let Katie get away with this.

"Don't you believe me?" asked Katie, wide-eyed.

"No, I do not." Mavis dropped a lump of butter into a pan of peas. "Take your sweater off," she said mildly. "After supper you must write your grandmother a nice thank-you letter. And we won't be able to buy you a new sweater. We do not waste clothing in this household."

"Mommy," exclaimed Katie tragically, "I don't see why you don't believe me."

Mavis looked levelly at her daughter. "Supper is almost ready," she said.

After supper Katie went to her room without having to be told, and in half an hour she appeared with a sheet of note paper in her hand. "Is this all right, Mommy?" she asked.

Mavis took the letter and read it carefully. "Except that there are two *p*'s in *appreciate*, it is a very nice letter."

"O.K., I'll fix it," agreed Katie cheerfully.

"And when your grandmother comes to visit us perhaps she can reknit the part of the sweater that was torn," said Mavis.

Katie groaned, but it was a cheerful groan. She had worked something out of her system and as far as she was concerned, the incident was closed. She sat down on the couch and said softly, as she curled up beside her mother, "Mommy, tell me what it was like in the olden time when you were a little girl."

Mavis smiled down at her daughter and glanced toward Shelley, explaining in her glance that this was a family joke. "In the olden time when I was a little girl," she began, as if she were telling a story, "there were no nylon stockings or Kleenex. Ladies wore silk stockings and little girls learned to iron by practicing on linen handkerchiefs. And three times a week a truck came down the street bringing ice for the iceboxes in people's kitchens, and all the neighborhood children climbed onto the back of the truck to pick up bits of ice to suck. . . ."

Shelley smiled at Mavis and her daughter as she listened. So the argument about the sweater was all over. Neither had won. Mavis had not succeeded in making Katie wear a sweater she did not want to wear, and Katie would have to go without a new sweater which she needed. And yet somehow it made no difference in their feelings toward one another. Maybe that was the way it was with mothers and daughters. Nobody ever really won.

That sweater was to Katie as roses in the Disposall were to me, thought Shelley, stating the whole thing like an algebra problem. But this was a problem that could not be solved by algebra. That was the trouble with people—they didn't fit into formulas. Perhaps every girl had to throw roses into the Disposall at some time, because that was part of growing up. And suddenly Shelley knew that this was true. She did not understand why, but she knew that it was true.

Shelley knew then that she was not going to be haunted by those roses nearly so much, now that she knew she was not alone in her rebellious feelings. But she still had another problem to occupy her mind and she turned her thoughts to it now—how she was going to keep her mother from knowing why Philip did not come to see her any more. She would have to mention Philip less and less and write about Hartley more and more. . . . There must be some way she could make Hartley take an interest in her again. . . .

"And in the olden time when I was a little girl," Mavis continued, "cars did not have heaters or radios. Everyone carried an auto robe for people who rode in the back seat to put over their legs in winter. Some cars had little vases for flowers on the dashboard—"

"Flowers on the dashboard?" Katie murmured sleepily. "Mommy, you are just making it up."

Shelley was happier than she had been since the day she received her D in biology.

Chapter 12

At school Shelley set out to recapture Hartley's interest, not only to be able to write home about him, but because she missed the companionship of a boy. She managed to walk down the hall toward the journalism room a step ahead of him. Since they shared a common destination, Hartley naturally caught up with her.

"Oh, hello, Hartley," said Shelley, acting surprised to see him. "I liked that personal interview you wrote for class last week. It was different from what most of the class wrote."

"Thanks, Shelley." Hartley was pleased by her compliment. "I think a lot of interviews printed in the school paper are pretty silly. You know, the reporter always asks what was the subject's most embarrassing moment and who is his current heart interest. I thought I could make an interview with the janitor more interesting than that stuff."

"You did," Shelley assured him.

"By the way, have you decided what you are going to do for that informative interview assignment?" Hartley asked.

"Not yet," admitted Shelley, as they entered the journalism room. "Mrs. Boyce said it was all right to go to church and write up the sermon, but that doesn't seem like a real interview."

"I haven't thought of anything either," said Hartley. "I suppose I could interview my dad on the state of citriculture in California."

"But interviewing your father doesn't sound like a real interview either," said Shelley.

"I know," agreed Hartley, "but I haven't thought of anybody better."

"Me either," said Shelley, thinking that perhaps this was her chance. If she could think of a really good subject, she and Hartley might interview him together if she suggested it in the right way. But the subject would have to be interesting and unusual. Hartley was serious about journalism, as he was about all his subjects.

That evening Shelley was still trying to think of someone to interview as she picked up the *San Sebastian Argus-Report* and glanced idly through its pages. She was thinking that it was a gossipy little paper, compared to the newspapers she had grown up with, when the photograph of an elderly man caught her attention. "Bard to Appear" was the caption and beneath it, in smaller type, Shelley read, "Jonas Hornbostle, noted poet and winner of the Biddle Prize for Poetry, will appear at the Swancutt Hall of Music, Orange Belt College, Vincente, Saturday afternoon at two-thirty. Mr. Hornbostle will read from his own works, which include such distinguished works as *Litany for a Lizard* and *Prairie Depot.*"

A real live poet, and Jonas Hornbostle at that! Shelley meditated on this bit of information. She had not realized that Jonas Hornbostle was still living—so many people whose works were required reading in English were dead. Jonas Hornbostle, whose poem, *Buffalo Bones,* was included in the textbook for English 5. Shelley preferred the poetry of Edna St. Vincent Millay, but she was impressed by the works of Jonas Hornbostle, who rarely used rhyme and who wrote so vigorously about earthy subjects. Shelley examined his picture more closely. The poet had a shock of unruly gray hair and heavy dark eyebrows. The photograph revealed every pore and every line in his face as he appeared to be squinting into the sun at some distant object, an eagle perhaps.

Shelley dropped the paper. She knew exactly what she was going to do. She was going to tell Hartley that she intended to interview Jonas Hornbostle. If she told him in the right way, perhaps he would suggest they go together to the Swancutt Hall of Music, hear Jonas Hornbostle read his poetry, and then go backstage to interview him. That would really be something to write home about!

The next morning, in their registration room, Shelley turned around to Hartley the first thing and said, "I have a marvelous idea for that interview assignment."

"Who's your victim?" asked Hartley.

"Jonas Hornbostle," Shelley announced.

"Hey!" exclaimed Hartley. "Smart girl! I read about him in last night's paper and didn't even think about interviewing him. I guess I thought he was too famous."

"There is no reason why two members of the class can't interview the same person, is there?" Shelley hoped this would give Hartley the right idea.

"No, I guess not." Hartley frowned. "Darn it all, anyway. This is the one Saturday afternoon that I can't go. But it sure is a good idea and I wish you luck. Meeting a famous poet should be interesting."

"Yes," agreed Shelley, with less enthusiasm. Somehow it had not occurred to her that she might have to do this interview alone. She had counted on Hartley's presence to give her courage, and now she was frightened at the thought of facing the famous man without him.

"Be sure you let me read the interview before you hand it in," said Hartley. "I'd like to see it."

"Of course," agreed Shelley. Letting Hartley read her story should be an inspiration to her, because she would not want to show him a poor piece of work. She valued his opinion too much.

When Saturday afternoon arrived, Mavis's insistence that she take the station wagon rather than the bus added to Shelley's pleasure and excitement at the afternoon before her. It was one of those California days that seemed to belong to no season at all. She felt very mature to be driving alone past the groves where crews on ladders were picking oranges, past the used-car lots and the Giant Orange on her way to meet a famous poet. Mr. Hornbostle? My name is Shelley Latham, she would say. And he would answer, Shelley—a poet's name. Well, no, he probably wouldn't, because he was an earthy poet, but it would be nice if he did. And if he did, could she put it in the interview without sounding as if she were bragging? Yes, of course she could. Anything he said would be part of the interview. Such a remark was full of human interest and belonged in the interview with a real live poet. Accuracy, accuracy, accuracy Mrs. Boyce always stressed in journalism class. Shelley mentally sharpened a pencil and prepared to be accurate, accurate, accurate.

Shelley began to recite in ringing tones as she drove toward Vincente:

> " 'Highway 30 bisects the sod where once they
>   lay.
> Bison bones
> Bleached by sun, leached by rain. . . .' "

She wished she could remember more than the first three lines of *Buffalo Bones*. What she did remember was looking up "leach" in the dictionary when she studied the poem. It would be so much easier if Jonas Hornbostle wrote poetry with a regular rhyme scheme. Oh, well. " 'Highway 30 bisects the sod,' " she repeated.

Driving to Vincente was easy enough, but finding a parking space near the Orange Belt College was not so easy. So many people had come into town to shop on Saturday afternoon. Every time Shelley thought she had found a place to park, the space turned out to be occupied by a small foreign car. Time was getting short and Shelley, eager for a good seat, finally drove around behind the Swancutt Hall of Music and held up honking traffic while someone backed out of a space. Glad that the streets were wide enough for diagonal parking, Shelley slid into the space, jumped out of the station wagon and carefully locked it before she ran around to the front of the auditorium and up the steps to purchase her ticket along with the rest of the crowd that had had difficulty finding parking space.

It was after two-thirty when Shelley slid past a long line of knees and into a seat. The audience, which was not as large as Shelley had expected for such a famous man, appeared to be made up mostly of college students and women who were removing their flowery hats. Shelley had not seen so many hats since she had come to California. As she sat down, the president of the college was finishing his introduction to the poet and the sound of applause gave Shelley a moment to catch her breath.

Jonas Hornbostle rose from his chair, walked to the lectern, laid down a sheaf of papers, removed a spectacle case from his pocket, opened it, put on a pair of dark-rimmed spectacles, removed them, took a handkerchief from his pocket, and wiped each lens carefully, to a ripple of sympathetic laughter from the audience. Shelley settled back in her seat. She was, at last, in the presence of greatness. It was too bad Hartley could not be there to share the experience with her.

Jonas Hornbostle put on his spectacles, hesitated, removed them, and meticulously wiped the right lens to the accompaniment of more sympathetic laughter. At last the spectacles were settled on the bridge of his distinguished nose and Jonas Hornbostle began to read. Shelley was thrilled. A truly famous man speaking famous lines and she was lis-

tening! And before the afternoon was over she, Shelley Latham, would actually speak to him. (Dear
Rosemary, You'll never in a million years guess what
I did today! I interviewed Jonas Hornbostle—you
remember from English 5. Yes, little old me. I
walked right up to him and . . . .)

Shelley was only slightly disappointed when she
had difficulty understanding Mr. Hornbostle. He did
not exactly mumble, neither did he speak with an
accent, but it was not easy to catch his words. The
audience coughed a lot and that did not help. Even
so, Shelley admired the poet wholeheartedly. That
famous shock of gray hair, the loose knot in his tie,
his suit rumpled as if greatness had no time for
sending a suit out to be pressed. How wonderful it
would be if he really did say, "Shelley? A poet's
name." Shelley caught the familiar words, "Highway
30 bisects the sod," and a thrill went through her.
Little had she dreamed when she was studying English 5 that someday . . . .

Intermission came, and it occurred to Shelley that
from her present seat in the center of the auditorium she might have some difficulty reaching Mr.
Hornbostle when his program was over. She peered
around the auditorium for a seat on an aisle.

"Disgusting, isn't it?" Shelley was startled by a
voice beside her. She had been only vaguely aware
that the seat was filled. Now she turned to look at

the fairly young man, probably a college student, who was sitting beside her.

"Disgusting?" she echoed. "What's disgusting?"

"Hornbostle. The whole performance," answered the young man who, like the poet, was wearing dark-rimmed glasses.

"Jonas Hornbostle?" asked Shelley, in the rising inflection of astonishment. Jonas Hornbostle disgusting? This man must be mad.

"Of course," answered the young man disagreeably. "Can you hear him?"

"Well, not every word, but—" admitted Shelley.

"You see?" said the young man. "The whole thing is an insult to your intelligence. He's really on exhibit."

Shelley looked shocked.

"Don't look that way," said the stranger impatiently. "What good is it to listen to a poet if you can't understand a word he says? And all that nonsense about wiping his glasses. I tell you he is just on exhibit. He and his manager think we are lucky people because we paid a dollar and a half plus tax just to look at him."

"But—" protested Shelley.

The young man was not going to listen to a protest. "Anyway," he went on, "just because he once wrote passable poetry doesn't necessarily mean he can read it."

Jonas Hornbostle's poetry *passable?* Shelley

stared at this person beside her, who by this time was collecting frowns as well as smiles of amusement from the other members of the audience.

"I'm glad I didn't waste my money on that LP record he made. I'll bet he's even worse on hi-fi," said the young man. Suddenly he rose from his seat. "I've had my intelligence insulted enough for one afternoon," he announced, and left.

At least Shelley was able to move one seat closer to the aisle. I don't care, she told herself. He *is* a famous man and his poetry *is* good and I *am* lucky to be listening to him and my intelligence feels just fine. But Shelley had difficulty even trying to listen to the second half of the reading. The moment of her interview was drawing closer. She folded back the cover of her notebook and fumbled in her purse to make sure she had not forgotten her pen. Mr. Hornbostle? I'm Shelley Latham. May I ask you a few questions for my school paper? She did not have to tell him that she was only a first-semester journalism student. First she would ask him a few factual questions to get him started talking and then she would ask what advice he had to give to students who wanted to write poetry. That would be the most important part of the interview. Accuracy, accuracy, accuracy, Shelley repeated to herself for reassurance and, from her journalism textbook, who, what, when, where, why?

Shelley sat on the edge of her seat waiting for

the reading to end. She would have to move quickly to reach the poet before he left the auditorium. When at last applause filled the auditorium, Shelley did not wait for the clapping to subside before she whispered, "Excuse me, excuse me," and edged past knees and over toes to the aisle. She struggled against the tide of the departing audience and made her way to the front of the auditorium, where Mr. Hornbostle, a taller man than he had appeared to be from her seat, was surrounded by important-looking people who were, she supposed, members of the college faculty.

Shelley edged as close as she could. This was not going to be easy, she could see. Maybe she had better skip her name and start by asking questions. Still, she did not want to do that. She peered anxiously through the crowd at Mr. Hornbostle, who was busy signing autographs. He was considerably older than his photograph in the *Argus-Report* and he looked tired. The price of fame, thought Shelley.

When the last autograph was signed, and the last lady thanked for telling him she liked his poetry, and only a few members of the college faculty remained with the poet, Shelley clutched her courage, moistened her lips, stepped forward, and spoke to the man, who was about to leave. "Uh—Mr. Hornbostle?"

"Yes?" Was that impatience in his voice?

"My name is Shelley Latham." No response.

"Could I—that is, do you have time to answer a few questions for my school paper?" Shelley sensed the amusement of the faculty members, but it was too late to back out now.

"Well?" said Jonas Hornbostle.

Apparently the poet meant this to be consent. At least he was looking at Shelley instead of moving toward the door. Encouraged, Shelley quickly decided she had no time for notes. She would have to remember what he said.

"Mr. Hornbostle, what do you think of Vincente —this part of the country?" she asked, looking up into the tired, impatient face.

"Does it matter what I think?" he asked ironically but not unkindly.

Shelley felt confused. Probably what he thought really did not matter, but that was not the sort of answer she expected him to give. "Well . . ." She gulped and tried frantically to think of a question that would sound intelligent and start him talking about himself. "Uh—how old were you when you wrote your first poem?"

Mr. Hornbostle raised one of his famous black eyebrows. "Poem?" he queried gently. "Have I written any? I am not so sure of that."

I'm getting no place fast, thought Shelley, uncomfortably aware that the college faculty members found the whole scene amusing. "Mr. Hornbostle," she began, determined that this time she was going to get a definite answer out of the man. "Where were you born?" That was a question that he could not evade.

Before Shelley's eyes the tired, impatient face grew more tired and more impatient. "My dear young reporter," said Jonas Hornbostle, "the answer to that question can be found in any one of a number of standard reference books that I am sure are available for your use in your school library. Have you never heard of *Who's Who in America?*"

"Yes," Shelley managed to whisper, unable to take her eyes from the poet's face. This could not be happening to her. No, no. Not to her. Things like this did not really happen. It *was* happening, though.

"Then if you expect to gain practice in interviewing, I would suggest that you never ask a question that can be answered in your library. *Who's Who in America* will not only tell you where I was born, it will also tell you how many children I have and give you their names. That, I presume, was to be your next question."

Shelley managed to tear her horrified gaze away from the famous face. She looked at the floor and whispered, "Thank you." Then, with tears in her eyes, she turned and walked halfway up the aisle until she could stand it no longer. She broke into a run and ran the rest of the way out of the building.

Safe inside the station wagon, Shelley sat trembling behind the steering wheel. Outside the world still seemed serene. A breeze moved the pendant branches of a pepper tree in front of the car, and down the block two little girls were playing hopscotch and laughing. Shelley rested her forehead on the steering wheel. What did I expect, she asked herself bitterly, the whole world to change because she had made a fool of herself in front of a famous man and a good part of the faculty of the Orange Belt College? And she had thought herself so smart, starting out to interview a celebrity. She had planned to impress Hartley and to knock the whole Journalism 1 class right back on its heels with her cleverness. And who got knocked back on her heels? Shelley Latham, the girl who was too stupid even to be a cub reporter. Shelley Latham, sub-cub, that was what she was. Whatever would she tell Hartley? She had promised to let him read her story and now there would be no story.

Shelley lifted her head from the steering wheel. She could not sit there all afternoon trying to pull herself together when Mavis was expecting her to return with the car. Automatically she inserted the key in the ignition and as she turned it, anger toward the poet swept over her. What a rude man he was! And where would he be without a public to admire him? And she had been his admirer. That was what hurt Shelley most—she had truly admired the poet, and then to have him be so curt to her . . . .

Shelley drove slowly home and as she turned into the familiar streets of San Sebastian, the anger drained out of her and she felt suddenly very tired. She could no longer be angry with Jonas Hornbostle. He was right. It was she who had been rude in expecting a tired and busy man to take time to answer her inexpert questions. Why, in every town he visited he probably met at least one journalism student along with the autograph seekers and the ladies in flowery hats. And probably they all asked him the same questions.

The words of the young man who had sat beside her came back to Shelley and she now felt that perhaps he had been right after all. Jonas Hornbostle was a poor reader of his own poetry, and for that reason she began to feel sorry for him. It must be difficult to read badly in front of an audience and then to be pestered by journalism students. He had really not been angry with her so much as terribly, terribly weary.

Shelley turned into North Mirage Avenue and then into the Michies' driveway. She had failed. On Monday morning she would have to admit to Hartley that she had failed. Hartley, of all people. If he had gone to Vincente he would have come back with an interview. He would have gone prepared with a list of interesting and intelligent questions, because Hartley was the kind of boy who always knew exactly what he was doing.

Early Saturday evening the telephone rang. "It's for you, Shelley," said Katie. She added in a whisper, "It's a boy."

"Hello?" said Shelley, wondering what boy could be calling her. Maybe Philip's father had relented after all.

"Hi, Shelley," answered Hartley. "Did you get the interview?"

"No," answered Shelley reluctantly, but feeling that she might as well bring to an end the whole unpleasant incident as soon as possible. And just when she had succeeded in attracting Hartley's interest once more, too.

"How come?" There was disappointment in Hartley's voice. "Wouldn't he talk to you?"

"Oh, he talked to me all right," said Shelley, not wanting to admit what had happened.

"Well, come on, tell me about it," persisted Hartley. "If he talked to you, you must have an interview."

"Oh, no, I don't," said Shelley.

"What happened?" asked Hartley.

Shelley was silent a moment. "Wait a minute!" she exclaimed. "Maybe I do have a story after all." Briefly she described the episode. "And how do you think it would be," she concluded, "if I wrote it straight and told what really did happen? I mean, wouldn't that make a story?"

"Sure it would," said Hartley enthusiastically. "That would be a better story than if he had answered your questions straight."

"Do you really think so?" asked Shelley eagerly.

"I know it," said Hartley.

"Then I'll do it," said Shelley. "It will make me look like an awful idiot but I don't care."

"Don't worry about that," Hartley reassured her. "We all have to learn sometime and besides, the fact that you had a hard time asking questions will make a good angle. You know, a headline something like 'Famous Poet Gives Cub Reporter Lesson in Interviewing.'"

"That's so," agreed Shelley. "I hadn't thought of that."

"Say, Shelley," said Hartley, as if he had just had another idea. "If you aren't doing anything this evening, maybe I could come over and help you write the story."

"Why—I'd love to have you come over," said Shelley truthfully. She had not expected this much.

"Swell. I'll be over in about an hour," said Hartley.

"Do you have a date?" asked Katie eagerly when Shelley had hung up. She had been following the conversation from the living room.

"Yes," said Shelley happily. "At least a sort of

date. Hartley is coming over to help me with my journalism."

"That counts as a date," Katie assured her. "Would you like me to bake a cake?"

Shelley laughed. "I'm sure Hartley would enjoy a piece of cake."

"I can make cocoa, too," said Katie. "Like we made at school. Of course at school we called it breakfast cocoa but I don't see why it wouldn't taste all right at night."

"It will probably taste better," said Shelley. "And now I've got to change my dress." Blessings on thee, Jonas Hornbostle, thought Shelley, as she ran up the stairs to her room. Poor tired old poet.

Chapter 13

Dear Mother and Daddy, Shelley mentally wrote, as she opened the door for Hartley. This evening Hartley, the boy who took me to Vincente that time when I first came down here, came over to see me and we worked on our journalism assignment. . . .

"Hello, Shelley," said Hartley as he entered. "I hope you won't write like the *Argus-Report* and call a poet a bard."

Shelley laughed. " 'Bard' is a funny word to use, now that I stop to think about it, but the *Argus-Report* uses a lot of funny words. Like 'tot.' They use that a lot—I suppose because it is easy to fit into a headline."

"There is a 'Dog Bites Tot' or a 'Tot Lost' story in almost every issue," Hartley agreed with a grin.

Tom was attending a meeting and after greeting Hartley, Mavis excused herself, saying she was going to her studio. Shelley produced the rough draft of the interview that she had managed to write, and she and Hartley sat down in the living room at the long table below the handmade hooked rug that hung on the wall—Tom could not bear to see anyone walk on Mavis's hard work, so the Michies had hung the rug on the wall. Shelley felt perfectly natural sitting there with Hartley, almost as if they had sat there together often. This rather surprised her, but she decided she must feel at ease with him because he sat behind her in her registration room at school.

Shelley was not disturbed by Luke's sitting in his favorite chair studying a catalogue of motorcycle parts nor was she annoyed when Katie, in a fresh cotton dress, wandered in and out of the room. She was amused that Katie had dressed up for her date and she knew that Katie was interested in everything she and Hartley said. Katie was thinking that someday she could have a boy come over to study, too.

Hartley read Shelley's interview and they talked it over. He made suggestions, Shelley made suggestions, and they had one argument. Hartley thought that after the first sentence she should refer to Jonas Hornbostle as Mr. Hornbostle.

"But I never think of him as Mister," Shelley protested. "Of course I called him Mr. Hornbostle when I spoke to him, but writing is different. Nobody writes about a poet as Mister. They are called by their full names or just their last names."

"But he's a human being," Hartley pointed out. "Why shouldn't he be called Mister?"

"It doesn't sound right. Did you ever hear anyone call Shelley—Percy Bysshe, that is—Mr. Shelley?" Shelley asked. "Of course not. It is always just Shelley or Percy Bysshe Shelley."

"I guess that's right," admitted Hartley. "But on the other hand, I'm sure that I have read about T. S. Eliot as Mr. Eliot."

"That does sound sort of familiar." Shelley ran through the names of all the male poets she could think of. Browning, Keats, Longfellow, Sandburg —Mr. Sandburg? "Hartley, you're right!" she exclaimed, and wondered why she sounded triumphant when she had lost the argument. "It's dead poets that you don't call Mister. Jonas Hornbostle is alive so it is all right to call him Mister."

Together they rewrote the interview. Hartley read the new version. "That's good," he said seriously. "Mrs. Boyce should give you an A on it. It tells a lot about the poet—about his being tired and impatient and all, possibly because he knows he is not very good at reading his own poetry—most people don't think of a poet as being that human—and it tells what was wrong with a cub reporter's interview. It is different from most school interviews."

"Thank you, Hartley," said Shelley, pleased by

his approval. "The *Bastion* does seem to publish a lot of silly interviews." She should know. She was still embarrassed by the memory of the interview she had given.

"A silly interview in the school paper is such a permanent fixture in San Sebastian that nobody really sees it any more," said Hartley jokingly, "just like—"

"—a cannon from the first World War in the park," finished Shelley.

"Exactly," agreed Hartley, laughing.

"When I first arrived I thought a cannon was such a funny thing to put in a park," Shelley said, "and now it seems a perfectly natural part of the landscape."

Luke closed his catalogue of motorcycle parts and stood up. "Good night," he said.

"Good night," said Shelley. "I hope we aren't driving you away."

"No," answered Luke good-naturedly. "I smelled cake baking and I thought I would see if Katie had taken it out of the oven yet."

The room was silent. Shelley and Hartley had no reason to discuss the interview any longer. Shelley looked at the boy beside her and a tiny thought, a thought that she felt was disloyal, intruded. It was a relief to be free of ping-pong, to sit and talk to a boy about something that interested them both, instead of batting that exasperating little ball back and forth. Why, I'm having fun, thought Shelley, surprised—more real fun than I ever had with Philip.

Katie appeared, bearing a tray with two pieces of cake and two cups of cocoa. Shelley, touched by the sight of her in her fresh dress and carefully cleaned shoes, said easily, "Katie, why don't you join us?" When Philip had come she had always wanted to show him off to Katie and then get him out of the way before Katie could do or say something awkward. It was different with Hartley. He would understand about Katie. Of course he would, and Shelley had been foolish not to explain about Katie on the refrigerator long ago.

Katie was obviously delighted to be invited to share Shelley's evening with a boy. She carried in another piece of cake and another cup of cocoa and sat down at the end of the long table.

"Blue frosting looks sort of funny on a cake," she said shyly. "I thought it would look prettier." She ate carefully, taking small bites and sitting up very straight. Just watching her made Shelley feel good.

"Blue frosting is good," said Hartley. "You could call it Surprise Frosting. Everyone expects something flavored with mint to be green so when you bite into blue frosting and find it mint-flavored, it is a surprise."

Shelley could see that Katie was pleased, and she knew that Hartley understood that Katie was thrilled to be included and was trying to act grown-up. Katie was even more pleased when Hartley ate a second piece of cake.

Shelley studied Hartley thoughtfully. She liked a boy who would go out of his way to be nice to a junior-high-school girl. When they had finished eating they all carried their dishes into the kitchen. Hartley was the kind of boy who was at ease in the kitchen. He rinsed and stacked the plates as if working at the Michies' sink was the most natural thing in the world. It was easy to picture him helping with a batch of fudge and enjoying himself if a girl could think of no better way to entertain a boy.

When they had finished with the dishes, Shelley and Hartley returned to the living room. Katie went upstairs to her room, and from the garage came intermittent pop-pops from Luke's motorcycle. At last Shelley felt that she could talk freely to Hartley. "Do you remember that night we went to Vincente to eat the doughnut holes?" she asked, determined to be forthright.

"Of course. The night you talked about the pomegranates," said Hartley. "Does San Sebastian still seem like a beautiful place to you after the smudging we went through?"

Shelley spoke seriously. "It was unpleasant at the time, but you know, I think it was exciting the way the whole town cared about the oranges. Every time I eat an orange I'll think about that cold spell and the way the boys who worked in the groves came to school greasy and tired and fell asleep in class and the teachers didn't even say anything. I've never lived where people were concerned about crops before. I mean, I have read about damage to wheat or something in the papers, but I never understood how the people felt before."

Shelley was silent for a moment. She wanted to bring the conversation to its starting point. She looked straight into Hartley's dark eyes. "I've always wanted to explain why I acted so sort of funny when we said good night that time after we went to Vincente," she said, and noticed Hartley suddenly look as if he were on his guard. She did not care. She had to explain, because the matter had been on her conscience so long. "That night I happened to look up and see Katie looking through the open transom —you know how the refrigerator is against the door we never use between the living room and the kitchen. She was kneeling on top of the refrigerator watching us say good night so she would learn how to act when she has dates. I was so embarrassed I —well, I just acted funny is all. It seems silly now, but that is the way it was."

Hartley threw back his head and laughed. "So that's what was the matter! I didn't know why you were suddenly acting so stiff and formal. I thought you had had a good time and I didn't know what was wrong. I thought maybe you didn't like it when

I came right out and said I liked you so soon, or something."

"Oh, no," said Shelley, relieved that she had finally explained. "I was terribly pleased to come to a strange town and get to know a boy who liked me right off."

"And then you seemed so interested in Phil," Hartley went on, "that I didn't feel I should ask you for another date."

"I was interested in him," admitted Shelley, looking down at the table. This was touching on a painful subject. "He is one of the nicest fellows I have ever known, but I don't know—I guess we don't have an awful lot in common." Until Shelley spoke the words it had never occurred to her that she and Philip did not have much in common. They had really found very little to talk about. She had not enjoyed Philip himself as much as the admiration of the other girls who liked him and the thought that he looked like the kind of boy her mother would like her to know. She frowned a moment before she said, "You know, now I'm not sure it was Philip I liked so much after all. I think maybe it was just that I saw him that first day of school and I was so excited to be in San Sebastian with real palm trees and oranges growing on trees and everything. He was so good-looking I just thought he was the boy I had always wanted to meet. In my mind I turned him into the boy I wanted him to be. And he wasn't at all. He doesn't even want to go to college. I really feel sorry for him." She stopped, afraid she might have said too much. She did not want to criticize Philip.

Hartley raised one eyebrow and said wickedly, "You looked at me the first day of school, too."

"I don't mean that you aren't good-looking, too," Shelley said hastily. "You are, you know, in a different way."

Hartley grinned at Shelley, enjoying her discomfort. "I understand exactly what you mean about Philip. And you know something else? I think maybe you liked him because he was not the boy at home you were telling me about—the one who always said, 'Penny for your thoughts.'"

"I guess you're right," said Shelley thoughtfully.

Hartley leaned closer and spoke softly. "I still like you, Shelley."

Shelley looked into Hartley's serious brown eyes and was ashamed. She had maneuvered this evening just so she could write to her mother about another boy to make her mother think she had lost interest in Philip because of Hartley. She was trying to use him to shield her own mistake. And that was all wrong.

"I like you, too, Hartley," said Shelley honestly, realizing how much she really did like him. How foolish she had been not to understand this before. Little things should have told her, things like her boredom with ping-pong and the way she rushed to confide in Hartley about her D in biology because she knew he would understand how important good grades were. She recalled a remark Mavis had made about the boy she called the Great White Hunter, something about girls in their teens always fancying themselves in love with the wrong boy. Shelley had not really fancied herself in love with Philip—her feeling had been excitement at knowing a new boy and pride in showing others that he liked her—but now she understood what Mavis meant.

Hartley put his hand over Shelley's. "Good," he said. "We like each other. That makes it unanimous."

Shelley laughed. "Two votes and it is unanimous." She felt a sudden urge to talk to Hartley about everything in the world—school, and their plans for the future, and people they had known, and the mistakes they had made that had once seemed painful and now seemed funny. She wanted to make up for all the time they had lost.

But as Shelley sat with Hartley's hand over hers, she was disturbed by an elusive unhappy feeling. She liked Hartley, but Philip still liked her. Poor Philip, who had flunked biology and lost his chance to play basketball because of her

Chapter 14

Spring, warm and gaudy, came to San Sebastian. One day was no season at all and the next day was spring—a spring unlike any Shelley had ever known. Wild flowers bright as paint spilled by children colored the hills. Geraniums washed clean of dust bloomed brilliantly while vines and low plants that clung to the ground brought forth crimson and magenta flowers that shimmered in the bright spring light. The orange trees, covered with bridal blossoms, filled the town with rich perfume. Shelley had not known that anything in the world could be as fragrant as San Sebastian in the spring.

The perfume of the groves grew stronger at night and as she lay in bed consciously enjoying every breath, Shelley thought how different this was from spring at home. An Oregon spring meant fresh green leaves unfolding on the birch trees that lined Shelley's street. It meant rain soft as pussy willows and fat robins pulling worms out of the wet lawn. It meant trilliums in the woods and lilies of the valley in the back yard. Shelley was happy, now that she was rid of homesickness, to lie in bed and enjoy two springs, gaudy and delicate, one in reality and the other in memory.

Hartley replaced Philip on Saturday nights and Shelley was not sorry. She felt gloriously free of that plonking little ping-pong ball. When she and Hartley discovered they both enjoyed working double-crostics, they spent several evenings prowling through the Michies' reference books trying to find Cotton Mather's wife's maiden name or a colloquial expression of three words meaning to be in good health—the second letter had to be *n* and the last letter *k*. Shelley was delighted. She had always enjoyed puzzles and word games but she had not expected a boy to enjoy them too.

Once when one of the puzzles called for the name of the chief room in a Roman house, Shelley printed the word *atrium* in the proper spaces and was reminded of her first school dance a long time ago. "Hartley, is this a peculiar way to spend an evening?" she asked suddenly.

"Of course not," he answered. "We're both having fun. Why do you even ask?"

"I was just thinking about the first time I ever went to a school dance," she explained. "I went with a boy from my Latin class, the studious type, and we spoke Latin as much as we could."

Hartley laughed delightedly. "Whatever did you find to say?"

Shelley giggled. "I don't suppose our conversation was exactly witty. I remember saying that the floor of the gymnasium was divided into three parts. You know, like all Gaul in Caesar, but I had to cheat a little, because I didn't know the Latin for 'gymnasium,' so I just pronounced it with what I hoped was a Latin accent. And we said things like, '*Is* drummer *cum diligentia laborat.*'"

"Don't all drummers work diligently?" Hartley asked, laughing.

Shelley laughed with him. "It was funny, wasn't it?" she remarked, thinking that now the whole incident seemed like something that had happened a long time ago when she was practically a child, and she wondered why she had been so upset by her mother's amusement. Because she had felt so unsure of herself, probably.

Shelley enjoyed Hartley's companionship. Once he arrived late in the morning with a picnic lunch and drove Shelley to the mountains to see the wild lilac covered with blossoms the color of blue smoke. They picnicked beside a stream. "So you can see that we really do have water in California," Hartley explained. Shelley, who had always had to pack the lunch when she picnicked with a boy, was charmed. She did not, however, talk about her dates with Hartley to any of the girls at school except Jeannie. She could not help feeling guilty, with Philip working doggedly beside her in the biology laboratory and—she supposed—studying with equal doggedness at home on week ends. When Hartley asked her to go to the school carnival with him, Shelley accepted although she did not feel quite right about it, knowing that Philip could not go.

It was on the Saturday of the carnival that Shelley received a letter from her mother in the same mail in which Mavis received a letter from her mother, Mrs. Stickney.

Shelley's letter concluded with a worrisome paragraph. "Jack came over this evening," Mrs. Latham wrote. "I was so glad to see him. He is such a nice boy and I have missed him while you have been away. He wanted to know when you would be home. I told him Daddy and I were going to drive down to get you and that we planned to take in Yosemite and the redwoods on the way home but we expected to be back the end of June. He was pleased to hear this and said he wanted you to go to the mountains with him and his family over the Fourth of July."

Jack. Shelley read the paragraph again. Her mother did not say she had accepted the invitation for Shelley, but Shelley was sure she had. Naturally her mother would not want to see her sitting at home on a day when other girls would be away on picnics or trips to the beach or mountains. But Jack —oh, well, as Rosemary said, a boy in the hand was worth two in the bush or any old port in a storm. But Shelley was not entirely successful in persuading herself that this was true. She might have believed it at one time but not since knowing Hartley. However, if her mother had accepted for her, there was not much she could do about it but go to the mountains with Jack and his family. She knew what it would be like, though. A crowd of people would come up from the city and there would be whispered questions about Shelley and Jack. Jack's mother would smile and whisper that Shelley and Jack were going steady. Everyone would smile back and there would be half-heard remarks about that was the way kids did things these days—now when I was in high school . . . . Shelley would hate every minute of it.

"Goodness!" exclaimed Mavis, looking up from her letter. "Mother will arrive this week end. Honestly, I can't understand why she absolutely refuses to send letters airmail." There was considerable exasperation in her voice. "Shelley, I wonder if you would mind picking some fresh flowers for the dining room and for the coffee table while I make up the bed in the corner bedroom. Mother is apt to turn up at any hour of the day or night."

"I'll be glad to," said Shelley, and went about the

pleasant task. She chose some wild California poppies that were blooming among the weeds at the
back of the Michies' property and arranged some of
them in a brown mug that Mavis had made. The
rest she set in a green pitcher of Mexican glass for
the dining-room table. She was pleased with the effect of both her arrangements. They were gay and
casual, suited to the Michie household.

Not long after Shelley had finished with the flowers, an old car pulled into the driveway with a
crunch of tires on gravel.

"Hello, Mother!" called Mavis from an upstairs
window. "I'll be right down."

Shelley joined the family at the side of the house,
where a tall gray-haired woman was getting out of
the car. It was obvious that she knitted. While Mrs.
Stickney kissed her daughter and grandchildren,
Shelley stared at her dress. It was knit round and
round in random stripes of yarn of every imagin-
able color.

"That's some dress you are wearing," remarked
Tom, after he had hugged his mother-in-law.

"I call it my coat of many colors," replied Mrs.
Stickney. "I told myself there must be something I
could knit out of all those odds and ends of yarn,
so I knit this. It's the most practical thing in the
world for traveling. Nothing shows on it and I just
keep turning the skirt around and it never bags in
the seat."

"That's my girl," said Tom, and kissed Mrs. Stickney on her cheek. "Luke, get your grandmother's luggage out of the car."

"And this is Shelley," said Mrs. Stickney, taking Shelley's hand in hers.

"How do you do?" said Shelley, as she took her eyes off the fascinating dress.

While Luke pulled three suitcases out of the car, and a large knitting bag that Katie eyed with distrust, Mavis said, "Mother, aren't you ever going to get a new car? That one is so old I worry about your driving it on the highway."

"Nonsense," said Mrs. Stickney. "I understand that car and that car understands me."

"It's a car, Mother," said Mavis. "Not a horse."

"Anyway," said Mrs. Stickney, "if I keep it long enough, some old car collector is bound to offer me a lot of money for it." It was easy to see she was a woman with a mind of her own.

The afternoon seemed unusually lively, even for the Michies, so lively that Shelley had little time to think about her mother's letter. First of all Shelley was dismayed to see that the poppies she had arranged so carefully had folded their petals as if it were night and instead of two gay bouquets, they became stiff bunches of pointed buds. Probably in protest against being picked, Shelley decided.

"That's all right," said Mavis. "Just put them in

a dark cupboard for a while and they will open up when you bring them out into the light."

Amused at the idea of trying to outwit flowers, Shelley did as she was told. This crazy mixed-up California vegetation!

After Mrs. Stickney had unpacked, she settled herself with her knitting needles and some bright green yarn which Katie could not help staring at so apprehensively that Shelley, to end her suspense, finally came right out and asked Mrs. Stickney what she was knitting.

"A pull-over for Luke," she answered. "I am making it out of his school colors."

Shelley and Katie exchanged a look of conspiracy, while Luke's expression became worried. Only letter men wore sweaters in school colors but a grandmother could not be expected to know that.

"Luke, what are you up to these days?" asked Mrs. Stickney, pausing to measure her knitting.

"I'm helping Dad in the grove and using the money I earn for parts for my motorcycle," answered Luke. "I'll get it running one of these days."

"Now, Luke," protested Mavis. "We've been through this a dozen times. You're just wasting money on that old wreck and even if you do get it to run, which I doubt, you are too young to get a license."

"Nonsense," said Mrs. Stickney. "The boy has to grow up."

"I'm going to be sixteen," Luke told his mother.

Mavis looked as if she were about to say something but thought better of it. Instead she told Katie that she had to practice her piano lesson, both the rhapsody and her scales, before she could go over to Pamela's house. Katie observed that she never had any fun and began to play the *Hungarian Rhapsody*. Suddenly, as if she had had an inspiration, she speeded up her playing until the music sounded as if it were being rattled out by an old-fashioned player piano.

"Katie!" shouted Tom in his basketball-court voice.

The playing stopped. "Mommy said I had to play it through before I could go over to Pamela's," answered Katie plaintively.

"Now Katie," said Tom. "Time is just as much a part of the music as the notes. You know that. Now play it properly."

The music continued with only one lapse into *Pop Goes the Weasel*. Then Katie went to work on her scales. Shelley was the only one who noticed an open copy of *Betsy Devore, Girl Sleuth* resting on the music rack while Katie's fingers flew up and down the keyboard.

When Mavis went into the kitchen to put the roast into the oven, Mrs. Stickney went along to visit with her daughter. Soon Shelley heard their voices rising through the transom.

"Mother, I know what I am doing," said Mavis. "This isn't the first roast I have ever cooked, you know."

"Mavis, I have been cooking roasts longer than you have," said Mrs. Stickney, "and I can't bear to see you ruin that meat."

"I know you have been cooking longer than I," said Mavis. "And sometimes the roasts were too rare and sometimes they were overdone. That is why I am doing it scientifically. By inserting a meat thermometer into the roast I can tell exactly when the meat is medium-rare."

"If you plunge that dagger into the bosom of that roast," said Mrs. Stickney dramatically, "all the juice will run out."

"Oh, Mother," said Mavis, and laughed.

Things were equally lively at dinner. The roast was excellent. The confused poppies opened their petals when brought from the cupboard as if they were greeting the morning sun. Everyone argued with everyone else.

Katie said it was Luke's turn to feed the dog and cat, because she fed them the night before. Luke said it was Katie's turn, because the only reason she fed them the night before was that the night before *that* he fed them when it was really her turn and she had gone off to that creep Pamela's house and he couldn't let the animals starve, could he? Shelley said she would be glad to feed the animals if it would settle the argument. Luke and Katie told her to please keep out of their affairs. Mrs. Stickney said when she was a girl, children did their chores cheerfully and did not argue at the table. Mavis said she and her brother always argued at the table and every place else. They still did. Tom told Katie to feed the cat and Luke to feed the dog and now couldn't they introduce a new topic of conversation?

They did. Mrs. Stickney said she was thinking of a trip to France next year—she had always wanted to see the château country. Mavis asked her mother please to promise not to ride a bicycle in France, not at her age. Mrs. Stickney said nonsense, she might be getting on in years but her bones were not that brittle yet.

Tom changed the subject by asking his mother-in-law who she thought would be elected the next president. Mrs. Stickney said she did not believe in discussing politics, especially with relatives, but . . . . Mavis did not agree. She believed the man was more important than the party, but . . . . Katie said her social-science teacher, who was not even supposed to discuss politics in the public schools, said . . . . Luke said Katie was only in junior high and what did she know about it anyway? His history teacher said if a man was to be elected president it was essential that he be born east of the Rocky Mountains. Mrs. Stickney said that was nonsense. The way the West was expanding, it was high time the East realized the United States included the West.

"Whew!" exclaimed Shelley, when supper was over and she and Hartley were on their way to the carnival which was being held on the school's tennis courts. "I didn't know families could argue so much. And the funny part of it is, the Michies argue a lot but it never really seems to make any difference."

"I guess that's the way it is with families. Some families, anyway," said Hartley. "My dad and my brothers and I are always hacking away at one another but it doesn't really mean anything except maybe that we like one another. It would be different if we all kept still."

"I suppose," said Shelley thoughtfully, "that when there are a lot of arguments going on, no single one seems so important." She rode in silence awhile before she said, "I got into the silliest argument with my mother once over a raincoat. At least it seems silly now. I got so mad I stuffed a whole bouquet of fresh roses into the Disposall and ground them up."

"Why, Shelley," said Hartley, after they had laughed together over the incident, "you always seem so composed, it is hard to picture you doing such a thing."

"I guess I usually seethe within, but that time I

boiled over," said Shelley, as Hartley parked the car near the tennis courts. She could laugh about the incident now, but could she, she wondered, when she returned home? She hoped so but she was not sure.

The tennis courts were a square of light in the fragrant night. Music poured forth from loud-speakers and mingled with the shouts and laughter of the crowd that wandered from one booth to another eating candied apples and popcorn, yelling encouragement or derision at those who were trying their skills at various booths.

When Shelley and Hartley entered the tennis courts, Shelley wondered a little uneasily what others would think at seeing her with Hartley when Philip had to stay home. Then she told herself she was worrying unnecessarily. Philip had never said anything about going steady, had he? But she could not help feeling that she would have a better time if Philip were here, with his usual crowd of boys —or even with another girl.

Shelley and Hartley wandered about, pausing to watch the boys from the print shop fill orders for calling cards, lingering at the nail-driving booth. "Oh, look," cried Shelley as they moved on. "The Gavel Club is selling personalized shrunken heads —it says so on that sign."

"The debaters must have been hard up for something to sell," remarked Hartley, as they walked across the tennis courts to look at the shrunken heads.

"Step right up, folks!" yelled the barker. "Have you ever wanted to shrink the head of one of your teachers? Don't miss this golden opportunity, the chance of a lifetime! Just twenty-five cents, one quarter of a dollar! Get your shrunken heads here!"

The heads were walnuts with faces painted on the wrinkled brown shells and black string glued to the top for hair. Hartley bought one of the heads, wrote something on the attached tag, and presented it to Shelley.

Shelley laughed when she saw Mr. Ericson's name on the tag. "Since I got ninety-six on that last quiz, I'm not so anxious to shrink his head," she said, "but I'll take this home as a souvenir of San Sebastian."

Shelley and Hartley wandered on to the Block S Club's booth, one of the most popular concessions at the carnival. Members of the football team were taking turns wearing a helmet and poking their heads through a hole in a blanket. Students bought three balls for a dime and tried to hit the football player's helmet before he could duck. Shouts went up when a ball slammed against the top of a helmet. The crowd booed when the player ducked out of the way of the ball. Hartley paid his dime and picked up three balls. The first hit the blanket to the left of the player. The second was close but landed to the right. The crowd booed, and Hartley took careful aim. The third ball landed square on top of the helmet. Shelley cheered with the rest of the crowd. One of the nicest things about Hartley was that he did everything well, even throwing a ball at a carnival.

"Hartley, do you suppose I could hit a football player?" Shelley asked.

Hartley laughed. "I don't know, but you could try." He laid down a dime for Shelley's three balls.

"I'll bet she can't even hit the blanket," said one of the girls in the crowd.

Shelley laughed, picked up a ball, and threw as hard as she could. It hit the blanket, but that was about all you could say for it. The football player laughed at her. The crowd groaned. "She throws like a girl," someone commented.

"Well—I *am* a girl," said Shelley, and picked up her second ball. This time the football player grinned at her and did not even bother to duck. "Hey," protested Shelley. "Don't just stand there sneering. It's bad for my morale."

She aimed carefully the third time and came close enough so that the football player was able, by straining against the blanket, to lean over to the right and bump his head against the ball.

"See?" crowed Shelley. "I hit him."

"With a lot of co-operation from your target," scoffed someone.

"Shelley is an excellent shot," said Hartley. "She just has an individual style."

"Thanks, Hartley," said Shelley, flushed and laughing. Then as they started to leave, because the crowd was growing, they turned and found themselves face to face with Jeannie and Philip. Shelley stopped in surprise when she saw Philip, but the surprise did not last. Of course Philip had to go out sometimes. A boy's father could not keep him prisoner because he flunked biology. She should have known that.

Philip's face turned red with embarrassment. Shelley was aware that the crowd was watching to see what her reaction would be. Jeannie was looking at her and at Philip with bright-eyed interest, a little detached as if she were observing a scene instead of taking part in it. Shelley found that her only reaction was one of relief. Philip was not shut up at home with a pile of books while she was out having a good time. "Hi," she said, feeling uncomfortable only because so many people were watching. "Having fun?"

"Uh—Shelley," Philip began. "Jeannie and I got together at the library so she could go over my biology notebook before Mr. Ericson looks at it and then we—we decided to drop in here for a few minutes." Those were the words Philip spoke. He was silently asking Shelley not to mind.

"I'm glad you came," Shelley answered sincerely.

"We've been having a lot of fun." She was happy to see the tense look on Philip's face relax. Now she knew where they stood. It was over for both of them. She need no longer have that vague, guilty feeling that had bothered her so often when she was with Hartley. Shelley's heart was light as she turned to Jeannie and said, "I hope you have as much fun as we've had."

Jeannie smiled and her eyes told Shelley how happy she was to be with Philip. It was a look that only another girl could appreciate. Philip looked at Shelley and gave her his slow, shy grin, a grin that no longer made Shelley catch her breath. It was just a nice smile from a boy whom she had once liked and still liked, but in a different way.

"I just hit a football player," said Shelley.

"Jeannie, do you want to try?" asked Philip.

"Good luck!" said Shelley.

Hartley put his hand on Shelley's elbow to guide her through the crowd. "You really didn't mind what happened, did you?" he remarked into her ear, when they had left Jeannie and Philip.

Shelley smiled over her shoulder at him. "I'm glad," she said honestly, and when they were out of the crowd she faced Hartley and said, "I guess I have felt sort of guilty about Philip. As if it were my fault he flunked biology and was not allowed to date or play on the basketball team. And now I don't feel that way any more." Shelley knew that she had been mistaken to have felt that way in the first place. Philip had earned his F the same way she had earned her D—he had not studied enough. His grades were not her responsibility.

Perhaps the whole unhappy incident was really for the best. If it had not happened she would have gone on dating Philip and eventually, because he was not really the boy she had wanted him to be, she would have come to feel about him the way she felt about Jack. Not that Philip would have said, "Penny for your thoughts." It would have been something else that he did—ordering those greasy grilled peanut-butter sandwiches, probably—that she would wish he would not do, and then she would know that she was tired of him. And by that time it would have been too late. Everyone would have assumed they were going steady, and her beautiful year in San Sebastian would have ended in disappointment.

"I know what," said Hartley. "Let's get out of this madhouse and drive over to Vincente for some doughnut holes."

"In memory of our first date," agreed Shelley. It was all over with Philip now and she knew that her year would not end on an unhappy note. Her wonderful year that made her feel as if she were seeing the world for the first time. Because she was so happy, she smiled at Hartley, suddenly and radiantly.

He looked down at her with a mixture of tenderness and amusement. "You always have fun, don't you, Shelley?" he asked.

"Yes," Shelley answered, as the noise and the crowd of the carnival became a bright spot behind them in the darkness, and the perfume of the orange blossoms hung heavy on the night. "Yes, I do have fun." And that was the way it should be when a girl was sixteen.

It was then that Shelley knew that she was not going to the mountains with Jack and his family over the Fourth of July, no matter what her mother had said. She would write him a nice note. . . .

She did not have time to think about the note, though. Hartley leaned over and kissed her on the tip of her nose.

Chapter 15

Suddenly the days were going much too fast for Shelley. She wanted to catch each hour and hold it just a little longer. The green hills were turning to gold, the sky was blue, laced with the vapor trails of jet planes, and Shelley's spirits were high.

Shelley found that even biology, after weeks of memorizing definitions and classifications, became interesting. When the class reached the chapter on heredity, she was fascinated. It seemed marvelous to her that Luther Burbank could decide that he wanted a large white daisy with a smooth stem and by working with three different flowers from three different continents, could in fifteen years of controlled breeding, produce the Shasta daisy, which was exactly what he wanted. If Luther Burbank had wanted a California poppy that would stay open after being picked, he could have bred one by crossing the sleepy poppy with some wide-awake variety.

Journalism was Shelley's favorite subject and when the Journalism 1 class put out the cub issue of the *Bastion,* Hartley was chosen editor—an honor that certainly meant he would be made editor of the paper in his senior year. Shelley had been made feature editor because Mrs. Boyce had been so pleased with her interview with Jonas Hornbostle. It was fun to stay after school working on the paper in the untidy room that students had decorated with signs that said, "Thimk" or "Don't just do something—stand there." It was fun because she and Hartley were sharing a real interest. Each moment spent bending over the dummy of the cub issue was precious.

The one flaw in Shelley's happiness was the thought of leaving San Sebastian so soon. She tried to stuff this thought into the back of her mind and slam a door on it, but the thought slipped out at the most inconvenient times. When Hartley tossed a paper from another high school onto her desk and asked her what she thought of its feature page, she picked it up and looked at it but she had trouble really seeing it. She was thinking that this was probably the last time in her whole life that Hartley would toss a paper onto her desk. Surely something would happen to spare her having to say good-by to him. If only she had not wasted so many months before getting to know him better!

The same sort of thought pursued Shelley at the Michies', too. When a letter arrived from home, Shelley's first thought was, Only two or three more letters from home before I have to say good-by to Hartley. When she joined Tom and his two children in packing their lunches for the next day, she thought, only ten more lunches on the lawn with Jeannie before I have to say good-by to Hartley. When Luke and Katie argued over whose turn it was to feed the animals, Shelley counted the number of times that were left for her to hear this argument.

When Katie began to talk about the last dancing class of the season, the class that was to be a party, Shelley shared her anticipation, hoping that this time Katie would not return from the party dejected because there were not enough boys to go around, or because all the boys were too short, or because Pamela had danced three times with Rudy while she had to dance with a boy with clammy hands, whose shoes made black marks all over her new white slippers.

It was over Katie's last dancing class that a crisis arose in the Michie household. Two days before the party Katie discovered that she had outgrown her best dress. Naturally she had to have a new dress. Katie requested what she called a store-boughten dress. Mavis said she could make a dress for half the price of a ready-made garment, and wouldn't

Katie like yellow organdy? Katie said she would die, absolutely *die*, before she would go to the party in any old organdy dress. Organdy was for kindergarten. Mrs. Stickney suggested white dotted swiss. Dotted swiss was always so sweet, she thought. Katie did not actually disagree with her grandmother. She merely stared at the corner of the living-room ceiling with a stubborn, sulky look on her face.

A last dancing class was so important, and Shelley wanted so much for Katie to have a good time. "Maybe white piqué would be nice," she suggested cautiously.

"Yes!" agreed Katie enthusiastically, to everyone's relief. There was some argument over the pattern, but they finally settled on a princess style because there was no sash across the back. Katie would absolutely die before she would wear a dress with a sash to the party. She did not want any old ruffle around the neck, either.

Saturday morning passed in a flurry of pattern and material on the dining-room table and basting threads on the living-room rug, while both Mavis and Mrs. Stickney worked on the dress. When they were both busy sewing, Katie called Shelley into the laundry. "Shelley," she whispered, "can't you persuade Mommy to let me get a permanent? There is still time before the party and maybe she would listen to you."

Shelley was in a difficult position. She felt that

straight hair was more becoming to Katie, whose face was round, and she knew Mavis would agree. At the same time she wanted Katie to feel she looked her best that evening.

"Please, Shelley," pleaded Katie.

"Katie, you know it wouldn't do any good," said Shelley, and then she had an inspiration. "Why don't you ask your mother if you could have your hair cut in a beauty shop?"

Katie was elated with this suggestion. Her mother and grandmother agreed that a professional haircut was a good idea, and for once something was accomplished without argument. Shelley made an appointment for Katie and drove her downtown in the station wagon because Mavis and Mrs. Stickney were too busy sewing. Katie emerged from the beauty shop with her hair thinned and trimmed into a sleek little cap.

"Katie, you look darling!" exclaimed Shelley. She could tell that Katie was pleased by the way she held her head higher as if she were proud of it.

Somehow Katie's dress was ready to try on and Mavis was marking the hem with a yardstick and a row of pins ("Katie, stand still. How do you expect me to get this hem straight when you stand first on one foot and then the other?") when from the garage came a loud popping noise and then the unmistakable sound of a motorcycle running.

"Luke's motorcycle!" cried Katie. "He's finally got

it to run!" She jumped down from the stool she was standing on and ran to the window.

"There he goes down the driveway!" Shelley was excited over Luke's success after all these months.

"Oh!" The exclamation escaped Mavis as if this were the last straw.

The motorcycle turned at the corner of the house, crossed the front lawn, proceeded under the pergola, and around to the back yard and the garage once more. The whole family was on the back porch when Luke arrived, grimy and triumphant, his face and hands smudged with grease. He stopped, with the motor idling. "She runs!" he shouted.

"Oh, I never thought—" began Mavis.

"Well done, son," said Tom. "I never thought you'd do it but I'm proud of you."

"But he can't ride it," insisted Mavis. "He isn't old enough to have a license."

"I can ride it on our own property if I don't take it out on the road," Luke informed his mother, with the air of a boy who had inquired into the subject. "And next month I will be sixteen and can get a license."

"But Luke," protested Mavis, "I can't bear to think of you riding that dangerous contraption on the highway."

Luke looked stubborn.

"If the State of California lets him have a license to operate the motorcycle and Luke can earn enough money to support it, we will have to let him ride it," said Tom. "What is there for a boy his age to do? I would rather have him tinkering on a motor-cycle than hanging around the drugstore like some boys."

"That's right, Mavis," agreed Mrs. Stickney. "You have to let your children grow up, you know."

"Sure, Mommy," said Katie. "He'll be all right."

"Sure I will," said Luke.

"But he's—" Mavis began. She stopped, defeated.

"We can only hope that we have brought him up to have enough sense to use his head," said Tom.

"I hope we have." Mavis managed a shaky smile.

"Mommy, my *hem!*" cried Katie. "We've got to finish my hem."

"This seems to be one of those days. If it isn't one thing it is another," said Mavis with a sigh. "Come on. I'll have to start pinning it all over after the way you have been jumping around."

Somehow, while Luke rode his motorcycle around and around the house, Katie's dress was finished and a meal prepared. After supper Katie showered, admired her hair frequently in the mirror, slipped her dress on over her best petticoat, and was ready for the party. She twirled around in front of her family. "Mommy, I just *love* my dress," she exclaimed. "And you know what? Pamela's mother can't sew a *thing*. She's awfully dumb about a lot of things."

"I am glad you are pleased, Katie," said Mavis. "But I don't think you should talk about Pamela's mother that way." Mavis sat down, rested her head on the back of the chair, and closed her eyes. "Shelley, is Hartley coming over this evening?" she asked.

"Not till later," answered Shelley. "Probably not till nine o'clock. They are having a family dinner for his grandmother's birthday and he has to stay around."

"Would you mind driving Katie to the party?" Mavis asked. "I'm too tired."

"I would love to," answered Shelley, who enjoyed driving.

When she had deposited Katie at the junior-high-school auditorium, Shelley said, "Have fun!"

"I will," said Katie, smiling. Then she turned and ran toward the auditorium before she remembered how grown-up she was and slowed down to a walk.

Shelley drove slowly back to the Michies', looking at all that had grown familiar in the last months —the cannon in the park, the big old houses along the main street, the high school's mission tower that had never contained a bell, the pomegranate trees, the groves that had shed their petals. She must remember every bit of it always.

At the Michies' Tom and Luke were washing the dishes while Mavis and her mother recovered from their frantic day of sewing. Mrs. Stickney's bright

green yarn lay in her lap and everyone seemed too
tired to argue about anything.

Shelley decided to go to her room to answer
her mother's letter. She picked it up and glanced
through it once more. "We are looking forward so
much to our trip to California. We can hardly wait
to see our daughter again. It seems as if you have
been gone more than nine months. Mavis writes that
Hartley is one of the nicest boys she has ever known
and that is such a relief. I do worry so about you
way off down there. What has happened to Philip?"

Shelley's feelings were a mixture of tenderness
and irritation. Honestly, the way her mother acted
as if she were still a child! Shelley picked up her
pen and stared thoughtfully at a blank piece of notebook paper. "Dear Mother and Daddy," she began.
"Of course Hartley is a nice boy. I don't know why
you think I would be interested in any other kind.
You really did not need to write for references—"

Shelley sat with her pen poised above the paper.
She did not want to bicker with her mother, any
more than her mother wanted to bicker with her.
She could not understand why they behaved the
way they did. She wished the situation would be
different when she returned but she was afraid it
would not. Her mother would still tell her she should
wear the blue dress instead of the green or the green
instead of the pink, she would still insist on helping
Shelley select her clothes, she would still say she

thought Shelley should not go over to Rosemary's house so often. And Shelley would still object to everything her mother said. She laid down her pen. Darn it all, anyway. Why did things have to be the way they were?

A little before eight-thirty Shelley went downstairs and asked, "Would you like me to go get Katie?"

"Why don't we all three go?" suggested Mavis. "Mother, wouldn't you enjoy a little ride?"

"I think it is a fine idea after such a hard day," agreed Mrs. Stickney.

"Oh, I forgot," said Mavis, when they arrived at the junior-high school and saw no sign that the party was ending. "Since this is the last class of the season, it lasts until nine o'clock." They sat in silence in the station wagon awhile until Mavis said, "Let's go in and watch. The girls always look so pretty in their spring dresses."

Shelley realized she was going to lose some of her precious moments with Hartley, because now it would be after nine o'clock when they returned. There was nothing she could do about it.

They walked up to the auditorium, slipped quietly through the door and silently joined the parents who were standing along one wall watching. It seemed to Shelley an exceptionally pretty party. The girls were all dressed in pastel cotton dresses and each was wearing a *lei* of pink carnations. The boys wore carnations in the buttonholes of their best suits. They were all very dignified as they danced around the auditorium to the music of a band of four high-school boys. Shelley located Katie dancing with a boy who was shorter than she was—so many of the boys were shorter than the girls Shelley thought Katie was having as good a time as it was possible to have with a short boy, but she could not be sure. Like all the girls Katie looked rather solemn. Not as solemn as the girls who were wearing their first high heels, but solemn for Katie. Shelley was glad to see that Katie's next partner, who had bushy hair, was taller. Katie's expression was one of elation suppressed by anxiety about not stepping on her partner's feet. Shelley was sure that this boy must be Rudy. Katie did not appear to recognize either Shelley or her relatives.

Eager not to miss any time with Hartley, Shelley glanced surreptitiously at her watch every thirty seconds and was glad when the party ended and Katie joined them.

"Did you have a good time?" Mavis asked.

"Oh, I guess so." Katie spoke coldly as they left the auditorium.

Shelley and Mrs. Stickney exchanged a glance. What had gone wrong? Shelley shivered in the cool night air. She should have worn a sweater.

Katie walked to the car in silence. She slid into

the seat beside Shelley, filling the station wagon with the spicy fragrance of her carnation *lei*.

"What happened, dear?" Mavis asked.

"I was having a perfectly marvelous time and then you had to come along and spoil everything," Katie burst out.

"*Now* what have I done?" Mavis's voice was weary.

"You brought Shelley and Nana in and watched as if we were all a bunch of animals in a zoo or something," Katie accused her mother. "You spoiled everything."

"But there was nothing wrong with that," protested Mavis. "Other parents were watching, and I thought it was a very nice party. You girls looked lovely in your light dresses with your *leis*."

"I was the only one there with three people watching," said Katie. "And nobody who is anybody lets his parents come and watch anyway."

Of course, thought Shelley. She had felt exactly the same way at Katie's age about her mother's visiting school. How well she remembered those arguments. "But Shelley," her mother would say, "the board of education wants parents to visit school and at P.T.A. we are urged to visit." "I don't care, Mother," Shelley would answer. "Nobody's mother visits school in the eighth grade." Now she wished she had remembered and somehow kept Mavis and her mother from watching the party. She could have made some excuse about her date with Hartley and asked them to drive her home. Now they were wasting precious minutes.

"Katie, that's ridiculous," said Mavis, inserting the key into the ignition. "The parents pay for the series of lessons and there is no reason why they shouldn't see what their children are doing."

"Mommy, you don't *understand,*" complained Katie.

"Katie, I wish you would stop saying that," snapped Mavis, her patience at an end.

"I understand," said Mrs. Stickney. "What Katie is really saying when she complains about our watching is, 'I am trying to grow up—I want to be free of my mother and grandmother and so I don't want them watching me.' And what Mavis is saying is, 'Katie is still my little girl and so I have a right to watch.'"

"I guess you are right, Mother." Mavis sounded tired. "Children do have to grow up."

Everyone was silent as the station wagon traveled up the main street. Why, of course, thought Shelley. It was all as simple as that. That was all she and her mother ever really argued about. She was trying to grow up and her mother did not want to lose her little girl. The argument might be disguised as a disagreement about a slicker, or visiting school, or how late she could stay out, but it always meant the same thing. Shelley wanted to grow up and her mother felt she was still her little girl. And that was the reason she had stuffed the roses in the Disposall. She had been trying to say, *Now* I am going to grow up.

"I am at a very difficult stage," said Katie, in a voice that suggested everyone should sympathize with her problems.

"Not really?" said Mrs. Stickney, and laughed.

Shelley could see that Katie felt her grandmother was being most unsympathetic.

"Tell us about your difficult stage," suggested Mrs. Stickney.

"Well, I read an article—" Katie began defensively.

"She's read an article," chortled Mrs. Stickney. "And I suppose the article said a thirteen-year-old girl is going through a lot of difficult changes."

Mavis shared her mother's amusement. "It must have been that article that said a thirteen-year-old girl is half child, half woman."

"You don't have to make fun of me," Katie said crossly. "What I mean is I am not like Shelley, who doesn't have any problems."

"Why, I do, too," said Shelley, surprised at this view of herself. "Lots of them. I had a terrible time with biology."

"Oh, school." Katie was scornful. "School doesn't count. I mean you have dates and things."

"But school does count," protested Shelley. "It's

terribly important. And just because I have dates doesn't mean they are always with the right boys."

"Don't you like Hartley?" asked Katie.

"Of course I like Hartley," said Shelley. "I mean . . . boys at home. And I have other problems, too."

"What?" asked Katie.

"Katie, do you think because you are thirteen you have all the problems?" Mavis asked.

"Well, the article said—" began Katie.

"I don't care what it said," snapped Mrs. Stickney. "Look at me. My hair is gray. I wear bifocals. I have bridgework. All because I have changed."

"But you're . . . grown-up," Katie pointed out, hesitating just enough so that Shelley knew she had been about to say, "But you are old."

"Katie, just because a girl grows up doesn't mean she stops feeling," Mavis pointed out.

"And take your mother," said Mrs. Stickney. "Her life is difficult too. Her children are growing up whether she wants them to or not. She will have to let Luke ride his motorcycle whether she wants to or not. And probably the hardest part of all is having a daughter too old to read *Winnie-the-Pooh* but young enough to misinterpret articles in women's magazines. That is a terrible stage for a mother to go through. I don't know why someone doesn't write an article about it." Mrs. Stickney and her daughter both thought this was extremely funny

"I never read *Winnie-the-Pooh*. Mommy read it to me," said Katie grumpily. "Why does this family have to argue all the time?"

"Yes, for goodness' sake, let's stop arguing," said Mavis. "Let's get Shelley home for her date with Hartley, and then the rest of us can go downtown for an ice-cream soda."

"I'm starved," said Katie, as they turned into the driveway behind Hartley's parked car.

"Mavis, I've been meaning to tell you—I think you're putting on a little weight," said Mrs. Stickney. "Don't you think you should cut out desserts?"

"Mother, you say that every time you come to visit us," answered Mavis. "I think I am old enough to know what I should eat."

Shelley stifled a desire to laugh as she climbed out of the station wagon. She found Hartley in the garage examining the motorcycle and talking to Tom and Luke. "Hi," she said, feeling the pang she had felt so often lately. This was her next-to-the-last date with Hartley. "The others have gone downtown for a soda."

"That's a good idea," said Hartley. "Why don't we go for a ride and then stop in for a soda?"

"I'd love to," agreed Shelley. "Wait till I get my sweater."

She ran upstairs and as she turned on the light in her room, her glance fell on the unfinished letter on her desk. She picked it up and read it over be-